Praise for *The Names of the Dead*

"There is no denying the book's overwhelming power. . . . In scene after scene, O'Nan's understated prose conveys the war's brutality with a remorseless, eerie majesty . . . an excellent novel."
—*Newsday*

"A dense and richly concentrated meditation on how the past rises like a flood to saturate the present. . . . Stewart O'Nan is an old-fashioned realist in the best sense of that term . . . he creates a complete, sculptural texture of verisimilitude that few contemporary writers could attain or even conceive."
—*The Boston Sunday Globe*

"Ambitious . . . *The Names of the Dead* offers a gruesomely particularized evocation of war's horror. . . . Like Tim O'Brien's novel *The Things They Carried*, *The Names of the Dead* takes up both the grim reality of war and the problematic task of communicating that reality."
—*The New York Times Book Review*

"*The Names of the Dead* is disturbing—as is anything we know, but would sooner forget. . . . It is also lovely, and heartbreaking, full of sympathy and humor. It should be required reading for anyone who studies war. It should be required reading for us all."   —Alice McDermott

"Stewart O'Nan is a fabulous storyteller, with a spare, dramatic style. He creates wondrous sentences, masterpieces of design that neatly weave separate themes."   —*The Houston Post*

"A confident, gripping narrative, as well as some of the most searing wartime storytelling in recent memory."   —*Publishers Weekly* (starred review)

"A credible and moving account of moral failure and regeneration: thrilling, mature, and thoughtful."   —*Kirkus Reviews*

"A real winner of a book. . . . O'Nan's language is powerfully restrained; his word pictures of the war and its effect on the men who fought there are fresh and vivid."   —*Booklist* (starred review)

PENGUIN BOOKS

THE NAMES OF THE DEAD

Stewart O'Nan's award-winning fiction includes *Snow Angels* (Penguin) and the short story collection *In the Walled City*. In 1996 *Granta* named him one of the 20 Best Young American Novelists. His latest novel, *The Speed Queen*, was published in 1997. He lives in Hartford, Connecticut.

THE

NAMES

OF THE DEAD

STEWART O'NAN

PENGUIN BOOKS

PENGUIN BOOKS
Published by the Penguin Group
Penguin Books USA Inc., 375 Hudson Street, New York, New York 10014, U.S.A.
Penguin Books Ltd, 27 Wrights Lane, London W8 5TZ, England
Penguin Books Australia Ltd, Ringwood, Victoria, Australia
Penguin Books Canada Ltd, 10 Alcorn Avenue, Toronto, Ontario, Canada M4V 3B2
Penguin Books (N.Z.) Ltd, 182–190 Wairau Road, Auckland 10, New Zealand

Penguin Books Ltd, Registered Offices: Harmondsworth, Middlesex, England

First published in the United States of America by Doubleday,
a division of Bantam Doubleday Dell Publishing Group, Inc. 1996
Reprinted by arrangement with Doubleday,
a division of Bantam Doubleday Dell Publishing Group, Inc.
Published in Penguin Books 1997

1 3 5 7 9 10 8 6 4 2

The author wishes to thank Terry May, Doug Anderson, Grant Shirley, Matthew Link,
and Sung J. Woo for their invaluable assistance.

Thanks, too, to the MacDowell Colony and the Sewanee Writers' Conference for the time and
opportunity to complete this book.

Chapter 1 appeared in a slightly different form in *Whirlwind*.

Lyrics from "Ain't That Peculiar" by Robert Rogers, William Robinson, Jr., Marvin Taplin,
and Warren Moore, copyright © 1965, reprinted by courtesy of Jobete Music Co., Inc.

PUBLISHER'S NOTE
This is a work of fiction. Names, characters, places, and incidents either are the product
of the author's imagination or are used fictitiously, and any resemblance to actual
persons, living or dead, events, or locales is entirely coincidental.

THE LIBRARY OF CONGRESS HAS CATALOGUED THE HARDCOVER AS FOLLOWS:
O'Nan, Stewart, 1961–
The names of the dead/Stewart O'Nan.
p.   cm.
ISBN 0-385-48192-6 (hc.)
ISBN 0 14 02.6309 8 (pbk.)
1. Vietnamese Conflict, 1961–1975—Veterans—New York (State)—Ithaca—Fiction.
2. Married people—New York (State)—Ithaca—Fiction.
3. Stalking—New York (State)—Ithaca—Fiction.   I. Title.
PS3565.N316N36 1996   95–36745
813´.54—dc20

Printed in the United States of America
Set in Goudy Old Style
Designed by Claire Naylon Vaccaro

Honey, you do me wrong but still I'm crazy about you.
Stay away too long and I can't do without you.
Every chance you get you seem to hurt me more and more
But each hurt just makes my love stronger than before.
I know that flowers grow from rain
But how can love grow from pain?
Ain't that peculiar?

—MARVIN GAYE

I love you too much.

—SAIGON BAR GIRL LINE

THE

NAMES

OF THE DEAD

ONE

Larry Markham's wife left him while he was asleep. Between four and six, he figured as he made himself an egg, because at three he'd gotten up and, before looking in on Scott, turned the overhead light on and stood naked in the middle of the rope rug, amazed at the safeness, the pleasing security of their bedroom. The vacation pictures on the dresser, the wicker hamper, Vicki's breathing—the whole instant filled him with relief. Before he'd flicked the switch he'd been prepared to see the musty inside of his poncho liner, his rucksack smashed against his cheek.

"Skull," Carl Metcalf was saying, prodding him with the tip of his jungle boot, "time to motate, bro."

No, this was home, not Odin, clean sheets instead of red dirt. The sudden jump pleased him. He looked down at his new foot to confirm it, and there was the prosthesis, perfect, not a single nick in its skin-toned rubber coating. He was alive. It seemed, he could admit, standing there soft and a little paunchy, an overwhelming piece of luck.

He'd stood looking at Vicki curled and warm under the covers. Now, at the stove, he wondered if she had actually been asleep. The gas hissed, rushed and flowered into a blue flame. Outside, the rain made a sound he had not quite learned to ignore. She was the only woman he'd ever made love to, a fact he was secretly proud of. He thought he should feel worse about her leaving, about Scott, but he only felt incredibly tired, leaden. It was unfair; October was his favorite month—home to his father's birthday, Halloween. He could not think of what to do. The house was quiet, his coffee steaming. There were only a few crusts of bread left. It was enough today, now. He had work to go to, and after, his group at the hospital.

It was not the first time Larry Markham had woken alone to the radio and gone to Scott's room and found his bed mussed and his drawers empty. It wasn't a mystery. They'd had trouble early that summer, after a long good stretch. Since she'd come back they'd been trying, but lately every effort seemed to take all their patience. There were nights after Scott was in bed that they didn't talk.

He'd called down the stairs, not expecting anything. She had leaving him down to a routine. The fight Friday night over who always drove Scott to his Rehab had not been merely to set the mood for the weekend but a formal way of saying good-bye. How many times had she done it, yet it still surprised him. She'd risen—he knew—a few hours before he was supposed to get up to run and, guided by the weak beam of a penlight they'd received for subscribing to *Time*, made her way through the house. She'd skipped work the day before to pack a bag each for herself and Scott and then hidden them somewhere—Scott's closet or among her summer things in the attic. She'd gone to the bank just before it closed and arrived home at the same time as if she'd finished her shift at the Photo USA. There were variations of this, but it came to the same thing. He imagined her sneaking through the cold downstairs, noting the photographs she would miss, the plants she knew he'd ruin. Scott was upstairs, asleep, his huge head resting like a prize vegetable on the pillow, his disquieting eye open and sightless. The Ruster waited outside, its tank full. He'd have to take the bus today, probably be late.

"Great," he said.

The egg butted the side of the pot, dinging, and Larry spooned it out. He ran cold water over it and knocked it against a wall of the sink, picked bits of shell away from the dent. He set it gingerly in a dish, sat down by himself at the kitchen table, and chopped it into bits with the side of the spoon, the yolk too runny, disgusting. He sat there, spoon in hand, and looked at the egg as if it were a sign, a reminder.

He wondered who it had been in the dream this time. He wondered if he'd called out the man's name in his sleep—if, creeping down the stairs holding Scott's hand, Vicki had heard him, and if because of that (not in spite of it), she had felt even more sure, more at peace with what she was doing.

He'd dreamed, he knew, because he was exhausted, but which one?

"Doesn't matter," he said, and took a gluey spoonful and a bite of heel and sat there chewing, trying not to think, to focus on the positive, as he counseled his group, on the immediate, the real. It didn't work for them either.

There was no real. There were the dreams and there was what Larry Markham remembered. They did not change. In both, his platoon all died. Pony, Bogut, Lieutenant Wise—all thirteen, night by night, died, and Larry was grateful to wake to the ceaseless Upstate rains, the day laid out ahead of him like the puzzles his mother pieced together those long, drizzly fall afternoons, familiar and somehow comforting, a way to hold off the cold and the gathering evening.

Some nights it was one—Leonard Dawson or Fred the Head. Bates. Jesus, he thought, Go-Go Bates. Larry had fixed him twice, and still he died. He cut their fatigues off in dripping swatches, guided the syrette into their jumped-up veins. After he popped them with morphine he drew an M in grease pencil on their foreheads so the doctors would know back at the evac hospital. Dumb Andy, Smart Andy, Magoo. Carl Metcalf.

"What's it look like?" Lieutenant Wise asked when they'd thrown a perimeter around the downed man, and before Larry could answer, the face strapped into the helmet or cinched into the boonie hat changed, became all of them, none of them. Dust clung to their bloody trousers. They never looked down to see what had happened; they gripped his arm and looked him in the eye and waited for him to tell them. Nate looked up, the Martian looked up, clutching his elbow so it hurt.

"You're gonna be all right," Larry Markham said then.

"Truth, Skull." And still they wouldn't look. He did because it was his job, just as he ran to them when all he really wanted was to hug mud. "Medic up!" someone not hit called, and Larry saw his man and flung himself forward, his own skin burning in anticipation of the round. Sometimes there was nothing but a rag, a red flap, the unreal white of bone. With body shots, if there was more than one most likely the guy wouldn't make it much past dust-off, but you couldn't just let the guy go, not in front of everyone. Blood bubbled up between his fingers, ran over his hands. The dust could only soak up so much, then it flooded like a Coke knocked over— a gush and little rivers.

"Man," Larry said, sticking another pressure dressing on, "it don't mean nothin,'" and he couldn't tell from the change that came over their faces then whether they were grateful or hated him.

Other nights they came in bunches, the gloom of monsoon season filling the chill bedroom as he screamed into his pillow—or moaned, for their blood and stunted breathing no longer shocked him (as it had not shocked him originally, after the first few), but rather struck him with dread and, unable to stop or even slow the approach of the next one, he could only protest feebly, leaching out a "No, no" that drove Vicki to the living room sofa.

She knew not to wake him with an elbow or by nudging his shoulder; once, coming out of it, he punched her in the throat and had to drive her to the emergency room at Tompkins County, where he knew his father would hear of it at shift change. That she had intentionally broken Larry's nose during an earlier, less desperate period (with an ashtray stolen from the club where she waitressed, drunkenly and furiously hurled with absurd, almost comic precision) was held not to his credit but as further evidence that the entire marriage had been, as his father maintained, a mistake in the first place.

He let the spoon drop and sink into the yellow mess. She never left him for more than a few days. That was what this was. It was Monday, and he was sure to have a full truck, big deliveries at Tops and Wegmans and the three P&Cs. The IGA in Dryden, then the loop of gas marts south of town. Group. It would be a full day, a good day.

He left his dish in the drainer, assembled a bologna-and-cheese sandwich and bagged an apple. He liked having the house to himself, liked the silence. He thought of not going in, but brushing his teeth he walked by Scott's door and noticed his ham radio, the happily colored map of the world stippled with pins—all the places Larry had called and given the mike to Scott so he could say his name. He was a big eight but would always be four, five, the doctors weren't sure. Larry went back into the bathroom and spat. At the last second he remembered to put the answering machine on.

On the porch he fumbled with his keys, dropping his lunch with a thud.

He was going to be late, which he hated. The trees had just begun to turn and a first layer of wet leaves filled the ditches. Rain hung from black branches across the road; the cows were out, breathing steam. Farther up the hill a gray barn leaned as if gently stepped on. The rain made him listen harder; it pricked his face but from habit he didn't blink. The chill of Ithaca had not lost its ability to surprise him. He could never get warm enough, even in the height of July. There was no reason; he'd lived here his entire life except for his tour. He knew that that one year shouldn't have such pull, yet often it seemed equal to the other thirty-one, a balanced half, and sometimes, the worst times, he was convinced it meant everything, summed him up and finished with him before he'd had a chance to understand. In its lostness, its distance, it was something like childhood, vivid yet irretrievable, precious. Occasionally he thought he wanted to go back, to visit the paddies and dusty hills and meadows of head-high elephant grass with the amused, sentimental appreciation of someone visiting his elementary school home-room. At other times he wanted the country burned, scraped and sunk. Either way, like his father's paralyzing mix of love and disappointment, it was his.

Next door, Donna Burns's old Monte Carlo sat with its nose against the rotting lattice of the porch, its bumper jutting over the sidewalk. SAVE THE EARTH begged an exhaust-filmed sticker. Taking up the back half of the drive, Wade Burns's nearly restored Camaro wintered under a cloth tarp dotted with pockets of black water, and Larry thought that if Vicki couldn't stay for him, at least she shouldn't have run out on Donna.

She was tall and intimidating, the daughter of an Air Force colonel. In the summer she tanned deeply, ate nothing but fruit. She knew how to dance, when to exit a stalled party. Since Wade had left she drank fitfully. They hadn't seen her this weekend, but the car had stayed where she parked it around two on Friday morning, crookedly, getting out loudly by herself and hooting at something utterly private. He'd complained to Vicki that she was getting worse.

"What else is she supposed to do?" she'd said, and rolled over, away from him. That he and Wade had been close—had talked about his leaving over cold Schaefers in their garage months before Wade had gotten up the courage to actually do it—was a fact Vicki could not forgive him, and which he, seeing how Donna had fallen apart, now helplessly defended to himself.

"She's nice, she's the sweetest woman in the world," Wade admitted, then shook his head. "But she's not right. There's something very basically wrong with her. I've tried but I can't fix it." Larry promised that he and Vicki would keep an eye on her, which consisted of making sure she refilled her prescriptions and, occasionally, when she forgot, bailing her out. She had the habit, in the grip of her mood swings, of getting wildly drunk and smashing windows. One Easter morning they'd seen her in the backyard wearing nothing but a pair of tennis shoes and menacing Wade with a rake. Her waist was a girl's, her arms muscled.

"I don't care who Jesus is," she shouted. "I want my own radio show!"

She was better by the time Wade left, but they worried about her. Friday when she'd gotten in, Larry had seen her lights come on and lain in bed looking for her shadow, waiting for the crash and tinkle of glass. She crossed the windows and pitched forward, fell without a sound. At three, when he rose up in the thick of the jungle to find himself saved, her lights were still on.

Now it almost seemed funny that they were both alone, a weird coincidence. He'd had a crush on her once, a vision of her in a swimsuit at some summer barbecue, her dark hair halfway down her back. The children were little then. The judge had given them to Wade, and there was nothing to argue about, even she knew. After all their plans, it had come down to two houses, two people.

"Fucked up," he said.

He detoured around the Monte Carlo, wetting one leg of his jeans on the bumper's rubber strip in keeping to the asphalt walk. He could walk on grass now, but only when the weather was dry, and he would not step on dirt—it always appeared freshly turned and tamped. He could not explain why he still distrusted the ground; his foot was only the most obvious excuse. Early mornings, running the road, he had to pick his way through long puddles and ruts, herringbone patterns of mud laid by tractor tires, and when he accidentally touched one and his Nikes slipped an instant before regaining traction, his heart would spike and he'd swear out a cloud. He'd seen Dumb Andy fly backwards over Carl Metcalf and then himself into a banana tree where pieces of him hung like drying laundry. Weeks ago, cruising by the bus stop, he'd caught the toe of his new foot on the lip of a pothole and was sent stumbling, and two girls smoking cigarettes had laughed. Dizzy with fear, he'd nearly had to stop to vomit.

The walk began to disintegrate, then ended in chunks of asphalt. He followed the road's tarred, irregular edge, listening for cars behind him. Far off, the pitch of their tires on the concrete mimicked the shifting rush of a Phantom dipping its nose for a run. It was a pleasing sound, but one that made him flinch, a shoulder hunching to protect his face, like a sleepy duck tucking its head under a wing. From a klick off, the heat of a ville going up warmed his cheeks like the fire in his father's den. When he'd first caught himself in the gesture, running with his old foot, he'd been ashamed. There was so much of the world he didn't trust anymore. For months he taught himself not to look over his shoulder, to let the noise grow behind him and not see the canisters tumble from the rack, leave a smear of fire a block long. A stage passed where he could laugh at it; now it was a rare day that he gave it a thought, usually the sign of a bad one.

There was no one at the stop, for which he was grateful, only the *Journal* machine chained to the telephone pole. Something about the town trying to cut a last-minute deal. Typical Ithaca—nickel-and-dime politics. Cars came by with their lights on and their wipers arcing, each bringing its own small squall as it passed. One of them honked for some reason. Too late, Larry waved. Wind slipped under his collar, reached down his back. He fitted his lunch into the crook of his elbow and jammed his hands into his pockets. He could feel the warm lint in there. The cows seemed to be looking at him.

"Got a problem?" he called, but they didn't look away.

He checked his watch—there was still time, another ten minutes maybe. His luck. One must have just come.

Another car honked.

He waved.

"Why don't you stop and give me a ride," he muttered, watching it go.

A Duster passed, the wrong color and younger, hardly rusted. Vicki would have dropped Scott off already. She'd be at her mother's in Trumansburg, getting ready for work, rolling her stockings on, clipping her name to her uniform. He imagined what his father would say when he found out—and he would, Ithaca was that kind of town. Vicki would probably call his father to explain. Larry imagined him in the den after dinner, listening with that polite, untiring patience he used with the dying, thanking her for calling and then hanging up, continuing with his *New England Journal of Medicine* and half finger of Dewar's. He would not be surprised; he'd wait a day or two to call Larry to see if he was all right.

I'm okay, Larry would say.

If there's anything . . . his father would say.

No.

All right then.

Okay.

By Friday his sister Susan in Boston would know the whole story and give him a consoling lecture of a call. She had divorced, remarried, divorced again and remarried her first husband, and she had advice.

From the barn came the bright clinking of a bell, and the cows sauntered away in a group, their tails flicking. He turned from the road and kicked at the base of the telephone pole, his boot leaving a smudgy ghost of its waffle design in the creosote. He made another print directly above it and practiced hitting the two, as if warming up for a more difficult exercise. With his hands in his pockets, he imagined it was good for his balance. He could feel the rain sitting in his hair but didn't mind. He thought with a bitter kind of pride that he'd seen worse.

A Cougar came by flashing its lights.

"What the hell," he asked, but waved. The driver—a fat, bearded man he didn't recognize—waved back furiously.

"Everybody's friend," Larry said, "that's me."

He gave the shaft of the bus stop sign a spin kick, and the metal head shivered tinnily. Jesus, he hated being late. He hadn't been late for work in three years, and that was a snow day. He showed up to find the store locked, the parking lot trackless. Vicki had teased him for his loyalty, then speculated bitterly on the chances of him ever becoming a manager. For years they'd waged the same two or three fights, resting only for a special dinner, a present, an inspired night of lovemaking.

A pair of headlights the right height flared in the distance, but it was a rental truck, college kids. DISCOVER AMERICA! the panel urged above a lumpy Mount Rushmore. At least the little snots didn't honk.

"Come on," he said, and looked at the sky, the wind cold on his throat. Above him, clouds tore themselves to bits, shredded like sopping handfuls of gauze. It was an all-day rain, the kind that seemed to follow him around the globe. He'd liked them as a kid, liked sitting inside the dark house while his mother knitted to the radio. Susan was at school. His mother had a stack of heavy 78s—The Budapest String Quartet, Glenn Gould, Charles Munch and the Boston Symphony. On the covers were palaces and women in skimpy, exotic costumes. Her cane rested in the gap made by the couch cushions, its curved handle worn thin from her touch, the varnish smooth as glass. She had to try several times to get up. "Come give me a lift," she'd ask him, and he'd carefully place one sneaker on the empty tip of her shoe and take her hand and lean back with all his weight. Other times she called for Mrs. Railsbeck, their housekeeper, and he had to go outside or upstairs. "I'm all right," she assured Larry before sending him off, but her eyes were tired and wouldn't smile. His first day, getting off the plane at Bien Hoa, he'd seen an entire line of men with those eyes. They were going home. In a year he would leave with the same drained expression, yet he would never catch up to her. They would have to be in the same room—the dying woman and the spared man—on a day like today, endless and unchanging. They would talk of what his father, her husband, could not know. How, though there were years, great plains and deserts of life left, one only hoped to die.

It was official, he was going to be late. It angered him like a defeat. He thought of what he could say to the bus driver, something about being paid by the hour. A bead of water hung iciclelike from his nose; he blew it off and rubbed the tip with the back of a sleeve. An orange Volvo shot by, flashing its lights, hauling behind it a wall of spray that settled on him like a net.

"For Chrissake," Larry Markham said.

He was wiping water from his eyebrows with a knuckle when a large white car with its lights on slowed and stopped beside him. It was the Monte Carlo.

Donna Burns leaned across the big bench seat and opened the door for him with what he thought was too much of a smile. For a second he imagined she had just stopped laughing. She was brightly made up and had on sunglasses, a purple scarf, tan trenchcoat and black kneeboots, and Larry thought he didn't have the energy to deal with her.

"That's all right," he said. "One's due any minute."

"I don't think so. Don't you know?" She grinned at him as if he knew the answer but was playing dumb. She had an aggressive calm he associated—

from his group—with lunatics. He wondered if she could tell from his face that Vicki had left him again.

"No," he said blankly, "I don't know."

"They're on strike."

"Jesus Christ."

"Come on," she said.

He got in and they started off. She'd just gotten out of the shower and was wearing too much perfume. On the dash a red plastic coffee mug with a Cornell logo sat wedged into a matching base; in the trough of the defrost vent rested a bottle of Tylenol. She worked as a secretary for an obscure department, something to do with plants and psychology. He could not imagine how she dealt with people on an everyday basis, yet she did, and had even during her weird years. She turned down the radio—new wave, all synthesizers and chilly English accents.

"They just started today."

"That's what I get for not reading the paper," he said.

She turned up the heater for him, offered him the coffee. "It's got a kick," she warned.

It had some sort of mint in it, creamy and intensely sweet. The heaviness reminded him of schnapps, the first thing he'd learned to drink. She laughed at the face he made.

"Too sweet for you?"

"Nope," he said, and thought of riding around all day drinking the way he had when he first came back. A line of cars passed them in the other direction, people intent on getting to work. It pleased him to see life going on, even without him. It made his problems seem smaller, insignificant. It was important to know that not everyone was fucked up.

"Crummy day, huh?" She looked from the road to him. Her lipstick was smudged from the mug.

"Yeah," he admitted, and looked at the ranches and split-levels drifting by. Some had pumpkins on the porch steps, headless scarecrows made of old jeans and flannel shirts stuffed with hay. They slumped in lawnchairs or against coachlights, lay sprawled and fallen like dead VC. He had to buy candy—or Vicki would. Scott was going to be Superman, she'd already made the cape.

"So how are you doing?" she asked.

He wondered if she knew, if she'd figured it out or if Vicki talked to her the way Wade did to him.

"I don't know," he said, "okay. How about you?"

"Great. Never better." She took her hands off the steering wheel and put them over her eyes, leaned her head back as if rinsing her hair.

"Hey!" He took the wheel and brought the car back into the right lane. It was power steering, and hard to make it go straight. She took the wheel again, chased him away with a hand.

"I suppose you didn't hear me come in Friday night either."

"We did. You sounded like you were doing all right."

"Wade's moving to Oklahoma. Isn't that nice? Tulsa. I'm not going to see Brian and Chris except for Christmas and two weeks in the summer. I think that's fair, don't you?"

"I'm sorry. What's he doing in Tulsa?"

"Fucking some redneck bitch. And he's got a new job. Oh, everything's going great for Wade. He says hello."

"Say hello back."

"You do it," she said. She took a long shot of the coffee and pushed it into its holder again, frantically lit a cigarette and stabbed it at the windshield, the wipers slapping the rain away. "You don't know how fucking glad I'll be when this year is over."

"Tell me about it," Larry said, and for a moment hoped she knew. They were coming into Ithaca, passing the long prefab barns of Cornell's vet school before the hill dropped into town proper. The dash clock gave him an even chance of getting there on time. All the roads east of town funneled into Route 79, and he was glad she had to concentrate on traffic. Behind the wheel, she bobbed and weaved as if slipping punches from the other cars. He thought of spending the day riding high in Number 1, the simple deliveries, stopping to off-load a tray of Donettes and Hohos and Ring Dings to people he didn't know beyond a polite greeting.

"Well," Donna said, "what are you gonna do, y'know?" She seemed to wait for an answer to this, then asked, "What time you need to be there?"

"Doesn't matter," he said, but at Seneca and Aurora he gunned it through a long yellow. He would punch in before he put his uniform on, get a coffee at his first stop. Over the years he had not lost a taste for the crumb cakes, and one of his great pleasures was driving with an open box on the dash, washing the bite-sized treats down at stoplights and feeling the caffeine and sugar kick in. He always paid himself for them, and the next morning ran them off, fifteen calories a minute, but every time he tore the perforated strip from a new box, he accused himself of a sinful decadence, an intemperance indicating far greater weakness—which only made him eat more. Like everything, they tasted better in the rain. He knew he would polish off a whole box today, and it didn't bother him, in fact made him grateful to Hostess for the very existence of crumb cakes and for making them bite sized.

They didn't say anything for a while, and he liked her for it.

Coming down Seneca they got caught behind a school bus picking up some kids. One had a camouflaged backpack that made Larry look away.

"Hey," Donna said, "I know it's none of my business, but are you gonna be okay?"

He looked back to the school bus, willing it to move. In the emergency door a crush of little girls Scott's age were giving him the finger. They smeared their faces against the glass, blew their cheeks up monstrously. Donna looked at him pityingly, as if she understood. The dash clock's red second hand swept around.

"I've done it before," he said, "Christ, I don't know how many times now."

"I know," she said. She stubbed her cigarette out and frowned. The conversation seemed to have taken all the life out of her.

"Why," he asked, "is this time going to be different?"

She looked at him as if what she had to say would hurt him, but said nothing.

The bus pulled its stop sign in, its lights went from red to yellow, and it pulled out with a burst of diesel smoke. Donna passed it and, after, paid too much attention to the other traffic. They turned left at Meadow Street and headed south down 13. The Wonder Bread outlet was less than a mile, wedged into the sooty gauntlet of used car lots and fast food franchises, muffler shops and budget motels. If they hit every light they might still make it.

"I don't know," she said, ducking a blue Buick. "I just don't think it's the same this time."

"What did she say?"

"Nothing new, really." She grimaced apologetically. "She told me to keep an eye on you."

"Oh, great. When was this?"

"Thursday."

"Thanks for warning me," he said.

"She said you'd understand."

"I don't understand anything," he said, though even she could see it was not true. Just to piss him off, the lights ahead of them dropped sequentially to green, and silent, the radio playing some maudlin song about the difficulties of love, they ate up the mile to the outlet.

It was a white cinder-block building infected with the product's red, yellow and blue dots. Today they made him feel especially clownish; he hoped she wouldn't notice.

"Hey," she said, dropping him off. "Maybe I'll come by later, okay? Or vice versa, whatever."

"Sure," he said, and thanked her and closed the door, and for a few seconds walking to the rear of the building he was completely, blissfully alone.

He punched in precisely on time. The locker room was empty. Marv's gold Eldorado was in the lot, which meant he was in his office. Derek was up front, taking care of the earlybirds; Julian wasn't in yet, his card still on the OUT side. Larry was surprised the kid hadn't been fired. He was nice if a little spacy—a Deadhead and a computer nerd—and unlike Derek, seemed impressed that Larry was a vet. Julian was always after him for stories, and not obnoxiously, not kidding, he really wanted to hear them. Larry put him off— so much that it was a joke between them—but still it was good to have someone acknowledge what he'd done. Last week, Marv had asked Larry to talk to Julian about being late. Larry thought he'd gotten through.

Now he was late himself. This second he was supposed to be loading up the truck, ticking off his customers' orders against his invoices. Wonder White, Wonder Wheat. With a finger he flipped his locker open and began changing into the blue-and-white-striped uniform. A picture of Vicki helping Scott onto a pony was stuck to the door. She had on red short-shorts and a peppermint tube top; you could see the white lines from her bikini. He began to remember the day at the lake, the trip to the gift shop, how Scott had been excited by the windmill and the water hazard at the miniature golf

—and stopped himself. He clipped on his bowtie and zipped his Hostess jacket to the neck. Beside the picture hung a piece of Scott's art, a collage of fabric, macaroni and cotton balls signifying earth, sea and sky. Larry closed the door and pulled his cap snug on his head, took the keys to Number 1 down from the pegboard. He checked himself in the mirror, setting his jaw and tipping his chin up, then, satisfied, made for the front, untouchable, ready for the day.

He gave Marv a wave as he passed his window, up front said, "Hey," to Derek.

"Hey," Derek said, bagging a couple boxes of Suzy Q's for a stout woman Larry had seen before. Probably a teacher putting on a Halloween party—or Columbus Day, that was a holiday, a half-assed one. Scott had tomorrow off. Larry tried to think if she'd ever left on a Monday before.

He filled the orders on his clipboard, counting out cupcakes and Hohos, arranging the plastic trays in the dolly. Wegmans alone took fifteen minutes, and as his hands played over the soft bags and cellophane-windowed boxes, he remembered Leonard Dawson and Go-Go Bates eating pound cake at some night position in the hills. Nothing had happened, it was just a picture his mind coughed up, the skinny black man with his thick, issue glasses, beside him the giant Bates, spooning contentedly from their cans. They played hearts together with a deck Leonard's sister had given him; he sent a card home every Wednesday, one for each week of his tour. He'd started with the hearts, so by the time they left LZ Odin, the only card they had to watch out for was the queen of spades. Leonard said he was saving the deadly ace for last, that, defying all odds, he'd take it with him on the plane, pin the sucker to the peephole in his skivvies and play peekaboo with the stewardess. At Cocoa Beach everytime they heard a 707 he'd jump up from the table where he and Bates were playing, race halfway down to the green sea and wave whatever cards were left in his hand at the departing Freedom Bird, prophesizing in a voice uncharacteristically bold with rice whiskey and Tiger beer, "You are *mine*, motherfucker. Ace of motherfucking *spades!*"

Larry finished the last rack of fruit pies, added an extra box of crumb cakes, then took it off again. He remembered he'd left his lunch in his locker, and retrieved it before rolling the dollies onto the truck. Behind his window, Marv lowered his newspaper and pointed to his watch; Larry nodded.

"Eat me," he said when he was past, then did an immediate about-face, thinking of the crumb cakes, but saw instead Leonard Dawson's small hands, the high school ring he was so proud of, and stopped himself. On the way out he gave a lariat-twirling cardboard cutout of Twinkie the Kid the finger.

It was still raining; it was Ithaca. From the side of Number 1 the same boggle-eyed cartoon smiled down upon him, in full chaps and spurs yet horseless.

"Yahoo," Larry Markham said.

He checked the rear doors, got in and settled himself, letting the engine warm. He tugged on the knuckleless driving gloves Scott had given him for his birthday, snapped the snaps. He would call her at the mall, and then her mother if he didn't get her. The way he was going he'd barely have time to eat. He threw Number 1 into first and headed across the lot and clicked his turn signal on. As he was waiting to take the left, Julian's rusty Subaru turned in beside him and beeped. Larry honked back and goosed Number 1 across Route 13.

Sometimes he thought he was happiest driving, with his mind only half connected to the rhythm of bumpers in front of him, the flow of lights and signs. His eyes flitted over the road as if on ambush, picking out movement, gauging and dismissing it. The truck heated up. He got the defroster going, put the wipers on low and tuned the radio to WSKG, which had the last movement of Schumann's Rhenish Symphony blasting. He liked Schumann, unlike his mother, who called him "that nut," and when told by the announcer that he'd composed a piece she'd been interested in, responded to the room at large, "Oh, *him*." As a child Larry liked how the music forced him out of himself, took him somewhere else completely. Now he let the rain and heavy strings sweep him along to his first stop at Wegmans, insulated from the day.

The first thing Ron the assistant manager asked was "How's it going?"

"Good," Larry said. "You?"

It was all he had to say. Everyone else in the half-lit back of the store was busy tossing boxes or hosing down produce. They all wore the blue Wegmans uniform and responded to his with the edgy, mutual tolerance natural between different branches of the service. He rolled his dolly along, following the yellow-and-black caution tape on the floor through a tangle of hanging plastic strips that swallowed him like a car wash. It was cold on the other side, and he heard the ring, clash and clatter, the high, grinding whine of a saw from the meat department, but passed the gleaming steel doors without looking in either porthole. Above the last doors before the actual store hung a sign that said COURTESY FIRST. Beneath, behind violet-tinted windows, shoppers and their carts glided silently as fish. Larry paused an instant and straightened his cap. He liked the whole pageantry of entering from within, as if hustled from his dressing room through the chaos backstage to emerge perfectly from the wings. He took a breath, put on a game face and pushed through.

The lights were blinding, the air warm, the Muzak immediately lulling. It took him an instant to recover, as if he'd bumped a piece of scenery. No one noticed. He guided the dolly up the cookie aisle, set up shop and did his shelves.

No one approached or interrupted him. Shoppers pushed past, oblivious, as if he were invisible. The company was featuring a seasonal orange-and-black jack-o'-lantern cupcake, and to make room he had to tighten everything on that shelf. Someone had left a half-eaten Sno Ball on top of its wrapper; he laid its pink remains on a tray to toss in the garbage on his way out. The new chocolate-filled Hohos weren't moving, there was a form to report that. He checked everything against his clipboard and rolled on toward the bread corner.

His donuts and Donettes were fine, his iced honey buns. He could have easily shorted them a box of crumb cakes, but didn't, instead buying a huge styrofoam cup of black coffee at their deli. When he switched the hazards off and headed Number 1 for Tops, he was on time.

"Larry," the manager there said, "how are you, buddy?"

"Great," Larry said.

At the first P&C, the woman at the bakery counter asked, "How's the family?"

"Fine," he said, but this time questioned his enthusiasm, wondered if it gave him away.

"And your wife," inquired the woman in the second P&C's courtesy booth, "she still working up to the mall?"

"Sure is."

"Your boy, how's he now?"

"Goddammit," he said in Number 1, throwing his clipboard against the dash so hard his pen flew. He went into the back and grabbed a box of crumb cakes from someone's tray. No one would notice; no one really cared.

At lunch he stopped by the IGA in Dryden and tried Vicki at work. He stood in the rain-beaded booth, a chill sneaking through the accordioned doors.

"Photo USA," another woman answered—Cheryl maybe, or Katie, he could never tell them apart.

"Is Vicki there?" he asked.

A hand clamped over the mouthpiece. He heard someone muffled in the background. "Is this Larry?"

"Yes," he said.

"She didn't come in today." She waited, as if challenging him.

"Not at all?"

"Nope."

"Okay," he said, "thank you," and hung up.

He let her mother's phone ring nine times before he retreated to the oily warmth of Number 1. He sat there in the parking lot of the IGA and looked at the puddles and the phone booth while he ate his sandwich and his apple and three more crumb cakes, and thought again of Leonard Dawson, how he had disappeared from his foxhole one night to pee and they had to go find him. He was just a little guy, Bates kept saying afterward, showing how the ring wouldn't fit his own pinky, but nobody really wanted to hear it. He wasn't the first and wouldn't be the last, and maybe if he'd showed around that picture of his fine sister, more guys would have liked him.

Larry wrapped the core of his apple in a napkin and stuffed it into the bag, balled it up, got out and threw it in a barrel by the electric doors. He tried Vicki's mother again but came up with nothing. At her work he got the same answer from what he assumed was the same person, which meant nothing. She could still be either place, and with the car she was mobile. He decided to zip through his afternoon stops and catch her picking up Scott at school —not to argue with her but just to show he missed them. It was a plan, and enough to keep him moving.

It was a slow time at the gas marts, and everyone wanted to know how he was, whether he'd had a good weekend, who he liked between the Cards and Milwaukee.

"Fine," he said, "yep, oh, the Brew Crew," but kept his eyes on his merchandise, and hiding his rudeness behind work, hurried the clerks into signing his clipboard, refused their offers of coffee and swung Number 1 across the empty lots. It rained all day, as he knew it would. He finished early in Danby and rocketed back to town with his lights on, accompanied by a murky, Scandinavian tone poem. Below, to the north, an appropriate mist hung gloomily over the lake.

Pulling into the lot of the Special Children's Center, he was pleased to see the numbered buses waiting nose-to-tail with just their running lights on, chuffing out exhaust as their drivers caught a smoke under the overhang. Evening had begun to come down; a warm light filled the windows, made the emptying classrooms seem rich and busy as a hive. Only a few parents had shown up so far—no Ruster.

When they first sent him there, Scott had wanted to take the bus; they'd even tried it for a week, but Vicki found herself going to get him anyway, haltingly following the bus home. Larry joked with her about it, but now— and whenever he drove past the Center during the day—he felt just as helpless. It was his fault the doctors had to reroute Scott's intestines as an infant, his fault his son had no sense of smell. Often when Scott looked at him with his mismatched eyes, his brow so large it appeared ripe, almost soft, Larry wanted to take the boy's face in his hands and with a power drawn not from God but simple justice miraculously heal him. Instead he taught him how to turn the sound down on the TV so the cartoons he loved but would never understand wouldn't wake them up Saturdays. Two years ago, when he was picking up his first words, Vicki got him to say "Smells good" whenever she creaked open the oven door. It was a highlight of holiday get-togethers at her mother's. The one time Larry's father had witnessed it, he said, "Jesus," and turned for the living room where he'd left his whiskey. He never said it, but Larry knew he wanted another grandson to keep up the line. Susan's two girls didn't count.

Larry took the last crumb cake from the box, then put it back as a brace of cars pulled up and double-parked beside the loading zone. One man in a Toyota took out a book and began to read.

A few students pushed through the doors and scattered, then stood dazed in the rain, trying to identify their rides. He recognized some from their coats and canes, and one from the steel halo bolted into his head. He was so used to seeing the contraptions at the hospital that he had to remind himself it wasn't normal.

A rush of students spilled onto the walk, and the bus drivers ground out their cigarettes. A mother flung open a car door and knocked a lunchbox from her son's pincer of a hand, then waited patiently while he retrieved it. Larry didn't see anyone from Scott's class yet. Still no Ruster.

The children sprinted and skipped and wandered, some holding their coats despite the cold. One stood forlornly by the doors, resting his hooded head against the brick wall. A mother struggled with a science project made from aluminum foil and a large cardboard box. The first bus pulled out and the other two moved up. He thought he spotted a girl named Natalie that Scott had invited over to play once, and there was Jeffrey, and Matthew with his Smurf backpack. The second bus was loading, heads filling the windows. A cheddar Chevy van swung alongside the curb, picked up one kid and zoomed off again.

The headlights of the second bus came on, showing how hard it was raining now. They swept across the lot as the bus wheeled around, followed by the third.

No one else was coming out; most of the cars were gone. Two teachers stood by the doors, a man and a woman hugging themselves against the cold, occasionally waving. He strained toward the windshield to see if Scott was among the stragglers on the walk, and when he didn't spot him, undid his seat belt, got out and picked his way through the puddles.

"I'm looking for my son?" he asked the man and woman simultaneously. "Scott Markham?"

"Wait here," the woman said, and went inside.

The man was young and wore a thin leather tie and pointy shoes. Larry could feel him looking at his uniform.

"How's it going?" Larry asked.

"Good," the man said defensively, and asked him the same thing.

They stood side by side watching the last cars go off, the clouds slide dramatically across the hilltops. Now the children were all gone, the lot empty except for Number 1. The lights inside went out.

"He wasn't in today," the woman explained when she returned. "The office says it was an excused absence."

Larry tried to come up with something—a mix-up, crossed wires—but could only thank them. He knew they would watch him back to the truck and talk about him as he pulled out. What the hell, at least he had tried.

He started Number 1 and pulled his gloves on and, looking at his fingers, saw Go-Go Bates with Leonard Dawson's class ring on a bootlace around his neck. When they came to medevac him the second time, the doc on the chopper automatically went for his tags. He squatted there with the ring in his hand as the skids rose and tilted. "B plus!" Larry hollered up into the rotor wash, "He's B pos!" and when the other medic held a hand to his ear, he gave up and pointed to his boots, where Bates had stashed his tags—one laced into each—so they wouldn't clink and give him away on ambush.

"Jesus," Larry said in wonder, and gently thumped a fist against the steering wheel. "Go-Go, man. B pos." He opened the last crumb cake and sat there eating it while the rain trickled down the windshield. When he was done, the man and woman were gone, the doors shut.

The lights of Ithaca were on now. Rush hour had begun, and Larry had to jockey across several lanes to make the turn into the Wonder outlet. The front was busy with people picking up cheap loaves on the way home. Through the windows he could see Julian and Derek at the counter, and he thought he would have to ask Julian for a ride to his group at the hospital and then fend him off in the car. There were these two guys in our platoon, he might say. A little guy and a big guy. A black guy and a white guy. A smart guy and a dumb guy. Then group, where it was his job to hear their stories, and later he'd have to catch a ride back with his father, when all he wanted was to be alone with Leonard Dawson and Go-Go Bates for the evening. Vicki would show up at her mother's eventually with some loopy rationale for Scott missing school. Christ, it was tiring.

Marv's Eldorado was gone. Larry fit Number 1 into its space and locked up. Inside, the picture of Vicki in her tube top ambushed him, and he banged the door shut so hard that it opened again.

He called her mother's from the front; while he was listening to it ring, the lights flickered twice, signaling last call. When Derek had closed out his drawer, he chopped the lights off, vaulted the counter and locked the front doors. He had his apron and uniform shirt off before they made the locker room.

Julian said he could give him a ride but first he had to clean up.

"And *he's* going to open up tomorrow," Derek said, hauling on his leather jacket, "and all week. Word came down."

"All talk," Julian said, but glumly.

"I don't know," Larry warned.

"I will see you gentlemen tomorrow," Derek said. He punched out and a minute later crossed the front window holding an umbrella and leaning into the wind.

Larry helped Julian wipe down the counters and stayed out of the way while he swabbed the floor. A car turned into the lot, realized they were closed and swung back onto the road. Larry peered out at the traffic, the lights going both ways.

"Wanna get stoned?" Julian offered, pinching a roach between his fingernails.

"Can't."

Julian took a last hit and tossed it into the mop water, rolled the bucket to the sink and muscled it up and in. While he cleaned the sink, Larry picked their cards out of the rack and checked Julian's time in.

He looked at the phone with its twisted cord hanging beside the time clock and thought he would have to call his father eventually. He picked it up and dialed the number, waited for the operator and then the receptionist to switch him to the office.

"This is Doctor Markham," his father answered, as if prepared for the next, more difficult question.

"Dad, Larry. I was wondering if I could get a ride with you tonight."

"Again."

"Again," Larry admitted, though the last time had been a month ago when the Ruster dropped its muffler.

"Car trouble?"

"Basically," Larry said.

"Eight-fifteen?"

"That would be great."

"Meet you in the lobby."

"Okay," Larry said, "thanks," and they hung up without saying good-bye. Larry stood there looking at the phone for a second, the swinging cord. It hadn't been bad, and yet he knew his father already counted this—however small—as another failure.

"Don't punch me out yet," Julian called from the front.

"Right," Larry shouted.

"So what did Marv say?" Larry asked in the Subaru. Julian had the Dead blasting—Red Rocks '73, he said. In the backseat the components of a computer rested haphazardly among old newspapers and fast food trash. Julian darted between lanes, making Larry press an imaginary brake pedal. Behind them, plastic clattered every time they stopped short.

"Fucking Marv," Julian said. "I just can't be late for a while. I can do that. Don't get me wrong, but it's not like my dream job, you know?"

"Yeah," Larry admitted.

"I don't know, 'dream' and 'job' don't really go together for me. I'd rather just sit in a room and work at my terminal."

They turned onto Fulton and then State, headed for the Octopus, where the roads from the west side of the lake came together at the bottom of the hill.

"So what's up with your group?" Julian asked.

"The usual," he said, deadpan, to keep him from going further. The usual —and what was that?

A dead guy and a dead guy.

No one would touch Leonard Dawson until Carl Metcalf went over him for booby traps. Larry cut him down and fit him back together. They'd sliced off his tattoos and made new ones.

"Fuck," Lieutenant Wise said when he saw him.

"Fuck is right," Bogut said, holding his own jaw as if it might fall off.

Bates came stumbling through the brush, half awake. Larry saw Pony look away, saw the Martian turn to give the big man space. Carl Metcalf went to stop him, but Smart Andy held him back with a hand. Bates stood there.

"Aw, Leonard," he said, and knelt down. "Aw, Leonard." He put his sixteen aside and reached for his boonie hat to put over Leonard Dawson's face, but he wasn't wearing it. He used his hands to cover his friend, as if the torn skin were a blinding light, something not to be looked upon, and after a minute Magoo came back with Leonard Dawson's hat with its jaunty Australian curl and handed it to Bates. Everyone stood around in the dark while Nate trained his red-lens flashlight on his miniature Bible and whispered a quick prayer. They couldn't get a dust-off until morning, and all night Bates sat beside Leonard Dawson as if he were only sick, feverish, and when the chopper came and they tagged him and bagged him up, Bates laid him on the floor of the Huey himself, and while the rest of the platoon watched, unfolded the poncho for a last look, closed it again and patted Leonard Dawson on the chest as if he'd done a good job and clambered out. The chopper lifted, dipped its nose and powered away, leaving a cloud of red dust that made them claw at their eyes and spit.

"He couldn't fucking hold it," Bates said a few weeks later. "Fuckers probably got him in mid-squirt. Fucking Leonard. I told him, save that water for the middle of the day, drink your Cokes early on to get your motor going, but he'd have 'em with dinner. He liked his Cokes, that was one thing he liked all right. Weinies and beans and a Coke on a shitty day."

A day like today, Larry thought, watching the blurry taillights through the wipers. They were going up the long hill of 96 to the hospitals, the route the ambulances took, past Vinegar Hill. Below on their right lay the dark blot of the lake, the far shore defined by a few tiny lights. On the way down with his father they would see the burning grid of Ithaca. What would Larry say to him? So often his life seemed without explanation, utterly defenseless, though he knew—deeply—that he was trying.

Fucking rain. If she was gone for good, maybe he'd leave, go somewhere dry—Arizona or New Mexico. But she wasn't gone, it was just another false alarm.

"Emergency entrance?" Julian asked, turning into the highly lit grounds. The VA and regular hospitals were connected and shared parking.

"Right next to it."

They pulled up ahead of a darkened Bangs ambulance. It was a local joke; downtown the Bangs family ran an EMT service and right beside it a funeral home.

"Thanks," Larry said, getting out. "I'll see you *early* tomorrow."

"Okay, boss," Julian said. As the Subaru looped back to the entrance, Larry could hear the Dead thumping through the doors and thought that it was inevitable and best not to get involved. One way or another, he would lose him too.

IT WAS ALWAYS the goddamn Wall. All summer the ward had seen it being built on TV, on the Armed Forces Network—a big black V engraved with the names of the dead. It was being built not by the government but with private money raised by a vet, which they liked. They wanted Larry to go for them when it opened, to make sure their buddies were there. They joked about getting up the money to send him, like the Fresh Air kids from the city. They wanted him to take pictures of names, whole panels, and though he said flatly—laughing—that he would not go, each of them was drawing up a list of friends.

It was what discussion drifted to in rap group. They'd lose what they were trying to say about the war and go off into stories about people he'd have to find.

"Man," Mel White would say, or Cartwright, "this dude you *got* to get. He was one bad-ass Sergeant Rock motherfucker."

Sponge was the worst, because of the old hematoma. His memory wasn't good but it was full, and since he'd started talking again, no one could shut him up. On top of that he was a juicer, and an old radioman, and something about stories got him going. The rest of the time he played Othello and penny poker with Rinehart and Meredith and, like everyone on the ward, watched the game shows with a mixture of disbelief and scorn for not only the host and contestants but any country that would permit such abominations. He had a dent in the side of his head like a little shelf, and sometimes he'd rest a pen there and forget it. He'd been in the Ia Drang Valley early on, a place Larry Markham even now considered himself lucky not to have seen.

"I wish I could remember his fucking name, this A-gunner. Everyone called him Dog 'cause he had this German shepherd he slept with. Couldn't sleep without him 'cause he was afraid of rats. Frank Something. I remember the dog's name was Toad. He was supposed to be able to sniff out tripwires and shit from the fish oil on the gooks' fingertips."

"And this Toad stepped on a package and waxed Frank Something," Trayner guessed.

"Emulsified his master, is that right?" Cartwright baited him.

Around the circle the rest of them waited for Sponge to come up with his usual sparkling bullshit. It was a game, and okay because Sponge knew it too and was good at it. It wasn't like trying to listen to Rinehart, who they all knew was telling the truth but couldn't make it interesting. They all wanted to see what Sponge would come up with, all except the new guy, Creeley, who picked his nails with mock concentration. His face was subtly two-toned, the skin grafts from his thighs lighter, with bristly hairs. Across his forehead the contrast between shades made his hairline look crooked, as if he'd had the top of his head cut off and all but a small strip put back on, which in fact he had. He'd been on the neuro ward less than a week, and it was his first time in group. He could talk, but slowly and with a slur. His file was frightening in its poverty of detail; all it said was that he'd been a SEAL working in the Phoenix program and that he'd been wounded in action, though it seemed obvious that he'd tried to eat a .45. He had no hometown, no birth date, but sprang fully grown and half healed from Bethesda Naval Hospital. As a counselor, Larry had been briefed on the Phoenix program, but vaguely, as if it was unlikely he'd see any of its survivors. It was totally covert. Assassinations—basically murder—working with Vietnamese cons paid by the CIA. It was something nobody wanted to admit to anymore. Larry drew a line next to Creeley's name on his clipboard. He'd have to talk to him one-on-one in conference, be patient with him.

"VC haul him off at night and boobytrap his ass," Meredith offered.

A beat behind, Johnny Johnson laughed, for no apparent reason. He had a Teflon plate and no ears and was subject to long, exhausting fits. On his bedstand his mother had propped a picture of himself before the war wearing a floppy velvet cap and giant sunglasses edged with rhinestones and playing the bass. "Is it hot?" he would ask at any time, referring, Larry supposed, to the landing zone or village he was continually approaching. He'd been walking behind a man who stepped on a fifty-pound antitank mine. The man was instantly vaporized. Johnny Johnson lost his right arm, right leg, right kidney, his spleen, half his pelvis, his testicles and his penis. The others considered him the worst off, and gave in to him on small matters such as extra desserts and what to watch on TV.

"It's a rat story," Mel White tried. "The rats chew his nose off and old Frank loses it."

"Unh-unh," said Sponge, "wait," and tipped his head forward as if to call for quiet or gather breath. As he did, he discovered a mechanical pencil sitting on his dent. He pinched it off and admired its intricacy with such smugness that they knew he was done stalling.

"So we're out on night ambush—"

The circle as a whole ridiculed this pat opening with snorts and puffs of breath just short of a mass raspberry—save Creeley, who seemed annoyed by the entire process. His chart said he was heavily medicated for pain, Dilaudid three times a day. He looked off down the ward as if any minute a car would turn the corner of the nurses' station and pull up for him. Sponge acknowledged their derision with a nod, but kept on.

"We're patrolling around for a while and haven't found a juicy position, no contact, nothing. You know, prime time, everybody's spooked—"

"And the dog barks," Trayner said earnestly. He was the baby of the group, a month short of thirty. He'd caught a dud rocket grenade in the face, though—as Meredith said—you couldn't be sure he wasn't like this before.

Sponge stopped as if pondering Trayner's suggestion, honestly trying to remember. "No, I don't think he did. He might have, I don't know, 'cause all of a sudden we get some fast fire from the right and everybody hits it. Like a year later it's over and you can hear Toad crying, and you know he's got one in him. Sounded just like somebody real, swear. Frank's trying to shut him up and calling for the doc."

"Fuck's the doc gonna do?" Cartwright said, partly to rib Larry. They knew he'd been a medic; it was in the files. He'd never told them, just as he'd never told them his nickname. He never told his own stories in group. It was not that his own were either special or dull or that he thought he would not do a good job of telling them, but that they were not all his to tell, though (and this they did not know, Vicki didn't know, even his father did not know) he was the only one left to tell them. This was their time, not his. It was enough, Larry thought, that they knew he'd been in-country and seen some shit, but like Julian they were interested in him. They always wanted more.

"So the doc goes over and slaps a dressing on him and shoots him up and has me call for a dust-off, and by the time they come in there are tracers zipping all over the place. We get Toad in a poncho and up and in, and the door gunner is all bullshit that his wounded is a dog, and the pilot wants to toss him until Frank *makes* him understand, know what I'm saying? So Toad goes to some evac hospital and we bust caps at them for a while and that's that. Back at base they call in and tell me Toad's okay, but Frank can't sleep. Do a bone, I tell him, have a nice warm brew, but he can't sleep. This goes on."

"I've seen it," Rinehart seconded.

"Three, four days, and Frank's a fucking zombie. The LT asks the doc to give him something, and it works, but it's not the same kind of sleep, it's like fake sleep, and Frank is just as messed up as before. Make a long story short, he steps on an unfriendly device and goes home in a jar."

"But the dog lives," Trayner said.

"Course the dog lives, Jughead," Mel White said. "That's what the story's going to be."

"Right. 'Cause when Toad comes back from the evac, his pal Frank's gone."

"So now the *dog* can't sleep," Meredith said.

"Or he barks all night," Cartwright said.

"Bingo," Sponge said, pointing. "We couldn't take him out anymore. We'd leave him back at base and he'd howl like a coyote all night long. It was obnoxious. Finally someone in Bravo greased him while we were out. Tore half his fucking head off and burned him in a shit barrel. End of story."

"Damn," Cartwright said, and nodded.

Johnny Johnson giggled. Rinehart tapped his shoulder and held a finger up to stop him.

There was a silence, as if in honor of the dog or, more important, the moral truth of the story.

"A boy and his dog," Mel White said, "that's what we'll call that one."

"Bull . . . shit," Creeley squeezed out. It was an effort, as if he were dredging the words from his lungs, muscling them up and pushing them out. The jagged line of the grafts made it hard to look at his face without staring, wondering how they fit the top back on. It looked like a rush job, the stitches obvious. Sponge shrugged as if Creeley were nuts and it was impossible to take offense.

They waited for Creeley to go on.

"No . . . dog."

"What the fuck are you talking about?" Rinehart said.

"No dog. Bullshit."

"Were you there, mister?" Cartwright said. With his legs on he was half a head taller than Larry Markham; he squeezed a handball constantly, even while eating. His only problem was that from time to time he held hands with a friend he'd left behind, a guy from his hometown named Mobley. "Mobley's tired of five-card," he'd say after conferring with him, or "Mobley's got a case of the fuck-yous today."

"I was," Creeley said, "everywhere." He turned to Larry and pointed. "I know you."

"Listen to this shit," Mel White said. "Hey, Captain America, you got a story for us or you just gonna piss on our party?"

"Yeah," Meredith said. "Doc, make the newbie tell us a story."

"*His* story," Cartwright said. "That's what I want to hear."

"Fair enough," Larry said. "Mr. Creeley, would you like to introduce yourself?"

"You know me," Creeley said. "You remember." He stood and hobbled down the ward to his bed and drew the curtain violently about it, the rollers protesting.

"Yeah," Sponge said reminiscently, and looked at the pencil, "Frank Something. Wish I could remember his name."

"Fuck Frank and fuck his dog too," Cartwright said, pointing to Creeley's bed. "I'm putting *his* name on my list. Fucking brain-damaged two-tone Frankenstein motherfucker."

All but Johnny Johnson laughed.

"All right, gentlemen," Larry said, "back to business. Whose turn?"

Before he could check his clipboard, Meredith said, "Okay, I got one," and the group settled in to hear it. Meredith had been a lurp, and his stories always began a few weeks into the deep bush. The jungle's triple canopy and birdless silence gave his tales a mystery the others couldn't resist. Looking for lost choppers, his squad would stumble over an NVA base camp with the rice fires burning, or come across an underground hospital full of VC hooked to empty bottles of blood, their throats cut. He was also wholeheartedly Born Again, and at some point in the story, by way of explanation, the Lord would be called in to set things right. It was an annoyance someone like Rinehart wouldn't get away with. Tonight they were in the Arizona Territory, and Larry kicked back and listened. He remembered the jungle, the heavy air and the wet sponge smell of fungus, the dusk in the middle of the day. Meredith led them in.

It was here, among the other men, that Larry felt most himself. He felt welcome and understood without having to explain. He could rest, stand down, as he did now, barely marking Meredith's progress into the foothills of the Que Son Mountains. The thought of Vicki and Scott, of riding home with his father, no longer bothered him, and though he knew that would change when he left the ward, that the world would come flooding back with all its problems, he would not let it intrude and ruin this quiet time. It reminded him of his mother's radio, how those afternoons alone he didn't want the music to end. Now he wanted the stories to go on and on.

Like every Monday, they ended when Shaun the orderly came in to give night meds. It was past eight but he waited a minute by the swinging doors for Meredith to finish. It was a tiger story, how both sides stopped in the middle of a firefight to watch it lope through, how no one dared shoot.

" 'Cause, dig, the animal was majestic," Meredith preached. "It was better than us and we knew it. It was purer. We knew we didn't have the right so we just let it walk on by. See, I didn't know it at the time, but I see now that that was a holy experience."

"Fuck," Mel White said. "Should of lit his stringy ass up."

"A tiger," Johnny Johnson said, awed like a child.

"Musta been something," Trayner said.

"It was okay," Sponge complained. "Not a lot of action."

"No . . . tiger," Cartwright stuttered, mocking Creeley. "Bull . . . shit."

Larry looked to Shaun and nodded.

"Okay, guys," Shaun said, tapping his watch, and they muttered and swore.

Mel White started to roll away.

Larry checked his clipboard. "Next week we've got Cartwright and an open spot. Who wants it?"

"Anybody but Rinehart," Mel White tossed over his shoulder.

"Eat shit," Rinehart said, but didn't volunteer.

"Give it to Mobley," Sponge said.

"Come on," Larry prompted, standing. They were scattering to their beds. The World Series was on in twenty minutes. "Train, you haven't been up in a while."

"You tell one," Trayner said.

"Yeah," Meredith seconded.

"Yeah, c'mon, Larry," Shaun pitched in.

"You owe us, Doc," Sponge said.

They all looked at him hopefully, and he wondered which one he would tell first if he were going to. His own, or just the beginning of his. Getting

29

there. And then who? Fred the Head and his little girl? The day Nate tried to fly. The first and then the second. He'd have to put them in order. It was hard to remember exactly but he'd have to do it. Once started, he'd have to tell them all.

When Larry didn't answer, Cartwright said, "Okay, then the new guy."

"Jesus," Mel White said, "it'll take all fucking night."

They looked to the curtains around Creeley's bed as if he might answer.

"I'll just leave it open," Larry said.

He always had trouble leaving. Often he wished he could stay, bring a case of beer and watch TV with them till lights out. He stowed his clipboard and papers in the one drawer the hospital gave him and locked up. Later in the week Dr. Jefferies would open it and look at his notes; once a month they had a meeting in her office. She was interested in the men, but she was Chinese, and they distrusted her.

Shaun rolled the meds cart between beds, handing out pleated paper cups and, for a few, shooting prepared syringes into their IV drips. The drips hung from wheeled stands so they could roll them down to the lounge to watch the game. Trayner was helping Cartwright on with his legs.

"I'll see you in a week," Larry announced, and waved to both sides of the aisle. He was always tempted at this point to salute, but as usual fought it off. He made for the doors, not looking at anyone. Good men. It was not bullshit.

He thought of stopping to look in on Creeley, then decided against it. Give him time, room to move. It wasn't like they were going anywhere.

HIS FATHER was not waiting for him in the lobby, as he'd promised. Larry checked the clock behind admitting, then went outside to see if his New Yorker was in the lot. His father was the first person in in the mornings and parked nearest the doors. And there the big Chrysler sat in the rain, waxed and sleek as a speedboat, its windows dark. Last week Larry had seen an equally big Oldsmobile south of town with former prisoner-of-war plates, and thought maliciously that his father would never advertise, never admit that fact to the world. Why did Larry want him to?

He retreated inside, and as he watched the Brewers bat, the day returned, as he knew it would. He thought of calling Vicki's mother again, and only pride and not wanting his father to know kept him from doing it.

Across from him, leaning forward and staring at the floor as if she'd been benched, sat a teenage girl in a basketball uniform, glumly holding a plastic bag of ice to her wrist. Beside her a friend was filling out her paperwork, and though the girl did not seem to be in any real pain, Larry turned away. There were no outs and the Brewers had already scored four runs. Someone had liked baseball a lot—Nate, maybe. *Stars and Stripes* had the box scores a week late.

"Are you allergic to anything?" the friend asked, and Larry had to get up and move to the other side of the room.

It was one of those days nothing was safe. The first magazine he picked up had a picture of British soldiers patrolling the streets of Belfast, the second a model with an elaborate version of Vicki's perm. He moved to the back part of the hallway, where there was nothing but aerial photos of the new wing being built and, at the far end, a rain-lashed window looking out on the night and the cold lake, the shivering lights of Ithaca. He paced and thought of the Wall, how they would make him go. He supposed he owed it to them. He would have to make his own list. Look up their names, take pictures. He almost wanted to. He'd take Scott. Vicki would have to lend him the car. It would be simple. The hard part would be the drive.

Behind him, farther up the hall, the elevator rolled open. His father got out first, already wearing his hat, and turned for the lobby without noticing Larry. Behind him came a pair of families exhausted with visiting; the children spread across the hallway and Larry had to tag along behind. His father walked purposefully, as if in a hurry, outstripping them. He had his keys out, jingling, and carried nothing but a pair of gloves. The tasseled end of his white scarf flopped rhythmically against his back. He had no reason to look behind him and see Larry, but when they got to the lobby, he didn't stop or even hesitate. He waved to the uniformed guard, drove straight for the automatic doors, hit the mat that made them fly open and marched off into the dripping night, still in stride.

Larry caught him before he opened the driver's side.

"Hey," he called across the roof.

His father looked at him quizzically, surprised to see him but pleased.

"We were supposed to meet in the lobby," Larry said. "I needed a ride?"

"Right," his father said, still catching up to it. He pointed to show he did remember. "Sorry."

He opened the door and reached across the seat to lift the knob, and Larry got in.

"Sorry," his father said, "I've been dealing with Margaret Cushing all day —Mrs. Cushing who used to live on Linn Street? She went around dinnertime and it's been crazy. So where do you need to go?"

"Just home."

"Can do," his father said.

As they exited the lot, an ambulance pulled in. Its lights weren't strobing, but the back compartment was lit, and Larry could see a blue-shirted EMT moving within. She wore rubber gloves and had a ponytail. He concentrated on the knobs of the radio, making the orange line slide across the dial, but couldn't stop the vision of Fred the Head from coming—his own hands pushed into his chest, the lung wound bubbling a pink froth with every breath, hissing and sighing, squeaking like a leaky tire.

"Truth, Skull."

"Don't mean nothing, man."

"Shit," the Martian said, staring at the hole where Larry's hands disappeared, shaking his head. "There it is, man."

"Get him the fuck away from me," Larry told Bogut, and he did.

"Don't mean a thing, Fred," Larry whispered.

"Truth."

"Truth, bro. All right?"

"All right, man."

"All right, man, you're gonna fly them friendly skies. This is gonna pinch a little."

"S'all right, I can't feel shit anyway."

"You're all right, man."

"M'all right."

Larry rubbed his eyes as if he were tired, and it disappeared, replaced by the glare of oncoming traffic. His father leaned back in the seat, steering with his gloved hands resting near the bottom of the wheel, a mannerism he and Larry shared. His chin was lined with white stubble, his neck a soft wattle disappearing into the debonair scarf. The news was on—another flood in the Midwest—and Larry wondered if the prison camp came back to him every time the Japanese were mentioned. The wire, the mealy rice, the friends who didn't survive—where did it all go?

They'd never talked about it; his mother wasn't allowed.

"He will tell you," she'd say when pressed, "when he thinks you need to know those things."

It was too late now, Larry thought, though he couldn't pinpoint when he could have used his father's wisdom. Before he signed up for the fucking medical corps and Fort Sam Houston. But that wouldn't have stopped him, only made him want to go more. He sat back in the seat and watched the dark farms slide by, the lights of oncoming cars mimicking the firefly wobble of a rocket grenade.

"Car trouble?" his father asked.

"Oh yeah."

"Bad?"

"Don't know yet."

"How old is that thing anyway?"

"Younger than this," Larry said, and then regretted comparing the two.

"Just tuned her up," his father boasted. He'd been driving it since Larry was in high school.

"She sounds good."

It was a lesson, like everything between them. He thought if they made it to the Octopus without his father asking after Scott that he'd be all right. They coasted down the hill toward town; below, a string of lights described the jetty running out into the black lake. Probably rain again tomorrow.

"So how is everyone?" his father tried.

"Okay," Larry said. "How's Mrs. R.?"

"Maddy? As usual. She keeps trying to get me to retire. Hates the weather here, always has."

Larry half ignored his answer. He'd asked after her only to change the subject. He didn't need to imagine their life together in the old house; besides a few new appliances, everything was the same—the paintings in their heavy gilt frames, his mother's furniture, the color of the walls. And for his father the days were the same. Mrs. Railsbeck laid out his clothes and made his breakfast, as his mother once had. While he was at the hospital, she did the laundry and the cleaning and the food shopping. His father had bought her a Volkswagen Rabbit, and occasionally Larry would see her around town, squinting at the traffic, her chin almost touching the steering wheel. Back home she watched the little TV while preparing dinner, and when his father came home, ate with him, cleaned up and sat reading magazines before the console in the living room while he retired to the den. They slept in separate rooms, just as his mother and father had, though everyone in town presumed to know.

"She wants to have you folks over for my birthday."

"Sounds good," Larry said. They were just being polite; it was the one day his father had them all over, at Mrs. Railsbeck's insistence. Usually when he asked if Larry would like to come over, he meant just Larry, at the most Larry and Scott. Vicki hated his endless courtesy. "Why doesn't he just say it to my face?" she'd complain. "I don't understand all this pussyfooting around. He doesn't like me. That's okay, I don't mind, I just wish he'd be upfront about it."

They breezed through the green of the Octopus, and Larry tried to imagine riding with him every day.

He'd call her mother when he got home. Maybe they could work something out with the Ruster.

Downtown, his father missed the turn to take him up the hill.

"You mind taking me home?" Larry asked. "Or you can just drop me at the stop up here."

"Sorry," his father said, "woolgathering," and tapped the brim of his hat. He changed lanes and made a quick left to get back to where they'd been. He didn't seem to be all there, staring over the wheel like a trucker too long on the road. He'd had a patient die today. Larry thought it was foolish to worry about him; it was the last thing his father would want. He was tempted to think that after so many years you got used to losing people, but Larry knew that each one bothered his father, even if he'd never admit it.

"Who was it today?" Larry asked gently.

"Mrs. Cushing—Anne Cushing's mother. Anne was there."

"She was in Susan's class."

"Nice girl. She's with Therm now."

"How was it?"

"Oh," his father said, perking up, "it went well."

"Good," Larry said, equally cheerful, but his father was done talking.

They cruised up the hill, past students' ramshackle houses with over-stuffed chairs and hibachis perched on the porch roofs, the gutters stuffed with beer cans. The New Yorker climbed easily, shifting into low for more torque. They hit the long level and the streetlights gave way to fields and woods, night. The road was shiny and pasted with leaves. They sped through the black, wipers lashing.

His father slowed to read the mailbox numbers. It was a guess.

"Another mile or so," Larry corrected him, then had to point it out.

The house was dark. His father pulled into the empty drive.

"So," his father asked, "more car trouble, huh?"

Larry looked to him to see if he was kidding. He didn't seem to be.

"It's in the shop," Larry said.

"How old's that thing again?"

"Five years younger than this."

"Just tuned her up," his father said, and patted the dash.

"She sounds good," Larry said, as if following a script. He opened the door, but paused. He wanted to ask his father if he was all right, then decided he was just tired.

"Let me know if you need a ride tomorrow," his father offered.

"That's okay," Larry said, "thanks," and clunked the door shut. He got the mail, bravely sticking his hand in the box without looking first. He watched his father reverse out of the drive and tool away, then walked toward the porch, digging for his keys. Next door Donna Burns's windows were lit.

Inside, before he even turned the lights on, he saw the red flicker of the answering machine. Once, twice, three times. At least one of them would be her. He'd call her and then they could start working to fix it. He hung his jacket up, went into the kitchen and sat down at the table to go through the mail.

He piled her catalogs to one side, and the *Pennysaver*, which she liked to look through. All he'd gotten was a postcard from Wade. It showed a green trout dwarfing a railroad flatcar. *They grow 'em big out here!* it said. Wade said hi. The kids were healthy, he was doing well. He'd send an address as soon as he had one. He was thinking of Ithaca. Larry stuck it to the fridge with a magnet.

He looked in the freezer and then the cupboard. He ate a few of the chocolate chip cookies he packed as part of Scott's lunch, washing them down with a beer. He got another handful and went into the living room and stood above the answering machine, chewing.

He punched the play button and the machine whirred, reversing the tape. The cookies and beer made a thin, sweet gruel going down his throat.

"Vicki," a woman said. "This is Cheryl. Ron wants to know if you're coming in or not, so call, okay? Bye."

It gave the time.

"Vic," Vicki's mother said, and he leaned closer to the machine and turned the volume up, stopped eating. "This is Mom. I thought you might be trying to call me. Nothing new, just wanted to talk."

That had been five-thirty, late enough for her to pick up Scott and make it to Trumansburg. The machine clicked complicatedly. He took a slug of beer to brace himself; it gave him a chill, the fine hairline beginning of a headache.

"Larry," a woman said, "I was wondering how you're doing." It took him a minute to figure out it was Donna. She went on talking, concerned; he turned the volume down and went into the kitchen.

He sat and rested his arms and hands flat on the table, palms down, and looked at the space between them.

"Goddammit," he said, and tilted his head up and eyed the tile ceiling as if it were a sky full of answers. He sighed and picked up the beer can, took it to the sink and rinsed it out.

He called her mother and stood there listening to it ring, wondering what he would say to her. The truth, it occurred to him. If they'd really taken off, she'd want to know.

"Larry," Mrs. Honness said, surprised.

"Are Vicki and Scott there?"

"No." She made the question sound absurd. "They're not there?"

"No," he admitted. He told her about finding them gone, about Vicki missing work, Scott not showing up for school.

"I'm sorry, Larry, but I honestly haven't seen them. I wish I had. Now you've got me worried."

"I'm sure they're okay. I thought she'd call is all."

"You let me know if she does," her mother said, and he wondered if she was lying.

"Same here," he said.

After he'd hung up, he wanted her to have been more concerned, and not only her but himself. The way they talked about it was too routine, as if Vicki's leaving had been expected, or worse, that it had lost the power to hurt him.

He didn't feel like eating, which he thought was a good sign. The World Series was on, and though the score was 10–0, he watched for another beer, from time to time glancing over at the phone.

As he was cleaning up, it rang. He flew across the room, answering before the second ring.

"There you are," Donna said, and he hated himself for hoping. "I was wondering if you'd pick up. How are you doing?"

"Okay."

She waited for him to say more.

"Have you heard anything?"

"No," he said, "nothing."

"She said she'd call you."

"She didn't," Larry said, and wondered why he was so angry with her.

"Hey," she said, "do you want me to come over, just to talk?"

"No," he said, "I'm going to bed," and then felt guilty for being short with her. "Thanks."

"That's all right," Donna said.

He had almost put the phone down when he remembered he needed a ride.

"Sure," she said, relieved, and they agreed on a time.

When he hung up he stood there a second as if it would ring again. When it didn't, he battened down the house for the night, going through the rooms, double-checking the locks on the windows, even the ones upstairs. In the dark of Scott's room the power indicator of the radio threw a weak red sheen over the world. He thought of how far they could have gotten. Sixteen, seventeen hours. He missed them, but not enough, he thought. He could picture himself living like this, eating alone at the kitchen table, seeing no one. In the bathroom mirror he was surprised he didn't look any different, and shrugged.

He turned on the bedroom light before clicking off the one in the hall and undressed in the yellow glow. The hamper was empty; she'd done the laundry. Small favors, he thought, and got into bed, the covers snagging his new foot. On the dresser stood their pictures; he rolled over so he wouldn't have to look at them. Tomorrow was Tuesday. He had no idea what he'd do. Call her work, drive by Scott's school, talk to Donna. He lay there looking at the bright leaves and flowers of the wallpaper, tracing the vines' false progress toward the ceiling as if reading a map.

She was the one who turned out the light every night, and now, without her, he thought it fitting that he leave it on. When they came to him later— when Pony came, or Bogut, or Carl Metcalf, and he woke with his hands miraculously cleansed of blood, when he missed his dead so much that he wanted to be alone with them, if only in sleep—he would need the light. To remind him that there was another world. To remind him that he was alive.

TWO

In Honolulu they wouldn't serve them in the USO lounge, so Larry didn't begin drinking until the NO SMOKING light pinged off and the stewardess came around with the bar cart. As they neared the International Date Line, he tried to figure out what day it would be and how the hours worked. It was simple—today would be tomorrow—but he couldn't hold it in his head long enough to understand it. He knew the line from the *National Geographic* maps his mother unfolded for him, the black dashes splitting the ocean like a seam. He expected cheers when they crossed it but there was nothing. The men around him looked up from their meal trays to hear the announcement, then went on spooning, chewing. The salad was warm; he didn't know what to do with his unused packets of salt and pepper. It seemed a waste, so he snuck them into the pocket of his uniform top.

It was the third time Larry had been on a plane. The first had been six months ago, the flight from Syracuse down to San Antonio where he'd received his advanced training, the second just yesterday, cruising high over the spectacles of the West—the ranges and canyons and mesas he knew intimately from the movies—finally slowing and dropping into foggy Oakland. The motion made him sick, but he liked how bright and solid the tops of the clouds were, spread out like tundra, another, higher set of clouds above them.

Today they'd been herded onto the charter at Travis ticketless, and he'd been too tired to fight for a window seat. The beefy private beside him said they could switch in Hawaii, and so they had. His name was Loomis, and for a thousand miles he'd been smoking and handing out cigars pressed on him by his father. He had a chapped face and was too big for his uniform, spilling over the armrests on both sides. Like Larry, he was drinking Jack Daniel's, but twice as fast, and his jokes had become unfunny. On the fold-down tray he had his little square bottles arranged like bowling pins. They were in an exit row; at Travis the stewardess had briefed them on how to pull the door in toward them and then heave it out sideways. "Can you lift thirty-seven pounds?" she asked, and Larry and Loomis looked at each other soberly and agreed, as if it might be up to them to save the entire plane.

It was as close as they'd come to an understanding. They'd exchanged all the necessary information in the first hour—hometown, MOS, girlfriends—and now sat and drank wearily, leafing through glossy magazines, Loomis occasionally making lame fun of their plush surroundings. They were taking Flying Tigers; Loomis didn't get the irony, and Larry didn't explain. You had to be a student of the other war, he thought, a fan, and wondered what that said about his childhood, leafing through books filled with pictures of the freshly dead.

He decided he didn't like flying. He had a headache, and with every jog and yaw of the fuselage his stomach bobbed as if filled with helium. The air in the cabin wasn't quite right, and the pressure; bubbles seemed to drift in his blood, float up between his organs. The spring-loaded ashtray in the armrest was cemented shut with gum he'd been chewing to clear his ears. Earlier he'd tried to sleep, propping a miniature pillow in the corner formed by the headrest and the wall, but it was too thin and his head kept shaking with the frequency of the plane. It reminded him of dozing off in the backseat while his father drove them home from Christmas dinner at their grandparents'. Susan slept against the other window, their feet tangled in the middle. Their mother sang along with the carols on the radio, looking back over her shoulder hopefully, as if they'd join in. Sometimes their father hummed.

Sun blazed off the wing, stripes of light reaching across the ceiling. The air was clearer up here. Below, the Pacific shone unbroken, the horizon a flat line. Somewhere out there lay their destination, Okinawa. Larry thought of

40

his father, the months he'd spent as a prisoner. Even if Japan was an ally now, he could not separate the country from his father, from the tortures he'd pictured as a child. His father had never gone back after the war. At Fort Sam Houston when they'd read his name off the levy, Larry thought this trip would be something of a homecoming, a vindication like MacArthur wading ashore. He imagined, vaguely, with the desperation of a wish, that he was going in place of his father. In Oakland he'd doubted it, and now, closing on the moment, he saw the connection as false, something he'd wanted that had never existed.

Last night in the transient barracks they'd given everyone five minutes to call home before lights out. In line by the wall of booths, Larry thought he would spend all five minutes on Vicki. His father did not want him to go, because of his own war, and school, and because his mother was sick. And Larry didn't have to go. It was clear to both of them—before and after—that Larry had done nothing to prevent his being drafted. Whether he truly wished to go or gave in to simple inertia was never determined. Only Vicki stood by him, resigned but trying to be cheerful. His father called his decision irresponsible, deliberate. They had argued all spring, and finally in the car on the way up to Syracuse, as if at the last minute Larry could refuse.

He wanted to serve, didn't his father understand that?

No. Don't you know what war is?

No, but I will.

You don't want to know that.

Waiting for the plane at Hancock, his father asked him questions he couldn't answer until Larry stopped talking. They sat with his bags at their feet, watching the other people at the gate chatting, reading, smoking. A number were guys like him, hair already buzzcut, ringed by family. The crowd kept checking the toteboard above the ticket counter, and over it, wheeling tirelessly, a numberless, futuristic clock. As departure neared, their boredom gave way to impatience—the rattling of newspapers, sudden shifts of position—a controlled, low-level panic.

A pleasant yet mechanical woman's voice came over the PA, asking for passengers who needed assistance boarding.

His father sighed. "Well, I tried," he said. "Don't ever say I didn't try."

And how could Larry explain that all he wanted was to get away from him, from Ithaca, from his mother in her rented hospital bed? It seemed he

41

would always be ungrateful, that again and again he would do exactly the wrong thing.

The only person he thought he would miss was Vicki, which proved untrue, because last night when she'd asked if he'd called his father yet, he didn't laugh like he sometimes did but said, "I wanted to call you first."

He dialed his own number, wondering if his father would be at the hospital, if all he'd get would be Mrs. Railsbeck. Someone picked up in mid-ring.

It was him.

"Larry!" he said, as if he were happy he'd called—as if he hadn't expected it. "Hey, how are you?"

"Good," he said, and suddenly felt ill. "We're leaving tomorrow."

"Are you ready, do you think? Did they teach you anything down there?"

"Enough," Larry said.

"You'll be all right. You pick things up pretty quickly. Just watch what everyone else is doing. And remember what I said about shock. Always watch for shock."

"I will."

"Your mother's asleep, otherwise I'd give you to her."

"How is she?" Larry asked. It was unspoken between them that she would not last his tour of duty, that he was running away from her the same way his father did when he went to work on Sundays, giving his patients what she needed.

"Good," his father said. "She's worried about you. So's Susan."

Mercifully, the operator came on, saying they had a minute.

"I'll write when I get there but I hear the mail takes awhile."

"We'll be thinking of you."

They didn't say anything. It was Larry's turn. He sat examining the scrawled numbers and obscene graffiti. JARHEADS DO IT WITH SQUIDS. The guy behind him peered through the door.

"You take care now," his father said.

"I will," said Larry.

"All right. We'll see you soon."

"Okay," he said, and they hung up.

Now, with the Pacific stretched endless beneath him, Larry wondered why he had called at all, if they'd really said anything. What time was it in

Ithaca? It didn't matter. Today was tomorrow. Up front, the movie wa
to start. The stewardess had opened the doors for the screen and was ask.
them to lower their window shades. The cabin lights went down and everyone let loose a spooky "woooo" like a roomful of third graders.

Loomis gestured woozily to the shade with his elbow, and Larry closed it.
For a moment it was as if someone had clamped a hand over his eyes. The
plane smelled like the end of a night-long party—all spilled beer and dead
cigarettes. The bones in his back hurt from sitting so long. Loomis took
control of the armrest, and Larry wondered if he'd switched not out of
courtesy but to get a better seat for the movie.

It was *One Million Years B.C.* with Raquel Welch as a hot-blooded troglo-
dyte. Headphones were free; he seemed to be the only one not interested.
The other men roared during her scenes, paid homage with groans and
whistles, slippery sucking sounds. Larry looked apologetically for the stewardess but she'd disappeared. The cabin hummed with the cyclic roar of
engines, a steady hissing and rushing of air, as if the plane had sprung a leak.
He fingered the lip of the shade, picturing islands floating below—volcanos,
reefs, brilliant fish. The green of jungle. In training, doing booby traps, they
told them not to let the injured man see what had happened to him. And
don't ever, the instructor said, pointing to a chalk drawing of an arm, don't
you ever let them see the missing body part. Chuck it in the woods, kick it
down the trail, just don't let 'em see it.

"Would you fuck Jane Fonda?" Loomis asked, too loud, chummily elbow-
ing him. His breath pressed against Larry's face like a balloon. "I'd fuck her
in a minute." Loomis contemplated his cigar, the smoke rising in a line. "I
wouldn't feel good about it, but I'd do it. You?"

"I don't know her that well," Larry said, loud enough to get through the
headphones.

"It's a yes-no question."

"No then."

"Your fucking loss," Loomis shouted, as if she were meeting them at the
airbase, then groaned as the camera peeked down Raquel Welch's fur-lined
bikini. At the end of the sequence the plane broke into applause.

Larry inched the shade up and curled forward to peek out the crack.
Nothing but the silver wing and the sea. Wind had worn the paint from a
row of rivetheads in neat circles. He imagined the wing shearing and the

plane spiraling in, how he'd flip the armrest up, pull the door toward him and sling it out, watch it skid across the bright metal like a riderless sled. He tried to remember what the stewardess had said about his seat cushion being a flotation device—something about sticking his arms through the straps.

Fuck it, he thought, let them drown. He closed the shade and opened his last bottle of Jack, tipped it to his lips. The heat spread deliciously, like forgetfulness. He tilted his seat back as far as it would go, stretched agonizingly and closed his eyes.

His stomach bobbed and he swallowed. He wondered if they'd get another meal, if he'd be faced with more useless salt packets. Probably not, they were that close now. Every place he'd been in the last three days was farther than he'd ever been from home, and that would keep happening, he thought, until he came back. He had the feeling that in the next year he would learn everything about himself, that after this he would not have so many questions, and how that could only be good. And yet, still, there was something missing, nagging at him, something that didn't fit. Japan, Vietnam—he needed them in some way to be equal and for the first time now, on the cusp of sleep, he was sure they would not be. He was sure that his father was right. The funny thing was, it didn't matter. This was his, no one else's.

"Oh, fuck me," Loomis crooned to Raquel Welch. "Fuck me."

Right, thought Larry. Exactly. Fuck you.

AS THEY NEARED Japan, the stewardesses picked up speed. Half an hour from Okinawa they came around with coffee. The cups were paper cones fitted into a gray plastic base. Larry ordered two for himself and one for Loomis, who was asleep, headphones still on, a cigar between his fingers. Forward, others snored, heads tilted, dreaming of Raquel Welch. By the time the stewardesses collected the empties, everyone was awake.

Stretching, Loomis knocked over his bottles. He was drunk but didn't laugh. A stewardess with a bouffant hairdo knelt, piled them into a garbage bag and sped off down the aisle.

The intercom crackled, and the captain came on. "We're just now beginning our approach to Kadena Air Force Base, Okinawa," he said with a confident Texas accent. "We should have you on the tarmac in about twelve minutes. Ground temperature on the Rock is ninety-seven degrees and sunny. Good luck to all y'all and thank you for flying with us today."

"So what happened?" Loomis asked.

"What do you mean?"

"The movie, how'd it end?"

"I don't know," Larry said. "I wasn't watching."

"Jesus, you're a medic, you're supposed to be helping me." He groaned and scratched at his tongue with his fingernails. He leaned across Larry to look out the window—nothing but blue. "It's gonna be hot as shit."

"That's what the man said," Larry said.

Below, a rocky toe of land appeared, the surf breaking white around it.

"There," Larry said, and Loomis strained against his seatbelt for a glimpse.

"Yep," he admitted, as if presented with evidence, and collapsed back in his seat.

The plane rolled and banked to the left, the wing tilting skyward so they couldn't see anything. Larry swallowed to no effect and stuck a pinkie in his ear.

Loomis dug the cigar box from the seatback in front of him and offered it to Larry. "Take as many as you want."

"I don't smoke."

"Come on," Loomis said. "For luck."

Larry took one and thanked him.

"I don't either normally," Loomis said. "The old man, y'know? It's a big deal for him."

"Oh, yeah," Larry conceded. "I know how that is."

"Fuck, is it gonna be hot."

The plane slowed suddenly, as if the captain had let up on the gas. The stewardesses, he noticed, had vanished like gulls before a storm. Below, the island reappeared, the whole coastline. Beneath them the landing gear rumbled and dropped, locked into place with a hydraulic whine. They were diving—sharply, it seemed to Larry, the angle between the wing and horizon comical. He could see fields and the green rings of terraces climbing hillsides. His ears filled with pressure. On a road a dot of a car slid along as if attached to a track. The engines didn't pulse so much now; they seemed to be coasting in, the green land rising to meet them. They cleared houses and clumps of tin huts, a line of mountains in the distance taking shape. A boy guiding oxen through a muddy canal lifted a hand and waved vigorously to the plane. The land began to speed alongside them, dizzying, though he saw no sign of an airport. The captain goosed the engines as if realizing that they needed more power, but the plane kept falling steadily. Cordoned oil tanks, another, faster car, a checkered water tower at what seemed eye level. His stomach hitched and tightened, puckered into a ball, as if, once small enough, it might fly up his throat and out of his mouth. The engines surged, pushing him back into his seat. He gripped the armrests, ready for a collision. He was prepared—after the crash—to pull the emergency door in toward him, turn it sideways and toss it out when they hopped a fence and a concrete runway began to glide by alongside them, dotted lines flitting down the center. He had to close his eyes. They floated over the ground for an alarming distance before touching down—just a bump, so that at first he wasn't sure if they had really landed. To keep from overshooting, the captain threw the engines into reverse, jerking Larry against his seatbelt. The cabin rattled, filled with sound like a subway station weathering an express. Finally the noise died and the plane slowed. He opened his eyes.

Loomis was looking at him, leering as if he'd found out a hilarious secret. He wouldn't stop but wouldn't say anything either.

"What?" Larry said.

"Man, this is easy," he said. "You ever been on a chopper?"

"No."

Loomis gave a little hiccup of a laugh, a single cluck or tick of his tongue, as if he pitied him, as if no one could be so dumb.

"What?" Larry said.

"Man," Loomis said, pointing what was left of his cigar at him, "you're in for a world of hurt."

It was hot. Even before they made the door, the air reached in and gripped them. They shuffled forward, nodding good-bye to the stewardesses, then turned and ducked into the sun.

The brilliance hurt, made Loomis and then Larry behind him shield his eyes as if holding a salute. Clumping down still in file, Larry could feel the heat in the railing of the stairs. Far off, a jagged graph of mountains loomed, dusted with gray haze. Closer, the quonsets and streets of the base lay spread neatly behind a concrete-block terminal. Palms lolled beyond the fence; on the tarmac sat several empty jeeps. A uniformed crew was already digging their bags from the 707's hold, and after several minutes in the still air of the terminal, they were reunited with their gear, which, as they started the march to their new barracks, they cursed as if it were an old enemy. Larry was on the end of his rank, the last in the file. He liked bringing up the rear, keeping the formation tight. Being on the corner afforded him a good view, which pleased him. He thought that he needed to see everything.

As they passed the corrugated, evenly spaced huts and turned through the vacant parade grounds, the base began to seem familiar to Larry, disappointingly like Fort Sam Houston—the red dust and whitewashed rocks and manicured grass. It was not his father's Japan at all. Instead of precisely creased officers hustling between buildings with clipboards and whistles, they passed clumps of enlisted men wearing sunglasses and smoking, their hair over their ears, their trousers unbloused. The whites among them were deeply tanned. Some were wearing sandals and walked on the roped-off grass as if it were natural. No one approached them; the MPs acted as if they didn't exist. One of them shot the formation a left-handed salute, meaning *Fuck you,* and Larry smiled. These men had been there; like his father said, he would have to watch them if he were to learn anything.

A patch of sweat had begun to grow where his duffel pressed against his back. After sitting on the plane so long, his hips and knees felt out of joint. He was wondering which hut would be theirs when a private with a full-blown afro and granny glasses got up from where he was lounging under a tree, crossed the lawn, high-stepped over a hedge and began marching stride for stride beside their formation. He marched with his chin up and chest out, but not exaggeratedly, and though some of the men laughed, Larry recognized that he was not making fun of them.

"Chuck the Duck!" another man called from the sidewalk, but the private paid him no attention, went on as if he belonged with them. The group the other man was with followed them in a pack, laughing and calling out "You tell 'em, baby! Tell the future, Duck-man!"

"Duck sees the future!"

"Duck knows all!"

The private was on Larry's side of the file, menacing the man in the front rank with something that looked like a gun—except he was holding it not on the man but himself, pressed against his throat as if he were going to blow his own head off. Larry could see his lips move; he was close to the man, nearly whispering in his ear. The man didn't look at him, marched as he'd been taught, impassive, eyes front. Far ahead, the buck sergeant leading the formation trudged on, oblivious.

"Chuck the fucking Duck!" the man's followers called, and Larry saw they were drinking cans of beer.

"Don't listen to him, newbie!"

"Tell the truth, Duck-babes!"

Chuck the Duck dropped back to the next rank and stared at the man on the end. He touched him on the shoulder, whispered to him and dropped back farther. Larry could see that what he had wasn't a gun but more like an electric razor—a black handle and silver head. They trudged along under the palms, the strap of the duffel cutting into his shoulder, Chuck the Duck falling back toward him.

The soldier in front of Larry was Loomis. The big man glanced to the side as Chuck the Duck slowed and waited for him to draw even. Loomis hesitated as if he might sidestep him and escape.

"Chuck-man, give it up, you can't save these greenies!"

"Meat, Chuck, they're fucking meat!"

Chuck stared at Loomis, brought his face close to his, cocked like a dog's, questioning him. He nodded sagely, as if satisfied, sure, and put his hand on Loomis's shoulder. Loomis didn't flinch, didn't look at him, and so close, in the heat, Larry smelled Chuck—a gamy, curdled scent, like the goose fat Mrs. Railsbeck rendered and then pressed into suet every Christmas. In his afro were white bits of lint, dried blades of grass.

Chuck brought the razor up and pressed it to his own throat, keeping his hand on Loomis's huge shoulder like a coach talking with his star player.

"I'm sorry," Chuck said, but it wasn't a voice coming from his throat, it was a buzz the razor made that his lips shaped. It took a second to decode what he'd said, like at the airport, a fuzzy public address.

"I'm sorry, man," Chuck buzzed behind his green shades. "You ain't makin' it back."

The razor came away from his throat, his hand sloughed off Loomis's shoulder.

"Oh, that is cold!" a beer-drinker called from the sidewalk.

"One-way ticket!"

"Meatloaf, Chuck, fucking dogfood!"

"Bag 'em and tag 'em!"

Chuck slowed and waited for Larry to catch up. Reluctantly he kept in step. They drew alongside each other. Larry tried not to look at the face inches from his, but involuntarily caught a glimpse of the pink hole below the private's chin. His skin looked greasy in the heat. Ahead, Loomis kept his eyes front, and Larry wondered how he'd taken it. It was just bullshit, the same stuff Loomis had given him on the plane.

Chuck the Duck put a hand on Larry's shoulder. He held onto him as they walked, staring at Larry, and for fifteen or twenty yards did nothing, as if unsure of what he was seeing. Larry wanted to laugh, to respond somehow to let everyone know it was okay, but merely kept in step.

"He's a tough one, Chuck!"

"You're losing your touch, man!"

"Live or die, Duck, what's it gonna be?"

The gang drew closer, crowded around them, some walking backward, keeping pace. A few men ahead glanced back to see what was happening, but no one intervened; the buck sergeant marched on.

"Tell it like it is!"

"Tell the truth, babe!"

Chuck the Duck brought the buzzbox up to his throat uncertainly, dramatically slow, and Larry thought that it must be a joke, that part of the act was keeping the last man in suspense. Larry waited for him to say he would die, to confirm what he had so far willfully ignored but that he now saw could too easily come true. It was a joke, and he could take a joke. It was all right. It was funny.

Chuck the Duck said nothing. They walked along, all of them, and then he reached across Larry with his buzzbox and took hold of his other shoulder so that they were face to face, still moving continually, as if dancing. Then he stopped. Larry tried to stay in step—to move through him, carry him—but couldn't, and slowed, fell away from the formation.

Chuck the Duck stared at Larry's face and gripped him hard. He wouldn't let go, and Larry saw his eyes behind the shades, and realized that he could not see Larry, that he was looking both into him and far beyond him at once, and Larry believed—as he believed in his love for Vicki and his mother and, grudgingly perhaps, his father—that this man could see the future.

Chuck the Duck's eyes rolled back, showing just the white. The buzzbox dropped to the asphalt. He began to shake, a tremor at first, as if he were shivering, then harder, teeth clenched, a current surging through him. The tendons in his neck went hard; his fingers bit into Larry's skin.

"Chuck, what the fuck, man?" the ringleader asked.

"Hey!" they said. "Hey, Chuck!"

They tossed away their beer cans and grabbed fistfuls of his shirt, trying to haul him off Larry, whose arms were pinned in the crush. His duffel was dragging him backwards. There was grunting, as if together they were lifting something incredibly heavy. "Goddamn crazy fuck," someone complained. An arm shot past Larry's face and Chuck the Duck's glasses flew. Someone's shirt tore. They danced and spun, wobbled and almost fell. While they grappled in the middle of the street, the formation marched on, and then at once—as if a referee had blown a whistle—everyone let go and stepped away from Larry.

Chuck the Duck was on the ground, his body arching, hands clawing at the sandy street, face stretched in a lipless, maniacal smile. The buzzbox lay beside him in the road; with each spasm a long hiss of air escaped his lips, made the hole in his throat open and close, a perfect black circle like a fish vacuuming food.

Larry had been trained in this; he knew what to do, but stood there frozen, speechless, watching the man's feet flop, his arms slap the pavement.

"Look at him fucking go," someone said.

"You're supposed to stick a pencil in his mouth or something."

"No, that would just fuck him up. Let him get it out of him."

"That's right," Larry said, remembering the procedure, then explained, "I'm a medic."

"Hey," someone said, "nice fucking job."

The buck sergeant and an MP in a white helmet and gloves sprinted down the street toward them.

Someone pushed the bag at Larry, and he took it.

"Go," the ringleader said. "Get the fuck out of here."

"And leave Chuck alone," another man warned. "Just stay out of his way, all right? Don't look at him, don't touch him, don't nothing."

"I won't," Larry promised.

The man's legs were still kicking weakly. Larry stood there a second watching the others kneel and begin to tend to him, then turned and ran after his formation, gasping in the humidity, clutching the bag to his chest like something he'd rescued.

THEY CALLED it going down south, and though it was inevitable, they needed to be surprised by it. They were shipping out tomorrow, everyone said, Friday at the latest. They believed everything they heard; they believed nothing. It was just excitement—the possibility, any minute, of leaving, of joining the war. They were going to the 90th Replacement Center at Long Binh, someone said over breakfast. By dinner, rumor was most of them were headed for the 101st Airborne.

"What's the word?" the private ladling Salisbury steak onto his tray asked, and Larry told him.

"That's not where you want to be," the guy on vegetables said. He spooned noodles and goop on top, then ridiculously green peas. "That's I Corps."

"Fucking Khe Sanh, man. A Shau Valley. You don't want to mess with that shit."

"One-oh-first Airborne."

"Screaming Eagles."

"Can I get one of those twisty rolls?" Larry said.

"The Puking Buzzards."

"You want to wear your cup up there," the vegetable guy said.

"You just don't want to go there period."

"Worse than Two Corps."

"Worse than the fucking Marine Corps."

"And some butter," Larry said.

They both pointed to the basket of pats behind him.

"The one-oh-worst, man. That is a bum fucking deal."

"Thanks," Larry said.

The first day was full of training lectures and insects, the listless, diseased heat of the tropics. Around ten the mist burned off and the sky stayed the same high, perfect azure until sunset. For a few minutes the whole barracks braved the mosquitoes to soak in the display, the pinks and purples and cool blues graduated in layers like a fancy cocktail, but after that only Larry and a pair of homesick westerners bothered.

That night they played cards and dice and dominoes and told boring stories about drinking and thrilling stories about women that no one believed. One guy had a guitar and another could almost play, so they took turns. The MPs bought Japanese whiskey at the PX and smuggled it into the transient barracks, and there were fights; Loomis was in one, acquiring a mouse beneath his eye, latrine detail and several new friends who'd been owed money by his opponent. Larry bet light and folded early, listened and didn't say much. He tried to remember everyone's name, yet spoke to no one, with the result that no one spoke to him, and he felt snubbed and alone, though he knew it wasn't true, or if so, it was at heart his own fault. He'd thought he would make good friends here but apparently he wasn't going to; that was supposed to be better anyway. Don't get too close, everyone said, you don't want to lose someone.

During the day they joked about these things, at night spoke the very same words gravely, confessed to their shared fear with the nervous credulity of virgins. It was then, long after taps, when the poker game dwindled, with the rest of the men asleep in their racks, that they told each other what they'd heard about the war.

The stories were from brothers and uncles, friends of friends, guys a grade higher. It was not clear if these men had witnessed or only heard of the events secondhand, but in the dark barracks, with the faces of both teller and audience lit by the flaring tips of cigarettes, it didn't matter. If anyone had reservations about the truth—and they all did, knowing that the war for them would not be a story but something they would have to live through—they kept their doubts to themselves.

First were the horror stories, the parts flying off, hair on fire, flesh shredded; then the funny ones, the embarrassment, the humiliation of death—exploding latrines and officers shot jerking off; and next, everyone's favorites, the ghost stories—whole battalions of gorillas trained to shoot AKs and rip out windpipes, GIs blown apart and sewn together again, zombies stumbling drug-eyed through the deep bush. And just then when their disbelief was piqued and they began to scoff, someone would mention yet another rumor, a secretly feared destination, a departure date, hour, and grounded again, they would pool whatever shaky information they had with a gravity and respect for the war completely absent during the day. Sobered, they decided it was almost time for bed, but because the night could not end on such an earnest note, they told one more story.

These last were cautionary, about men who'd come back different, missing pieces or, worse, messed in the head. "That's not the worst," someone else said, and told them about the ones who lived but didn't come back—the ones who had been captured and had everything cut off and cauterized, or the poor bastards who'd caught the Black Virgin strain of VD, incurable. There was a hospital full of them on an island off Japan; it was common knowledge. The Army sent telegrams to their families saying they were dead. Of all the stories, Larry believed these the least, though in their details—the limbless, faceless patients eating through tubes, wired to throbbing monitors —they were by far the most terrifying. Bitter laughter passed around the circle; a few men protected their nuts.

"No way," someone said. "Just fucking shoot me."

The man next to him put his finger to the man's temple and said, "Boosh."

Larry had to think about it, how badly he'd have to be hurt to ask that, and couldn't answer himself. After a while the jokes died out and silently, one by one, they picked their way through the maze of bunks and slid under the scratchy olive bedrolls, contemplating the shock of being wounded and the slow approach, the long, brimming plateau of pain. Then, astonishingly, they slept, heavy and deep as children.

In his bunk Larry wrote Vicki by flashlight, long, pointless letters on ricepaper stationery. He held her picture and consulted it between sentences, remembering her voice, making the wallet-sized face speak. On the corner of the envelope where the stamp was supposed to go, all you had to do was write FREE. He composed a shorter, more optimistic one for his mother. When he still couldn't sleep, he wandered outside and gazed up at the unfamiliar sky. He could find Orion's belt but nothing else. He could not tell what season it was. They were going to leave here. He did not know if he hoped it would be soon.

Breakfast, lunch, dinner. Flies and sunshine. Care and operation of the M-79 grenade launcher. He read his manuals and practiced his bandages.

53

Everyone was superstitious, so he tended to the head wounds of volleyballs, the broken limbs of softball bats. It was too hot for games. There was nothing to do but spread rumors and hide in the air-conditioned library, alternately ducking the eyes of the happy, ragged men who had already served their tours and surreptitiously inspecting them with a self-conscious mixture of dismissal and adulation Larry associated with being a freshman. The veterans lounged at the tables while the fresh meat skulked among the stacks, leafing through tattered magazines filled with glossy shots of muscle cars. Though there were empty seats, no one was bold enough to sit in them.

The two groups said little to each other. A rigid courtesy separated them, a respect for one's elders and for the war. In the mess, the replacements deferred to them, the entire line stepping aside to let one grunt to the head, who then did not even acknowledge their presence. The men returning to the World ate separately and left early, as if on their own schedule, free, meandering about the base at dusk, sipping on their endless supply of Budweiser. None of the new men thought it odd, no one remarked on it—because, Larry thought, they themselves hoped to be that way eventually, to deserve the same admiration and fear.

He saw Chuck the Duck that morning, sprawled serenely on the lawn by the communications building, and later in the day, as Larry was hosing off the sidewalks as part of some makework detail, witnessed him greeting a planeload of new recruits. He had the same audience as before, and gave them the same routine, except that at the end he did not accost the very last man and drop to the ground writhing, but merely told the man—comfortingly, Larry thought, despite the ominous buzzbox—that, yes, he would be coming back. The gang following the show gave him shit for letting the kid off easy but toasted him anyway. Chuck the Duck walked back through them to his tree and lay down in the shade.

He did not seem to notice Larry; neither did the ringleader or any of the gang, most of whose faces he knew. It was disappointing, though Larry was unsure why. It should have been a comfort, but he felt cheated, and late at night, listening as the stories made their way around the circle, he understood that Chuck was just cracked, that the whole thing had meant nothing. And really, he'd never said anything about him one way or the other. In his rack, Larry lay awake, agreeing with this, boiling it down logically until he was convinced. The man, even if he could see the future, really hadn't said anything.

The new rumors were that on Friday they would be sent to the 90th Replacement Depot, and from there most of them would go to the 1st Infantry Division at Lai Khe.

"The Iron Triangle," said the private dishing out creamed chipped beef.

"Hey, it's better than up north," said the guy on hash browns with a shrug.

"Not much."

"Rocket City."

"Black Virgin Mountain."

"What's there?" Larry asked.

"Oh shit," the first guy said, and laughed.

"For real," Larry said, and the guy doubled over, letting out a whoop.

"Hey, Cherry," the other said seriously, "don't let him shit you. It's bad all over, just some places are worse than others."

"Fuckin' A," the first guy said, still chuckling.

"So what's there?" Larry asked.

The first guy wiped his eyes and stirred the creamed chipped beef around the steamtray as if Larry didn't exist.

"Bad shit," the second guy said. He looked at Larry as if he knew the answer, as if he were intentionally playing dumb. "You know," he explained. "The war?"

After chow, Larry went to the library to look it up. The only books on Vietnam were field manuals published stateside for Officers Candidate School, full of flow charts on division hierarchy and diagrammed pincer movements. They reminded him of the books he'd had in health class—way out of date and trashed with obscene graffiti. The newest was from 1964. It had a map on the inside cover that someone had elaborately defaced, blacking out the name of each city, North and South, so all that was left identified was the thin belt of the DMZ. Beside this, it read Ain't. Under VIETNAM, the same hand had penned in *Land of Enchantment*. The inside of the back cover had received the same treatment. Over the table of contents, someone else had written: *Everything in this book is a lie*. Another person had crossed out *lie* and added *joke*. All the other books were from the fifties, the bigger cities in

French and Vietnamese. Larry found Saigon, then next to it Long Binh, and higher, to the west, Lai Khe. They were just dots on the map, but far south enough, he thought. Like the vegetable guy said, it was better than up north.

At lunch, the rumor came true. After they'd mustered at their tables, before saying grace, a staff sergeant read the manifest over the PA. They were officially shipping out tomorrow at 1100, destination TBA. At Larry's table there were cheers, smiles, a few friendly bets settled over the jugs of Tang and platters of Wonder bread. They all hollered the blessing. In line, Loomis slapped Larry on the back as if congratulating him.

It was sloppy joes. The guys behind the steamtable remembered him. The first one wouldn't look at him, gave him a hard face as he covered the bun.

"So," the vegetable guy said, "First Infantry. There it is."

"I looked it up," Larry said. "Lai Khe, I mean."

"Too fucking much," the first guy muttered into his steamtray, and Larry thought of tossing his sloppy joe at the man.

"So what's it say, professor?" the second guy asked.

"Nothing. I just found out where it is."

"Hey," the first guy said, smirking, "I got an idea. Why don't you call us and tell us if it's still there when you get there, huh?"

"Fuck you," Larry said. He took his plate off the tray, set it on the counter and stalked off.

"What," Loomis said back at the table, "you're not eating?"

"Not that crap," Larry answered, and buttered a piece of bread.

"TBA," someone said.

"The Big Asshole."

"Hey, to the Big Red One," someone else said, and they toasted it with Tang.

"The south!"

"The fucking South Pole isn't south enough for me."

"Got that right," Loomis said, and they ate.

They spent the afternoon squaring away their duffels to be put in storage, to wait for them in the dim humidity of a warehouse for a year. While they stood in formation, each one was tagged, logged onto a clipboard and locked into a wall of wire cages. It seemed foolish to Larry to bring them so far only to leave them, but no one complained or even joked about it. The building reminded him of the cellblocks in prison films—steel catwalks and railings painted gray. As they stood there at ease, he noticed their formation was sharper than usual—no one playing grabass or cracking wise.

"If, in the event you will not be returning for whatever reason via Kadena," a staff sergeant lectured them, "your gear will be shipped after you regardless of circumstances. It will not be lost."

The sergeant gave them his name, saying he would be personally responsible, then dismissed them.

They had an hour till chow. A contingent of men—Loomis among them —headed for the PX and the snack truck, stocking up for the flight down. Larry wandered through the sandy streets toward the barracks, taking a last look, composing letters in his head. *The sunsets here are beautiful. Haven't seen a Japanese yet. They don't have an army anymore.*

He detoured by the airstrip to see if anything was taking off. The Marines had Phantoms, hawk-nosed and muscular; their afterburners shot a soft cone of flame, blue at the center like that of a gas stove, the tail a transparent orange. He liked to stand with his eyes closed as they rocketed by; the noise shook him, left his face flushed and his insides jangled. Though the violence of it terrified him, he thought he needed the practice. In-country, choppers were like the bus; every day he'd ride one to work.

On the flightline the only bird stirring was a fat C-130. A few Hueys and Chinooks sat on the tarmac, blades scissored and battened down against the wind. Shithooks, everyone said now, as if they were intimate with them. They knew their purpose; maybe that was enough to curse them in advance. Larry walked the fence, hoping, then turned down the street he'd first seen two weeks ago, utterly familiar now—the palms and quonsets and sandstone buildings. Chuck the Duck lounged beneath his tree; otherwise it was deserted, the sun throwing shadows over the grass.

Larry could have easily slipped past him, but crossed, walked along the low hedge protecting the lawn. He was asleep, an arm thrown over his face, and Larry stopped. Chuck the Duck was wearing the same stale fatigues as before—grease- and grass-stained; his afro was dented like a punctured ball. Beside him in the grass rested his glasses, his buzzbox and a portable tape recorder, running almost inaudibly, only a mumble.

Larry looked both ways before stepping over the hedge. The lawn kept the imprint of his boot. He hadn't walked on anything but hot concrete since his arrival; even through his boots, the grass felt cool and delicious. He crept a step toward him and found he was holding his breath. The tape player was saying something; it wasn't music, just a voice, the kind of tape they encouraged you to mail home. Closer, he could see the hole in Chuck's throat, and around it, overlapping patches of scar tissue in different tints, like the meat scraps Mrs. Railsbeck boiled and then pressed into head cheese.

"We been here a month and only gone out once," the tape player said in a rich, soft drawl. "People gettin' itchy."

Chuck the Duck's hand shot out and smacked off the recorder, stopping Larry in midstep. He groped for the buzzbox and held it to his throat. The other arm stayed over his face.

"You think I ever sleep?" His voice was like the droning of locusts at the end of a hot day, a radio coming in fuzzy.

"No," Larry said.

He laughed, a burst of static. "You boocoo green." It took time for him to make the words, his mouth shaping each sound. "Get away from me, green."

"I wanted to ask you something."

"*Didi mau*, motherfuck." He pointed the buzzbox at Larry like a revolver, pretended to shoot him.

"Am I going to live or die?" Larry asked.

Chuck the Duck pursed his lips, shook his head in disgust. "If you fail to react," he said, "you fail to come back."

"They say you can see the future," Larry said. "I just wanted to know."

"What did I tell you?"

"You didn't tell me. You told everybody else."

"Tough titty," Chuck the Duck said. The time it took for him to deliver the words robbed them of all comedy or menace, gave them the flat authority of a proclamation. It was like on *Star Trek* when the enemy was a computer. "I can't do all y'all greenies."

"But you did me," Larry said. "You were going to tell me and you had some kind of fit."

Chuck the Duck blinked at him over his arm. He was stoned, his eyes veined. He reached for his glasses, held them in front of his face and peered at Larry. He sat up as if he'd discovered something and hooked the curved stems around his ears.

He was on his knees now, examining Larry, open-mouthed. He put a hand on Larry's shoulder as if for balance. His eyes drifted into that un-focused zone where he was and was not seeing and, panicked, Larry thought he should not have asked, just kept on walking. Chuck the Duck shook his head vaguely, as if listening in disbelief. His lips moved, but he hadn't put the buzzbox to his throat, and nothing came out.

"What?" Larry said, hoping to snap him out of it.

"I saw the fire," Chuck finally said. "I was at the end of the world with Jesus. I hid everything in here." He pointed shakily to his forehead, then touched Larry in the same place, his fingernail denting the skin. His gaze swept the street, the buildings and the deepening sky, then stopped, rested on a nodding palm above them. He closed his eyes and lay in the grass like a dead man.

"You're gonna live," Chuck the Duck said.

"That's all right," Larry said, as if it no longer mattered.

Chuck shook his head. "Naw, man, it's gonna fuck you up. It don't matter if they're dead, they come get you anyway. That's the bitch, you know? Motherfuckers come for you every night."

An MP walking the opposite side of the street noticed them and started over.

"Don't believe old Chuck," Chuck said.

"I don't," Larry lied.

"Hey, you're the one that asked. I felt sorry for your green rabbit ass."

"Trouble here?" the MP said, leaning over with his hands on his knees.

Chuck pushed the buzzbox away and lay back in the grass, an arm across his face.

Larry stood, making the MP straighten up.

"No," Larry said. "Everything's fine."

THAT NIGHT the poker game broke up early. Suddenly it was unlucky to win. No one bet anything past the ante. The same guy—a big Swede missing his front teeth—took the first two hands uncontested before he figured it out.

"Oh shit," he said, and laughed, trying to twist it into a joke. The other players gave up at once. The whole thing was dumb, they seemed to agree, muttering, and pitched their cards in the middle. The dealer collected the deck and turned off his flashlight. They were playing on someone's bunk, and when the Swede tried to leave his winnings, the owner called after him.

"It's not mine," the Swede said, and walked away.

The owner shook out his bedroll and a shower of coins jangled and rolled across the concrete floor. In the morning, when Larry laced up his boots, even the quarters were still there.

It was raining and surprisingly cold. After the weeks of heat, he thought he would appreciate it, but for some reason it annoyed him. He had slept briefly throughout the night, dropping off and coming to sharply, like someone in a train station. Near morning he'd heard thunder and stepped outside to watch the sky light up. Under the eave of the barracks stood ten or fifteen men in their skivvies, like him, some smoking, faces raised. He found a spot against the cinder-block wall; it was still warm from yesterday's sun. With each strike, the mountains jumped out of the night and died, their green afterimage lingering. The storm was nearly on top of them, the gap between the flash and the rumble down to just a second. The noise seemed to test them, standing there, and in the quiet between crashes, Larry watched the others bracing for the next one, trying not to flinch. It was a relief. Finally there was something here he wasn't afraid of, something he knew. In Ithaca the living room would suddenly darken toward mid-afternoon. He'd go out on the front porch and listen to the storms walk down the lake. His mother couldn't bear them. "Oh," she'd say at the first blast of static, as if the Beaux Arts Trio had been interrupted, their feelings hurt. She summoned Mrs. Railsbeck, who would pull the blinds to her bedroom and bring her tea and Melba toast rounds. Mrs. Railsbeck checked on him, lined the plants up on the railing to catch the rain, then hustled upstairs to be with his mother. The windows rattled; branches clattered down from the honey locust. He rocked on the old steel glider, making it squeak and bang against its frame until he remembered her upstairs, cringing as the thunder crashed. His loving the sheer force and glory of Ithaca's relentless weather wasn't bravery, just as her terror was not cowardice; there was just something wrong. It had always been wrong and it would always be wrong, and there was nothing he or his father could do to fix it. She was sick. But wasn't his father a doctor?

A blast like a great tree cracking split the night, making him blink.

"Oh yeah," someone said matter-of-factly, as if verifying its grandeur.

It was funny now how everything reminded him of Ithaca—its summer thunder, the seat of the glider checkered with holes you poked your fingers through, hoping they wouldn't get chopped off when you rocked. He wished they would be allowed a phone call tomorrow but it wasn't going to happen. He thought of Vicki sleeping in her parents' house—her flannel pajamas, the heart-shaped pillow he'd won for her at Immaculate Conception—when she would actually be awake; it was the middle of the day there. A chill wind picked up. Across the road, a palm thrashed beside a streetlight, and soon a lukewarm rain began to fall, softly at first, spotting the asphalt, and then steadily, drumming the gutter above them. No one spoke. The private beside him blew smoke rings into the falling drops. Several men came outside, letting the screen clap shut behind them, and leaned against the wall, and shortly a few more, and without doing the math, Larry understood that there was no one left inside, no one sleeping. They all stood there and watched the rain gather and run through the streets, pool brown at the sewers.

Now, waiting as the staff sergeant pointlessly called their names off the flight manifest, Larry thought that if the other men were not his friends at that moment, he was at least one of them, accepted, and it saddened him to be leaving. He waited for his name, when it came, said, "Sir!" then relaxed.

When the sergeant was satisfied everyone was present, he marched them out into the rain and through the empty streets to the airstrip. They were getting soaked without their ponchos; the shoulders of Loomis's khakis had gone dark. As they passed the mess and then the library, Larry noticed several veterans leaning out of windows and in doorways, solemnly watching them go. He wondered where Chuck the Duck was, or if he even bothered seeing them off. Everyone else was: the cooks and counter men, the supply clerks and base NCOs. For the first time since they arrived, Larry felt at the center of attention, as if both he and the men around him had become greater, charged, more real than the rest of the base. Selfishly, he understood that the men who served here didn't matter, that this was limbo; there were only those who had been there and those who were going. He wished the vets would laugh at their ragged formation, flip them the bird—the simplest acknowledgment. One flicked a cigarette in their direction but his face didn't change, stayed grim and pitying. A few others turned away, and Larry thought that it was unfair, that the least they could do was salute.

A gloved MP rolled a section of fence open, and they marched onto the runway. The wind made him squint. At the base of the glass-crowned control tower lurked a flock of emergency vehicles topped with red and amber lights, all pointed toward the runway, poised for disaster. He looked back toward the terminal but its windows were empty. In Syracuse his father had waved silently behind the glass, had stayed there, a dark blot, until the plane taxied away. As they banked, turning south, he searched the parking lot for the familiar shade and bulk of his father's New Yorker. Beneath them slid the hills and farms of the Finger Lakes, the gorges with their waterfalls, the vineyards running down to shore. Larry was surprised at how much of the land he knew and how long it had been since he'd really seen it, and though the distance between him and the land—his home, he realized—though that separation felt if not irrevocable then lonely, he thought it was a perfect way of saying good-bye.

Here there was no one—Loomis, the few men he sat with at the mess table. They splashed across the tarmac and up the metal jetway. This time it was Braniff, the fuselage of the 707 swirled puce and canary yellow like modern art. The stewardess who met them was a blonde, and tall as Larry. The seating was the same; Loomis gave him the window, and again Larry wondered if he'd misjudged him.

After they were completely buckled in, the staff sergeant borrowed the intercom.

"Gentlemen," he said, to quiet them down. "I don't know where you get *your* information, but Flight Golf Six-One-Niner has a terminal destination of Bien Hoa, where you will be processed through the 90th Replacement Depot and then on to your line units. Somewhere someone got it into their head that a fair number of you might end up with the First Infantry. This is a rumor and I can assure you now it is untrue. You will be assigned to your units individually, not as a group. I wish you all luck. God bless you."

He gave the microphone back to the stewardess, who began to explain the safety procedures, but no one was listening to her.

"Fuck me," Loomis said.

"The north," Larry said.

"Might as well be in fucking Hanoi."

"You don't know, it might be all right."

"Shit," Loomis said.

"Due to United States Military and Republic of Vietnam regulations," the stewardess broadcast, "we will be offering only our limited beverage service," and went on to explain there would be no liquor. The troop protested as a whole, then shut up as the plane began to move. Outside, in the rain, two privates were soaping the bubble front of a small chopper, shooting each other with the hose. Beyond the fence, palms nodded.

"We're basically fucked is what she's telling us," Loomis said.

"I heard," Larry said.

They bumped over the tarmac, turned slowly to get into position at the end of the runway. The red light on the tip of the wing blinked. The pilot tested the engines and then, as they wound down, checked the flaps.

"Aw Jesus," Loomis said to himself, and hung his head, covering his ears as if to block out some terrible news. "That guy was right," he said. "I'm not coming back."

"Bullshit," Larry said. "That guy was Section Eight all the way. You saw what he did to me."

"Oh man," Loomis said. He rubbed his face.

"Hey. It was just a game. He said I'd get it too."

"Well, maybe," Loomis said, as if relieved that Larry might die.

"Sure," Larry said. "The guy's battle-whacky."

"Yeah," Loomis said, unsure.

They traded nods, as if to say it could happen to anyone.

"North, south," Loomis said, and shrugged. "What the fuck. No going back now."

The engines powered up again, shaking the plane. Larry twisted the nozzle above him and aimed the cold air at his face, leaned back and closed his eyes. He'd meant to buy a book at the PX to take his mind off the flight. At least it would be short.

The plane jerked, then started down the runway. Larry gripped the arm-rests like an astronaut taking g's. The pulse of the wheels jolting over the expansion joints quickened with the pitch of the engines, then suddenly stopped as they lifted off the ground.

Loomis tapped him on the arm, and Larry opened his eyes. He couldn't look out the window or he'd be sick.

"Here," Loomis said, and pressed into his hand a tiny bottle of Jack Daniel's. "I was gonna save 'em but what the fuck." He already had one uncapped and raised above the armrest. Larry clinked his against it.

"To old age," Loomis toasted.

"To old age," Larry said, and drank with his friend.

THEY CAME IN over the sea, a fleet of fishing boats sliding beneath them thin as gondolas. His first sight of the country was a white beach, palms, then the green of jungle running smooth as carpet into the shadowed foothills, the soft bulge of a mountain. It was raining; scarves of mist drifted above the trees. The plane rose now, inland, cutting uneasily through clouds. Silently, a Phantom pulled even with them, an escort. Loomis leaned across Larry to see. The fighter was so close they could see the pilot give them the thumbs up. It was like driving neck and neck down Route 13, how Vicki used to lean out the window of his Fairlane and pass a cold Genesee to the other car. On the left side of the plane the same thing was happening, the guys in the aisle straining for a better look.

After a few minutes, the pilot of the Phantom saluted and shot ahead. The stewardess came on and announced they were beginning their descent into Bien Hoa. They dove into the clouds, the angle ridiculous, his stomach a balloon; streaks of water trembled across the windows. The gear clunked beneath their feet and the overhead lights blinked. They fell blindly through the white.

"How you doing there, bud?" Loomis asked, and Larry found that he was gripping the armrests.

"I'm all right," he said.

The mountains suddenly rose up beside them, still misted, and he could see the same jungle as before, interrupted by clumps of brown pockmarks. He wanted to look, to savor his arrival, but the speed of everything flowing past made him dizzy. He closed his eyes again.

"Aw, man," Loomis said. "You're missing the best part."

"I don't care," Larry said, and held on.

They touched down harder this time, on one wheel, as if they'd tip over. The pilot corrected and threw the engines into reverse. Larry had thought it would be easier this time. He hitched and tasted Jack Daniel's, barely avoided retching on Loomis, who had leaned over to look out the window.

"Man," Loomis said.

Queasy, braced upright against the headrest, all Larry could see was the wing and the edge of the runway. From far off, muffled by the rain, came a dull boom like a shotgun on a distant hill, and Larry thought of his father, the quail he stuffed into the game pockets of his hunting jacket, how his mother couldn't look at their kill. They had to clean them in the garage. As a boy he'd liked their iridescent feathers; he kept one from every bird strung on a copper wire above his father's workbench. They were there now, waiting in the still, oily air, gone brown with dust like the shell reloader. At Fort Sam the program required him to qualify with a .45, which he'd done almost nonchalantly; it had been three or four years since he'd picked up a gun. Lead them and squeeze, his father said, and clapped him on the back when he brought one down cleanly. At Fort Sam the instructor warned that they might be offered an actual weapon, meaning an M-16. "Under the current convention," the sergeant said, "you are under no obligation to accept this weapon. However," he said, "you may deem it necessary for personal reasons of safety or overall unit morale. I hope there are no questions."

When the plane had slowed and turned to taxi back to the terminal, they heard another explosion close by, and several men jumped up.

"Please remain seated," the stewardess announced, still buckled into her jumpseat. "In all likelihood what you are hearing are outgoing artillery rounds. For your own safety, please remain seated until the plane has come to a full stop."

Sheepishly the men sat down.

Another round went out, and both Larry and Loomis flinched. They looked at each other as if waiting for the next one, then let out a breath and leaned back in their seats.

"We're here," Loomis said.

IT WAS COLD. Larry had been ready for more of the steamy heat of Okinawa, but after the stewardess nodded good-bye, he stepped out into the same gray drizzle his father would be getting in Ithaca. The air was sharp and

65

heavy and fetid, a swampy mix of gasoline, wet ashes and rotting garbage. Fish, mildew, shit. It stopped Larry an instant; he had to recover from it.

"Goddamn," Loomis said ahead of him, waving it away from his nose.

The stairs were slippery. At the bottom stood a sergeant with a clipboard, motioning them onto an olive-drab bus beyond the fence. Going down, Larry held the railing and glanced out over the airfield. Sandbagged artillery positions lined the runway, across which sat a fleet of Hueys, each with a red cross on its nose. In an open hangar a jumpsuited crew was working like a team of surgeons over an engine of a C-130.

"Move it, troop," the sergeant called, and Larry hustled down the stairs. He caught up to Loomis at the door of the bus; it had wire mesh over the windows, like the ones for the protesters in Chicago. A line had gathered, and they had to wait. Along the road sauntered GIs in jungle fatigues, all carrying rifles and draped with grenades, crossed bandoliers of brass-jacketed bullets.

Another round went out, making them duck. Some of the GIs walking past laughed, but most looked right through them into some middle distance. The line in front of them had vanished.

"Come," the driver beckoned, "you be safe in Vinh bus," and Larry saw that he was Vietnamese.

Inside, it was air-conditioned; his dogtags felt cold against his skin. The bus was newer than the ones in Ithaca. The sergeant followed them on, and the driver closed the door and started off.

"Ammons," the sergeant read, "Present, Sergeant!" a man said, and they went through the whole roll again.

Outside, long quonsets and wooden barracks slid past, occasionally a guard hut or bus stop. No garbage, just puddles. The road looked new, freshly lined; beyond the fence the ground was brick red, reminding him of San Antonio. Behind them the artillery continued, buried in the deep diesel of the bus.

"Gentlemen," the sergeant said, standing in the aisle with his arms behind his back, swaying. "Welcome to Vietnam, Republic of. We will process you inbound as fast as we can, verify your assignments and get you outbound toot-sweet. For some of you that may take several days. That time counts toward your DEROS, or date of estimated return to the States, so enjoy it while you can. Now then, who do I have here that's Eleven-Bravo?"

Loomis raised his hand, as did five or six others.

"I expect you men will head out sometime tomorrow. What else have I got?" He looked at his clipboard. "I've got a doc here?"

"Here, Sergeant!" Larry said, and raised his hand, both proud and surprised that he was the only one.

"They'll want you too. The rest of you may be here awhile. Now listen up. I want you to remember two things and only two things while you're here. If you do have the misfortune of being subject to a mortar attack, number one: get down on the ground. When you hear someone yell 'Incoming,' do *not* look around and try to find where it is coming from; get down on the ground. Number two: you will have a bunker assigned to your barracks. Know where this bunker is located. When you hear the sirens indicating incoming rockets or other sorts of rounds, get to this bunker and do not leave it until you hear the all clear. One: get *down*; two: get *in* the bunker. It's that simple, gentlemen. I do not want you dying on my time."

"It figures," Loomis said when the sergeant had sat down. "We're first, then you."

"Could be worse," Larry said, out of habit. It was a phrase his father used when things went wrong. Thankfully, Loomis didn't ask how.

They turned off the main road and headed for a large compound of wooden barracks, where the sergeant herded them out, still in alphabetical order. Again, the smell made them shake their heads. He looked around for a source—a latrine or cluster of garbage cans—but there was nothing; it was as if the ground itself had gone rotten. Gravel paths and wooden ramps led through the heavy red mud. Above the doorway hung a horseshoe painted gold and pointed up. They double-timed it inside, but not before another round made them duck.

"You are pitiful green," the sergeant said.

The processing center was a switchbacked maze of ropes. They stood in single file like customers at a bank. It was stuffy, suddenly warm. After the bus, Larry expected air-conditioning, but only a pair of ceiling fans rotated slowly overhead, any breeze trapped in the rafters. The building reminded him of the mess in Okinawa, all rough lumber with a long serving window at the front. Men were emptying money out of their pockets and piling it on the steel counter. He was trying to see what the clerks were giving them in exchange when Loomis turned around and pointed to the side wall.

"Funny, huh?" Loomis said.

Above a bulletin board, the numbers two feet high and on placards like at a gas station, hung the date—Friday, September 13, 1968—and in cheerily slanted letters, as if advertising an unbeatable price, a banner that read: WELCOME TO VIETNAM.

THEY WERE WATCHING *Star Trek* that night when the rockets started. There was a TV in the enlisted men's club, and slot machines if you were stupid. The shows were commercial-free; the army taped them. It was almost over. Mr. Spock was in the transporter, his body going opaque, when the men around the set heard a blast—a crack like a nearby lightning strike.

"Fuck," someone said, almost a question. They hesitated a second, then a man jumped up, knocking over his soda, and everyone followed.

They scrambled to the door to see a jeep burning across the compound in the rain, its hazards flashing as if in protest. The siren they'd been instructed to listen for wound up from nothing, like the ones Larry knew from the movies, one note soaring and falling, insistent. Running for the bunker, he glanced up, expecting planes, and the man behind him ran him over, knocked him facefirst into the mud. The aproned barkeep jogged past as if unconcerned.

Larry was the last one in. Everyone laughed at him. In the dark, he leaned against the packed sandbags and wiped mud from his cheeks. He waited for another sputtering whoosh and crash and clattering shower of debris, but there was only the rain. The bunker smelled sweetly of dried, dead mice.

Beside him the barkeep uncovered the radium dial of his watch; it was not quite nine—twenty-one hundred. "We got one more coming," he announced, and everyone stopped talking. "VC rocket. You new guys listen for it."

As predicted, it came, the flash of impact visible through the low opening, dirt and rocks falling for an instant afterward.

"Gentlemen," the barkeep said, getting up, "*Star Trek* has been brought to you by Luke the Gook."

As he was leading them around the smoldering jeep, the sirens died and the all clear sounded. Inside, *Gunsmoke* was already on. They watched it to the end, and then *Bonanza*. Larry bought a Coke; they'd all traded their dollars for pink and blue scrip—funny money. Handing over the bills with their old-fashioned, heroic pictures of Indian chiefs and Greek-robed women didn't feel like spending anything. He thought of a beer but decided against it. Some of the others were determined to get drunk, going outside every few minutes to whiz into a reeking pisstube. He wanted to be sharp for tomorrow in case they sent him north. Loomis had the same idea, and they walked back to the barracks together.

"Fuck," Loomis said in the rain, "did you see that jeep?"

"Yeah" was all Larry could say.

They waited for a truck to pass, then crossed the road.

"Think we might get sent the same place?" Loomis asked.

"Probably not," Larry said, then, "you never know."

"I don't like it here. The whole thing gives me a bad feeling. I don't know, I think maybe I should have gone Navy. Too late now though."

"You'll be okay," Larry said, wanting to believe it.

"I hope," Loomis said. "What the fuck, if it's gonna happen it's gonna happen."

They turned with the road; the barracks behind them had lights mounted on the corners of the roof that threw their shadows onto the bare ground inside the wire.

"Hey," Loomis said, "dig this," and pulled a bead chain out of his shirt. It was like the one for their dogtags except it had a bullet on it the size of a lipstick. "Seven point six two millimeter," he said, "the kind the gooks use. I got it at the PX. And check it out."

He turned it to the light so Larry could see an inscription on the casing: *Howard Loomis,* it said.

"They say there's one with your name on it," Loomis explained. "This is it."

Larry pressed his thumb against the tip, hefted the weight of it in his palm.

"I sure as hell hope so," he said.

Inside, the other six infantrymen were sitting on the edge of their cots talking; they waved Loomis and Larry over. Two of them had purchased life insurance from Hawaii Mutual listing each other as the beneficiaries. They were trying to convince the others it was a good deal.

"Maybe," Loomis said, "but it's like betting against your own team. I won't do it."

"Same here," Larry said.

The rumor was all seven were going to rifle companies tomorrow.

"What about the doc?" Loomis asked. It took Larry a second to understand he meant him.

"No idea. All I know is they need legs."

"What the fuck," Loomis said, "we're not here for the TV."

THEY STOOD formation at 0800. It was warmer but still drizzling. Not all of the mud had come out of his shirt, and as the sergeant passed with his clipboard, he shook his head at Larry as if he were hopeless.

Beside him, Loomis had to look at his boots to keep a straight face.

"Ten-hut!" the sergeant called when he was done with the roll, and they all snapped to. He flipped his papers to a new page and read it silently, making them wait.

"This is it," Loomis whispered.

"Maybe not," Larry said.

The sergeant looked up from his clipboard and, as if reciting something too familiar to be of interest, announced, "The following men will report to myself immediately upon dismissal. I will be reading the name, MOS and full serial number only once, so listen carefully."

The first and second were infantry. When he read Loomis's name, Loomis looked at Larry and shrugged as if it were just bad luck. Larry nodded in sympathy. The sergeant called all seven 11-Bravos and dismissed the rest of them. The men had ten minutes to get their gear together. Larry sat by uselessly on his cot while Loomis dug through his bag.

Outside, under the eave, they shook hands.

"Hey," Larry said, "you'll be okay."

"You too," Loomis said. "Maybe I'll see you up there."

"Maybe."

He watched Loomis and the others go off with the sergeant. They boarded a deuce and a half; the sergeant gave a piece of paper to the driver and walked back to the processing center as the truck drove away. From inside the canvas-covered rear a hand waved, and though Larry did not know if it was for him, he waved good-bye until the truck was out of sight.

At 1700 hours they stood formation, and again at 0800 the next morning, when the sergeant called his name and put him on a truck by himself. On its way across the base the truck stopped at several barracks, picking up others, all of whom were infantry. The consensus was that they were headed for the 101st Airborne in Phu Bai, and when they checked him onto the flight manifest, it proved true.

"Screaming Eagles," someone in line behind him said, already impressed with himself.

At the airstrip a different sergeant marched them across the tarmac and up the tail ramp of a C-130. Inside, nose-to-tail, sat several jeeps strapped to steel rings in the floor. The sergeant instructed them to take a canvas-webbed bench along the gray wall of the fuselage and went through the roll once more. A few heads turned when the others heard Larry's MOS, and again he felt an untested pride and thought of his father and then Vicki and how his mother was doing. The sergeant wished them luck and two jump-suited crewmen hydraulically retracted the ramp and closed the door. The crew chief handed out yellow foam rubber earplugs from a coffee can. Larry searched the webbing for seatbelts and found there weren't any.

"Damn," he said, and sitting there waiting for the plane to move, thought that Loomis was right, that somehow he would have to learn to do this. Next to what he would really have to do, this was easy.

THE PLANE was freezing and loud, and as they came down he could feel the heat building. A mist hovered inside the hold, soaking their clothes. He'd tried to sleep but managed only a few fitful beginnings of dreams, all of Ithaca—the kitchen door open on the grassy backyard, his mother's Oriental rugs, the delicate prints in his father's medical texts. He was younger, the boy he'd been. The house was quiet and he was the only one around; he could look through the cupboards or in his father's dresser, in Susan's closet where she hid her magazines and cigarettes. He'd been moving through the rooms as if searching for something when the plane shuddered and he came awake, rigid, gripping the webbing beneath him in both fists. The hydraulics groaned, a rushing in the hoses. With each bump the jeeps bounced in their restraints. A few men slept, read; the others stared sullenly at the floor, trying to disguise their fear. No one really knew where they were going.

He closed his eyes and began walking up his block, doing the paper route, every name and face a comfort—yet how desperately he'd wanted to leave. And then all he could see was Vicki riding beside him, her hair whipping out the open window, the lake winking blue through the pines. All summer she cried after they made love, and he had to reassure her. They rarely talked of marriage. He would have understood if she insisted, would have gone against his father's wishes, but, no, she said, it would be better if they waited. She just wished he didn't have to go. He could not quite explain to her why he needed to, but it was all right, with Vicki he didn't have to.

On landing, they were counted, as if one of them might have jumped. It was still drizzling, but hotter, and the air smelled. The plane kept its engines running, like a getaway car. Across the runway a medevac chopper was coming in, the rotor wash kicking up trash, rippling a muddy puddle; two uniformed stretcher bearers leaned against the rear doors of a boxy, olive-drab ambulance, arms folded, bored. Above, another chopper hovered. The man in front of Larry stared.

There were bunkers everywhere, sandbagged artillery positions. The run-way was newer here, disintegrating at the edges, as if laid in a hurry. Over the gate at the lip of the tarmac arched a gold-on-black sign that read: RENDEZVOUS WITH DESTINY. They marched beneath it and down a gravel road to the only wooden building in sight, a barracks similar to the one at Bien Hoa, where the supply clerks welcomed them to the division and gave them jungle fatigues with the Screaming Eagle patch on the shoulder and new rubber-soled boots. Emptying his pockets, Larry discovered the salt packets and Loomis's father's cigar. It seemed months ago.

When they came out, a deuce and a half was waiting for them. Though it was drizzling, the back had no cover. The floor was packed with sandbags. They bumped along, getting wet. The base went on forever. A few prefab tin buildings stood out from the mud; the rest were tents soaked a deep green. Larry expected they would be assigned temporary quarters and then sent to the mess, but the driver passed row after row of tents, and when he finally stopped, it was at a guardhouse at a gate that separated the base from a native village.

The fence here was topped with concertina wire, from which flew skeins of plastic bags, tatters of clothing. Outside, a crowd of barefoot children had gathered by the side of the road. Two GIs with M-16s, helmets and flak jackets climbed in the back. Larry noticed they both had grenades hanging from their web gear, and smoke canisters for signaling choppers. One took a second to check his weapon, snapped the bolt back and let it clash forward.

The truck started off and the gates closed behind them. Children scampered in their wake, calling, hands lifted. One of the soldiers took out a pack of gum and began tossing sticks to the children. The other reached into his flak jacket, pulled out his hand and gave them the finger.

The road stopped at an asphalt highway—Highway 1, someone guessed. "No shit, Sherlock," the soldier with the gum said.

In minutes they were in the jungle, the humidity suffocating. The soldiers rested their rifles on the slatted sides of the truck, leveled them at the dense brush, sweeping the barrels back and forth as if tracking an unseen enemy. All but a few of the new men got off the benches and sat on the wet sandbags, peering out like cattle through the slats. On each side the engineers had cleared seventy or eighty meters to the woodline, making them feel even more exposed. Larry watched the trees for movement, and thought it was like hunting; you concentrated, waited for a mistake. Though he could see birds, all he could hear was the grinding of the truck. Palm fronds dipped and nodded. The greens deepened with the clouds; farther in it was all darkness. He wondered if he would be offered a rifle and if he would accept it.

A village formed in the distance—thatch huts and shacks fashioned from rusting advertising signs and uncut sheets of beer cans. They sat up on the benches to see. Blatz, Schlitz, Budweiser. Charcoal fires spiced the air, along with a hint of sewage. They passed shrunken old men squatting by the road like frogs, smoking; silent women in coolie hats cinched under their chins, carrying baskets; slim girls on bicycles, avoiding their stares—all small as children, none showing the slightest sign of welcome or even acknowledgment. The soldiers swept their weapons over the treeline, sighting through the civilians. There were no young men, no older boys. Larry wanted to see more but the next minute they were back in the shadowed thick of the jungle, the berm on both sides empty of traffic. The soldiers knelt down and buckled their helmets, and the other men slid off the benches.

A mile farther they came upon an armored trac guarding one end of a bridge. Poking out of the hatch was a GI with sunglasses and no shirt behind a heavy machine gun; he waved, and the soldier beside Larry waved back and shouted out, "Happy?"

"All the time!" the gunner called, holding his arms out wide, as if to show that all this belonged to him.

The driver sped across the bridge. All Larry could see beneath it was mist. At the far end another trac and another gunner commanded the road going north.

"Happy?" the gunner called, and the soldier returned the same greeting. When the trac was out of sight behind them, the soldiers knelt down again, and everyone hugged the floor. They had yet to see anyone coming the other way.

A mile or so later, the driver suddenly slowed and swerved into the left lane. Larry peered over the tailgate to see what he'd missed—craters three feet deep and filled with water.

"Mines," the same guy guessed.

"Is he brilliant?" the one soldier asked the other.

Larry thought he saw someone ahead duck into the brush, but as they neared the spot, he saw it was a small stone shrine, a seated Buddha raising his hand in blessing; the head had been knocked off, the belly chiseled and pockmarked with bullet holes. Farther on, another lay toppled and crushed like chalk. Larry ducked down again and watched the clouds pass overhead.

They slowed even more, taking a curve, the truck's momentum throwing them to the left.

"Cherries gotta see this," one soldier said, cracking his gum, and Larry looked up again.

Off the road, in a heap, rested the burnt and rusted wreckage of several trucks similar to the one they were in—also a jeep, a bladeless grader and a trac crushed like a shoebox, all a dark orange in the rain. Bent and snapped axles lay strewn about the ground, the smashed cab and flatbed of a tractor-trailer.

As they stared at the damage, the soldier beside him let off a burst of rifle fire into the woods, and Larry covered his head. The soldier on the other side let loose too, a clanking sound like a rivet gun. Larry wanted to see but kept his head pressed to the wet sandbags. A few spent cartridges clinked off the tailgate and hit him in the back. They were hot. He found he was holding his breath, and exhaled, then discovered he had to pee.

"Nope," the one soldier said. "Musta been nothin."

"Better safe," the other said. They knelt down and slipped in new magazines, popped up again, ready. The road was straight now and the driver put his foot down. It was almost cold with the wind. From nowhere a Phantom threw a shadow over the road, shredded the air above them, its jets deafening, then disappeared behind the treeline.

They passed one more torched car—a large, older model, humped and curved like a '34 Ford. It had nearly made the gate of the firebase they were being taken to, and now a band of children had claimed it. The doors burst open when they saw the truck, and while the driver waited for the guards to walk apart the razorwire gate, the same soldier produced another pack of gum and threw it piecemeal to the crowd. The other smirked and shook his head as if he should know better.

A sign above the wire said the Rakkasans of the 3/187th welcomed them to Phong Dien; sky peeked through a few bullet holes, and several letters were obscured by clots of what Larry hoped was mud. Inside the wire the guards had their weapons ready. Only after a German shepherd had sniffed the undercarriage of the truck did they push the two sides of the gate open with their free hands, letting the truck in, then retraced their steps backwards, closing it again, never taking their eyes off the treeline.

A sergeant was waiting for them—or Larry, because his name was first on the list. His papers had already been cut for Echo company, operating out of LZ Odin. He was sent to the supply tent with an escort from battalion medical and orders to be on the chopper pad at 1500. Larry knew it was well past lunch and wondered if it would be easier to simply not eat. He was still queasy from the plane.

Besides skivvies and socks and a new toothbrush, supply gave him a full aid bag—sealed battle dressings and sterile gauze, plasma and albumen, trach tubes and scissors and tweezers. They pressed extra morphine on him, and a month's worth of tetracycline and penicillin and Dapsone and ringworm pills, tape and copper-wired tags to identify his casualties, Dexedrine and vitamins, hydrogen peroxide. They fixed him up with a used helmet and flak jacket and, lastly, a scuffed .45 with one seven-round magazine, which he loaded before going outside.

It had stopped raining while he was inside, and the sun was out. The chopper was waiting for him, churning up a storm of grit. As Larry hustled to the pad, the pistol knocked against his hip. He thought he'd be taken in on a medevac, but he climbed in beside a gunner hunched over a can of ammunition. The gunner wore a crash helmet with a built-in headset and what looked like dirty golf gloves. Though it was impossible to hear anything but the rotor, Larry tried to say hi. The gunner pointed to a bench, and as he had so often lately, Larry sat there and waited for take-off. The belly of the chopper smelled like an engine, all hot metal and burnt air; the vibration of the floor shivered through his boots. When the gunner was done fixing his ammunition, he came back and helped Larry take his flak jacket off so he could sit on it, then gave the pilot the thumbs-up.

The ship didn't lift straight up, as Larry had anticipated. It dipped its nose and lunged forward uncertainly, slid and jerked, hesitated as if it weren't getting enough gas. Only pride would keep him from being sick, he thought. They jumped suddenly, accelerated away from the earth, and the gunner looked back to check on him. Larry waved feebly. The gunner pointed to the other door, in which the jungle sped dizzyingly below. Larry shook his head; he did not want to get close to it. The gunner pointed again, ordering him, and Larry shifted on the bench and leaned into the opening.

The wind here was freezing, his fingers numb against the steel frame. Beneath them the shadow of the chopper darkened the treetops, hopped and shifted with the green hills. He could see white flocks of birds soaring below and streams pouring down mountainsides, charred patches of forest, black and tan bomb craters. The gunner was right; watching the land roll slowly beneath him, Larry didn't feel sick. Here, far above the jungle, he felt a strange appreciation for the country, a rapt detachment, an invulnerability. He followed tributaries to a muddy river, the river into a narrow valley, and forgot about himself. It was like cruising in his father's old Packard those long-ago summer vacations, watching the farm stands and Lake Ontario slide by.

The gunner signaled one with a finger and, when Larry didn't understand, pointed to the bald top of a hill in the distance. The pilot kept the chopper steady, heading straight for the LZ. One minute, he meant. It hadn't taken long at all; to his surprise, Larry found that he wanted to keep flying.

They came down in a wide spiral, the camp below growing, rows of tents and fortified bunkers coming into focus. It was larger than he'd thought, all red dirt, like San Antonio, the earth unexpectedly bright. The bulldozer they'd used to scrape the place out of the jungle sat beside the chopper pad, as if waiting to leave; the pad itself was readymade, perforated steel plate, like the runways the Seabees laid on Tinian. Toward the center he noticed some large artillery pieces and a sandbagged position bristling with antennas. Around the perimeter, guard bunkers faced a moat of concertina wire; like the sides of Highway 1, there was nothing for seventy or eighty meters down the hillside, then a solid wall of jungle. The gunner swept the barrel over the green below, then when they were a few feet off the pad, helped Larry balance his ass on the doorframe and drop his feet to the skids. A sergeant in jungle fatigues waited for him, shielding his face from the dust with a soft hat. The gunner tapped Larry on the shoulder and pointed to the pad. Larry nodded uncertainly and jumped.

The weight of his aid bag knocked him down, and his helmet clanked against the steel plate, dazing him for a second. The sergeant lifted him up by one arm and hauled him away from the chopper, which was lifting off, its turbine whining.

"Welcome to Echo," the sergeant shouted, and shook his hand hard, as if he was happy to see him. Larry remembered to salute. "Your platoon's out on recon, so we'll get you set up first and take you over to the hootch."

He followed the sergeant through the camp, glancing at the view—green humps of mountains to the horizon on all sides. He thought of the Adirondacks. The heat he'd anticipated down south had waited until now to hit him. In minutes his fatigues weighed on him, and he desperately wanted to remove his helmet. No one else was wearing one.

Again, they went to supply. Here they gave him insect repellent and extra canteens, an olive-drab towel and a ratty fatigue jacket, a large, new poncho and a coil of rope. He was issued a bag of pale blue heat tabs for cooking C-rations in the field, Halazone tablets for purifying water, a fresh bedroll and an old pillow packed in a flimsy foot locker. The sergeant helped him lug some of the gear; there was so much that Larry had to cradle a heap of it in his arms as he walked across the compound. The crew manning one gun was shirtless and wore headbands fashioned from parachute silk; it seemed to Larry that they were staring as he passed. Somewhere a generator hummed, and the air smelled of diesel. The sergeant pointed out the commo bunker with its antennas, and the mess, then started down a row of tents with sandbags stacked halfway up their sides. He called them off as they passed until they came to his—first platoon. He held the door for Larry.

It was one large room with a wooden floor, a row of cots on each side of an aisle. An unframed mirror hung on a post, a shaving brush in a tin canteen cup nailed beneath it. Far in the back, one bunk was sectioned off by a curtain of mosquito netting. The air smelled stale but sweet, like the cherry air freshener Vicki's mother sprayed on the carpet after cleaning Jojo's mess.

"They ought to be back any minute," the sergeant said, but Larry was more interested in what he was seeing.

Playboy centerfolds decorated the canvas walls; above one bunk, Willie McCovey stepped into a pitch. Closer to the beds, farther down, next to the pillows, there was no one famous, only framed pictures of girlfriends and families, brothers in dress uniforms, jumped-up cars in backyards. Several beautiful suits hung beside bunks. One cot was empty, and after a glance at the sergeant, Larry dropped his gear on it and took off his helmet.

"We're a little undersized right now," the sergeant apologized. "We expect that to change soon." He told Larry where the nearest pisstube was, then shook Larry's hand again, as if they'd made a deal. "I'll just let you get situated."

As Larry fixed his rack he looked around the tent, taking in the transistor radios and Cinzano ashtrays, the sandals mustered at the head of each cot. The pictures of loved ones, the souvenirs of Sydney and Hong Kong arranged as neatly as Vicki's mother's knickknacks—everything seemed laid out like the effects of the dead. He wondered who had slept in what was now his cot, and when he'd finished squaring the corners, found he couldn't sit on it. He paced between the bunks, careful not to disturb anything, then went outside without his helmet and searched for the pisstube, then stood above it, self-consciously draining himself into the olive-drab cylinder. Back inside, he snooped for a while before finally sitting on the bunk and then, wondering when they ate, lay down. It took him only a few minutes to realize he couldn't sleep, and so he sat back up, opened his pack and began writing Vicki a letter that began: *I'm here.*

He was writing to his father when he heard several men outside loudly cursing each other. "Because you're a simple motherfucker, that's why," one said, and the others laughed. Larry stopped, listening, waiting for them to pass, but the voices grew until the door of the tent opened, and in walked a short, balding man draped with grenades and carrying an M-14.

He hesitated a second when he saw Larry, then continued in, followed by the rest of the platoon. They were all dark—that tan he'd seen before, or actually black—and he wondered how long it would take his skin to turn. Their boots were crusted with red mud and their fatigue jackets fraying, some literally in ribbons. Larry stood and saluted when their leader came over to the bunk, but the man only patted him on the shoulder. His eyes were red and he seemed tired, slumped under his load; the patches of sweat beneath his arms connected with the one down his front. He examined Larry's face and then his uniform, his gear; Larry kept at attention, trying to appear competent. Around them, the others were leaning their weapons by their cots and tugging off their boots, shucking their gear. Very softly, the older man said, "Son, how long do you think it will take you to figure out you are in exactly the wrong place?"

"Sir?" Larry said.

"You college?"

"Sir? No sir."

"Then you've already figured it out, haven't you?"

"Yes sir."

"Good," he said, and introduced himself as Lieutenant Wise. He turned to the rest of the tent and said, "We've got a new pecker checker here— Markham," and before he'd finished, everyone had gone quiet and was staring at Larry. "I know everybody misses Rosie but we're lucky to have Markham here. I want you all to help him out, he'll be a good man." He patted Larry on the shoulder and headed for the back of the tent, where he disappeared behind the mosquito netting.

The others came by his bunk to greet him, giving their names and shaking his hand. Bogut, Salazar, Leonard Dawson. The smell of them reminded Larry of a locker room after gym class. They all seemed older. "So you're the Band-Aid man," one guy with long blond hair asked; someone called him

Fred the Head. Larry tried to remember them, put faces to names, but there were too many. He'd have to stay alert, pick them up in conversation, make a list.

"Andy Kazmirski," one of them said—tall, with blue eyes and almost white blond hair.

"That's Dumb Andy," a tiny black man added, and the blond shrugged in mild annoyance. "This is Smart Andy."

"Andy Falco," the other said, also tall, but with dark hair. They were both lean and slightly hunched, as if ashamed of their height. In a strange way, they could have been brothers.

"Hey, yo," someone said. "FNG gets the brews."

"Yeah, I'm dry."

"No, man," a heavyset black man said from the other end, "that's bad luck—a doc?"

"FNG gets the brews, that's the rule."

"What?" Larry asked the small man. His name tag said STARGELL; everyone called him Nate. "What am I supposed to do?"

"It's tradition. The new guy has to bring the platoon a cold beer. They're in the connex around back."

"Okay," Larry said.

Nate counted how many they'd need. Everyone was laughing as they left.

They walked between the tents and up a rise toward a shacklike metal box with a door and what looked like an air conditioner attached to one side.

"So you were just on recon," Larry asked.

"Around the LZ it's a skate," Nate said. "Local VC at the most—snipers and shit. Don't worry. Get your ass in the grass and you'll be fine. All you need's a little on-the-job training."

Nate pulled a key and popped the lock, then stepped aside.

Larry had to duck going in. The cold air prickled the hair on his arms. There was no light, only what filtered in around him, and it was hard to see. Larry thought it might be a nice place to steal away, maybe take a flashlight and a good book.

"It's back and to the left," Nate instructed.

Larry had to squeeze between two shrinkwrapped pallets—plasma, one looked like. The beer was in the corner, already opened, a few spent six-pack rings sitting on top. Pabst Blue Ribbon—familiar and somehow comforting. He lifted two sixes out and turned to go when his boot caught on some plastic. He kicked free of it, and as the plastic resettled, Larry saw that lying beneath it was a man—a Vietnamese with part of his head shot off, the blood and tissue coagulated black. A piece of skull jutted from the mess like a broken bowl.

He dropped the six-packs and fell backward across the plasma and scrambled for the door. He shot past Nate and kept going, down the hill and between the tents and up the dusty walk the sergeant had brought him across from the chopper pad, until he stopped, short of the artillery, and stood there dizzily in the heat, bent over and breathing hard, and vomited on the ground. He hadn't eaten, and it hurt, bitter yellow strings. One side of the man's face was fine, the other sheared off and crusted. He spat and cursed Nate and the rest for doing this to him, and at the same time was ashamed of being afraid and, more acutely, of trying to hide it. Impossibly, he'd hoped no one would know.

When he'd composed himself he went back to the tent, where they were drinking beer. They gave a cheer when he entered; the laughter followed him to his cot. Nate walked over and handed him a cold can, but kept something behind his back.

"This," he said, laying a hand on Larry's shoulder, addressing the entire tent, "is what this man looked like coming out of that box," and showed them what he'd been hiding—a plastic skull with the eyeholes poked out. Nate waited for the laughter to stop. "Seriously, I thought I was gonna fucking die. Dude still looks like he could use some blood."

Larry tried to smile and took a sip of his beer, stared down into the opening, the bubbles coming up. The one eye was gone, the socket scraped clean as a shucked clam. The rest of that side was missing, ragged, gone black.

"Hey," one of the Andys said—the dark one, the smart one—and Larry raised his eyes. "Cheer up. You'll see a lot worse."

"A lot and a lot more," Nate said, exaggeratedly waving the skull over Larry's head like a voodoo priest.

"Come on, Nate," the heavy black man at the far end said, "just do it and get it over with," and Larry resented his protection.

"Doctor," Nate said, addressing Larry with mock seriousness. "The vote was not close. It would have been unanimous except a bunch of us wanted to go with 'Larry the Cherry.' But a doc's gotta have a handle. And so," he said ceremoniously, "with the power invested in me by first platoon, I hereby pronounce you 'Skull.' " He bowed and offered Larry the plastic one.

Larry took another sip of his beer.

"C'mon, Doc," Smart Andy said.

"Might as well take it," the heavy man advised as if he were on his side. "They'll call you it anyway."

And so Larry did.

"They're okay," the man said later, coming over to his bunk. "Carl Metcalf," he said. Like Leonard Dawson and Lieutenant Wise, he didn't have a nickname. He was the squad leader, a corporal, which impressed Larry. There had been a sergeant, Carl Metcalf said, but didn't explain. He was from Syracuse, and so they talked for a minute about snow and Ernie Davis and how cool it would be there this time of year. He seemed older than the others, projecting a calm Larry recognized in his father.

"Just be there when they need you," Carl Metcalf said, "and they'll do anything for you."

Later, when they were all asleep, Larry lay awake listening to the other men. He'd had three beers and no dinner and his anger had softened and turned and become first a grudging and then an easy camaraderie. He noted the sleeper in each bed and memorized their names, their faces—Magoo, Bogut, Pony. This was his platoon. It was his job to keep them alive, though he did not know them at all—like his father taking anyone in off the street. It was not generosity, Larry thought, only the acceptance of one's responsibility. He hoped he would be good enough. He rolled over and closed his eyes but still could not even entertain sleep. At least he could stop moving. It was not odd or strange to be in this tent, among these men, about to become part of them. He'd been trained; he'd worked hard. He had thought of Vietnam for so long and now he was here. Looking at the skull and his picture of Vicki, at Loomis's father's cigar and the handful of salt packets he'd carried across the Pacific, Larry thought that the lieutenant was wrong; though he did not know exactly what he would be asked to do—or how, after seeing the face of the dead man, he would be able to do it—Larry thought that finally he was where he was supposed to be.

THREE

They called from the hospital—Mel White, Rinehart and Sponge, all on a party line. Larry had just come back from running, sweaty and cleansed; he was crossing the front yard when he heard the phone and dashed inside, thinking it might be Vicki.

In the past, she'd never left long enough for him to appreciate the fact that she was gone—the chores and boredom of living alone. The solitude was still novel; it would have been pleasant except that he worried desperately about Scott. His radio had gone off in the middle of the night, jerking Larry up from a well-rehearsed dream of the A Shau—the mountains, the all-day rains, the clots of congealed fat lurking pearllike in his cold can of turkey loaf. Magoo was taking pictures while they were eating, pissing everyone off. The radio squawked and, without looking up from his ham slices, Bogut reached for the handset clipped to his shoulder.

It took Larry a second to realize the static was coming through in the next room, that he was dreaming. The ceiling light was on, blinding. It was nearly three; he'd be up anyway, he reasoned. This morning he'd found a careful clicking on Scott's answering machine, just a Morse code hello from Rudy, his friend in Fiji. Larry logged it in, thinking Scott would want to see it when they came back.

He was expecting Vicki, no matter what Donna said. Usually she called to tell him what he'd done. They'd argue over how they each deserved to be treated, talk about Scott and how they were a family, and finally come to some truce and schedule her return. She'd never left for more than three days, always to her mother's and always—before—on a weekend. It was convenient. Sometimes Larry wanted her not to call, to give him a few days by himself, but when she did, any thought of them actually breaking up evaporated, and after they fought, he needed to see her, to make it up to her in person.

He was ready to apologize, though he didn't quite know what it was this time. Not touching her enough. Spending too much time on the ward. Bolting one too many Genesees before dinner at her mother's. He was guilty on any number of counts, but willing, too, to set things right again. He'd take the whole family out on the town—even her mother if she wanted. He'd take them to Joe's, where both Vicki and Mrs. Honness ordered the bottomless salad, and the waitress kept hot garlic breadsticks coming for Scott. Even the wine was cheap there; he'd order a bottle of chianti and all of this would be forgotten.

He picked up—still winded from the run, sweat dripping from his chin—and they all started talking at once. He was confused and then disappointed. It took him a minute to listen to what they were saying.

"It's fucked up, Doc," Mel White said. "Your buddy Creeley booked on us."

"We thought you ought to know," said Rinehart.

"Typical covert shit," Sponge put in. "Middle of the night. When they came around for meds, they opened his curtain and there was Benny the night guy spread-eagled with a towel in his mouth. The dude is a fucking menace. I mean, we didn't even see him."

"He left a note," Mel White said. "The cops took it but basically it said he was going out on a recon, some kind of final mission."

"Yeah," Sponge added, half in admiration, "real melodramatic."

The memory of a VC cadre chief beheaded with a wire garotte came to Larry and he didn't listen to what Rinehart said next. The Phoenix was ugly when it wanted to send a message, otherwise it was silent. At night they came out of the thickets and plucked men from their sleeping families. The canals were full of soft, fish-kissed bodies; to sink them they slid the blade of a K-bar into the lungs, watched the water bubble.

"You said the cops were there," Larry asked.

"Still are," Mel White said. "I don't think they want to mess with him. Benny says he never saw him, just blacked out and woke up like that. There wasn't a mark on him."

"And Benny's a load," Sponge reminded him. "He's no pushover. The cops definitely do not want any part of our boy."

"They think he'll try to go back home," Rinehart said.

"Which is where?" Larry asked. He wiped his face with the hem of his muscle shirt.

None of them answered, and Larry remembered the blank spaces in Creeley's file. Birth date, birthplace, permanent residence. Jesus, he thought, he's just out there.

"They're going to check the bus station," Rinehart said.

"Okay," Larry said. "I'll do what I can."

"Hey, Doc, do us a favor?" Mel White asked.

"Yeah."

"Don't let this dickhead embarrass us. I see enough of this psycho shit on TV."

"What do you want me to do?"

"Find his rabbity ass and neutralize it."

"I'll look."

"Fucking get some," Sponge instructed.

"I said I'd look," Larry said, and when he'd hung up, swore and headed upstairs for the shower, thinking that he didn't need this shit. He already had enough people to look for.

HE'D HAD the last of the eggs yesterday. He killed the silty dregs of Scott's Count Chocula, drowning them in Vicki's skim milk. The radio said the union had walked out of the talks but the Gadabout and the Ithaca School District buses were following their regular schedules. Officially he could use the Gadabout; he had a DAV card they'd mistakenly issued him. Vicki was always on him about taking advantage of their insurance rates, but it didn't seem right to him; there were people who'd really been hurt. He stood at the front window, spooning the chocolatey balls in, keeping an eye on Donna's Monte Carlo. He'd pay her back for gas, maybe rake her yard, fix something around the house.

Coming up her steps, he saw a perfect opportunity. The buzzer beside her door hung by its wires. Wade had been gone less than a year and the paint was already peeling. Even when the family was together the house had never been in good repair, a fact his father harped on. Wade was well-intentioned but half-assed, the Camaro symptomatic. The boys' plastic pool and their two Labs had destroyed the backyard. Larry and Vicki never said anything to them, though occasionally they complained to each other, and even then they couldn't get worked up about it, as if admitting there were larger problems. Near the end, they could count on Donna to smash out the windows once a week; about suppertime they'd hear the shouting and wait for the noise, up one side of the house and then around back, and later, Wade hunched over in the dark, picking up the larger pieces with work-gloves and dumping them in a steel trashcan. She was actually better, Wade said, cautiously ironic; she was just angry now. He stapled plastic over the broken ones, which only provoked her. Vicki once saw a kitchen chair tear feetfirst through a new sheet, and behind it, suddenly public, Wade and Donna wrestling each other for a lamp. She and Larry bickered over who should go see if they were okay and then, finally, when they didn't hear them anymore, decided it was not their affair.

Wade had left. Now Vicki had left, again. It made Larry wonder what made him stay. Susan left for college and never came back. He wasn't angry about it, or bitter, it was just curious. He liked the town, he didn't love it. He could live anywhere really. Not Vietnam. Donna stayed. He wondered what inside them could possibly be the same. Was it out of duty, paying back the place and people that had made you, or was it just inertia, the ease of familiarity?

On the welcome mat Larry hesitated, his thumb over the button, wondering if he'd be shocked. Before he could summon the nerve, Donna opened the door for him.

She was ready, her purse over her shoulder, Cornell mug in hand. He almost didn't recognize her. Her hair was pulled back and she was wearing wire rims and very little make-up. It was warmer today, but she had on a heavy tweed ensemble—a jacket with elbow patches and knee-length skirt.

She laughed at his reaction. "Big meeting," she explained, and smirked, making fun of the get-up. He wished he'd put on a clean pair of jeans.

"So," she said in the car, "any word?"

"Nope."

"It's early."

"Oh yeah," Larry said, as if he weren't worried. The aspirin still rested in the vent, sliding sideways with every curve. She didn't offer him coffee and drove as if they were late. He was glad she hadn't cleaned the car for him.

"Are you eating?" she asked, surprising him. It was a question he expected from Vicki.

"Yep," he said, and as proof held up his lunchbag.

"What?"

"Everything. Whatever's there."

She clicked her tongue as if she didn't believe him.

"Really," he insisted.

"What did you have last night?" she asked, and when he hesitated, waved her hand as if he needn't bother. "I'll make dinner for you sometime this week—not tonight. There's no sense both of us cooking."

"That's okay."

"No," she said. "You've got to eat. How about Friday? I'll pick up some fish."

He didn't want to argue.

"It'll be great," she said.

They headed for downtown, the sun cutting through the trees, warming his hands. Her offer was generous, but too cheery. He was comfortable with her, which was her doing, and he appreciated it, yet he missed the intensity of yesterday's conversation. He thought he should be more worried, Donna more concerned. He wondered if she'd heard from Wade.

"Beautiful day," she said, and as if obeying, he nodded and turned to look at it, separated from her solely by his concentration. The bus strike was only in its second day.

Fat leaf bags stamped like jack-o'-lanterns smiled from the neat lawns. A skeleton hung from an oak just going gold; the maples were blazing. It seemed that other people put their decorations up earlier every year, while he was content to wait till the final week. What had happened to his enthusiasm, his high spirits? He'd need candy—and before that he had to find something for his father. It was harder now that he'd stopped playing golf. Larry used to rely on a box of Titleists, the promise of the coming spring. In June when he went over to help bring up the wrought-iron lawn furniture, he'd come across an unopened box beneath the toolbench, the plastic wrap dusty. His father offered him his clubs; Larry said maybe he'd change his mind.

"At this point I think you're more likely to," his father said.

"We'll see," Larry said, turning it—like everything between them—into a victorless battle of wills.

Scotch was boring. His father still fished occasionally but hated the new gear—the acrylics and graphite shafts—and wouldn't entertain the idea of buying flies. His hands were still good, he boasted. Something for the car maybe; he had a weakness for its luxury, its plushness. Larry had seen him and Mrs. Railsbeck tooling around one Sunday in July, going nowhere in particular, Mrs. R. bundled up against the air-conditioning. He'd wanted to honk but didn't, just watched the New Yorker glide regally through the intersection, like a great and ancient fish on the verge of extinction.

He watched the houses and trailers speed by, the brief bursts of woods. An old woman in a blue sweatsuit was taking a letter out to her mailbox, moving impossibly slowly down her drive, tottering, taking baby steps. A German shepherd had worn a perfect circle around a tree.

He tried to imagine Creeley out there somewhere, field-stripping his cigarettes as he prepared to break camp at the edge of someone's back pasture, but it didn't fit with the day, the slow stirring of people getting ready for work, the lunches that needed to be made, the patient drawing on of socks. Knowing he was out there among the still houses and gravel backroads made Larry uneasy. As a child, he waited for this time of year, the forests brilliant, going cold at dusk, leaves racing scattered beneath the streetlights. The autumn and the land here seemed one, unlike summer, with its raw brightness and unnatural heat. Fall's pleasures were furtive, risky, short-lived —buckeye fights, the smell of woodsmoke, the endless recipes for the apples

Mrs. Railsbeck asked him to fetch from the cobwebbed crate in the basement. He waited for the season as he did the flap of a sideshow tent to be lifted, ready to be utterly, gleefully terrified. That had passed too; he no longer wanted to be frightened, he did not see the need. And he was frightened of Creeley. He could discount Rinehart and Sponge, but Mel White wasn't a storyteller. None of them knew Creeley was Phoenix.

It wasn't something he'd have to worry about. The state police had probably already picked him up hitching east on 17, hungry after a night by the roadside. Larry hoped so. Right now Vicki was all the drama he could handle.

"You do like fish," Donna asked, glancing over at him.

"Sure."

"What's wrong?"

"Nothing," he said, and shrugged to make it seem heartfelt.

"Hey," Donna said, "cheer up. It's already Tuesday."

He appreciated her trying, but for some reason she was no comfort today. Yesterday they both seemed to have problems; now it was only him. It was just the clothes, he thought, that and having Creeley on his mind.

They had time. Downtown she took it easy at the lights. He would have to rush through his deliveries if he wanted to check the camping areas at all the parks. He'd call Vicki first, try her at work. He'd load Number 1 and get on the road. He'd have to see Dr. Jefferies, talk with the police.

Donna let him off in the parking lot.

"Same time tomorrow," she said, and rolled away, not looking back. Larry wondered why he'd thought she might. In a corner of her rear window nested a bleached Marriage Encounter sticker, a pair of rings entwined beneath a single heart, and he wondered what had happened to his crush on her, if he'd let go of it coldly, because of her troubles. Her arms were thin as a girl's, her shoulders bony; she had the feet of a child. It was funny, he'd never talked to her that much back then, only about her, with Wade. He'd felt sorry for her, mostly; now he understood she didn't need that. She was capable while he felt lost, and he hoped that that self-reliance would come to him in time—if this was really it. It was strange, and cheering in a way, to find that after all these years he really did like her. He liked the idea of having dinner with her and hoped, perversely, that Vicki would not be back by Friday.

He was early and Julian was late. Up front Derek was engulfed in the donut rush. Marv stuck his head out of the office and told Larry to get dressed and give him a hand.

"Fuck," Larry said, loud enough for him to hear.

"And Larry," Marv said, holding up a finger. "One more and he's gone. I don't have time for this shit."

"Bite my butt," Larry said when the door had closed. "Laziest man in the world," he muttered, and for a second saw Lieutenant Wise spread out on the ground under his poncho, safe from the midday sun, drooling onto his rucksack. He was a good six years older than anyone in the platoon and forty pounds overweight, and by midmorning in the bush the towel around his neck was sopping. They called him the skipper, or skip, or the LT, or the Old Man. When anyone asked a question, he had the answer. Do I look like a shitbird? he often asked Higher on Bogut's radio, without pressing the send button; do I look like some ninety-day wonder? He had been there a long time and he would be there a long time after their young asses were gone. He could sleep sitting up in a Shithook, the big bird's motion making him sway, scarily trancelike. Once Fred the Head bet Smart Andy whether a frag would wake up the LT. It hadn't, and Fred the Head had to hump the extra belts Smart Andy carried for Pony's sixty.

"You gotta be numb," Nate scolded Fred the Head. "I mean, you gotta be a real shitwit to bet someone whose name starts with Smart."

The fifth day at Hamburger Hill the laziest man in the world caught a claymore across the head and chest. Part of a leaf spring stuck from his cheek, as if, robotlike, he'd burst from the inside. They took him down the hill to the aid station and put a poncho on him. By that time there weren't many of them left, but Smart Andy was still there to say something. When he was done, Magoo took a picture.

"There it is," Go-Go Bates said, "the big sleep," though the LT looked anything but peaceful. It was muddy and they'd dropped him coming down and Carl Metcalf was angry.

That was all gone, Larry thought, that didn't exist. He looked at the pictures of Vicki in her tube top and Scott on the pony, closed the locker and tied Julian's apron on over his uniform; in the middle of it sat a child's idea of a house—square with a chimney—inside of which rested a bright red heart. On his way to the front he passed the phone by the timeclock. Eight-oh-five and he was already behind. He had to mask his scowl before he hit the counter.

Five or six people stood in a loose line, keys in their hands. One man in a red-and-black mackinaw had a scar across his forehead and a few days' worth of stubble. Outside, traffic whipped by.

"Hey," Derek said.

"Hey," Larry said, and got in beside him. "I can take the next person over here."

The guy with the scar bought a carton of moon pies, all cherry, probably for a month of lunches. He was too old for the war, just as the man behind him in the jean jacket was too young. Larry could tell at a glance, though he had no idea—except in rare, flamboyant cases—whether a man had been or not; it was a secret army, he thought, invisible and in a strange way undefeated.

There was a run on the pumpkin cupcakes. Every time someone came in, an electronic chime binged from a speaker. Larry rang up his customers, the cash drawer kicking out, hitting him in the gut. He had to open a roll of nickels, cracking it against the side of the drawer like an egg; he swung too hard and the coins showered the floor. Some of the customers clapped.

"Leave it," Derek ordered, and they skated around behind the counter, the nickels clicking underfoot.

It was almost nine when Julian came in. Larry bagged a box of crumb cakes, made change and left the next customer waiting at the counter.

"Big help," Derek said, and Larry gave him a forget-it wave.

Walking toward the back, he untied the apron and replaced the scowl. Julian was punching in, his hair flat on one side, his clothes the same as yesterday.

"Don't *ever* fucking string me out again," Larry said, and shoved the apron into his chest. The boy cringed as if he'd been hit. Larry stalked past him into the back, giving the lockers a gratuitous, booming slam with a fist.

Loading Number 1, he kept dropping things, the cellophane bags slipping through his hands like fish. He banged his trays in and checked the invoices on his clipboard, hopped up on the seat and tugged his gloves on over his knuckles. Nine-fifteen. Christ, the morning was almost gone. He backed her up too fast and the trays clattered, then he couldn't find first. The gearbox crunched; the shift buzzed in his hand.

"No fucking slack," he said, and mashed the clutch, jammed it in gear, and revved across the lot.

Only later, caught in traffic at the Octopus, did his anger drain away. The big trucks coming down West Hill shook the bridge. Below, the inlet was still, a single scull pulling for open water. Up the lake, a vee of geese angled north toward the Montezuma preserve. Mendelssohn was on SKG, the Hebrides Overture, and Larry regretted shoving Julian. He supposed that eventually it was for his own good, but still, he shouldn't have taken it out on the kid.

It was just Vicki, he thought, how she could do this to him again. Her silence frightened him, she knew that, just as his frustrated her. After the last time, she had promised not to leave, to talk it out with him. Now he wanted to hate her. He came close, but it was an effort, a choice he had to make, a commitment. She knew he would plead with her, tell her he needed her. He was tired of it, and tired of feeling he'd done something wrong. This would be the last time, he thought, and vowed that it would be true, though in his heart he knew he was lying.

THE FIRST WORDS Vicki said to him were "Fuck you."

He'd called her mother's, and unexpectedly she picked up. He could not tell if she was angry with him or with herself for being caught off guard.

"Vicki," he said desperately. Already he was pleading.

"Don't," she said as if he'd hurt her, and hung up.

He called back, expecting it would be busy, the handset left off the hook or stuffed into the sofa, but there was the little trill, the waits in between. He thought of her listening to it in the empty house. She would go to the dining room where there wasn't a phone, or outside on the back patio where it wouldn't be so loud. He wanted her to answer, even if she'd only click it off again. After twenty rings he stopped and stood there in the lot of the Trumansburg ShurSave, questioning the deserted county fairgrounds across the road. He could be at her mother's house in minutes. He was already behind but that didn't matter; it was his long day—nearly two hundred miles. The new foot hurt like hell by noon, and if he blew off a few late stops, the managers would understand. He tried her again and, as he was dialing, felt his skin shiver, his breath catch the same way it had when his men called for him and he knew his legs would carry him there. Now, like then, he did not balk. He stabbed the last digit and let it ring another twenty, got back in Number 1 and headed for her mother's.

It was near the end of Seneca Street, a sea-green bungalow with an elaborate, rusted TV antenna and a whitewashed tractor tire in which, every spring, her mother transplanted her kitchen geraniums. In the years since the war Trumansburg had become a strange town. Her mother's neighbors on one side were a houseload of hippies, leftovers from Cornell; they painted their Gothic Revival an electric blue with lavender trim and drove an old roachlike Saab and a sputtering VW bus. The man who invented the Moog synthesizer lived two blocks over, looping xylophone scales and banshee screams like Psy-Ops flyovers escaping his barn. On Main Street, among the farmers and matron ladies, you'd see braless women in Indian print skirts and bearded men wearing sandals. Even the trip from Ithaca—itself a haven for aging Ph.D. students and waylaid Deadheads—seemed a kind of time travel.

The gates of the driveway were propped open on both sides by high weeds, the stems and heads splashed silver along with the fence. The Ruster wasn't there, just a pair of ruts Mrs. Honness's Volare had worn to the garage. After Larry had rung the bell several times, he took a closer look at the hump and noticed in a puddle no wider than a coffee saucer the telltale candy red of transmission fluid. The last year or so the Ruster took an extra second, a noticeable clunk, to find Drive. He smelled the viscous fluid to be sure, wiped his hand on the grass and rubbed the excess into his fingertips. In Number 1 he found a blank invoice and wrote her a note.

Why? it said. *Miss you. Please come home*. He signed his initial and wedged the bill behind the sheet-metal eagle screwed to the screen door, hoping the wind would be merciful.

In Number 1 he thought that he did not hate her, that whatever happened, he never would. Was that love? He cared for her, wished her well, but that wasn't enough. It puzzled him that he could think this way now, when all he wanted was for her to come back. There was something wrong with him, he thought, something in the way. After all their history, he did not know what he felt, or why, or whether he even wished he did.

HE TRIED her from Pete's, the Woolworth's downtown and the Lansing Foodliner before passing beyond SKG's signal and out of the local area code. He drove up the east side of the lake toward Aurora, through overgrown farms and crate-littered orchards, past a few surviving dairy herds and deco motels from the thirties. Here the Halloween decorations seemed needless; the day had gone dark, ragged clouds drifting low over the cornfields. Peeling Greek Revivals and asbestos-shingled Italianates sat back from the road under shaggy willows, their porches rotting off, windows broken and stopped with plywood. Everyone had firewood for sale, and acreage, kittens for free, rabbits, cleanfill. In the yards, posed so traffic could look them over, rested heavy sedans and tired pick-ups from the sixties, their paint sun-faded, fenders lacy with rust, the prices too small to read. A spike-finned Cadillac made Larry smile, and he imagined raiding their savings account, how he'd explain it to Vicki.

Usually he liked it up here, coasting through the speed traps of the backwater towns; he liked the sooty brick schools, the soft lawns and old oaks, the sense of being in some other time where happiness might exist, or at least quiet, but today the frost-heaved sidewalks and blank-windowed thrift shops only reminded him that he was missing the present, that his life was elsewhere, unraveling and untended.

He cleared a rise and the lake came into view alongside him, running thin and crooked to the north, subtly bending west. On the far side lay the state parks with their campgrounds, unheated summer homes on the water, more rundown motels. That was where Creeley would be, reconnoitering, getting ready to head south. Larry could not get Bethesda out of his head, as if there were any real connection there. He tried to remember the man's voice, to place it by state or region, but came up with nothing.

King's Ferry came, and Bromleyville, first the green sign, a clutter of houses, maybe a strip of dingy stores, a gas station with a gravel lot and a padlocked ice machine for fishermen, and then the same sign in the mirror, fields, forest, nothing but road. How easy it would be to disappear into one of these towns, to work for the gas company reading meters or tend bar part-time. He'd wear a hat or bandana to hide the scar, depending on his neighbors; say it was a farm accident, a stray blasting cap or augur gone haywire at the Cargill salt mine. He'd be left alone, the kids on his block suspicious, the adults sympathetic—a quiet guy, they'd say, good worker, did his service. But that wasn't Creeley, Larry thought; that was what *he* had tried to do. Still was, he admitted. It was the price of driving for a living, cornering yourself every so often, finding out what you didn't really want to know.

On the door of the Cogos mini-mart in Aurora was a poster for a missing cat. After he did his shelves he took a look. Banana, it said under the picture. Children had written it, their N's backwards. The tape holding it in place had gone a caramel brown; Banana had been missing since late April. Larry shoved the empty tray back in the rack, closed the doors and drove.

At lunchtime he was in Ithaca but still behind. He stopped after stocking the A&P in the Triphammer Mall and called the hospital. He gave the operator Mel White's extension and got Johnny Johnson.

"Larry," Johnny said, but nothing else. "Larry," he said.

"Okay, Johnny, put Mel on."

"Mel," Johnny said, and with a clatter, Trayner came on.

"He's in PT or somewhere," Trayner said dreamily.

"Did they find Creeley yet?"

"I don't know, man. He's not here." His voice was heavy like a drunk's, and he chuckled as if what he said was funny. After dessert the staff gave the worst ones meds, and all afternoon they floated around obnoxiously, interrupting card games, laughing at the soap operas.

"Who else is there?" Larry asked.

"Cartwright's here."

"Let me talk to him."

It took a minute. He could hear a radio going in the background, the Spinners or the O'Jays maybe. Johnny had a whole lettuce crate of tapes his brother made for him years ago; everyone was sick of them, whistled the old tunes out of the blue until someone told them to shut up with that Gladys Knight and the Pips bullshit.

"What's up?" Cartwright asked. He refused to take medication and—at his invisible friend Mobley's request—had once broken an orderly's nose.

"Did they get Creeley yet?"

"Who—those poges? Those sad-asses couldn't catch the clap. I'll snag his ass. The fucking nutty-buddy souvenired my K-bar. Took my poker money—cigar box and everything. When he comes back he better cover his ass 'cause I will bush that boy toot sweet, and you know that's a promise."

"What else did he take?"

"Fuck," Cartwright said, and blew out a puff of air. "You name it."

"How about Meredith's pistol?" It was an NVA captain's, a sweet old Colt from the thirties with dirty pearl grips. He wasn't supposed to have the gun and kept it hidden in a strongbox in the back of his night table's bottom drawer.

"Cranked. Outta here."

"Shit," Larry said, trying to think.

"He got into the doctor's office and did a bunch of shit there. The poges were all over it. Tell you, the dude knew where everything was, like after five or six days. What was he, a green beanie, a spook?"

"A spook plus some."

"Oh shit," Cartwright said slowly, as if he'd gotten a joke. "I guess I better hit my moms up for some more money."

"Probably a good idea," Larry said.

"Fuck," Cartwright said, still surprised. "Well, good luck, man."

"Thanks," Larry said. "You're really helping me there."

"He's your fucking boy."

"I guess he is, him and the rest of you fucksticks."

"There it is, Doc."

"Yeah," Larry said. "There it fucking is."

The police put him on hold; he started in on his tuna fish sandwich, ignoring a syrupy rendition of "Fall" from *The Four Seasons*. When they came on he was almost done. He explained the situation to a woman officer with rigid diction, gave her his name and his relation to the missing man. He wanted to know what they'd got so far.

"I'm afraid we can't give you that information, sir," she enunciated.

"What *can* you tell me?"

"If you'd like to come down with some identification," she said, "our offices are open till five o'clock."

"Who should I ask for?"

"Just ask at the front desk, sir."

She started to give him their location but he stopped her. He knew the building. There was a vending machine in the basement he filled once a month.

When he arrived—around four, neglecting his stops in Dryden—the desk was empty. On it sat a pair of in-out baskets and a bell like that at the front desk of a hotel. He rang with the flat of his hand. A pudgy officer came out and, after taking Larry's name, led him upstairs. The man's gun and silence set him on edge. He said nothing to Larry, just showed him to an open door where a small man with thinning, auburn-tinged hair and in a pinstriped suit with huge, obsolete lapels sat behind a desk, its blotter empty save a computer terminal and two manila folders. The man was alternately talking on the phone and drinking a can of Diet Pepsi. He wore a college ring and cuff links and a United Way pin on one of his winglike lapels.

"No one knows," the man was saying. His name was on the door: Det. Gene Clines. Larry knew his face vaguely from last year's campaign posters; he'd run for sheriff and lost, and instantly Larry was sorry he hadn't voted for him.

"I've got nothing," Detective Clines said, doodling on the green expanse of the blotter. "I've got somebody here who might be able to tell me something. If I get something I'll let you know, but right now I don't have anything so let it rest for a little bit, okay? Okay." He hung up and motioned Larry to come in and sit. "The *Journal*," he said, rolling his eyes. "Glad you came in." He leaned over the desk to shake Larry's hand.

Closer, Larry could see he was older than his photos, his forehead mottled, his hands lined and spotted like his father's. The hair was a spectacularly bad comb-over and dye job, and Larry wondered if the detective had a wife or friends, political allies, lodge brothers—anyone to tell him it looked ridiculous.

"Okay," Clines said, "so who is this guy? I know who you are." He patted the folder on the left. "I know your father, have for thirty years. This guy though." He turned the computer so Larry could see the screen. "This is all we've got."

It was an electronic version of Creeley's file from the hospital—the blank places and dates. He punched a button and another form came up. "Bethesda has him in their records but with a different serial number. When we run his real number through the VA he comes up deceased. No pictures, no driver's license, nothing."

"He was in the Phoenix program."

"So it could be deliberate." Clines took a swig. "Oh yeah. I'm sure somewhere in Washington there's a file on him thick as a phonebook."

"How about the other number, the fake one?"

"That one's real interesting." He opened the folder and turned it so Larry could see.

There was his address, his father, his mother, Susan, Vicki, Scott; his employment record; Ithaca High, DeWitt Elementary. They had his service record too. He knew it all by heart. The date of his discharge was circled, and his serial number.

"So?" Larry asked.

Clines opened the other folder and set it beside the first. The top pages were the same, the dental records and dates of immunizations; the only difference was the names—Creeley's instead of his. Victoria Honness Creeley, it said, Scott William Creeley.

"What the fuck," Larry said.

"You don't know this man."

"All I know is what was in his folder. He was brand new in my group. Last night I saw him for the first time in my life."

"Did he talk at all?"

"Not much. He didn't want to so I didn't push him."

"Did he say anything strange or threatening?"

"No," Larry said reflexively, though he remembered exactly what Creeley had said. He wondered why he was lying, and why, already, he had no faith in Clines. It wasn't just the clothes or the desperate hair, the Diet Pepsi. He'd had the feeling before, in the bush; they all had, and the stronger of them, like Carl Metcalf or the skipper or Smart Andy when he and Pony positioned the big gun, acted on it—a sudden certainty based on everything he'd learned, that taking the streambed would lead them into a sure ambush, or that tonight the Martian and not Leonard Dawson should be on LP. You could see the future in the eyes of the new guy coming off the resupply chopper, in the scuffed bark of a root beside the inches-thin game trail, and you knew. It was not luck or a hunch, not an intangible at all, and the man who waited for more proof was a fool. Detective Clines, Larry knew, was simply not going to get the job done.

"I was over to the hospital this morning. I got the feeling some of the other patients didn't like him, is that right?"

"He was new," Larry said. "It always takes a while with a new guy."

"Here." Clines lifted the top sheet of Creeley's file and handed Larry a playing card. "We found this pinned to the orderly's labcoat with a syringe. What do you make of it?"

It was a two of spades. Larry recognized the deck—Rinehart's red Bicycles. Across the card, Creeley had gouged in ink: REMEMBER ME. Below, under the inverted pip, he'd drawn a round-socketed, noseless death's-head.

"A suicide note, maybe," Clines prompted. "Saying good-bye to someone."

Larry handed the card back. "I don't know. A lot of the better outfits like the First Cav left a card on their kills so the enemy would know they'd been paid back. Some of them even had business cards printed up."

"Got it," Clines said, and made a note on Creeley's file. "But without his records we don't even know what outfit he was with. I've got a call in to the VA in Syracuse."

"I wouldn't count on anything from them," Larry said. He wanted to be honest with Clines now, knowing he had no clue.

"Would you say he's dangerous?"

"To himself, you mean."

"That too."

Larry thought of what Mel White had said. They were all tired of the psycho vet; the tag was an insult, a late movie staple. It was a bitch. Sometimes the TV made him want to disown all the alcoholics, the vets in prison, the suicides and guys whose cars mysteriously rolled over on empty straightaways; he didn't like the success stories any better—the celebrated novelists and first-term congressmen who were supposed to be an inspiration, the men whose businesses donated oversized checks to build Little League fields with their dead buddy's name on the scoreboard. That kind of shit made him sick; all he wanted was some respect and to be left alone. But Creeley had the gun and Cartwright's knife and knew how to use them.

"Yeah," Larry said, "he's a fucking menace to society."

"Seriously."

"Seriously. The man's Phoenix. He's armed and dangerous and probably happier that way. And heavily, heavily medicated, at least for the next twenty-four hours. Once the Dilaudid drains out of his system he's going to be hurting."

"So what you're saying is we've got a problem."

"That's what I'm saying," Larry said.

Clines kept him till five. When Larry came out, Number 1 was surrounded by cruisers, looking huge and clownish. He had parked in the wrong lot and they'd given him a ticket, which he knew Marv would refuse to pay. He was glad he hadn't filled the machine yet; it was one less stop he'd have to make.

He hit the middle of rush hour at the Octopus and got to the hospital later than he'd expected. He had to get back by six to catch a ride with Julian; he'd have to apologize for this morning.

"What say, Chief," Mel White greeted him, rolling his chair up the aisle. Johnny Johnson was asleep, Cartwright hunched over a wordsearch book, Sponge and Rinehart locked in a bitter endgame of Othello. Larry gave them a wave; only Cartwright nodded, tipped his eraser.

"So what's the story?" Mel White asked, following along. "Carty says he's CIA, is that right?"

"Worse," Larry said. "What's the worst thing he could be?"

"No," Mel White said, as if he was joking.

"Yeah," Larry said. "And he's all scrambled upstairs, you've seen him."

"Jesus, he could have done all of us, easy."

"If he wanted to," Larry said. "Obviously he didn't."

Creeley's bed was made, his night table bare. They'd taken his tray with the bronze water pitcher and the stack of sanitized plastic cups. In the top drawer were a pair of rubber handgrips used to strengthen the forearms, some VA stationery from Bethesda and a sediment of pennies.

"We need those," Mel White said, and Larry pinched them up.

Creeley hadn't been there long enough to be issued his own phone, but in his bottom drawer rested a combination white and yellow pages for Ithaca. Larry lifted it out and handed it to Mel White, who turned the book upside down and shook it. Larry tried to reach in behind the drawer but there was nothing.

"Nothing," Mel White echoed.

In Creeley's closet hung a terrycloth bathrobe, a brace of white Oxford shirts and an equal number of dark slacks. He'd also left behind a tasseled pair of brown cordovans, several solid ties and a stack of tastefully striped boxer shorts. Some still had price tags on them.

"No socks," Mel White noted. "You always take as many as you can get."

"How about a belt? I must have gone through ten over there."

"They're useful," Mel White said, and Larry realized that it had probably happened to him—the quick and dirty tourniquets, the call and then the long wait for a dust-off. He remembered tying Nate off, how the canvas slipped and then caught on his skin, pinching a big chunk in the buckle. Bogut had tackled him to stop him from walking on the stump.

"Well," Larry said, and stirred the shirts around so the hangers clacked, "doesn't look like he's coming back."

"Nope," Mel White agreed.

"Hey," Sponge called over, "big fucking loss."

"Anything else I should tell the cops?" Larry asked the room at large.

"Carty," Mel White said, "tell Doc about your buddy."

"Fuck you," he said, and went back to the wordsearch as if slapped.

"What's the deal?" Larry asked.

Cartwright wouldn't look up.

"It's Mobley," Mel White said. "He says he hasn't seen him since Creeley took off."

"Anyone else seen Mobley?" Sponge asked, his hand in the air, looking for a laugh, but no one joined him.

In his sleep, Johnny Johnson flinched and whimpered like a dog, his remaining limbs twitching.

"It's okay," Larry said. "I'll keep an eye out for him."

A HUGE Spiderman crouched on top of the Wonder Bread outlet, tethered to the roof by guywires, menacing Route 13 with a Honda-sized Twinkie. Hostess had just signed him for a few million. It was a dumb promotion; everyone knew there was no hole in his mask. Marv's Eldorado was there but the Subaru was gone, and Larry thought he must have finally gotten rid of Julian. He wondered if he should stick up for him again and thought, Probably not. But he would. He'd say something to get Marv pissed off at him. It didn't matter that Julian was a fuck-up, or maybe Larry stood by him for exactly that reason, the way Carl Metcalf had carried him. He wanted to apologize for this morning, and imagined that if Julian really was gone he'd call him at home, invite him over to watch the series.

Before the fire door clanked shut, Marv stuck his head out and told him to get up front, and again Larry threw Julian's apron on. Derek was punching the register as if the rush had been constant since morning. Someone had picked up the nickels.

"So what happened?" Larry asked as they bagged.

"When?"

"This morning with Julian."

"Nothing. His car got ripped off."

"Bull." They couldn't swear up front, it was a rule.

"That's what Marv said. Then about an hour ago the cops show up and say someone torched it. The kid was flipping out so Marv sent him home."

Larry shook his head instead of swearing. "He was my ride."

"Marv's still in," Derek joked.

"Right," Larry said, and thought that he'd have to call his father again. He shook his head. "What a day."

"Tell me about it," Derek said, already serving the next customer.

Marv was in his office when they closed up. Larry punched out before calling the hospital. His father sounded surprised to hear from him again so soon, and made a joke of it.

"What can I do you for?" his father asked, and Larry thought of walking.

"I wondered if you could give me a ride home. The car's still in the shop."

"When?"

"Whenever you're done there."

"It sounds like you're ready now."

"I am," Larry admitted.

"What about your Vietnam thing?"

"That's Monday night."

"Hang on then. I'll be right down."

The way he said it made it sound like an extra favor, but Larry was too tired to argue.

In the lot, he watched the traffic pass. Across 13 the lights of the used car lots glowed like a carnival. Some of the soaped-on prices seemed reasonable, within reach. If this was really it, he thought, and stopped himself. This wasn't any different from the last time; it was the same old shit. Fuck it. He could live by himself; it was less hassle.

He turned circles to keep warm, his new foot protesting the cold. Spiderman loomed huge over Number 1. The windows of the store were papered with crayoned drawings of Twinkie the Kid. The scrawls outside of the lines made him miss Scott, and he turned away. Everyone was going home. He wondered what there was for supper, if there was anything in a can, and by the time the New Yorker turned into the lot, he was starving.

"This is the last time this month," Larry promised when he was in.

"That's all right," his father said. "I was pretty much done for the day."

They drove along without speaking, past Tops and Wegmans and over Six Mile Creek, back toward town. His father had the heater and the fan cranked as high as they would go; the air smelled of dust and Larry unbuttoned his jacket. A newscaster jabbered away on SKG, something about taxing the unemployed.

"I told you Maddy wants you all to come next Wednesday."

"I don't know if Vicki will be able to make it," Larry said. "I'll try."

"How's Scott?"

"Good."

They turned up Green and headed for downtown, silent again. Pretending to be interested in the new bar in the old American Legion post, Larry stole a closer look at his father. He seemed tired, leaning back into the plush seat, the crown of his hat an inch from the roof. With his gloves and scarf he seemed from another time, his reserve earned and wise. Like Larry, he was a quiet man, and genuinely kind—something Vicki refused to see. His father did not mind being alone, Larry thought, was sometimes happier that way. He was not that different from him, and at times like these he thought they might cut the shit for once and really talk to each other, say flat out, "Here's the deal. I want to know what it was like for you, and I want you to know what it was like for me." He peeked at the white, whiskerlike hairs curling out of his father's ears and the soft, fallen jowl, the moles the color of giblets, and thought that he did not have long.

Never happen, Carl Metcalf said when anyone wished for something dumb.

The fire station passed with its black POW-MIA flag. He thought of telling his father about Creeley but immediately dismissed the idea.

"We should talk about the war sometime," Larry tried.

"What about it?"

"Both wars, I mean, yours and mine."

"Sure," his father said. He exaggerated his concentration on the road, gazed over the wheel imperiously. "I don't have much to say about mine. I'm not sure how much of it I even remember, honestly."

"I'd like to hear it," Larry said.

"We will someday, I'm sure."

"Not now though."

"Now?" his father said, and glanced over as if Larry had asked something absurd.

"I'd like to soon," Larry said.

"Before I forget everything."

"Yes."

"We will," he said, but just to pacify him, and then he was lost in the intricacies of driving. Larry sat back and watched the last streetlights go by, then the empty fields, the dark woods, a solitary chore light on a barn. Never happen. That was all right too, he thought. In group not everyone talked. And he'd never had a prisoner before. It was different, probably harder.

His father didn't remember which driveway was his from yesterday. He slowed early, waiting for Larry to say something, and when he didn't, accelerated back to speed. It was intentional, Larry thought; they'd been living here ten years.

As they neared his place, Larry saw that Donna wasn't home and that Vicki hadn't come back. He waited for his father to brake, but he didn't, instead shot by the driveway at full speed.

"You missed it," Larry said. "We're back there."

"Why didn't you say something?" his father scolded him, suddenly angry. "You know my eyes aren't good in the dark."

"It's okay," Larry said. "You have to turn around anyway."

His father swung the New Yorker off the road and back across, gassing it, throwing Larry against the door. The big V-8 raced, pumped up to overdrive.

"Where is it?" he demanded.

"There."

He didn't pull in, just stopped with the car running.

"It's enough I had to leave work early, you bring me out here to play games and talk nonsense."

"Dad," Larry said.

"I don't appreciate being made fun of."

"I'm sorry, I thought you could see our mailbox."

"Well I couldn't and I can't and I don't think you should expect me to. I was nice enough to give you a ride."

"I appreciate that. Thank you."

"You're welcome, but don't expect this everyday if you're not going to treat me with respect."

"I do," Larry said.

"If that's what you call what you did just then, you've got a lot to learn. Now close the door, I've got to get back."

Larry thunked it shut and his father took off, his lights disappearing over a low rise, the thrum of the engine dwindling into the night.

"Jesus Christ," Larry said, and fingered his keys. It was chilly but clear now, a wind in the trees across the road—October weather. He wondered where Donna was in her neat tweed skirt. He debated how wise opening the lid of the mailbox in the dark was, then, defying Creeley, grabbed the latch and pulled. Vicki's *Bon Appetit* had arrived, and some junk mail they'd arranged for Scott, nothing important.

The door was locked, as it should have been. No trip wires, nothing out of line. Across the living room the answering machine blinked twice. Maybe they'd found him. He dropped the mail on the couch and punched the message button.

"Larry," Vicki said, "I wish you wouldn't call me. I think we should talk because I need to explain what's going on with me, but I can't do it over the phone, and you're just making things harder here. This isn't easy for me to ask you and I know it's not going to be easy for you to do, but I want you to promise me you won't try to call again, okay? Okay? Please, for me." The machine clicked off. He thought of driving over but Donna was gone. He was stuck.

The machine beeped. It was Vicki again.

"Larry? Larry, I want you to come to my mother's this Saturday. We have to talk about what I need to do, and I want you to see Scott—he misses you. Please don't be angry with me but I can't do it anymore. I'm sorry, baby, I just can't." She began to cry and talk at the same time so that Larry had to bend low to the speaker. He could not figure out what she was talking about through the sobbing. "Goddammit," she said. She was sniffling, regaining her strength. "So please come Saturday, okay? Around lunchtime, and we can spend the afternoon together like we used to do. I care about you, Larry, I do, but I need to do this now and I need you to help me. So will you please help me? And don't call anymore. Please."

He stood there waiting for more but it clicked and stayed off. He lifted a hand as if to erase it, but caught himself, stopped, and pulled out a chair. He sat beside the machine awhile before running it again, listening, this time angry, astonished by her nerve, and yet when he finally did erase it, he did not call her. He turned the lights on and relocked the front door and went into the kitchen, and when the game came on, he had a hot bowl of chicken noodle soup and a cold beer and had already come up with what he'd say to her first. He didn't need a lot of time to choose the absolutely right thing. Like Dumb Andy used to say, it started with an F and ended with a Fuck you.

HE HEARD Donna come in around nine-thirty. In the morning he didn't mention it and she didn't offer where she'd been. He watched her as she drove, the bruised color of her eyelids, the petal-thin skin. She'd brought a coffee for him, and day-old cinnamon rolls; bits of icing clung to her upper lip while she laughed at the Spiderman, and Larry thought that his crush on her had never gone away, that if Vicki didn't want him, maybe his feelings for her were justified. He knew it wasn't true, but watched the Monte Carlo away just the same, and when Donna waved in the rearview mirror, he was there.

Julian's insurance wasn't enough to replace the Subaru. He was thinking of going home to New Jersey and writing software for his brother's company. Larry apologized for shoving him.

"It's bullshit," he said, buttoning up. "My car gets ripped off and Marv laughs at me."

"Where'd they find it?" Larry asked.

"Buttermilk, up by the campsite. They said it was probably kids. They took everything and then set it on fire. It sucks. A lot of those tapes can't be replaced."

Larry thought that Creeley couldn't have worked that fast, then was afraid of underrating him. Last night Julian had given him a ride. He imagined Creeley behind a curtain on the third floor, watching him hop out, taking down the license plate.

"I mean, what's keeping me here?" Julian was saying. "I don't have any friends, my roommate's a complete weasel, my job sucks and my car's history. Give me one good reason why I should give a shit."

"Spiderman?" Larry said. He pulled on his workboots, the laces loosened so the one fit over his new foot. Wednesdays he did everyone in Collegetown and the mom-and-pop stores right in Ithaca; there wasn't much driving. He snapped the thong of a heavy keyring around his belt and grabbed his jacket.

Julian was ready to go up front.

"Hang in there," Larry said.

"We'll see."

"Let's go," Marv called. "Quit playing grabass. It's hump day, I want to see you humps do some work for a change."

All day Larry wondered if he should call Vicki, if despite what she'd said she really wanted him to. SKG began with Bach, one of the partitas his mother loved; at the first notes she would sigh and shut her eyes and not open them until Madame Landowska was done. It was sunny, and he had to flick his visor down, switch on the tiny caged fan above it. Collegetown was teeming with students, and at every stop he locked the truck while he was inside. Downtown he emptied his trays one by one, kneeling to square the boxes, checking the expiration dates. Wonder White, Wonder Wheat. If she could wait, so could he.

He got through to Clines on his second try.

"*Nada,*" Clines said. "Not a thing, which makes me think he may have done something to himself. Either that or he's already five hundred miles from here."

Larry told him about Julian's Subaru.

"I've got that right here," Clines said, as if Larry had questioned his competence. "A car stereo and some computer equipment. From the picture, whoever tried to light it did a half-assed job. A rag in the gas tank. Doesn't sound like our man."

"I guess not," Larry admitted.

"Nope. He's either holed up somewhere or long gone. Either way we're going to have to be patient."

In the afternoon they always played the Scandinavians, whose combination of gloom and heroic bombast didn't fit the day. He finished his deliveries early, doing the strip of Route 13 south of the outlet, and decided to see where they'd burned Julian's car.

The booth at the entrance of Buttermilk was closed for the season, and parking was free. The lot was almost full; people had come to see the leaves. Couples strolled by the pond at the bottom of the falls, sat bundled up at picnic tables. The water didn't actually drop but ran frothing and white over the streambed's steep rock face; a narrow stone stair ran up the hill beside it. His father had taken him and Susan here on Sunday afternoons to walk the trails while his mother had her nap, and likewise Larry held Scott's hand and named the trees when Vicki needed some time by herself.

He cruised through the lot and up the switchbacked, shoulderless road to the campgrounds. Summers he'd gone to Boy Scout camp here. The cabins hadn't changed, the stone lodge with its giant fireplace where they sang rounds of "Frere Jacques" and listened to hokey ghost stories. In the A Shau he sometimes wondered if it had all been training—the games of Capture the Flag and Release and Indians and Settlers. Once a day, after lunch, they had a mandatory rest period before going on with archery or canoeing or arts and crafts, and he wrote his mother postcards she'd already stamped for him. A few years ago his father showed him a packet of them, tied with a baby-blue ribbon and tucked into a compartment of his mother's secretary. *For lunch we had hot dogs and baked beans*, it said. *Yesterday it rained.*

Each cabin had its own parking spot, an angled tongue of asphalt edged, like the road, with low creosoted posts. He was near the end of the loop when he saw the black smudge, a few pieces of debris. He stopped Number 1 short of the spot and got out, looking around. It was quiet up here, only the birds and the leaves scratching across the asphalt, and he felt like a target.

Along with the blot of the scorch mark, he could see the tracks of the towtruck and those of the Subaru. There wasn't much else: a blackened cigarette butt, the cracked shell of a lighter, some rubber stripping stuck to the ground. He imagined that they'd checked the cabin but couldn't be sure.

The grass was unmowed, cushioning fallen leaves. The police had trampled a path to the door. He paused at the edge of the parking spot as if contemplating a high dive, then lifted his good foot and let it sink into the grass. His new foot followed, though he noticed he was crouched now, ready to hit the deck, that he was tracking the crushed grass, slipping his feet into the trodden spots the way he fit the soles of his jungle boots into Carl Metcalf's steps.

The door was open, the floor mercifully concrete, with black patches of gum. Two webbed bunks jutted from the wall, their mattresses in storage for the season. A steel mirror hung over a wash basin. Dust coated the spigot; he turned the taps and the plumbing shook, coughed out a rusty splash. He sniffed and discovered he could no longer trust himself that way—just mildew, the damp musk of moss and rotting logs. Dumb Andy had been good at that, even when they were a few weeks in the bush and nice and ripe. When they searched a village he went from mama-san to papa-san, holding their shirtsleeves to his nose and breathing deeply. In the tunnels they worked by old-fashioned tallow candles and kerosene lanterns. Dumb Andy would walk down the line, inspecting, then come back the other way, touching mama- and papa-san in the middle of the forehead as if blessing them. "You VC. You VC. You no VC."

Larry followed his own tracks back to the asphalt and looked around at the other cabins before getting into Number 1. The news was on and he turned it off. The sun followed him through the trees, down the curves. He'd been foolish to think Creeley might be here, and realized he was no better equipped for this than Clines. He had been out of the jungle nearly fifteen years while Creeley, it seemed, had never left. It had come to him this morning while running, gazing off into the endless stretch of hills, rich with water and game and cover: A man like that would have to want to be caught.

When Larry got back to the outlet, Julian was gone; there was a scrap of a Hostess bag with a phone number stuck in Larry's locker door.

"He took off," Derek explained.

"What happened?"

"Marv was on him so he told him to go fuck himself. Marv told him to punch out. It was pretty funny. He didn't say anything, just took off his apron—real calm—and walked over and punched out. Cleaned out his locker and everything."

"I guess that's it for him."

"He didn't really want to work here."

"No," Larry agreed.

"He's too smart for this shit, not like us."

"Yeah, you're right," Larry said, but later, walking home, he didn't see why it was inevitable, or why Vicki didn't want him to call, or what Creeley meant by REMEMBER ME.

Donna was home, and he was tempted to go over rather than face the empty house again. His foot hurt; he shouldn't have walked so far. Fucking bus drivers. Tomorrow he'd see if she could give him a ride both ways; he'd offer to pay for gas. On the porch he tried not to think of the answering machine blinking.

It wasn't. Fine, he'd figured that. He clicked it off so if someone called it would come through.

He took his shoes and socks off and massaged the transition where his new foot started. That's what they officially called it at the VA—the transition. In Japan, when they'd taken the ruined part off, everyone said it was a good stump. Wednesdays his doctor came by with a flock of Japanese interns and lifted his bandages. "That's what we call a good stump," he'd say, and after the translator had finished, Larry would nod in agreement. It was not bullshit; the man had saved more than Larry thought possible. Now it stung from walking so far. He spread some Jergens lotion on his palm and rubbed it in deep, then put his foot back on.

He fixed himself a can of chili and buttered some bread. He needed to buy beer soon. He needed a gift for his father. The series wasn't on—it was a travel day—and the rest of TV was stupid.

He was sitting with the light on, eating, when he heard the unmistakable thumping of a Huey coming up the valley. The Army flew them out of the depot over on Seneca Lake, though not as often as the men on the ward claimed. He'd seen them all stop at once, freeze, looking to the ceiling as if it might fall; they waited as the blades boomed overhead and then faded to nothing before restarting the card game, picking up the fuck books. It was like a moment of silence, a kind of respect or gratitude. There had been moments they'd prayed for that noise, when they'd bargained with God for a cowboy crazy or brave enough to risk the dust-off no matter how bad the sitrep was. Without the Huey they knew they'd be dead, so even now they paid attention to it, welcomed it like a friend.

Larry limped outside and stood on the cold front walk, listening to the rotors pound the air, the nervous swish of the turbine growing. A trio of red and green blinking lights screamed overhead; he turned to watch them go. In a minute the lights disappeared, and the rush of the turbine, but the steady thumping remained, the long blades stroking almost leisurely, effortless, until that too grew faint and gave way to the rustle of leaves. He turned to go back inside and saw Donna on her porch, also looking up.

She leaned against a post, sipping from a coffee cup, the saucer held level with her chin. She had a skirt on, but no jacket, and he could see the closed toes of her stockings, her tiny feet. Larry nodded acknowledgment and retreated to the porch, where the shadow of the rail hid his feet. A sickle moon was out, the evening star a beauty mark beside it.

"Pretty night," she said, rubbing an arm against the cold.

"Yeah."

"How are you doing?"

"Okay."

She sat sidesaddle, balancing her saucer on the rail. "Did she call? She said she would."

"Not today."

"Yesterday?"

"She left a message."

"I asked her not to do that."

"Do you know what's going on?" Larry asked.

"Not everything."

"What *do* you know?"

"You should be talking with her, not me. I told her not to do this. Talk to her, then let's talk. I don't want to get caught in the middle of this."

"Looks like you already are," Larry said.

"I refuse to. I've got enough problems of my own, and I'm not objective."

"How do you mean?"

"I think she's wrong for doing this to you."

"Doing what?"

"See?" she said. "This is exactly what I didn't want to happen. I should have just kept my trap shut. Don't ask me anything, just call and talk to her. Maybe you can change her mind, I can't."

"Change her mind about what?" he asked, but she'd stood up and was collecting her cup and saucer. "Donna."

"Talk to her," she said. "I can't do this." She turned to go inside, then stopped, as if she knew he was still waiting for an answer. "I'm sorry, Larry."

"You're right," he said. "I'll call her."

Inside all he did was rinse the rest of the chili down the sink and finish his beer. He remembered Wade telling him he'd made up his mind weeks before they finally separated, and every time Larry saw Donna in the backyard or in the kitchen talking to Vicki, he felt sick with guilt, as if he were the one leaving. He didn't want her to feel pity for him now, partly because he was fighting it himself. After talking to her he didn't know how much hope he should have. He went upstairs early, trying not to think.

At 0300 he came off watch. Nate relieved him; he turned over the clackers and the Starlight scope and woke to the blinding light of the room, exhausted, as if he hadn't slept. He'd migrated to the center of the bed and had to shift his butt to swing his legs out. By the glow of Scott's answering machine he checked his window, across the hall tested the frosted glass of the bathroom, and then the downstairs, room by room. He turned the spotlight on the backyard, surprising Scott's sandbox, Vicki's wilted garden. The doors were chained, the windows closed, only the murmur of the furnace, the refrigerator, the wall clock. It was dumb, Larry thought; if Creeley really wanted him, he'd already be dead.

On his way back to bed, he passed the landing window and saw Donna's upstairs lights were on. Her shades were drawn and he couldn't see anything, and again he thought how funny it was, the two of them alone out here.

He hung up the phone twice before he dialed the whole number.

"Frank," she answered tearfully. "Thank God you called me back."

"Donna?" he said, and when she didn't say anything, explained, "It's Larry."

"Larry," she said, as if she'd never heard of him. "What are you doing on my phone?"

"I saw your lights on. I just wanted to make sure you're okay."

"I'm okay," she said. "I'm just awake."

"Me too."

Now he couldn't remember what he'd wanted to say to her, what purpose the call served. A car went by outside, its lights plowing a stretch of road, fence, meadow.

"I'm sorry," she said, "I was expecting someone else."

"It's okay, I shouldn't have called."

"No," she said, and then didn't explain.

"I guess I'll see you tomorrow."

"Yeah," she said, and they traded good nights.

Running, he wondered why he'd done it and what she thought of him. Why was she up, and who was Frank to her? His foot hurt but his legs were fresh. Trees floated overhead. A crow cawed atop a fencepost, and he spit in its direction—a lesson from Mrs. Railsbeck. He checked his split time, noted a rack of antlers fastened to the back of a garage. The lack of traffic pleased him. He could wait on calling Vicki. He'd see Donna in less than an hour. Bringing it in, he made his decisions for the day and pledged to stick with them, but once he'd slowed and started walking and the sweat went cold on him, Larry wondered which one he'd have to forgive himself for breaking.

On the way in, she didn't mention Frank or ask if he'd talked with Vicki. Her make-up couldn't hide the circles under her eyes, and he thought he shouldn't say anything, that he should be patient and wait for her to offer something. They cruised down the hill and through town. When she let him off, he thought he'd been foolish to think she considered him anything more than a friend, and after she'd driven away—though she did wave—he was so disappointed, dragging himself across the lot, that he had to admit the crush was back. Opening his locker, he confronted Vicki and Scott. You, Larry thought, are a stupid, stupid man.

He made it past lunch before calling her work. Katie or Cheryl picked up.

"I'm sorry, Larry," she said. "She doesn't work here anymore."

He called her mother's. It rang twice and then gave way to staticky silence; three mismatched tones introduced a halting recording. "The number you have reached . . . has been changed. The new number . . . is not listed."

"The bitch," he said, and whacked the receiver against the phone so hard it bounced out, clattered against the plexiglas and swung by its steel cord. It peeped insistently as he walked away.

He had machines to do at Cornell; on the way he tried to decipher what

Vicki was up to. It was too early to check the Special Children's Center, though he suspected Scott was not there. He should have gone over to her mother's yesterday. He needed a car. He thought of driving over now but knew he was too angry.

The two upper rows of the machine in the basement of Goldwin Smith Hall had to be refilled every few days. It was a high traffic area; the students ate the Donette Gems for breakfast and the cupcakes for lunch. Usually a few moon pies and Sno Balls went unsold, but not today; both rows had been picked clean. He laid his tray on the marble floor and searched his big ring for the key. He turned it and the front of the machine swung out, unseating a few stray coins. He stepped on a dime trying to escape, and as he picked it up, an elderly professor stopped beside him.

He had a full beard and a beret and a briefcase that appeared to have been thrown from a truck—also a folded dollar bill he reached toward Larry.

"Twinkies?" He enunciated the word, made fun of it.

Larry gave him one from the tray, shoved the bill in his pocket and made change.

"Thank you," the professor said, and bowed as if Larry had handed him an award.

He gently dropped the packages into the screw mechanism, careful not to smudge the frosting. Classes were changing, and several times he had to stop to sell a Suzy Q or a Ding Dong. He was surprised by the number of Asian faces among the students; he tried not to stare, to figure out which were Korean and which Chinese.

He kept getting interrupted. He only had sixteen slots to do but there was always someone lurking behind him with a dollar. They didn't understand that he was working. No one seemed to have exact change, and he was running out himself. He sold a pack of Hohos to a short boy and dug through his pockets. There was something in one stiffer than a bill, made of paper. He couldn't remember anything and fished it out.

It was hidden in a messy wad of ones, all but a single red corner. When he slipped it out he was surprised—not by the card itself but the fact that even before he flipped Rinehart's Bicycle over, he knew it would be the three of spades.

REMEMBER ME? it said, and where the death's-head had been, Creeley had made it plain, had scrawled instead: *SKULL.*

FOUR

They told him things he needed to know.

Always wear your pisspot. Never wear your pot on patrol 'cause you can't hear a goddamn thing with it on. Wear it backwards so the lip doesn't get in the way. Stay off roads; stay off trails; stay off paddy dikes. Don't bunch up on me or I will cut your fucking heart out. Cut the sleeves off that jacket or you'll sweat to death. Wear just the T-shirt. Wear just the jacket. Slit your pants so you get some air in there. Don't bother with underwear 'cause it just rots off. Don't eat the ham and mothers. Don't trade your spaghetti and meatballs for anything. Watch out for the kids. Watch out for mama-san. Watch out for papa-san. Don't go fucking with baby-san. Watch out for Salazar—he's a two-digit midget and earthquake shaky. Never bet with Smart Andy. Don't listen to any of Nate's shit. Don't call Go-Go Norman, it's his real name. Don't ask about Rosie. If it's bad, take me out. If it's my legs, take me out. If it's my head. If it's my thing.

"The first thing," Lieutenant Wise told him, poking the Red Cross armband on his fatigues, "is to get rid of this shit."

"Nothing the fuckers like better than popping a doc," Bogut explained. He was the RTO, and even inside the wire it seemed like he was beside the lieutenant all the time, tuned into his frequency. "They'll nail the point —not the Martian, he's too slick for that shit—but they'll take someone down and wait for you to show up. Then the rest of us are basically fucked."

"You want to get rid of the peashooter too. Stick it in your pack, it just makes you a target. Barclay'll get you a weapon."

"Magoo," Bogut translated.

Larry didn't say he did not want a rifle.

The lieutenant approved of the contents of his aid bag and the extra canteens. "What else?" he asked Bogut.

"The men."

"Markham, these are your men as much as mine. I hope you know what that means."

"Yes, sir," Larry answered truthfully. He was happy to be asked the question. So far in Vietnam it was the only thing he knew.

They told him stories with simple points. Pony was lucky. The lieutenant knew his shit. Fred the Head was too sentimental; Magoo was a sick fuck. Some were meant to scare him, Larry supposed, like the VC in the connex box, and some merely to enlighten.

One story was so fresh he heard it three times: how Salazar went ten days without saying a word after Rosie got shot. They had to take him off point and give it to the Martian; he just wasn't the same anymore.

It was a sniper in a tree with a carbine. He waited until Salazar and half the column walked right underneath him, then let loose at Bogut's antenna. Rosie took a round through the forehead.

"Real ugly," Leonard Dawson said, wincing. "The man's shit was all over Metcalf." He was the first to tell it to Larry, Go-Go Bates beside him, shuffling the cards and nodding at each turn of the story.

In Smart Andy's version Carl Metcalf had to spit, then after they'd emptied their magazines into the gook, rinsed his mouth out with half a canteen of grape Kool-Aid.

"It was bad" was all Carl Metcalf would say.

"But Jesus," Leonard Dawson said, "Sally went fucking nuts. The gook's tied himself to the tree and when we light him up he falls out and hangs there. Guy's dead, right? Guy is juicy. Sally walks over, changes magazines, clicks it on rock 'n' roll and just dices the guy. I shit you not—like a piñata and shit, guts flying all over the place. When he's done, what's left of the gook plops down in the middle of the trail and he starts hitting it with the butt of his sixteen. The stock breaks off so he throws it away and starts jumping on the gook with his boots. There's nothing left of the guy, I mean he's mush, and we're just standing there watching. By the time Bogut calls Rosie in, Sally's done. He goes back up the trail and sits down by himself and when we get Rosie in a poncho and head back with him, Sally doesn't get up, he just watches the Martian go past and gets in behind him. Next time we go out he's way back in the column and Nate takes slack, and when we come in, Dumb Andy says Sally was right behind him and it's funny 'cause that was Rosie's spot."

"Listen to him now," Smart Andy said. "Hear him whistle? Him and Rosie used to do that—'I Could Have Danced All Night.' "

"I think he's still messed up about it," Carl Metcalf said. "Guys on point get that way, think it's all their fault. They're supposed to be loners anyway. Look at the Martian, he never says anything."

"Sally's okay," Leonard Dawson said. "He's just too short for this shit."

"Thirty-eight and a wake-up," Go-Go Bates marveled.

"Whoosh, right the fuck out of here."

Larry listened as if in class. He popped his eyes and smiled at the wildest parts, tried to imagine the weirdness and the fear. He could see the round clipping Pony's elbow and Magoo obscenely posing the dead for his camera, but none of the stories had the punch of the VC's puffed and blackened face. The stories were real and for the most part probably true; they just hadn't happened to him.

"Just wait," Nate said. "You haven't *seen* shit so you don't *know* shit, so you just wait, and when the shit is over, then *maybe* you can talk. Fuck, my man Skull here is so green I spread his shit on my lawn."

"Play eight-ball on the boy's stomach."

"Sea-green."

"Pea-green!"

When they laughed, all Larry could do was smile. He wasn't used to being new. In Ithaca, everyone knew him—if not firsthand then through Susan or his father. They might not have liked him, all of them, but they knew who he was. Here he had to earn everything. Wasn't that what he wanted?

They gave him the shit details. He filled sievelike sandbags with the rust-red dirt and stacked them against the sides of the hootch. He helped string tanglefoot and concertina wire along the perimeter and tore up his palms.

He burned sloshing barrels of shit with a cologne-soaked bandana over his mouth and nose.

"Dues," Carl Metcalf said.

He couldn't sleep. They laughed and said it was normal and that it would go away in a few days, but it didn't. They told him how last Christmas Eve Salazar poisoned his grandmother's fruitcake with bug juice and left it in the middle of the floor and in the morning found three dead rats with red velvet bows around their necks. Swear to God, they said. They told him about five-inch-long cockroaches that snapped when you stepped on them and about the leech that tunneled up the Martian's dick. No lie. "Hey, Marsh," Pony called, "show him your worm."

Deep in the night he heard the crunk of explosions and the pop of automatic rifle fire nearby. Across from him, Dumb Andy woke up, looked around as if someone had called his name and lay down again. Larry waited for the enemy to burst through the door, but nothing happened. The firing slowed and then stopped. Someone farted, just a puff. His watch ticked. He didn't see how he could keep doing this.

In the morning the wire was hung with local VC. They were tiny and limp, their skin gone chalky, drained of color. The lieutenant said the platoon was responsible for body detail. He needed two men. Magoo said he'd do it and everyone laughed; he had his camera around his neck and a pair of yellow rubber gloves like Mrs. R. wore to do the dishes. Larry thought he should volunteer and began to raise a hand. Fred the Head stopped his arm and stepped forward.

"It's bad luck," Carl Metcalf explained. "We don't want you touching anything dead. It rubs off on you. And never volunteer for anything. I shouldn't have to tell you that."

Never look into the eyes of a dead man. Never leave your dead behind. Never fill your magazines all the way up because of the spring. Always bend the pins on your frags. Always call before coming in. Always be ready to hit it. Look out for tripwires. Look out for shit in trees. Look out for bamboo vipers—two steps and you're dead. They told him these things again and again. Alone, he tried to remember them, to keep them in his mind so when they hit the shit he'd know what to do. It seemed that he didn't know anything.

"That's right," Pony said. "Now you're gettin' it."

The first week they were on bunker guard and didn't go out. It was quiet except for the artillery. Every day they put out fire, the brass casings piling up behind the guns. The 105s weren't bad, but every time a 155 caught Larry off guard, walking across the compound, his entire body flinched against the concussion and his jaws snapped shut so hard that his teeth ached. When he asked the other guys how they stood it, they just shrugged, fixed him with a look of annoyance. What noise? Who cared? The war was hot and boring. They lay around the hootch, catching up on sleep and letters home; one day he wrote to Vicki three times. Nate and Pony and Magoo went down to the village at the base of the hill and came back half drunk and bragging about a trick this whore could do with her armpit. Carl Metcalf drew pictures of the hills on crinkly ricepaper. Fred the Head leaned over his transistor radio, drumming along with the hits Chris Noel and Hanoi Hannah dished up. Salazar had a short-timer's calendar, a big brunette sectioned into a hundred puzzle pieces; he was crossing her chest now, filling it in—38, 37, 36— headed for the heavenly 1. Secretly Larry was already keeping count.

Instead of dragging bodies off the wire, he was assigned to garbage detail. Below the LZ was a dump where they trucked it in a reeking deuce and a half. Larry showed up at the back of the mess tent wearing a pair of heavy gloves; the driver had a helmet on and a sixteen slung across his back.

"You never done this before," the driver guessed.

In the truck, the driver stuck his rifle between the seats. Larry glanced to see if the safety was on. The bulldozer had cut a road the width of the truck. They bumped over the muddy ruts in first, branches reaching in the windows.

"How long you been in-country?" the driver asked, and when Larry answered, whistled. "This is gonna be fun for you."

Like the LZ, the dump was surrounded by concertina wire. The crowd waiting at the gate didn't give way. They were mostly kids and women, a few old men stoically smoking. They swarmed the truck, banging at the doors and fenders, climbing onto the bed while they were still going to get at the hot slop from breakfast. They cackled and jabbered, called up to Larry, "GI number one." The driver inched the truck forward, cursing them. The children had learned to give him back the finger; they smiled as if it were a greeting. The driver stopped at the gate and several boys clambered onto the hood and slapped at the windshield.

"You know what we call these people?" the driver asked, hefting his weapon.

"What?"

"Friendlies," he said.

They showed him things. Pony showed him the groove below his elbow, how smooth the new skin was. Magoo showed him pictures of a dead woman with no clothes bent over a table. Fred the Head showed him the NVA rucksack he humped and explained why it was a better design. Carl Metcalf showed him his sketches of the village kids. All Larry could remember was the woman, how white the flash made her ass, the black braid a snake on her back. It was something, Larry thought, that he needed to see.

His fifth day he pulled bunker guard. Everyone did, Carl Metcalf said; there wasn't any luck attached to it. There were supposed to be two men to every bunker, but they were a little shorthanded. It was a joke—a little shorthanded. They were operating well below half strength.

"What if I fall asleep?" Larry asked.

"You don't," Carl Metcalf explained.

"Nothing to it," Magoo said, going over the breech of Larry's rifle with a toothbrush. "You sit there. You see something move, you shoot it."

"If there's more than one of them," Dumb Andy instructed, "you blow your claymores. You'll be all right. Remember, we'll be covering your butt the whole time. Just don't snore or the old man'll tear you a new asshole."

Before chow, Carl Metcalf walked with him down to the bunker he'd been assigned. Its sandbagged roof stuck out of the ground a foot. In front was a trench—a grenade sump, Carl Metcalf called it. He took Larry out into the dirt berm among the tanglefoot and showed him the tripwires—ankle high with noisemakers fashioned from C-rat cans and spent cartridges. He brushed one with his leg so Larry could hear it.

The bunker itself was three feet deep with an ammo crate for a bench. It was hotter inside; the floor was covered with a puddle the color of tomato soup that lapped at their boots. Carl Metcalf had him sit down on the bench and look out the slit. Shreds of fabric from the other night still clung to the wire. A bird called from the jungle. The clouds were beginning to pile up in the valley.

"You know how to fire that thing," Carl Metcalf asked.

"First you chamber a round," Larry began, repeating what they'd told him. It wasn't that different from any other rifle.

"No, here you already have a round chambered. All right, how about changing magazines?"

"Magoo showed me."

"Show me how you do it," Carl Metcalf ordered, and when Larry was done, shook his head. "You've got to be faster than that." He dipped into an ammo pouch and showed him his own magazines, taped end-to-end so he could flip them. He handed one to Larry. "Give me twenty," he said, and sat there with his arms folded while Larry clapped it in and popped it out until his palm stung.

"Okay," he said, "where do you shoot a man?"

"In the body," Larry said, remembering his father at the beginning of deer season stressing the clean kill.

"Where do you aim?"

"The heart."

"Not here," Carl Metcalf said. "No one's going to be standing around out there, they're going to be crawling. You fire ankle high, just above the tripwires. Now show me how you hold it."

Larry nestled the butt into his shoulder and laid the long, contoured handgrip of the barrel on his palm. The rifle felt light, not at all like his father's Winchester. He put his eye to the sight and brought the front post up to one of the fluttering pieces of cloth. He kept steady on it a long time, feeling himself breathe the way he did when he had a squirrel or a dove lined up and didn't know whether he wanted to shoot or just watch it, be with it a second before it spooked and darted away. The plastic pistol grip was getting sweaty beneath his hand, and he was aware of Carl Metcalf beside him. He lowered the weapon, ejected the magazine and handed it back to him.

"You ever hunt?" Carl Metcalf asked.

"No," Larry said, though he could not say why.

"Just a natural, is that it?"

"I used to when I was a kid," he admitted.

"It's true," Carl Metcalf said. "You never forget."

At chow they told him stories about guys falling asleep on guard, how when they called on the radio, some VC picked up. It was an old one, the crazy calling the babysitter from the upstairs phone. None of the stories scared Larry. He knew the slashed throats and empty foxholes from World War II, from the drugstore paperbacks with cracked spines and glue the color of pine sap he hid in the attic closet. Nights at home he sometimes put himself to sleep imagining the tortures his father endured and measured himself against them. This was nothing, a bunch of shaggy dog stories about peeled fingernails, genitals cut off and shoved into the victim's mouth, yet he could not stop thinking about the strips of cloth on the wire and how dark it was at night. Then they started talking about the old Special Forces camp at Lang Vei being overrun.

"They say it was just like Korea," Smart Andy said. "Human waves. Gunners burning the barrels out of quad-50s. Then it went hand-to-hand. They kept drawing the perimeter in and calling on the horn, hoping someone would come and extract them." He stopped to sip his coffee, then didn't go on.

"So?" Go-Go Bates asked.

"Nobody did."

"Come on," Salazar said. "You're scaring the kid."

"Skull can hack it," Nate said.

"Nothing the little people like better than you big dudes," Bogut joked. He'd shown Larry how to use the radio, wrote the command post frequency on his sleeve.

"You'll be all right," the lieutenant said, but it was his job to be positive.

Don't forget your bug juice, they told him. Don't look at anything straight on or it'll move on you. Don't wait till you see something; by then it's too late. Don't worry.

At dusk Smart Andy and Magoo came down with him to the wire and showed him how to rig his claymores. They were slightly curved, with FRONT TOWARD ENEMY on one side and BACK on the other. Smart Andy led them out into the no-man's land, careful of the tripflares. During dinner it had begun to rain in earnest and they all had their ponchos on—and their helmets, Larry noticed. Their feet sank in, made a sound coming out. Smart Andy showed him how to fit the blasting cap in, unfolded the legs and propped the mine in the mud so it would explode up into the midsection of someone running past. The rain tapped their pots harder and he had to shout. He showed Larry how to attach the leads and the three of them slogged back to the bunker, high-stepping over the tripwires.

Water was dribbling in through the slit, running down the front wall into the puddle. The three of them could barely fit inside, and it was still hot. While Smart Andy hooked up his clackers, Magoo told Larry about some of the claymore's problems. Sometimes, he said, the enemy crept in and turned it toward you, then hit the tripwire deliberately. Sometimes they picked it up and planted a grenade underneath, so it would blow when you retrieved it. Sometimes they stole it and left just the wires. Sometimes it simply didn't work.

"But when it does, man," he said, "you just sit back and watch the show."

Smart Andy made sure the clackers were on safety and clicked one in each fist. "All set," he said. "See you in about eight hours."

It was almost dark, the hills solid, cut from one piece. He checked the radio and got Bogut.

"Affirm," the speaker said, and told Larry to say "over."

It was too hot for the poncho, so he folded and then sat on it, rubbed bug juice into his arms. He was doing his neck when he thought he saw movement outside the wire—a reflection quick and tricky as a shooting star. An insect, he guessed. The wetness of a mouth or maybe a raindrop. A gold tooth. He pushed off the bench and knelt in the puddle, clicked the safeties off his claymores and stared into the rain. He reached his wrist up to the slit to see the time; he'd officially been on watch three minutes.

Listen, they'd told him, but all he could hear was the patter of leaves, the trickle running down the front wall of the bunker. He thought of Lang Vei and their calls on the radio, how they must have sounded just before they stopped. He felt his chest for his ammo pouches filled with the extra magazines he'd taped end-to-end and tried to see the treeline. The helmet made him wipe the sweat from his eyes every few minutes but Larry kept it on.

By midnight he'd stopped looking at his watch. He'd thought of some things he wanted to say to his father, things he couldn't tell Vicki. Looking out at the night, he pictured Ithaca under the same rain, the neon of the bars caught in the wet asphalt. He imagined stopping for a last Schaefer at the Chanticleer or the Royal Palm before going home and crawling into his warm bed. He wouldn't talk about the war, just sip his beer and shoot a game of pool and wave good night to the place. Yeah, everyone would say, he was there; bet he could tell you a thing or two.

Around three the birds stopped calling, as if they'd all fallen asleep, and later the noise of the rain lifted, because he could hear a choked, foreign voice out in the jungle, croaking "Fuck you, fuck you." They'd told him about this; it was a gecko—a fuck-you lizard. It wasn't as funny as they'd said.

"One-six," the radio whispered. "This is Echo Baker four, over."

He knelt again, the puddle cold now.

"Copy," the lieutenant said, "over."

"I've got movement. Request permission, over."

"Affirm," the lieutenant said. "Over."

He saw the shots before he heard them—a splash of red tracers cutting into the trees to his left. The lines stayed on his eyes like the ghost of a flashbulb. In the bunker beside his, Magoo opened up, pouring fire into the same place. Larry didn't see anything but shouldered his weapon anyway. Suddenly he had to pee; his dick shriveled, went cold as if he were swimming. Shoot first, they always said. He sighted on the spot where the two streams crossed and, as his father taught him, squeezed the trigger.

Nothing happened. The safety was on. In the dark he had to feel for it. His arms were heavy, his hands shaking, fingers numb. He didn't remember which way it clicked. A parachute flare blossomed above, silvering the treeline, making the wire and the night shimmer. Tracers ricocheted above the jungle. He leveled his rifle again and in one furious burst emptied the magazine. He clicked the selector back to semi and ejected the magazine into the puddle.

"Check fire," the radio said. "Check fire."

"What the fuck," the lieutenant asked, "over."

"We have a negative situation, over."

The flare dropped into the jungle; the night went quiet. Larry knelt there panting, listening to them explain why they'd been firing at nothing, and found that his trousers were wet from the crotch down. He pushed himself up onto the bench, the sopping, hot cloth sticking to his skin. Maybe he'd tell his father someday, and maybe not. In the puddle glinted a scattering of brass cartridges. He picked one up, reached under his poncho and tucked it in his fatigue jacket.

"Echo Baker eight, give us a sitrep," the radio asked, "over."

It took Larry a second to remember his bunker's number. He held down the button of the handset as Bogut had shown him. "Negative, over."

The geckos resumed their fuck-yous. There was a moon out now, and he tried not to look at his watch. He wondered if he would be too tired to sleep in the morning. An hour later, when the radio asked him again, his lap was still damp but the smell wasn't as bad.

"Skull," someone on the frequency said, "how you doin', over."

"I'm okay," Larry said, "over," and thought that despite wetting himself it was true, and that without their help he couldn't have done it.

"You know you still a cheesedick dumbfuck know-nothing cherry. Over."

"Affirm," Larry said.

When they could see the outline of the mountains again, the lieutenant came over the radio and gave the order to stand down. Smart Andy, Magoo and Nate were waiting for Larry when he crawled out of the bunker.

"Dag," Magoo said. "Someone forgot to change the baby."

"No big thing," Nate consoled him. "Little more of that on-the-job and you'll be good to go."

"Hell, he's ready now," Smart Andy said. "Hear him crank that thing? Fucking *I* was covering up."

After breakfast the lieutenant said that third platoon had run a check outside the wire and found a greasegun and a blood trail.

"Skull!" Nate said.

"Get some," Magoo said, and they traded an elaborate dap.

He couldn't sleep. He couldn't eat. He lay on his cot with his eyes closed, thinking of the heat of the bullet going in, the wetted leaves. He thought of the man stumbling, covering the hole with both hands, lying down on the soft, mossy floor of the jungle. It was not his work, he was sure. Just the same. It was strange; when he was aiming, he hadn't imagined hitting anyone.

In his aid bag he had some depressants—Seconal—and after dinner he washed one down with a beer. He slept through the night and in the morning couldn't remember dreaming.

For breakfast they had powdered eggs with powdered potatoes and powdered milk, and later the resupply chopper brought more. In among the ammo crates and shrinkwrapped pallets of C-rations and Sunday packages was a red mail sack. Pony, they called it, short for the Pony Express, and when the lieutenant gave the stack to Bogut to call off, Larry understood where their Pony's nickname came from. Each of his three aunts in Chicago sent a letter a day in rich envelopes still smelling of lilac water; he also had two younger brothers and a girlfriend, and every week his high school football coach saved him the sports pages from the Sunday *Trib*. He stood beside Bogut, the pile growing in his arms. Watch him, they said, he'll only open one, and it was true, he saved the rest for the coming days, left the unopened stack at the head of his bunk.

Leonard Dawson received a letter—from his sister, Nate said, and clutched his heart with both hands, pretended it was thumping with love. Dumb Andy got a cassette tape from his mother, which he listened to in the privacy of the latrine. Magoo got *Hot Rod* magazine; Salazar got *Playboy*. Carl Metcalf and Fred the Head got packages—smashed cookies, which they passed around. Half of them got packets of Kool-Aid, which they stashed in plastic baggies. Larry expected something from Vicki, if not from his father, but there was nothing.

"You won't get anything for a while," Bogut said. "It takes about a month."

Along with the mail there were free copies of *Stars and Stripes* and the *Army Times*, which he'd heard them make fun of. In the back was a list of that week's dead. It was a joke: "See you in the *Army Times*," they'd say. No one else took a copy, so Larry went back to his bunk and dug through his Sunday package, deciding what he'd save and what he'd trade.

They went through the boxes of C-rations in order of seniority, Salazar first, even before the lieutenant. Larry was left with nothing but ham and lima beans and ham and eggs, both of which he'd been warned not to eat. Carl Metcalf traded him a can of boned turkey and one of pears, gave him a bottle of Sneaky Pete hot sauce. Shake a little bit on, he said, you won't taste a thing.

They haggled with each other over tropical chocolate bars, miniature packs of Lucky Strikes, peanut butter, pineapple chunks.

"Got some vagina sausages," Nate called like an auctioneer. "Who can do me that pecan nut roll?"

In the middle of the bargaining, the lieutenant came out from behind his curtain and said the platoon had day patrol tomorrow. Larry thought it was bad news but everyone seemed pleased.

"Where we going?" the Martian asked from his corner. He didn't roll over.

"Just around the block."

"A walk in the park," Fred the Head said.

Skip's all right, they said. He was a mustang; he'd come up a grunt. Most of the other platoon leaders lived apart from their men. There was a saying the lieutenant used, a rhyme he'd bring out to remind Carl Metcalf of his duties as squad leader: Only the assholes live near the flagpole.

After dinner they cleaned their weapons, handing the rods and brushes and LSA oil from bunk to bunk. Pony and Smart Andy went over the sixty like doctors attending a patient. Rain played against the canvas roof, darkened the walls. Carl Metcalf showed Larry how to load ammo into his magazines. Never trust anyone to do it for you, he said. Do it every time before you go out. The rifle lay across Larry's knees. He listened intently and fitted the rounds in as he'd been shown, clapped the magazine in place and smiled when Carl said he was getting pretty good at this, but he kept checking the safety, kept looking to see if the barrel was pointed towards anyone. He didn't think he would fire it again.

"How about some frags?" Carl Metcalf asked.

"Not yet," Larry said.

At taps he popped a Seconal and in the morning didn't want to get up.

They walked out through the wire, down the red face of the hill and into the jungle. It was twilight under the canopy, and murky, the green ceiling keeping the mist in. The heavy air muffled their footsteps. Dew soaked their boots; creeper vines caught at their ankles. They pushed through clacking stands of bamboo, shouldered waxy leaves aside. The column wound far ahead, the Martian invisible, drawing them on. They tacked back and forth across the slope until he could not tell which way the LZ was. The new boots chafed his feet and his rifle was getting heavy. Carl Metcalf was in front of him, Go-Go Bates right behind. Larry followed Carl's back and remembered what they'd told him. Keep your intervals. Don't talk. Don't whistle. It seemed foolish. There were fourteen of them tromping through the bush, their gear rattling. He peered into the lush cover on both sides, glanced up at the trees, the strangling vines. He was ready to move with the shot, to get to his man, pack the bleeder, press the dressing over the wound. Don't think, they said. His father had said it too. Don't think, just react. He wouldn't have a choice, he thought.

There was a logic to the column. The Martian took point because he was the best and knew it. Nate walked his slack because he was almost as quick and didn't give a shit. Then came Pony with the big gun for when they made serious contact, and Smart Andy, his assistant. Once they set up and started working on the problem, the lieutenant and Bogut were there to think it through and call for support. Dumb Andy, Salazar and Carl Metcalf were the second wave; if the point element took a hit, they'd give Larry enough cover to get to them. You weren't supposed to bunch up your firepower, so Go-Go Bates, who carried a grenade launcher, stayed toward the rear, which was fine, since he liked to keep an eye on Leonard Dawson. Magoo couldn't see well enough to be up front, and Fred the Head—because he was weird, they said, as weird as the Martian on the other end—liked drag. Sometimes he would slow and let them get ahead, pretend he was the only one in the jungle.

Larry thought they would stop when they reached level ground but they kept going. All the blood in his body had migrated to his right calf and formed a hard ball. The small of his back ached from the weight of his aid bag. Mosquitoes circled his ear. Just the T-shirt, they said, or just the jacket, and now he wished he'd listened; the sweat made him blink, stuck in his lashes. He reached for a canteen and a creeper nearly tore his rifle out of his hand. He gripped it hard and marched, keeping in step with Carl Metcalf. It was a form of hypnotism, a dizziness. He no longer cared if the enemy was watching him, or what his father thought, or anything else.

Finally they stopped for water. Five minutes. He sat down on a mossy rock beside Carl Metcalf and undid his canteen.

"Markham," the lieutenant called. "Two sips."

"Sir?"

"What am I, a mute? Two sips. Get used to it."

"Yes, sir," Larry said.

The lieutenant stood there to watch him. He had an acetate map folded into the long pocket of his trouser leg, and his chest was heaving and slick with sweat. When Larry was done, he nodded and walked away.

"It's a good thing to learn," Carl Metcalf said.

"That's what I'm here for," Larry said.

They moved out, Bogut's bulky radio flipped upside down to hide the antenna. Stay away from it, they said, it's a great target. Look who's right behind it—think they call him Dumb for nothing? Larry watched how Carl Metcalf swiveled his head—slowly, as if he were listening—how he put his feet down. It was hard to concentrate but he knew he had to. He tried to read the jungle, freeze it the way his father had taught him the chilly woods, look for motion only. His hands were wet and he wiped them one at a time on his trousers, got a better grip on his rifle. He had the selector switched to semi-automatic. You can't hit shit on full, they said. You want to be locked and loaded at all times. You want to see him before he sees you.

They crossed a ravine with pricker bushes and slick clay banks. Behind him, Leonard Dawson swore, and when they stopped again for water, his arms and the stock of his rifle were smeared with red mud. The lieutenant didn't say anything to him when he came by, which Larry thought was unfair, and though the old man had passed out of sight, he only drank two sips.

They came out of the jungle suddenly, the light blinding, and crossed a meadow of chest-high elephant grass that ripped at his hands, pricked him through the wet shirt. As he looked up to see if he could find the LZ above them on the hillside, he stumbled and let out a yelp. Carl Metcalf looked back, then kept going.

A road ran by the meadow but they didn't take it; instead they marched along beside it in a wide, dry ditch, kicking pebbles. An old man on a bicycle passed and gave them an unsure wave. Farther on, they saw three girls walking down the middle, the tallest one carrying a trussed duck. The column fell in behind them.

The road led to the village at the base of the hill. Before they reached it, the column turned off, crossed another meadow and cut back into the jungle. The brush wasn't as dense here, and Larry could see the Martian pacing them far ahead. The dizziness had solidified into a headache behind one eye. They tacked uphill in the false twilight. Twice they stopped for water; the last time Larry didn't drink any. They halted to call in, then walked single file through the wire.

Taking his watch off, Larry noticed the crystal was fogged and the hands had stopped. He wanted to show it to someone but everyone was busy ripping their boots off and airing their feet.

While he was hanging up his socks, Magoo and Smart Andy came over and made a show of inspecting his lap. Magoo took a wad of scrip from his pocket and peeled off a bill.

"Easy money," Smart Andy said.

Later Larry would see his watch as a sign. He lost track of the days. It was late September, and occasionally he would come across the date, but whether it was Tuesday or Saturday didn't matter. Without his watch to consult, he relied on the sky or the temperature to tell him how far chow was. The days were baking; around four-thirty it cooled and the clouds moved in, then after dinner it rained till well past midnight. He asked if there was ever a day without rain around here.

Rain? they said. Is it raining? It isn't even the season yet, this is nothing. You haven't seen a goddamn thing. Shit, they said, you think you're in Vietnam? You haven't even got here. You're still on the fucking plane.

THEY WERE MORTARED nights and once even exchanged fire—the green tracers of an AK smothered in a storm of red—but the days were the same. Bunker guard, sandbags, garbage detail. They smoked Luckies and filtered Winstons when they could trade for them. They chewed gum and did crosswords. They talked and lied and spread rumors and sometimes the truth.

"Heard somebody in second platoon got waxed in Stupidville," Magoo said.

"Lang," Pony said. "He was all right."

"Guy in front of him hit a Tinker Toy," Magoo said. "One-oh-five round."

"Lang," Go-Go Bates said. "Fuck."

"Yeah," Pony said.

"Fuck," Bates said again.

"Yeah."

"Better him than me, I guess."

"No," Pony said, "I'd vote the other way on that one."

"We're supposed to be going out that way," Dumb Andy said.

"I hope so," Nate said. "My shit's getting freaky just hanging round the house."

"Why don't you go and we'll stay here?" Dumb Andy said.

" 'Cause you a simple motherfucker, that's why."

"Half the company's going out tomorrow," Smart Andy said, looking up from his book. He and Bogut and the Martian traded paperbacks, mostly sci-fi.

"Says who?" Magoo said.

"Second platoon already got a warning order."

"It'd be nice if you let us in on these things," Pony said.

"I knew it," Leonard Dawson said. "Things were going too good."

"The old man'll tell us after lunch."

"Stupidville. Goddamn."

"Hey, Skull," Nate said, "you ready for Stupidville?"

"Not really," Larry said.

"Wrong answer—you dyin' to go there."

Waiting in line at lunch, Carl Metcalf explained how the town got its name. It was a very unfriendly place, with a heavy VC presence. Echo had lost too many men to sniper fire or booby traps, and so they'd evacuated the residents and declared it a free-fire zone. Three times they'd relocated the villagers and their animals forty klicks north, but they kept coming back. It had been burned to the ground twice that summer—officially by airstrikes, Carl said, and lit his Zippo.

"They're still there, some of them," he said. "They don't understand what's going on."

"That's not being stupid," Larry said.

"No," Carl Metcalf said, "that's being ignorant. The whole thing is what's stupid."

The lieutenant and Bogut filled them in. Intelligence said a battalion of NVA regulars was digging into the hills above Stupidville. Last week the Air Force had run an Arc Light on them. Second platoon was doing bomb damage assessment when they were ambushed.

"They called in snake and nape on them," the lieutenant said, "so we don't know who's left out there. I'm thinking not many of them, but if you've been there you know you don't want to be there long."

"Where are we?" the Martian asked.

"Point." He said it as if he expected to be challenged, as if it was not his fault.

"Shit," Pony muttered.

That afternoon Bates went down to supply and came back with a sack full of extra grenades. He had a cache of gold-tipped high explosive and white phosphorous rounds—Wilson Picketts, they called them, because they made Sir Charles dance.

They had a better name for everything. Stupidville, bug juice. They called Bates's grenade launcher a thumper or a blooper, and a man killed in action a Kool-Aid. Pony's sixty was a pig, an air mattress was a rubber bitch. You didn't shoot someone, you popped them, or capped them, or made them see the light. Willie Peter make you a believer, they said, and called the ranking artillery NCO the King of Smoke. Fucking the duck was sleeping. It's a lick, they said. Cut me a huss with this ruck. Larry nodded as if he understood and listened for the word again, in context. It made sense, he thought; when you were in another country, you had to learn the language.

In the morning the sky was pink and Stupidville was on. The platoon went out with the first lift, the Hueys blowing dustdevils into the bunkers, covering everything with red grit. The door gunners wore helmets with shiny black visors. With all their gear, only six men could fit into each bird, so the platoon split, the lieutenant and Bogut going in the lead ship. Larry tried to forget his stomach by watching the others. Carl Metcalf rested against the back of the pilot's seat. Leonard Dawson sat on the bench next to him, dwarfed by his pack. They didn't look at each other, didn't say anything, like strangers riding the bus to work. The sun was low and mist still clung to the trees. Larry had taken the picture of Vicki out of his wallet and slipped it into his fatigue jacket over his heart; occasionally he touched it as they headed down the valley. The wind echoed in his helmet like a shell. Across from them in the other slick, as if in a passing car on the freeway, Magoo gave them the finger and took a picture. Pony looked around for something to throw. They rose and passed over a spinelike ridge, dipped into a valley split by a river. His rifle was cold and he hugged it and stuck his hands in his armpits, squinted against the wind. They dropped with the contour of the land and two Cobra gunships moved in to escort them, their cannons like stubby Gatling guns. Below, a narrow railbed twisted with the river, its bridges fallen. The jungle gave way to meadows dotted with haystacks, glassy paddies, lone banyan trees. Ahead he could see a cluster of huts sheltered by a fencelike hedgerow, the hills beyond it pocked with craters, scraped bare.

The Cobras peeled off. The crew chief turned and gestured over Carl Metcalf's head, pointed a finger at the floor. A road ran alongside the field below; Larry peered at the treeline but didn't see any movement. Leonard Dawson crossed himself and closed his eyes.

They spiraled in. The door gunner swung his sixty over the treeline, ready to let loose. The Cobras circled above. Below, the lieutenant and Bogut and the others were unassing the lead bird. Carl Metcalf scooted his butt to the door and hung his legs out, followed by Leonard Dawson. Larry waited behind them on the bench, then imitated them, holding his rifle by the pistol grip, his other hand on the doorframe. They were almost down now. There was no one in the field below, but as the whine of the turbine slowed and the tail dipped, he saw a discarded fatigue jacket and a length of gauze whipping in the thrashing grass.

Carl Metcalf pushed out of the door and dropped his feet to the skids, leaned his pack against the frame and crouched for the jump. Larry watched Leonard do it and followed him out, but his aid bag caught on the lip. His foot missed the skid and he fell, banging his shin. It flipped him and sent him headlong toward the ground.

He landed on his shoulder. The impact snapped his head to one side, knocking him out a second. He woke up on his stomach. He'd bit his tongue. His lips were dirty and he spat. He'd lost his weapon and his helmet. He was beginning to understand that he was all right when Carl Metcalf and Leonard Dawson grabbed him by the arms and dragged him into the high grass. They dropped him and knelt down, their rifles trained on the woodline.

"You okay?" Carl Metcalf said, then laughed. He watched the woods, giggling.

Leonard Dawson wasn't laughing. His eyes darted behind his thick glasses; he jerked his head like a bird. Larry knelt between them, weaponless, dust in his hair. Behind them the next chopper dropped its load, dipped its nose and powered away.

The LZ was cold. Leonard Dawson cradled his rifle and patted the sweat from his forehead with the towel around his shoulders. Go-Go Bates was beside him chewing a stick of gum. Larry had been told to listen for him but had forgotten in all the confusion; anytime they really hit the shit he was supposed to holler "Go! Go!" He was a good soldier, they said, a stone killer. So was Carl Metcalf, everyone said. You'd never know it, a dude that sweet, but he made sure—one round in the head, one round in the heart. The man could bring it, a real artist. The rest of them just did their jobs, got a surprise kill once in a while, laid out a stream on full auto and let the dinks run into it. The Martian could have been good but didn't give a shit, the same with Fred the Head—a pair of floaters. Salazar had lost heart, it was a shame, but maybe he didn't have it in the first place. You'd see it in their eyes, they said; watch them when they get motion on patrol, they just lock on, they're fucking hunters, it's in the blood. Larry brushed the dust off his weapon and thought of his father walking the jungle.

No one other than Carl Metcalf and Leonard had seen him fall off the chopper, but one of them must have told the lieutenant because as they were heading out, he dropped back.

"Markham," he said, "you all right?"

"Yes sir," Larry said.

"You understand what you're supposed to be doing out here?"

"Yes sir."

"Yes sir doesn't mean dick to me. Get your shit squared away and show me you're going to take care of your men. This isn't college; there are no second chances out here."

"Yes sir," Larry said, and the lieutenant went forward.

The Cobras jetted away, leaving behind a sudden quiet. The Martian led the company across the field and through a stinking paddy, and Larry discovered the fall had knocked his bug juice out of his helmet band. Though they were almost on top of it, Larry couldn't see the village, only the dense hedgerow. They crossed a dike and came upon a farmer behind a water buffalo. He kept plowing as if they weren't there, and no one stopped to check his ID. Officially they were allowed to kill him. Larry waited for someone behind him in the file to shoot but no one did.

Stupidville had been smashed flat but a new Stupidville had sprung up. It was smaller than the original, only seven or eight thatched huts. The few remaining villagers had rebuilt their hootches over the ruins of the old ones; the others were nothing but blackened frames of bamboo, scorch marks in the dirt. One had been a larger building—a schoolhouse, Carl Metcalf said. In the center of the village, children were kicking a deflated ball, stirring up the chickens. A few women with baskets had gathered at a well and turned to watch the column as it spread out. They had scarves wrapped around their heads and one was smoking a tiny pipe. They didn't stop talking, just followed the soldiers with their eyes as they went hootch to hootch, poking their barrels in the mud openings. The women's teeth were black from chewing betel nut; one spat what looked like blood at Larry's feet. He looked in two large clay urns that reminded him of his mother's planters in the backyard; they were half filled with rice.

"Check 'em out," Salazar ordered, and Larry pushed his arm in deep and felt around.

The *chieu hoi* with second platoon fired a shot in the air and shouted something in Vietnamese. The soccer game stopped. The tallest boy picked up the ball and the children huddled around the women. While the *chieu hoi* talked to the women and the lieutenant checked his map, everyone dug through the hootches. Under their reed sleeping mats the peasants had dug cubbyhole bunkers; in one, Pony and Smart Andy found what at first appeared to be a teenaged boy. He was unconscious, almost dead, a black pajama top stuffed into the hole in his back. They hauled him out by the arms and dropped him facedown in the dust.

Larry tugged the soggy top out to look at the wound. When he rolled him over, he saw the man was at least fifty, on his chin a grayed wisp of a goatee. The bullet had entered above the nipple and come out to one side of his spine, taking bits of rib and tissue with it. He was barely breathing and morphine would kill him, and though the man was going to die, Larry thought he should at least give him some blood, put a better dressing on. He took a can of expander from his bag.

"Save it," the lieutenant said, and went back to his map.

"You heard the man," Nate said.

Larry knelt there a second in protest, the can in his hand. Magoo took his picture. Smart Andy pulled off the man's Ho Chi Minh sandals, measured them against his feet, then left them there. The women were jabbering at the *chieu hoi* and pointing toward the hills. The boy with the ball came over, sat down beside the dying man and tried the sandals on. Larry put the can back in his bag.

"You ever meet Lang?" Carl Metcalf asked him.

"No."

"He was a good guy," Carl Metcalf said, and kept his eyes on Larry, as if it were something he needed to remember.

The company split up. Third platoon would stay and search the village while first and second snaked into the hills to find the bunker complex. They moved out past the dead man and through the skeletal hootches. Behind them the *chieu hoi* was screaming at the women; they sat on the ground, silent and blindfolded, their hands tied behind their backs.

The Martian led them up a muddy streambed, second platoon far off to their right, out of range. They could see the scars of the Arc Light on the hillside above them, but the lieutenant was worried about booby traps, and the Martian listened to him. It was slow going and they kept bunching up.

"Get off my ass," Carl Metcalf said.

"Get back," Larry asked Bates.

They were turning a bend in the stream when they heard an explosion off to their right. It was muffled by the jungle but still close enough to make them crouch down. Then nothing. Bogut motioned them to come on, so they did.

Farther on they heard choppers—a medevac for second, probably—and later a faint, sustained burst of rifle fire, no heavy weapons. The Martian and then the lieutenant put up a hand to stop the column. The radio chattered, filled with static. They listened to the distant snapping until it stopped, then moved on.

They smelled the bunkers before they saw them. No one had to tell Larry the stink was from the dead. The air grew greasy and sweet. Not like garbage, he thought, or the slop bucket from the mess; this was different, steady, inescapable. Carl Metcalf tied his towel around his face like a train robber, and Larry did the same. As they drew closer, the smell didn't change. He breathed through his mouth. He tried to compare it with things he knew— spoiled liverwurst, deer guts, skunk—but nothing fit. He noticed they were moving faster now.

Ahead they could see light where the jungle stopped. As they neared it they began to notice strips of black fabric hanging from the tamarind trees, wads stuck to the trunks like wet toilet paper. The ground was littered with fronds and branches amputated by the bombs' hot shrapnel. They passed a finger imbedded knuckle deep in the smooth hide of a banana tree, a piece of lung glued to a smashed bamboo thicket. The leaves of the bushes looked diseased, spotted with shreds of skin, blackened by flies. Carl Metcalf swiveled his head as if the flesh might suddenly unstick itself and fall on him.

They came out of the jungle into a plowed and cratered field. Among the charred slivers of bamboo and gobs of flesh and raw, shattered logs they found a mortar tube flattened like a tennis ball can—nothing more. The bunkers were gone, churned to dirt again, the treeline wilted. Larry felt unprotected so out in the open but the lieutenant didn't seem worried. "Smoke 'em if you got 'em," he said, and Pony stoked up a long cigar.

The lieutenant explained that Higher wanted a count of the enemy Killed by Air, so they spent twenty minutes rounding up body parts. Larry stayed with Bogut and watched them build a few corpses. There was no attempt at matching limbs because there were none. Salazar came up with the biggest find—an entire hand, complete with a sleeve; the skin was blistered, a translucent gray. "Luck Be a Lady Tonight," he whistled behind his bandana, and laid it down a proper distance from a gristly elbow. Magoo came back from the treeline with what looked like a rubber mask hanging from a stick; it was a face. He took his camera from around his neck and gave it to Larry, held the face up level with his.

"Come on, buddy," Magoo said. "Smile."

They made seven-and-a-half NVA. The lieutenant rounded it up to ten and they called it in and headed back to the village, the Martian taking them down a game trail inches wide. Larry realized the smell was gone, replaced by moss and rotting vegetation. Through the canopy they could hear more choppers, and when they reached daylight saw a column of white smoke.

By the time they reached the village, it was gone, the poles of the hootches smoking. The women were gone, and the children, and the body of the VC. The *chieu hoi* was gone. Chickens were splattered about the ground, rice spilled in the dust and covered with bootprints. They formed up and moved out, this time taking the road. The water buffalo stood knee-deep in the paddy, but the farmer was gone. The rear of the column took a few potshots. They walked along the road until all Larry could see behind them was the hedgerow. Above, two Cobras were circling, the platoon of Hueys spiraling down to the pick-up zone.

There was a sign beside the road in Vietnamese.

"You are now leaving Stupidville," Bates translated. "Population: zero."

THEY CAME to him for things. Bogut came to get Lieutenant Wise extra vitamins. Salazar had some bad jungle rot on his legs and wanted tetracycline. Magoo needed penicillin tabs for the clap. Some of them took everything, thinking it might protect them; each morning, along with the vitamins and penicillin, they'd take a Dapsone for malaria and two chalky ringworm pills and wash the rattling handful down with strong coffee. They hated their Sunday pill—the shitter, they called it, also for malaria. It was orange and the size of a quarter and sometimes it got caught, but Sundays they came and Larry dipped into his aid bag and had enough for everyone.

Every time they went out someone came down with something. Bamboo thorns tore through their trousers; when they came in he wiped hydrogen peroxide on the infected sores and bandaged them. The Martian had a rash in his armpits, and he had a salve for that. Smart Andy's hair mysteriously began to fall out. Leonard Dawson caught pinkeye. At some time, they all got the shits.

They came over to Larry's bunk and sat down, shook their heads and smirked at their own stupidity, their bad luck. He had to ask them what it was and then let them make fun of it before he could do anything, and he thought of his father talking with his patients, how he stopped when they were walking downtown to shake hands and chat, pat someone on the arm. It was more than care, Larry thought, and pledged to tend to their boils and sprains and splinters with the same patience.

Sometimes there was nothing wrong with them, they just needed his expertise. They figured he had to know how to sew—which he did—and brought him their buttons and—strangely—their broken bootlaces. Nate brought him a bamboo viper he wanted made into a helmet band and watched over Larry's shoulder as he worked with his scalpel and tweezers to peel the skin off in one piece. Fred the Head brought him a letter from his mother asking him to write about nice things, to be cheerier.

"What do *you* tell them?" Fred said, and Larry thought that he hadn't been in-country long enough to answer him fairly.

"That I wish I was home with them," he lied.

"Does it work?" Fred said, as if he'd take anything.

It rained for five days straight. They were on bunker guard, and everyone picked up a cold and the start of immersion foot, and Larry was busy. The hootch was hung with dripping socks and he ran out of foot powder. Dumb Andy's toenails fell off. The Martian came down with pneumonia, and Larry made him stay in bed and brought a hot tray from the mess tent through the rain.

"You're earning that ninety bucks a month," Carl Metcalf said.

"What about my sixty-five?" Larry asked, meaning combat pay.

"Junior," Nate said, "get back in that crib."

"Get back in your mama," Magoo said. "You ain't been born yet."

The rain lifted. Before they went out on patrol he gave them salt pills and, later, when they grew dizzy and had to lie down in the shade, undid his canteens and pressed aspirin between their lips.

They were doing bomb assessment south of Stupidville when they found a dead NVA. A tree had fallen on him.

"Now *that's* stupid," Magoo said.

The Martian knelt and checked the body for booby traps. Pony, Go-Go and Salazar lifted the trunk, and Dumb Andy dragged the man out. He was in khakis and canvas boots with a red bandana around his neck.

Larry elbowed in for a good look. He expected to be shocked—his first real dead—but it was like the wounded VC; there was nothing he could do. The man smelled, and they had to hump another three klicks back to the pick-up zone. The lieutenant was only a few feet away, seeing what his reaction would be. Larry didn't have one for him.

He had no idea how old the man was. The blood had pooled in him and gone dark; the bottoms of his arms looked bruised. The tree had been on him a long time; his midsection was inches thin.

"That's gotta hurt," Bogut said.

"I've seen guys worse," Dumb Andy said.

The man's weapon was missing but his ruck was full. While they went through the contents, flies settled on his lips, chafing their front legs together as if washing their hands before a meal. They found a pair of sandals and a roll of piasters, a pouch of rice and a tin of mackerel in tomato sauce. Pony showed around a picture of the man's wife or girlfriend; she was slightly cross-eyed, which inspired several lewd imitations.

Smart Andy pretended to read some of the man's poetry from a notebook. "How at nights I miss the lanterns of my village and its dark-eyed beauties. How I long to till the land of my family."

"How I wish I heard that tree," Fred the Head said.

In the brush Magoo found a cap with a metal star on it, but because the Martian had spotted the man, he had first choice of the spoils. He took the man's belt buckle.

"Aw, man," Leonard Dawson said. "I been trying to souvenir me one of them for months."

The lieutenant gathered the papers together for intelligence and gave the money to Bogut to pay for more beer. They dumped the rice and the mackerel out and ripped the thongs off the sandals, and this more than anything angered Larry—but for no reason, he thought, or the wrong reason. It didn't make sense; he didn't give a shit one way or the other. The guy was dead, it was simple. It wasn't sad or funny or anything really. It just was. Everything after that was up to you.

Magoo kept the cap; Salazar got the rucksack. Rigor mortis had set in, and with the help of Dumb Andy, Magoo picked up the body and propped it boardlike against a tree and asked Larry to take a shot.

"Okay," Larry said, getting them in focus. "Pretend like you're enjoying yourself."

There were still things to learn. Now that he could sleep without help, the platoon went out on night ambush. No helmets, they said, boonie hats only. And camo grease—have Bates do your face. No aftershave or deodorant, they can smell it. No talking, no snoring, no smoking—don't even try to cup one. We want good light discipline and good noise discipline. If they probe us, don't fire back, the muzzle flashes give your position away. Take extra grenades.

"Nothing's gonna happen," Dumb Andy explained. "You set up twenty of these for every one that works."

The Martian wanted Dexedrine. Larry thought he should check with the lieutenant first.

"Are you the medic?" the lieutenant asked. "Then it's your decision."

He gave the Martian two Black Beauties. The Martian looked at the pills in his hand and back to Larry as if he'd cheated him. He took the vial from Larry and poured a mound out, gave it back to him and walked away.

"He's just used to Rosie," Smart Andy said.

They walked out through the wire at dusk and down the mountain, the Martian on point. There was no moon visible through the canopy, no starlight. The lieutenant and Carl Metcalf had picked the intersection of two large trails. They waited until it was dark to lay out their claymores and take up position. Carl Metcalf checked to make sure they had proper fields of fire, then ducked back in the brush to wait for someone to enter the killing zone. They were hoping for the VC who'd been mortaring them, but they'd take anything.

They waited in the dark. Larry lay propped on his elbows, watching the trail, his safety on. The trees dripped. All day they'd been teaching him about leeches. Blouse those trousers, they said; rub on some extra bug juice. He couldn't see Smart Andy, whose shoulder touched his, and thought that it didn't matter if he fired or not. They'd let the claymores do the work. The jungle simmered with the chirps and ticks of insects. The camo grease made him sweat and the mosquitoes were thick. He could feel them land on his cheek and walk around looking for a spot to drill, but he was afraid to move. His head felt egglike in the boonie hat—huge and unprotected. Somewhere behind them, the lieutenant, Bogut and Carl Metcalf were facing the other direction, providing rear security, checking in with the command post by clicking the handset.

They waited, and he thought of how buggy the woods were in Ithaca, how at night spiders spun their webs between trees so that in the morning you walked into them facefirst. At camp once he'd been bitten by a spider in his sleep; the flesh under the red welt went hard. His father had used it to explain to Larry what was happening to his mother's cells. He would write her tomorrow, he thought; he would write her once a day—it was free. He clutched the grip of his sixteen. He was ready for the claymores to erupt in a sudden burst of flame, to show him the VC and the jungle behind them for an instant before everything went black again, but soon he began to drift again, to picture the drive to Vicki's—the summer camps along the shore, the silos and roadside diners—and wondered if he should have done some speed.

From somewhere far away came a thump, and Smart Andy shifted his arm. Seconds later, a mortar round screamed and crashed, close enough to make Larry's ears pop. Another thoomped, but the red flash of the tube didn't reveal itself, and they had to lie there and wait for the report. Artillery started putting out fire, walking it down the mountain, the shocks rippling through his body. The mortar kept thumping. He counted six rounds. When it was done they were all ready for the VC to walk through the killing zone.

They didn't. The night lengthened into morning, and Larry drifted. While Vicki was still taking him on a picnic table at the state park, daylight finally came. His knees creaked when he stood, his shoulders burned. The lieutenant ordered them to bring in the claymores and police the area before humping back to the LZ. The mortars had destroyed the deuce and a half they used for garbage detail but nothing else, yet they were still angry. They ate and then slept the day away, all but the Martian, who would have stayed up the night as well if Larry hadn't given him three Seconal.

"See," Dumb Andy said the next day. "I told you nothing would happen."

It rained and they didn't go out. On a routine patrol down the valley, third platoon ran into some local VC and their radioman got shot in the hip. They found a sack of Chicom grenades and two blood trails headed for Duc Pao.

"Bet you we sweep that ville tomorrow," Smart Andy challenged them, and nobody took him up on it.

Larry wrote his mother and then his father. *Doing okay*, he told him. *Haven't really seen any live fire yet. Hope you are well.*

When he'd finished writing FREE in the corner, the lieutenant came in and told them what Smart Andy had already guessed.

"Where are we?" Leonard Dawson said.

"We're in Vietnam," the lieutenant said, then sighed. "We're in the goddamn middle," he said, and disappeared behind his mosquito netting.

Salazar had his helmet on his knees and with a black Magic Marker was crossing *September* off the cloth cover. October was the only one left.

"I'm so short," he said, "they'll have to send me home with a micro-scope."

"Good thing your girlfriend's already got one," Dumb Andy said.

That night they had lots of advice. They passed the rods and brushes and the hootch smelled of LSA oil. It reminded him of his father's workshop in the basement, the tuna fish cans full of useless screws. Larry hadn't asked any questions, but they answered him anyway, told him what he needed to know. You won't see them, they said; you'd be really lucky to see them. If you don't see them, that's where they are. You can't worry about them. You've got to watch yourself, watch where you're walking, watch what you touch. You want to be smart, they said. You don't want to think about what you're doing. Somebody up front hits it, you hit it. Grab some cover. Figure out where it's coming from and return fire. Don't wait for a target, just pray and spray. Usually it doesn't last that long, usually.

Larry filled his magazines and slipped them into a cloth bandolier he could cinch around his waist. He kept his mouth shut and listened, waiting for them to say something about how he was supposed to get to his wounded, but they didn't, and he understood before Carl Metcalf whispered it to him that he was not supposed to go over his aid bag in front of them. Later, after they had all written their letters and gone to bed, he took it down to the shower and picked through it by flashlight. In the morning he went to supply for more battle dressings.

A platoon of Hueys lifted them out of Odin and down the valley about ten klicks. The rest of the battalion had been inserted from Phong Dien and was deployed around the village. Duc Pao was bigger than Stupidville, and deserted, with a ransacked bar and grill and a Catholic church whose stucco walls were covered with graffiti. Every other letter seemed to have an accent.

"American soldier," Smart Andy translated, "you are not something-something the people of our glorious nation."

"Killing enough of," Salazar offered.

The operation was a straight hammer-and-anvil. The other companies would drive the VC out of the hills and along the river. Echo would set up at the edge of an overgrown cane field just west of the village and act as a blocking force. There were Cobras in the air and Navy Phantoms standing by, artillery primed at Firebase Stephanie.

"A gook shoot," Nate said.

As promised, they were in the middle of the column. They moved out through the village and along an irrigation ditch to the field. Crossing it, they slowed, wary of booby traps. Larry had never seen sugarcane before. The rainy season was young and he was astonished by how lush it was; the leaves formed a knee-high plain of green that stretched to the treeline. Beyond the trees lay the river and then the jungle. Artillery was keyed in on the coordinates of the far shore, acting as a second blocking force. Echo was supposed to use the treeline for cover. The VC would come across the field, heading for the river and safety—just as they were doing now—and they would cut them down.

The rear of the column had just forded the irrigation ditch when the treeline erupted. Green and pink tracers blazed across the field. Larry saw men ahead hitting the ground, disappearing beneath the leaves. He dropped, arms wrapped around his helmet. He could hear rounds snapping overhead, ripping into the cane, and then answering fire.

"Go!" Bates was shouting at him, and he saw Carl Metcalf crawling for a slight rise—a culvert behind which Pony and Smart Andy were setting up the pig. Larry followed him on his elbows and knees, worried that his aid bag was sticking up, making him a target. He was panting, his mouth dry, leaves and twigs raining down on him. Bates was right up his ass, hollering. Carl Metcalf grabbed his arm and pulled him in behind Smart Andy; he rolled over and, without risking himself, raised his rifle above his head and let loose. Larry imitated him; the kick made the gun waver in his hands. For some reason it was funny. He looked to Carl Metcalf to confirm this, but his face had gone hard and he was busy flipping magazines. The sixty chugged, its belt clanking. Bates crawled in beside Larry, waited as if listening, then popped his head over the rise and ducked down again. He pulled a white phosphorous round like an oversized bullet out of an ammo pouch and thumbed it into the blooper, leaned his eye to the sight and waited, then popped his head up and shot it.

After a few minutes of light firing, Carl Metcalf, Bates and the Martian were all calmly taking aim, and Larry mustered the courage to peek. Third platoon had been walking point; their men were strewn about the field. The VC had an RPD machine gun, and each time its stream crossed the bodies, they moved a few inches backwards, as if lapped by an invisible tide. An acrid, gray haze masked the treeline. Larry ducked to change magazines and saw the lieutenant was on the horn calling for support, a finger in one ear. A minute later Bogut whacked Larry on the calf, screaming "Check fire!"

The gunbirds swooped in first, rocketing the treeline. Everyone stopped to watch them. A white phosphorous round threw up a cloud of sparks, giving them a target. The exhaust puffed behind the launchers, made a white line as the rocket darted into the woods and exploded, sending up geysers of dirt. There were two birds, and between runs the RPD opened up again.

"Little pricks never quit," Bates said. "Gotta give 'em that."

Both Cobras emptied their launchers, came around again and hosed the palms down with their mini-guns, shredding the fronds, then broke off.

Larry was about to ask Carl Metcalf if third platoon's medic was down there when a pair of Phantoms cleared the ridge. They were so low he couldn't hear Pony's sixty, just saw it spitting brass. Bates pointed to the treeline as if Larry shouldn't miss this. Nate had his fingers in his ears and his mouth wide open so his jaws wouldn't snap, and Larry did the same.

The first thing they dropped were bombs. The concussions weren't as bad as the 155 in camp but still made him flinch. The crown of a palm tree cartwheeled through the smoke; splinters and chunks of heartwood arced high and then showered down. It reminded him of the newsreels of Tarawa, the big shells lobbed in by the *Maryland*, making the camera shake. The jets pulled up, circled and came in with napalm. Two canisters tumbled and hit and, like a pair of struck matchheads, flared to life. The fireball swallowed the leaves and trees, lay a flaming streak across the river; it drifted boatlike downstream. Larry could feel the heat on his cheeks, the air suddenly devoid of moisture. The fire mushroomed into black, rolling smoke. The trunks of the palms flickered, smoldering. The Phantoms circled, came back and worked over the treeline with their cannons; after the show of firepower, it seemed anticlimactic, almost commonplace. Before the planes turned, the RPD clattered out a belt's worth, making all of them duck.

"Goddamn," Nate said, impressed.

The artillery took a few rounds to find their target. The first landed in the middle of third platoon's dead, flinging pieces into the air, but soon they found their range and the shells shrieked and crashed, giving second platoon enough cover to retreat. Several medevac choppers circled above, waiting for a break.

"Here's the story," the lieutenant said, giving Bogut the handset. "We're going in right behind the arty." It wasn't an order; he seemed to be asking them if it made sense.

"We're not doing shit here," Pony admitted.

They waited for someone else to speak but no one said anything. Leonard Dawson blinked behind his glasses; Fred the Head yawned. The artillery blasted the treeline, felling a tall palm.

The lieutenant split them in two. They would cross the field in staggered lines, running fifteen meters, then dropping, letting the other leapfrog ahead. Fire and maneuver, the lieutenant called it. He put Larry in the second wave, between Salazar and Leonard Dawson.

"Second platoon's on line," Bogut said, and listened, head bent, then gave the handset to the lieutenant.

"First team," the lieutenant said, and the six of them crouched on one knee as if at the start of a race. A shell shrieked overhead. "On my mark." He held a hand up, then without a word brought his arm chopping down, and Carl Metcalf, Nate, Pony and the others moved out across the field. "Go!" Bates shouted.

The machine gun didn't open up.

"Second team," the lieutenant said, and Larry found himself crouching, one hand on the ground, ready to throw himself forward. A fountain of dirt spouted above the treeline, the lieutenant's arm dropped, and Larry ran for the gap between Bates and the Martian, passed it and flung himself to the ground, gasping. He couldn't see anyone in the brush, no movement or muzzle flashes.

Bates hit the ground and Larry was up and then past him and down again. They were still sixty meters from the trees and his lungs were bursting, his grip on his rifle uncertain.

This time Bates passed him, hit the dirt and got off a grenade. It hit high in the treeline while Larry was running. He covered his face with one arm as if the shrapnel might carry back, then dove.

They were into third platoon's dead now. The machine gun had stripped the leaves from the cane and they were without cover or concealment. The artillery shook the ground, making him stumble and lunge.

He waited for the freight train scream of incoming but there was nothing. The Martian ran past, firing his sixteen from the hip. He didn't stop. Neither did Bates or Nate or Pony; they charged, laying down fire, and Larry found himself chasing them.

The Martian was the first man to reach the treeline. He leapt a ditch and disappeared into the heavy brush, then Nate and Carl Metcalf, Bates, Smart

Andy. The firing was done; Larry could hear birds and was stunned that anything had survived. By the time he jumped the ditch, Carl Metcalf was already coming back, the strap of his helmet undone.

"They *didi'd*," he said, and went to tell the LT.

In the woods, they looked through the singed and steaming bushes, stepping around pools of blood. Larry's mouth had been dry before, but now, out of danger, it filled and he had to spit. He needed a latrine, otherwise he thought he'd done well, that if not proud, he could at least say he'd done his job. He expected bodies or parts like at Stupidville, but the one foot and shinbone Magoo discovered wedged in a tree ended in a jungle boot and belonged to someone from third platoon. Smart Andy showed Larry where they'd set up the RPD, pointed to the holes the tripod had left in the dirt. Brass casings littered the ground, and a few cigarette butts. They followed a confusion of sandal prints and blood along the trail to the river.

"They just chuck 'em in and let 'em wash downstream," Fred the Head explained. "It's supposed to mess with our minds or something."

"It's good to remember when you're filling your canteen," Dumb Andy said.

In the cane field two medevacs were landing, whipping the haze into ram's horn vortices, and Larry wondered if he should have taken a look at third platoon's dead. It was probably bad luck but he thought it would be good practice.

They went back to the culvert to cook up some Cs. He noticed a few of them were spitting as much as he was and that Leonard Dawson had gone off to squat somewhere. Carl Metcalf showed him how big a pinch of C-4 to use, and Larry decided to live it up and have the can of turkey he'd traded him. He heated it until the metal burned his fingertips. The turkey bubbled and steamed; Larry dipped his plastic spoon in and blew on it. He took a bite, and it was rich and smooth and salty as his mother's Thanksgiving dinner. He took a bigger bite and burned the roof of his mouth but it tasted so good it didn't matter.

"This stuff's all right," he said, and they all laughed.

"Wait till you taste the fruit," Carl Metcalf said.

"You got a chocolate bar?" Pony said. "Man, that's the best after some action."

"Pound cake and applesauce," Fred the Head said.

"Peanut butter and crackers."

"Skull," Magoo said, and tossed him a can of pears. He opened it with his P-38 and took a bite and closed his eyes. Everyone laughed. Dumb Andy pitched him a tropical chocolate bar. Larry dug the one he'd brought out of his pack and made it an even trade.

"Is that beautiful?" Pony asked.

Though it was hot, they had coffee, then policed the area and saddled up. Third platoon was ahead of them in the column, and when the slicks came to pick them up, there were two extra birds. They lifted off empty and stayed with the formation all the way back to Odin, circled while the others ran their touch-and-gos.

They didn't talk about it that night, didn't recap the way they did after Stupidville. The hootch was quiet. Some of them finished letters they'd started the night before. It was a superstition Larry didn't understand; he felt as if he were a different person than the one he'd been last night. He thought of writing his father but could not imagine what he would say. That he had been glad not to be dead, happy even, when he ate the chocolate bar. He borrowed a paperback from Bogut and tried to read, but it was dumb—some story about an astronaut whose dreams became real. Though it was early, he was tired, and Bates and Pony had already crashed, so he felt justified in pulling the covers up and kissing Vicki's picture good night.

"You see Skull putting down that turkey loaf?" they said the next day. "See what he did to those pears? Got-damn! That's a hungry man, don't get in his way. VC saw him coming and beat feet out of there."

He went along with it because they needed to laugh and it *was* funny, but it bothered him that this was the way they would recall everything that happened. They would see him first, spooning the hot food, and then re-member crawling through the dead. It stung him because that was already how *he* saw it.

Later that week, a Shithook dropped off eight replacements assigned to third platoon, including a medic. His boots were new and his fatigues clean, and when he walked out the back ramp of the chopper he was hugging his aid bag to his chest like a schoolgirl. He still had his Red Cross markings and two brass caducei on his collar. Larry walked with him to supply and filled him in.

His name was Redmond. He said he was a conscientious objector and showed Larry that he didn't have a .45. It was almost a challenge, as if he expected Larry to fight him, make him change his mind.

"It wouldn't do you any good here anyway," Larry said. "But if you're an objector, what are you doing here?"

"I'm one-A-O," Redmond said. "I've got no problem serving my country, I'm just against the war."

"Okay," Larry said, already bored, trying to like the kid. "Glad to have you aboard."

He pointed him out to Carl Metcalf at chow. Everyone at the table looked in his direction.

"That's fine and dandy with me," Carl Metcalf said. "Long as he does his job and doesn't put me in jeopardy."

"I think the guy's a sweetpea," Nate said.

"You go outside the wire without a weapon," Carl Metcalf said.

"Guy doesn't sound too bright to me," Dumb Andy said.

"Skull'll straighten him out," said Bates.

"Yeah," Magoo said, "Skull was looking pretty dangerous the other day."

"Get some," Nate said, and held out a palm for Larry to slap, then pulled it away. Larry had learned not to fall for it, but only lately, so the joke was still on him.

"I don't know," Larry said, and it was the truth. "I'll keep an eye on him."

They were walking back to the hootch when a slick came in.

"Looks like pony," the Martian said, though the chopper was just a speck on the pad.

Salazar stopped and concentrated. "Oh yeah," he said, "two bags full."

"Guys walk point you think you're the fucking nuts," Magoo said, but later the company clerk came by with a stack for the lieutenant.

It was a ceremony, and Bogut made the most of it, dishing out a piece at a time. Pony got one from each aunt; you could smell the perfume. Fred the Head got a letter from his little girl with a smiling stick picture of Mommy. "Stupid bitch," he said, but tacked it up lovingly. His wife had sent him a Dear John letter a few months ago, and he was planning on fighting her for custody when he got back. Salazar got an application for a credit card, which he immediately filled out. Larry watched from his bunk, trying not to hope.

At the bottom was a rubber-banded wad thick as a dictionary with magazines and heavy manila envelopes. Bogut called everything until only the wad was left.

"Anybody here know a Markham?" he asked, then made Larry show ID.

It was a month's worth. He read Vicki's letters in order before anything, and wished he'd written her more. She sent pictures of their Labor Day picnic and a lock of hair and a monogrammed handkerchief she'd kissed, the lipstick going through all four layers. Some of the letters were smeared—tears, she apologized—and some illustrated with doodles. It was only a year, she said in almost all of them, and he felt ashamed; it was what he'd told her.

The *National Geographics* were a present from his mother, the form letter said, though he knew his father had thought of them. As a boy, whenever Mrs. Railsbeck took him to his father's office, Larry sat leafing through the glossy, sharp-smelling pages, thrilling to pictures of giant insects and entire cities. At home, his mother unfolded the maps across the coffee table and they followed famous rivers upstream from the sea.

His father also sent a clipping from the *Journal* that listed the men from Ithaca serving in Vietnam; Larry was surprised how many there were and how few he knew. In every letter, his father worried that his mother might have to go into the hospital again. He mentioned it as if Larry had something to do with the decision, as if he were waiting for word. Larry stuffed them into his ditty bag and reread Vicki's.

That was all the excitement for a while. It rained. The resupply choppers couldn't fly and they ran out of beer. They pulled bunker guard and hung around the hootch. Salazar marked off his calendar, filling in her stomach. They shot craps in a C-rat box, played solitaire and Michigan rummy and spit-in-the-ocean. Redmond got in a fistfight with someone in his platoon and surprisingly nobody was hurt.

The World Series started; Nate was from Detroit but was perversely rooting for the Cardinals. He was a Bob Gibson fan and did a great imitation, the big leg kick. "Dude throw a lambchop past a wolf. Throw turkey loaf right by my man Skull." He bet them both ways, so they all got interested. They gathered around Fred the Head's transistor and devoured the box scores in *Stars and Stripes*.

Dumb Andy had it figured. "Say it's real," he said. "In real life, who's gonna win—a tiger or a bird?"

"You are so fucking simple," Nate said, "that you make me want to kill you."

They ran patrols down the mountain and helped with a cordon-and-search operation in Nam Ong, a little up the valley from Stupidville, but nothing happened. The Martian uncovered a tunnel complex with a cache of over three hundred rusting cans of Spam, which Fred the Head destroyed with a block of C-4, leaving the walls glittering with jagged tin and pink meat. Bogut threw up from the smell but laughed at himself. Somewhere in there was Columbus Day, and lasagna and garlic bread for dinner. After Duc Pao, they didn't expect to step in any real shit for a while, and they didn't. When the rains lifted it was an easy time, and Larry kept after them to brush their teeth and use the extra foot powder he'd requisitioned. He painted their mosquito bites with cortisone cream and gave them their daily pills. At night they heard the war in the distance but it didn't worry them. "Someone's catchin' it," they said, watching the sky light up, the way you'd say "Nice day" or "Might rain."

The Tigers won the World Series, and though he lost money, Nate didn't mind; Gibson had pitched well and Denny McClain hadn't and the city deserved it. Even Dumb Andy couldn't rattle him.

"That's all right," Nate said. "See, 'cause even if the Tigers win, you still a dumb motherfucker."

Smart Andy started taking bets on the election. He even had an over-under for George Wallace.

One sunny day after lunch they were near Nam Ong walking patrol when they took some fast fire from the right. Everyone bailed. They'd taught Larry to know where you were going to go if they hit it. Carl Metcalf had practiced with him behind the connex box, running it like a football drill, and so before he could think, Larry took three small steps to get momentum and dove to his right, rolled on his shoulder and landed flat, the barrel of his rifle aimed in the direction of the sniper.

He didn't have a chance to fire because someone ahead to his left hit a booby trap and flew through the air.

They'd told him all along not to think, but he was surprised when he didn't hesitate, that he ran to where he thought the man would land. He was there an instant after Salazar hit. Larry knew it would be him, they all did.

He'd taken it in the chest. His flak jacket was shredded, and when Larry got it off, he could see his chest was riddled with pea-sized holes. The blood was fresh, bright lung blood pumping out, squirting inch-high streams like an old water cooler. He could no longer see the wounds and began tearing the foil packets with his teeth, sticking the dressings to his chest. He could see it was not working, and when Bates and Carl Metcalf scrabbled over, he didn't answer them. He kept working, trying to patch everything, but the dressings were already sopping. Salazar's eyes were open but unfocused; his vest was soaked. Larry checked his neck for a pulse and didn't get anything. He pounded his chest and listened. The sniper was still firing and they were answering, Bates and Carl Metcalf protecting his back. Salazar's eyes were filmed over, gone cloudy.

He was still bleeding and there was nothing Larry could do, but he started a heart massage the way they'd shown him at Fort Sam. He tilted Salazar's head back and stuck two fingers in his mouth to clear the airway and pinched his nose and put his lips to his.

He was on the second group of five breaths when a hot gout of blood filled his mouth like a gulp of wine. It hit him so fast it came out his nose. He gagged and, when he turned his head to spit, saw it pumping out of Salazar, flowing over his neck and into the leaves and moss of the jungle. He felt it hot on his chin and in his mouth and all over his hands.

There was nothing he could do, but they were still firing, still waiting for him to save their friend. He felt for a pulse and got nothing and started the massage again, leaned down and closed his eyes and put his mouth to Salazar's. He'd heard of this before, at Fort Sam; they had a name for it. It was a joke among the instructors, how sometimes new recruits didn't know when to quit. Kissing the dead, they called it. Don't do it, they said. You'll end up married to them.

FIVE

Donna met him at the door. She thought it was funny that he'd dressed up for her—sweet, she said. She had jeans on and one of Wade's old cable-knit sweaters and no shoes. Her hair was down and just brushed. Larry had brought a bottle of local wine.

"I'm sorry," she said, "I can't."

She took it as if to welcome him, then shouldered past him onto the porch and set the bottle down in the dark corner at the top of the steps. It was drizzling and her feet left prints.

"I should have told you," she said, then inside apologized again for not having any beer. "But really," she said, "I don't think I've ever seen you in corduroys."

Larry hadn't been in the house since Wade left. It felt strange, as if he were replacing him. The furniture was the same—the fat brown couch and the huge TV—but the clutter was gone: the boys' Matchbox cars and Gobots, the dogs' balls and rawhide bones, Wade's latest project. She'd taken up the rugs. A few new plants hung in the windows. On the mantel were two pictures of Brian and Chris hugging each other in the backyard, taken the same day. The endtables were empty, and the coffee table; the oak floors shone. The neatness made the place look big and unlived in, cold.

"Looks great," he told her.

"It's a lot easier to keep after," she said. "Though sometimes you don't feel like it. But you know that. God, I can't get over those pants."

At dinner they didn't talk about Vicki. That morning in the car he'd mentioned that he was going to see her and Scott tomorrow, and Donna just nodded. Larry had only wanted to be honest and was glad to let it drop. Now they sat with a single unclaimed piece of halibut between them and sipped their ice water.

"Bus strike's over," she said.

"Good."

"We should still ride in together—it's more fun."

"It is," he said.

He needed her to smile, and she did. He thought he had something to say to her, but they just sat looking at each other. She lowered her eyes and straightened her unused silverware with a fingertip, and he thought that if for nothing else he wanted her for her eyelids and the way she drove. When she looked up, he was waiting for her. She didn't seem surprised, only worried, as if this was wrong. Larry wondered if it was wrong if he loved her. He did. He could. He didn't know anything for certain.

"Help me do the dishes," she said, then broke a cup under the suds.

"I don't know why I'm so nervous," she said. "Look." She held her soapy hand out flat so Larry could see it shaking.

He held up his.

"At least I've got an excuse," she said.

They went into the living room to have coffee and she turned on the series. She wasn't a fan, but he'd mentioned it this morning and he didn't correct her. She folded her legs under herself, balancing her saucer on the arm of the couch, her toes inches from his hand. Brian and Chris looked down from the mantel. The sweater hid everything but her shoulders, the bones at her throat.

"I should go," Larry said.

"That's probably a good idea." She didn't look away from the game.

"I'm sorry."

"About what?"

"I don't know," Larry said.

"Then don't be sorry." She bit a nail and concentrated on the replay. "Talk to her—that's who you should be thinking about, not me."

"But I do."

"No," she said, "I'm just here. You're there. It's convenient."

"I don't think so."

"You'd be the only one who wouldn't."

"Donna."

"Please," she said. "This is how it always happens with me. You don't want to, really. I'll just fuck you up. So go, see if you can fix things with her."

"Okay," Larry said, and when she didn't argue with him, he got up.

She followed him to the door and, as he opened the screen to leave, laid a hand on his back so unexpectedly that he tensed as if shot.

"I'll see you tomorrow?" she said.

"Yeah. Thanks for dinner."

"Talk to her. Try."

"I will."

He stooped to retrieve his bottle of wine and waved to her as he crossed the dark yard, ignoring the Bouncing Bettys and toe-poppers and rigged 105 rounds. It wasn't a matter of courage, he thought, because he was already dead.

IT RAINED all morning and he was glad. Vicki would be coming around lunchtime with Scott. He kept busy, putting away the breakfast dishes and squaring the corners of her magazines. Making the bed, he tried to remember the last time they'd made love. It must have been a weekend, some morning while Scott watched cartoons. He recalled hearing a springlike sound effect as he was taking her from behind, his hands on her waist. She had laughed, and he rolled her over. He liked the way she threw her head back, the skin of her neck red from his stubble.

It had only been two weeks ago, though Vicki would say three. She was always after him to touch her, but lately she'd stopped complaining, instead read till she fell asleep. In the mornings he ran. He could not explain to her that sometimes he needed to be alone, that he liked it better. She thought he should see someone professional, that they should see someone together. He said he'd consider it, though they both knew he was just waiting for her to forget, to quit bothering him.

He tucked the corners, then straightened the pictures on the dresser.

There they all were in the rowboat, her wicker hat protecting Scott from the sun. Larry went to the bathroom cabinet for a can of Endust and a rag. When he finished the downstairs, the hands of the clock had barely moved.

IN THE ATTIC he hauled his old footlocker over to a musty recliner and sat there with the key in his hand. He liked the dimness and quiet, the drumming on the roof. He didn't really want to see Carl Metcalf's drawings or the class A's he couldn't fit into anymore. He didn't want to see Magoo's pictures or the bundles of letters from Vicki and his father. It was a ritual, almost looking, a way to waste time, drift out of himself. Often in the winter when Vicki took Scott to church, Larry would sit up there all morning, not even bothering with the key, just leaning elbows on knees in the cold and contemplating the locked box.

It wasn't a mystery; he knew what was in it, had catalogued each piece in his head. There was a picture of Salazar in the sling they made from his poncho and a length of bamboo. Bates and Dumb Andy had walked him out trussed and swinging between them like the spoils of some hunt. When they laid him down, blood rushed from the poncho. They undid the knots and, when the dust-off came, lifted him into the arms of the medics. A permanent medevac, they called it. Some of them watched the chopper away; others stood around silent, smoking, thinking of how to change or fix what had happened. Carl Metcalf gave Larry some Kool-Aid to rinse his mouth, but he couldn't get the taste out of his nose. That was one picture; he had two shoeboxes full, and though it had been years since he'd peeked, he knew every one, knew whose boot that was, whose muzzle pointing to the dead man's chest.

When he'd shown Clines the three of spades, the detective asked him if this thing might be personal.

"Think," he said. "Try to remember."

"The guy is fucked in the head."

"No chance," Clines asked. "Absolutely none."

I know you, Creeley had said that night. *You know me.* Now Larry thought of all the men he'd treated—not just his own platoon but other units at Dong Ngai and Hamburger Hill. He'd saved some and lost some but they were not his men, and he'd always done his job. He could say that if nothing else: he'd done his job.

"No," Larry said.

"He just likes you. Or he can focus on you. That group of yours at the hospital, what is it for?"

Larry explained.

"Suppose," Clines said, "someone doesn't want to remember?"

"Then they don't have to be in the group. It's all voluntary."

"Just a thought," Clines said. "I'm looking for any kind of tie."

He turned the computer screen to Larry and showed him what the VA had sent him. It was a file for deceased personnel. Creeley, it said, had died in August of '69 in Thua Thien province, where Larry had been.

"It's wrong," Larry said.

"You mean the date. No, it's right. Everyone has him listed as KIA, I don't know why. It's the rest that's fake. The computer guru up there said someone's been in the system. Their records show someone was in this file last week. Look at the address."

It was his father's house.

"Great."

"Yeah," Clines said. "So there's nothing personal?"

"Not that I know of."

"You *would* tell me if there was," Clines asked, and Larry had said yes, not sure if he meant it.

Now he turned the key in his fingers, ran his thumb over the teeth. He stood up and went to the window and looked down at Donna's car, the rain making circles in the puddles. Vicki would be here soon. He would ask her to come back again, though it wouldn't do them any good. So often there was nothing left to hope for, and while he knew that it was not true, at times all he could see were the years strung out ahead of him like winter fields.

The other day Creeley had been right next to him, could have driven a knife up under his ribs. It was something very personal, Larry thought, something forgotten. *Remember me.*

The wind shifted and the rain shook the panes. Across the road the lights were on in the barn, the woods black. He climbed onto the chair and hid the key back in the rafters.

Downstairs, he called Julian. He answered on the sixth ring, blearily, as if he'd just gotten up, but as Larry outlined the problem, he came awake.

"Just anything on the guy? High school, credit history?"

"I'll pay you," Larry said.

"That's all right," Julian said, but gave him time to offer again. "So give me the names of these places."

Larry listed them off.

"I'll get my friend Burt at school to run him through the Pentagon, that should give us something."

"One thing," Larry said.

"What?"

"Don't let him know you're looking for him."

"I think I can handle it," Julian said. "It's not like I've got anything else to do."

A LITTLE BEFORE lunch he heard the Ruster chugging up the drive. He'd saved all of Scott's messages, but when he went out on the porch to meet them, it was just Vicki. She got out of the car without looking at him and walked hard to the porch through the rain. She had on a windbreaker of her mother's with TRUMANSBURG VFD over the heart. She'd had her hair cut or done, feathered so only her earlobes showed. She had on the pearls he'd given her for her birthday, and fresh lipstick. He always thought he could hate her when she came back, but at the last minute his bitterness failed him and he was abjectly glad that she was safe. She climbed the stairs with her head down, as if concentrating. Larry wanted her to kiss him but she just stopped in front of him, a hand on the strap of her purse. She didn't have her ring on.

They both said hello, and he knew it was going to be bad, that they would have to squeeze out the words.

"Thank you for not calling," she said.

"I wanted to."

"I'm glad you didn't."

"Where's Scott, at your mother's?"

"Can we talk inside?" Vicki asked. "That's why I came a little early."

"Sure," Larry said, and let her by.

She put her purse down and hung up her windbreaker. She had on a lemon-yellow blouse he didn't remember; he could see the ghost of her bra beneath it. He waited for her to pick where they would sit—on the couch. He didn't know if it was a good sign; usually they fought in the kitchen so they wouldn't wake Scott. Without him, Larry felt unprotected, as if the rules had changed and anything could happen. He wished he'd put the stereo on, even the plinking harpsichords she hated.

"Sit beside me," she said.

She took his hands. She looked down at his fingers, rubbed them with her thumbs. She rubbed and rubbed and he did not want to hear what she was going to say.

"Vic," he said.

"No," she said, "I'm going to do this. I need to do this."

He tried to take his hands away but she wouldn't let him.

"Larry," she said, "you know I love you."

"It's okay."

"Shut up!" she said, crushing his fingers. "Jesus Christ, I'm trying to tell you this the only way I know how!"

"I'm sorry," he said.

"No." She began to cry and pulled away, buried her face in a Kleenex. He put his arms around her.

"What's wrong?"

"What's wrong," she said. She finished with the Kleenex and shrugged him off and took his hands again. Her eyes were veined, the wings of her nose pink. She tried to say something but her lips quivered and her mouth lost its shape and she turned from him again.

"Whatever it is—" he began.

"Please," she said. "Be quiet." She looked to the ceiling and bit her upper lip, and he knew he would forgive her anything because he loved her. He was suddenly ashamed of wanting Donna, saw that it was wrong.

"I've fallen in love with someone," Vicki said.

He looked down at the veins on the back of her hand, her slacks, the brown of the couch they were sitting on. The two of them in this room, in this house. Outside was the world, the trees, the rain.

She said it again.

"No," he said.

"Yes. I need to go away for a while to figure out what I need to do. I love you but I'm very confused right now, and I think the best thing is for me to be alone for a while."

"Bullshit." He took his hands away and crossed his arms.

She held him but he barely felt it. "I had to tell you."

"Fuck you."

"I tried to make it go away but it hasn't. We tried not seeing each other for a month but it didn't work."

"How long have you been seeing him?"

"It doesn't matter."

"Have you slept with him?"

"Yes," she said, "but that's not important."

"What's important?"

"You are."

He turned and she clung to him. He looked at the wall over the TV, a print his father had given them—a herd of cattle racing from a thunderstorm. It seemed stupid and he looked at the rug. She was trying to explain, but he stood up and she slid off him and he moved across the room and sat down in a chair. She knelt on the floor and hugged his knees, crying. "I'm so sorry," she said.

"It's not your fault," he said, so she would stop, but he didn't believe it. He could not see this other man, only Vicki beneath him. Donna must have known all along. He did not want to think, and got up again and made for the couch. She started to follow him and he turned on her and shouted, "Get the fuck away from me," and went into the kitchen and out the back door. He slammed it and the top pane gave way. He thundered down the porch stairs and tromped across the backyard, his heels digging in. He threw a kick at the sugar maple; the force of it brought down a shower of leaves. He held his head to stop picturing her beneath this other man.

"Goddammit," he said again and again, pacing. The trees were black with rain, the leaves bright. He was getting wet. Fuck it, he thought, and went back to the porch and stood there with his arms folded, thinking of what he could say that would hurt her.

There were things—women he'd coveted, things she did in bed that didn't work or were boring, idiotic—but none of those things really mattered, and in truth he did not want to hurt her, so he stood there breathing steam, not knowing what to do.

"Shit," he said. He should have seen it. He should have known and done something and now it was too late.

She came out and held him in the cold.

"Do you love him?" Larry asked.

"Yes," she said, without hesitation.

"What am I supposed to do?"

"I don't know," she said.

"Who is he?"

"You don't know him."

"What's his name?"

"I can't tell you."

"Why not?" he shouted, and she shrank back. "You love him, why can't you tell me his name?"

"Because I can't."

"You're willing to protect him, that's great."

"I didn't mean for this to happen," she said. "It just happened."

"I understand that. I just wish you'd talked to me when it started. It sounds like it's been going on a long time."

"Not really. A year."

He tried to think back to all the times they'd made love this summer trying to patch things up, the fights they'd had in the spring—it was all false.

"So you're leaving," he said.

"Just for a while. Until I know what I want to do."

"Why can't you just stay here and figure it out?"

"I can't do that," she said, but didn't give him a reason.

"How long is this going to take?"

"I don't know."

"A week, a month?"

"I don't know!" she said.

"Where are you going to stay—with him? Who's going to watch Scott?"

"We're going to stay at my mother's until I find a place."

"What about your job?"

"What about it?"

"They said you quit."

"I told them to say that," she said, as if he were a fool to believe it.

"What about Scott's school?"

"He's only missed one day."

"Why don't you leave him with me?" Larry asked.

"I know," she said. "That's been the hardest thing."

"The rest was easy."

"You know that's not true," she said.

He wanted her to talk more, but once they'd stopped, he thought it was better. He wanted to ask why, though he knew that at heart it was his fault. In the summer, when he told her that he loved her, Vicki said she knew that, as if it wasn't enough, and he had nothing else he could say. He thought he should have something more now, but he didn't. They stood there on the back porch watching the rain until she said it was cold.

Inside, she said her mother was waiting for them, but hesitated before getting her windbreaker, as if he might not want to go. He didn't really, not with her. He was suddenly exhausted, but thought of Scott and went to the front hall closet and pulled on his jacket.

"Do you want to drive?" she asked.

"No," Larry said.

Donna was still home, her windows dark. Before getting in the Ruster, he brushed Cheez-It crumbs from the seat. Scott had spilled grape juice on the rug, the stain faded but permanent. In back was a laundry basket with a jug of detergent, a few hangers and a single pink sock. She'd brought an umbrella but hadn't used it, and he thought that telling him must have been hard for her. While he could sympathize, he still didn't understand—or wouldn't. It made sense, yet it surprised him. She shifted into reverse and after a second the transmission clunked and they backed past the Monte Carlo.

"Who else knows?" he asked.

"No one. Just you."

He had questions he was afraid of. What they did and where. When. How often. Was it fun? Did they laugh? Did she say the same things to him—that she missed his smell, that she wanted him right here, right now? He lay back in the seat and watched the trees. Tomorrow was Sunday; there would be football on. Donna would want to know how it went. He wondered if he would tell her the truth so she would comfort him. He hoped not. She already felt sorry for him.

"I saw Mrs. R. at the library yesterday," Vicki said.

"Good," he said.

"She says she's having a party for your father. She wants us to come."

"You don't have to. I know you don't want to."

"I think we should—all of us."

"Don't do it just because of this."

"I'm not," she said. "Do you want us to come?"

"It's your choice," he said. "I'm not making you do anything."

"You know Scott would like it."

"Fine," Larry said. "I don't care."

He was tired. He didn't know what he was doing in the car with her. When they stopped at the Octopus, he thought he should get out and just walk away, like Creeley the other night. He reached over and turned on the radio, changed it to SKG. Saturday afternoons Texaco sponsored broadcasts from the Met—an entire opera plus highlights and a quiz in the middle. "We're not listening to that all day," Vicki would ask, and he'd go down to the basement or over to help Wade with the Camaro. When he came back she'd ask how it was, then hold her throat and yodel. Today it was an old *Tosca* with Joan Sutherland, and he sat back, daring her to turn it off.

They passed Vinegar Hill and the hospital and spun along through the farms, the reception breaking up. In the valley, clouds hid the lake, but up here it was only sprinkling. The road was crowded and slow; everyone had come out to see the leaves. Cars flocked around stands selling pumpkins and gourds and Indian corn, plastic jugs of cider and homemade pies. One winery advertised a haunted hayride.

"Probably too much for Scott," she said.

"I think so," he agreed.

"He misses you at bedtime."

"I missed him all week."

"More than me, I'm sure."

"No," he said.

"I did miss you."

"Obviously not enough," he said.

She slowed as they came into Trumansburg. Something was going on at the high school; cars were parked on the lawn, a trooper in a blaze orange slicker waving them in. They cruised through the empty downtown, past the church they'd been married in. It made him look away but she didn't notice. The hippies were home next door, Mrs. Honness's Volare in the garage. Vicki eased the Ruster over the sidewalk and turned off *Tosca*.

"Tell me when you want to leave," she said. "It's up to you."

Mrs. Honness and Scott were in the den, playing Candyland at a card table. Vicki's mother had her back to the door, so they stood and watched a moment. Mrs. Honness didn't see well and had a lamp pulled up to one corner as if they were doing a puzzle. She was helping Scott move his piece across the colored squares. He had trouble telling the orange from the red and sometimes he simply could not concentrate, lost track and went backwards. He sat open-mouthed, his blind eye looking off toward the ceiling. He was winning.

"One blue," she said. "And that has a black dot on it, so you have to stay there until you pick another blue card." She explained it patiently, checking to see if it registered.

Larry let Vicki lead him into the room. Scott looked up and saw both of them. "Mom," he said, surprised, "Dad," but didn't get up.

"Hey there, champ." Larry kissed him on the cheek; in response, Scott's lips smacked the empty air. He had on a nylon football jersey with Joe Ferguson's number and a T-shirt underneath. Larry stood behind his chair and kneaded his bony shoulders. He was thick around the hips but his upper body was scrawny, his arms stick-thin. As a toddler, he rarely moved; they had to turn him to prevent bedsores.

"Larry," Mrs. Honness acknowledged, and he returned the greeting.

"So who's winning?" he asked.

"Scott," Scott said, and pointed to the board.

"Look at that."

"Why don't you join us?" Vicki's mother said, and Larry pulled up a chair.

"Vicki?" Mrs. Honness asked.

"I've got to sort some laundry." She gave Larry a last look as if to make sure he was okay.

"How's your father?" Mrs. Honness asked as they were playing.

"Good," Larry said, noting she didn't ask about him.

"What a dismal day," she said. "A good day to stay inside."

They cheated so Scott could win, then switched to Chutes and Ladders. The rain picked up and the room went dark. The lamp seemed to warm them. Vicki brought in a bowl of Chex party mix and some hot chocolate. Scott immediately spilled his and she ran to the kitchen for the paper towels, bringing back the whole roll. He sobbed, gulping in air, and Larry had to soothe him. "Just an accident," he said, dabbing at the board. "Whose turn is it?"

Vicki asked her mother if there was anything she needed while she was out and took the Ruster, then half an hour later came back with a basket of folded clothes. From the front of the house came the sound of movie music —brooding bassoons and playful oboes.

"I gotta go potty," Scott said, and Larry pushed back his chair.

In the bathroom, he leaned against the sink while Scott went.

"Are you having a good time at Grammy's?" he asked.

"Uh-huh."

"That's good." He didn't know what else to say, what he could possibly ask him. "I miss you," he said.

Scott looked up at him but said nothing.

"I love you, I hope you know that."

Larry smoothed his hair and his good eye blinked.

"I need a wipe," Scott said.

"Okay, tiger," Larry said, and folded a handful. "Lean toward me."

He stayed until Vicki started dinner. The college scores were coming in from the west coast. Scott liked the highlights. Larry had given him a Nerf football; he flung himself around on the couch as if he were part of the play.

"I hope you're being careful in there," Vicki called from the kitchen.

She said there was enough Swiss steak for all of them. It was dark out now, and the house smelled of grease and onions, and he thought that if he stayed it would only be harder later. He thanked her for having him over and they made plans for her to pick him up Wednesday. He would get a gift for his father, he said, something from all of them. She tried to give him money. He thought it was silly until he realized they would have to split the account and probably the house and everything else, all of it. She would get Scott because she was the mother, and he would have nothing.

"Thank you for the Candyland," he told Mrs. Honness.

He knelt to hold Scott and, when he kissed him, smelled the hot chocolate on his breath.

"I know that was very hard," Vicki said in the car, and thanked him.

"That was easy," Larry said. "Not seeing you is hard."

"You never saw me when I was there."

"I did," he said.

"No," she said. "You were off in Vietnam or wherever it is you go."

"You're not going to start that again."

"It never stops, Larry. The littlest thing and you go into that shell of yours. It's my fault for letting you do it, but I'm tired of it. I don't want to live that way anymore."

"That's just the way I am," he said.

"No," she said, "you weren't like that before. You were funny and happy and then something happened to you."

"That's such crap. You're like everyone else, you want to blame the war for everything. It was one fucking year. I didn't even serve the whole thing. Eleven months. What about the rest of my life? And what's wrong with the way I am? I work, I sleep. I love you and Scott. I'm grateful to be alive, not like these zombies walking around worrying about money and shit. I've got my priorities straight. *You're* the one sleeping around."

"You really see it that way."

"I don't see any other way to see it. I'm trying. You're giving up."

"Are you happy?" she asked. "Because I'm not and I haven't been for a long time. Not that you'd notice."

"I noticed," he said, and it was true. All spring she'd been a bitch on wheels, and there was nothing he could do. "I wish I made you happier."

"You're missing the point."

"What's the point?" he said.

"Forget it," she said. "I'm not going to argue with you."

"You always say we should talk, let's talk. I mean, you pull this shit on me, what am I supposed to think?"

They passed beneath a streetlight, and he could see her biting her cheek. All afternoon she'd been quiet, oddly calm, and he wondered if some of this morning had been an act. She'd had a long time to think about it, while he

w... ...ng to realize what it meant—the lawyers, seeing Scott on
... ...ld add it to the list of disappointments. Susan

... sorry about the way it happened. I didn't know
...lk to you I don't know how many times; you just
...ing was wrong."

...t it's no excuse."

. I'm ready to take the blame for everything, that
n just worried about you."

.

... ...y do you think I asked Donna to keep an eye on you?"

"Because you're doing the same thing Wade did."

"I knew you'd say something like that."

"I hope he's at least not some fucking grad student."

"No," she said, "and I don't even know what's going to happen. I could be
back in a week. I just need some time by myself."

"I don't understand that," he said. "You know I'll take you back. That's
the sad thing; I promised myself I'd never do that, and here I am."

"I'm not asking you to."

"But there it is."

"Thank you."

"Wait till I make good on it," he said. "Then you can thank me."

Donna's lights were on, the Monte Carlo still there. Vicki swung the
Ruster in, splashing. The lights played over the yard, and for an instant he
thought he saw a pair of eyes in the bushes—a cat maybe, or a raccoon. He
had reason to be paranoid, he thought.

"Wednesday," Vicki said, and before he could open his door, she leaned
over and kissed him, a hand on the back of his neck. "Thank you," she said.
After he'd dug the mail out of the mailbox, he watched her taillights away,
wondering how big of a fool he was.

Donna was watching TV, the blue light swimming on the columns of her
porch. He stood there fishing for his keys, thinking of what he would say to
her, but once inside, he chained the door, threw the mail on the kitchen
table and unplugged the phone. He went through the rooms, checking the
locks on the windows and, once he was sure he was alone, lay down on the

couch. A few hours later when he moved upstairs to the bedroom, he hadn't made any decisions. He dreamed of Nate trying to fly and woke clutching the pillow. The light stayed on all night.

DONNA HELPED HIM pick out a gift at the Iron Shop downtown. "What does he like?" she asked, and the only thing Larry could come up with non-alcoholic was the fireplace. They looked up the store in the yellow pages and she drove him down there. She found a bundle of kindling cut from old bourbon barrels and a pair of horse-head andirons.

"Think they're stuffy enough?" she said.

They went shopping at Wegman's. Donna clowned for him, tossing cereal boxes, making fun of the Hostess display.

She knew he was down and insisted on making dinner, which turned out to be nothing but salad. They ate on the floor, listening to a frantic jazz album, all squealing saxes and random percussion. She was wearing neat cigarette-leg jeans and had her hair up, pinned with a tortoiseshell clip.

He waited for her to ask him how it went yesterday. He'd practiced in his mind what he would say: Not bad, or, pretty much what I expected. When the conversation finally drifted to it, he said, "How do *you* think it went?"

"I don't know," she said.

"But you knew what was going on."

"I didn't want to. I told her that, but she needed someone to talk to. She said you and Wade used to talk about us."

"Not much," he said.

"But enough."

He stacked their plates and stood. "It went the way she wanted it to."

"I'm sorry," she said. "Are you okay?"

"No," he said, "but what can you do?"

She washed and he dried, and after, she flipped the record and they sat on the couch. She tucked her legs under. She'd stopped smoking around him and started chewing gum. She could snap it in her back teeth, and laughed at how tacky it sounded.

"What did *you* do when he told you?" Larry asked.

"I don't remember. Smashed things. Hit him."

"You hit him?"

"Oh, yeah, I let him have it. The bastard deserved it. He knew it too. He didn't try to stop me, he just stood there and took it, like I couldn't touch him. And I couldn't. I wasn't strong enough to really hurt him, that was the worst thing. I hit him as hard as I could in the face four times and it just bounced off."

"I remember his lip," Larry said.

"That was a book."

The record ended and the tone arm lifted and clicked back into place.

"I had no right, really, with my history." Donna laughed. "It seems so long ago. You know, I don't care what he does anymore." She rubbed her calf with a palm as if working out a knot and frowned. "That's not true."

"It's hard to stop," Larry said.

"You do though, you just don't admit it. That's why they take so long to leave. They think they're going to save you or that you're going to change, and after a while they finally give up and start looking for someone else."

"Is that what happens?"

"I think so."

"What about us?" he said. "What are we supposed to do?"

"Forget it," Donna said. "We've already given up. I don't know about you, but I gave up a long time ago."

"You really believe that?"

He thought from the way she held her expression that she did.

She laughed and pulled the clip out of her hair and it spilled down over her shoulders.

"Come here," she said, and took his hand and drew him to her. She kissed him chastely on the lips and looked at him, inches away. "You're very funny," she said. "Will you promise me one thing?"

"Yes."

"Don't lie to me."

"I won't," he said, worried that he already had.

"Now go home," she said, "before we do something stupid."

THOUGH IT was still raining the next day, he got up early and laced on his Nikes. He needed to run, to let everything settle, and once he got out on the road and his calves loosened up, he debated whether he was in love with

Donna or just lonely. He wondered who Fred was to her and when she had quit drinking. He tried not to think of Vicki going home last night and dialing the other one's number, telling him she'd finally done it.

He passed a burst trash bag, its contents scattered along the ditch—chicken bones and french fry boats, coupons and toothbrushes. Sweat trickled through his hair; his windbreaker stuck to his arms. It made him think of monsoon season, the long days of rain.

After Salazar got hit, it rained for a week straight, and the walkway to the mess tent sunk in the mud. They didn't mention Salazar, didn't say his name. Bogut took down his calendar and boxed his pictures to go home. Pony claimed his bedroll and his canteens; Magoo secured his weapon and his ammo. The birds were grounded, and they stayed inside, playing cards and listening to "Chickenman" and "The Shadow" on Armed Forces Radio.

One day Bates turned from the pot of MPC on Dumb Andy's footlocker and asked, "Where's Sally?"

"Fucking the duck," Fred the Head said, as if it were a normal question.

"Twenty-two and a wake-up," Nate said. "Gone. Outta here."

On patrol, they stopped for coffee and Cs, and Pony asked, "Where'd Sally go?"

"Draining the snake," someone said.

"Man's so short he wears elevator drawers."

When his DEROS rolled around, they had a party, gathered around his rack. The connex had broken down and all they had was warm beer, but they got drunk and made speeches and told him not to take any of that stateside shit, and in the morning he was gone.

Larry focused on the road, the toes of his Nikes eating up the white line. He checked his split time and it was fast; it happened whenever he thought too much, the energy went to his legs. Vicki would have called the man and maybe gone over, let her mother watch Scott. It didn't matter—they'd already made love. He wished he knew what the man looked like; all he could picture was Vicki with her hands on his back, taking him in.

The best thing was not to think, to stay busy. He had Creeley to worry about, and group tonight, and Donna. He saw Scott playing Candyland in the lamplight and picked up the pace, concentrated on the leaves glued to the road. It was high autumn now, the air a familiar mix of mist and woodsmoke, the orchards bare. The season comforted him like a fire or a quiet room, a perfectly turned adagio.

It was dependable; even the fall he came home, he hobbled out the French doors to his father's back patio, still drunk from the night before, and marveled at the bright hillsides. In Vietnam when they came upon a flame tree, he told them it was nothing, that they should come see him in Ithaca. "What the fuck is an Ithaca?" Nate teased, but Carl Metcalf said, "It's something, all right," and Larry had been proud, as if he'd helped color the woods.

The leaves pleased him now, and it was not a small consolation, he thought—being alive and home—yet when he finally slowed to a trot and then walked it off and climbed the porch stairs, he no longer felt lucky or blessed but merely tired. The day ahead seemed long and pointless, and he had to force himself to fix his corn flakes, and then sat looking at them until Donna honked.

SHE DIDN'T KISS him or take his hand. She said good morning formally and started off before Larry could respond. He stayed on his side of the seat, trying to read her face. He wanted her to lead, to tell him she was happy with him, but she watched the road. She had her hair pulled back in a white scarf that made her forehead seem severe, her lipstick harsh. Outside, the decorated houses slid by, ghosts hung from trees.

"I'm sorry," she said finally, as if in explanation. "I'm not a stable person. I don't have any self-control, that's always been my problem." She didn't look at him, and he was suddenly tired, let down, as if he should have seen this coming.

"I understand," he said.

"Come on, don't get weird on me."

"I'm not," he said. He wanted to crawl back under the covers and sleep the day away.

"I just think we should think right now."

"You're right." He thought it was good of her to be worried, even if it was the worst thing she could say to him. In a way, he was relieved.

"I really do like you," she said. "Very much."

"It's all right," he said. "You were just trying to be nice."

"Don't think I'm so noble. I've been living alone a long time and I'm not very good at it."

"Neither am I."

"It's been what for you—a week? Try a year. And I wasn't that strong to begin with. Then you come along and I don't know if it's because I want you or just somebody. I'm tired of being by myself all the time. I like being with you, but you're not mine and you can't be."

"Why not?"

"Don't be stupid," she said.

"She's not mine anymore."

"She is," Donna said. "I know her, and she is. And where does that leave me? So let's think, okay?"

He agreed, though now he wanted her even more. They slowed and tagged along behind a bus.

"Look at that," she joked.

"Just in time."

In the parking lot, he said he'd think.

"Not too hard," she said, and waved as she pulled away.

Inside, Marv called him into his office. He had a pair of pink telephone memos on his desk. One was from the Price Chopper in Van Etten.

"They say you never showed up last Thursday. That right?"

"I didn't have time."

"Will you have time today? Can you fit them into your busy schedule?"

"I didn't have time because I had to help Derek and didn't get out of here till ten."

"You'll get there today."

"I will," Larry said.

"This other one's from the police. Guy called about five minutes ago."

It was Clines. Marv let him borrow the phone and went up front.

"There you are," Clines said. "How was your weekend, pretty quiet?"

Larry said yes.

"Good. Tell you why I'm calling. Guess whose desk the four of spades was on when he got in this morning. Yeah. It says: R, E, M, F. *You weren't there.* Any ideas?"

"That's REMF," Larry said. "It means rear echelon motherfucker, some-one who hasn't seen actual combat."

"I guess that's me."

"It means he doesn't consider you an equal."

"Not like you," Clines said. "You're his best friend."

"You have anything else new?"

"There's more every day. I just talked to Bethesda, and they say they can't find his transfer order. All your people have is a carbon and no one in Admitting is taking responsibility for signing off on it. It's beginning to look like he checked himself out of there and into here."

"How long was he in Bethesda?"

"Nine years," Clines said. "They finally sent me his medical file. It says he was catatonic almost all of it. One of those miracles, patient wakes up one day and asks for hot cereal. They think a bullet fragment migrated in his brain and relieved the pressure or something, I don't know. All I know is he's freshly hatched and we've got him—you and me. So help me out here. I've got your files so I know where you were and when, but you've got to tell me what you did over there."

"I did my job," Larry said.

"You want me to dig everything up myself, I can do that."

"I don't know this guy. I never met him and I never worked on him."

"You're sure about that?" Clines asked.

"Yes," Larry said.

"Then why's he so interested in you?"

Piloting Number 1 through the slick streets, he tried to answer Clines. Creeley was the size of Fred the Head but Larry had tagged Fred, had placed his arms at his sides in the poncho and popped smoke. He was smaller than Bates and taller than Bogut; there was no one else his size. Maybe a new guy later, when the replacements came, but that time was fuzzy, and he'd done his best—maybe better, because by then he didn't care, threw himself at his wounded whether he had cover or not. They protected him, gave him their chocolate bars and pineapple chunks, made sure no one fucked with his sleep. He did not want to remember that time, and because he had learned —too late—not to care about himself or his men, he didn't; his last month was a blur of red dust and blood and sunlight, the many greens of the jungle.

When he'd stepped on the toe-popper he was almost grateful. Finally he could rest and forget.

It was not someone he knew, he was sure of it. It was someone he'd forgotten, someone who had not forgotten him. He mulled it over between deliveries, but everytime he saw a Duster or a young couple pushing a cart together, his thoughts drifted to Vicki. She had a white cotton robe with lacy trim she wore in the mornings, and though he hadn't been interested lately, now he pictured her at the table, flashing him a nipple. He could not stop himself from seeing Donna in the backyard, waving the rake, her chest flushed, breasts swinging. He thought that she was right, that they should think. He pictured her on the couch, taking his hand, or their first day in the car, bitching with him.

He was supposed to be missing Vicki, but all day Donna followed him like the rain. He conjured her tiny feet, her shoulders, her hair. He worried that it was just lust or, as she'd said, convenience. She was smarter than he was, it was part of the attraction—and strange, unpredictable. She was new. They didn't know each other at all. She was right; it would only fuck them up more. All the gray afternoon he listened to SKG and restocked his shelves, and when he pulled Number 1 into the outlet, he thought that while he hadn't come up with any answers, he'd followed her advice. It surprised him; he'd thought the day would be harder.

He took the bus up the hill to the hospital. He resented paying the fifty cents, but it would save him a ride home with his father.

In group they all wanted to talk about Creeley. Mobley had come back on his own; beside Cartwright sat an empty chair. Larry hadn't told them about the three of spades or Julian's car. They thought the REMF was funny.

"So is this Betty Crocker doing anything?" Meredith asked.

"He's all worried about his Colt," Trayner explained.

"You might as well write it off," Cartwright said.

"I don't get it," Mel White said. "Why's Creeley hanging around here?"

"They don't know," Larry said.

" 'Cause he's a nutbag," Sponge said. "He's taking orders from the invisible radio."

"He hasn't really done anything," Mel White said, and they all thought about that.

Larry pretended to be stumped. He checked his clipboard. "Okay, who do we have tonight?"

"That's me," Cartwright said, and they settled in to listen. He was a Marine sniper, and his stories were about Kentucky windage and impossible shots. He and Mobley had been crossing a footbridge over a canal on the Plain of Reeds when the bamboo gave way and dropped them onto three-feet-long punji stakes anchored in the mud. Cartwright had been in front and only lost his legs, both high above-the-knee amputations. He always started with a loving description of his rifle—a bolt-action Remington 700 with a hunting scope—as if the M-16 was a toy and the rest of them amateurs.

Tonight they were outside of Pleiku, running security on Highway 19. A company of main-force VC had shot up a convoy, and Higher wanted some bodies. Larry relaxed into the twilight and the smoke of the rice fires, the rattle of bicycles on the road below. Beside him, Johnny Johnson laughed, and Trayner patted his hand.

He'd been so busy this last week that he'd forgotten how calm his time with them made him feel, how certain there was some greater good in the world that he could be part of, if only by sitting and listening, nodding acknowledgment that, yes, that was the way it was. He wondered why he could not agree with Vicki this way, or with his father, and wondered whose fault that was. When he talked to her about the war she had the same reaction every time, no matter what he was trying to tell her; it was awful, and he had been deeply hurt, and in time they would overcome it together—all of which was untrue and, worse, beside the point. Here, his brothers knew that it could not be so easily described, that they were lucky to be alive and that they did not wish to get rid of it, even if that were possible. It was not a choice. The war lived within them like an extra organ, pumping out love and terror and pity for the world—a necessary, sometimes unwelcome wisdom. After all these years he did not expect her to understand completely, or his father, though it seemed he had reason to, yet Larry still hoped they might recognize this difference in him as something other than crippling. Here, at least, there was no question of being misunderstood.

After Cartwright, Rinehart told a foot-still-in-the-boot story that everyone made fun of. In the next ward, Shaun trundled the med cart back and forth across the hall, disappearing into rooms. Larry asked for volunteers for next time.

"Are we going to have a Halloween party?" Trayner asked.

"If you want," Larry said.

They took a vote. Cartwright and Meredith and Rinehart were against it, Sponge and Mel White and Trayner for. Johnny Johnson wasn't anything.

"Johnny," Larry asked, "do you like Halloween?"

"Halloween," Johnny said.

"Fuck it," Cartwright said, "we'll have the goddamn party."

"What about the names?" Meredith said. "How many can we give you?"

"You guys going to fly me there?" Larry asked.

"Doc," Rinehart said, "you gotta go."

"Who else is going to do it," Mel White asked, "Dr. Jefferies?"

"Me no VC," Cartwright mimicked, holding his hands above his head.

"Maybe we'll all go after the excitement dies down."

"Right," Sponge said, disgusted.

"You're letting us down, Doc," Rinehart said.

Trayner gave him a puppy-dog look and gestured pathetically to Johnny Johnson.

"Son of a bitch," Larry said. "It's bad enough I've got Creeley out there without you guys on my ass. We'll see, okay? No promises."

"You're going," Mel White said.

On his way to the bus stop he passed his father's New Yorker in the lot. Its parking lights were on. The driver's side door was unlocked, which was unlike his father. Larry pushed the light knob all the way in, then rummaged through the glovebox for a pen and paper and wrote him a note.

At the stop, he looked back at the lit windows of the hospital and imagined Creeley walking out the sliding emergency room doors, the night orderly's keys in his pocket. It was still drizzling, and cold, the streetlights glazing the asphalt. His new foot hurt, as if they might get some weather. The first frost was long gone, and sugar snow wasn't uncommon this time of year.

The only other passenger was an old woman with a plastic rain hat and a ratty shawl; she sang to herself, rocking in time against the seat. She was too small to be Creeley, but Larry took a bench well behind her, across from the side door. If she turned with Meredith's pistol cocked beneath the shawl, he could either duck or dive for the doorwell. The second was better, though the driver would be no help. The light in the bus was grainy, fluorescents behind plastic advertising panels. He imagined his silhouette and moved away from the window. He thought of Donna's scarf and her bare forehead and scolded himself. They splashed through downtown, picked up a balding hippie and a few Japanese students and growled up East Hill in low.

He was the last passenger and, getting off, thought foolishly that Creeley might be the driver. She was a fat black woman with plum lipstick and a streaked blond wig. She said good night and folded the door closed behind him and motored off.

Donna's house was dark, the Monte Carlo in the drive. Inside, he wondered if it was a signal. He threw the mail on the couch and turned off the machine, went to the hall window and looked out at her porch, hoping for the strobing blue of the TV. There was nothing.

She wanted them both to think, she said, which was right. She was a better person than he was because of that, more thoughtful, considerate of Vicki. Yesterday he had been ready, despite everything, to make love to her on the couch, on the floor, wherever she wanted. When she'd sent him home, he was glad to go, if only to please her, to prove he would do anything to protect them. It frightened him to give her such power, but now that she had it, there was nothing he could do but hope she would be kind.

FRED WAS her sponsor from AA. Donna didn't know his last name, but when she felt shaky she called him and he listened. It was her third time and it was working so far, but it had been less than a month. She went to meetings once a week.

"Tonight," she said, "if you'd like to come."

Larry thought he should, but she took a hand from the steering wheel and pawed his arm as if she were joking. "You don't have to. God, you're so serious today."

"I've been thinking," he said. "I think I'm in love with you."

"Wrong," she said, and made a game-show buzz in her throat. "You're going to try to work things out at home."

"There's nobody at home except me."

"And why is that?"

"Do you know or are you asking me?"

"I'm asking you."

"It's probably my fault," Larry said.

"Because?"

He thought of the spring, and before that. It had been a year, Vicki said. He didn't think he'd changed. Their problems were typical, impossible to solve. She wanted him to pay more attention to her, to do more around the house. She complained that he didn't like her friends, that he didn't like doing things with her family. They never went out anywhere, they never did anything. When he tried, she didn't give him credit, made it into a test he was sure to fail. It was normal, he thought, just boring to listen to.

"I don't know why," he said.

"Honestly," she said.

"Honestly."

"She says it's like you're not even there sometimes. That you sit and listen to your music with your eyes closed."

"Sometimes," he said. "I like music."

"Like all the time," Donna said.

"Hardly ever. Once, maybe twice a week."

"How about sex?" she asked. Her window was open a crack, and her hair fluttered against the headrest.

"I'm happy," he said. "Or I was."

"What about her?"

"Should we be talking about this?"

"Should you be telling me you're in love with me?"

"It's true," he said.

"You're avoiding the issue."

"That's basically what I did with her."

"Do you like sex?" she asked.

"Yes," Larry said, "but it's not everything."

"In my entire life," Donna said, "in all the times I've made love, I've had one real, honest-to-God orgasm. One."

Larry thought that his record was probably the opposite but was unsure exactly what that meant.

"Do you still love me?" she asked.

"Why wouldn't I?" he said, and she shook her head and sighed.

He waited now for her to say his name, to turn from the road to dispute his answer and show him the face he would re-create later in Number 1— her dark eyebrows, her cheeks, the dimple in her chin.

"Larry," she said, "look at me. I'm exactly the wrong person for you to fall in love with."

"Isn't it funny?"

"No," Donna said. "It really isn't."

JULIAN CALLED as he was boiling some hot dogs for dinner. He'd gotten through to Creeley's file.

"That was quick," Larry said.

"It was pretty simple," Julian said. "The guy butchered it, real one-oh-one stuff. I can't believe the cops couldn't pick it."

"I don't think they tried."

"Five minutes and I was in. No back-ups, no alarms—it wasn't even fun."

"So what does it say?" Larry asked.

"You're on it—L. Markham, right?"

"That's the fake one."

"No, I trashed that one. This is his induction papers from the Navy. It has you down as the examining physician. It even has your signature."

"What year is it?"

"Nineteen sixty-eight."

"Is the signature perfect?"

"Really beautiful."

"Loops and curls," Larry said.

"Like in handwriting class."

"That's my father," Larry said. "So he must be from around here."

"Right here. Four-fourteen East Buffalo Street. He went to Ithaca High."

"I figured. What's his birth date?"

Creeley was a year younger than Larry, but two grades behind, which explained why he didn't recall him. His father probably could, probably knew the family.

"Anything else interesting?"

"I don't know," Julian said. "Personal stuff—father, mother. Medical records. You'll have to look at it. I'll be around all day tomorrow. Burt's got the Pentagon stuff going, but that's going to take a while. From the looks of this one, I don't think this guy could get in there. He just doesn't have it."

Larry thanked him and asked if a check was okay.

"Next time," Julian said. "This one wasn't even work."

Larry ate his hot dogs and mac 'n' cheese at the table, contemplating the news as he chewed. Creeley might be holed up with relatives or old friends. He'd have access to anything he needed. He knew the town, the land, the weather. He knew where Larry lived, and his father. If Creeley wanted to kill either of them, Larry didn't see what was stopping him. He couldn't finish his second dog and set the nub of it on his plate. What was worse, he thought, than being killed?

LATER HE SAW Donna pull in, but didn't go over, and in the morning they talked the same way, as if words could discourage him. She seemed serious and tired; though the morning was gray, she wore shades, and smoked with the window open. She had not forgotten his father's party tonight and, letting him off, wished him luck, but lingered at the window as if she had more to say, then instead of joking just said, "Bye," and didn't wave.

He swung by Julian's before his first stop and rang the bell, but there was no answer. He shared an apartment over the Chapterhouse, a bar near Collegetown that brewed its own beer; the halls stank of roasted malt. When Larry came back after lunch, Julian said he'd been asleep. He'd just woken up, his hair snarled, his face greasy. On one wall his roommate had painted a huge red and blue skull, a white lightning bolt splitting the frontal lobe. There were cigarette butts crushed out in bottle caps on the living room table, and empties underfoot. Julian gave him a few pages of print-out and followed him sleepily to the door. Larry sat in front of the Chapterhouse with Number 1 running, going over the pages.

Creeley's father had died in 1951, and though his mother had been alive at the time of his induction, the person he'd listed to be reached in an emergency was his grandmother, Ida Sizemore. Her address was in Varna, just outside of town. The Chapterhouse didn't open until four, so Larry had to wait until his regular stop at Powers' Red and White to give the number a call.

A man answered and said he'd never heard of her. Larry gave him the address, but the man said, "Nope, sorry."

He drove by 414 East Buffalo and was stunned. He knew the house, everyone in town did. It was a restored Victorian on the hill up to Collegetown, beige with grape and pumpkin trim. It had a cupola and brass coachlights and an involved garden in back. It was a landmark, a character; every year it was written up in the *Grapevine*. The editor of the *Cornell Alumni News* lived in one half, in the other, Peggy Haine, a local character who dressed like a flapper and sang raunchy standards with a Dixieland band. In the summer the porch roof was overflowing with plants, in the winter lined with plastic penguins wearing red-and-white-striped scarves. Larry didn't know why, but he was surprised that the Creeleys had had money at some point. In its majesty, the house didn't fit with the scar across his forehead, the lurching speech, while the dead father and the grandmother in Varna did.

He called Clines to tell him the news.

"Where'd you get all this?" the detective asked, and, without mentioning his name, Larry told him about Julian.

"I can't use it," Clines said. "Until we officially get it, I never heard of it."

"What good is that?" Larry asked.

"I'm just telling you it may take us a little while, so just sit tight."

"Is that your advice?"

"No," Clines said, "but that's what I'm telling you."

THERE WASN'T enough paper left from Vicki's birthday, and Larry had to wrap the andirons in smiling tigers and straight-legged zebras. He took his good suit out of the clinging dry-cleaning bag and hunted down a tie he hoped would go with it. The last time he'd dressed up was for the fortieth anniversary of his father's practice, right after Easter, and Vicki had helped him then. She'd worn a midnight-blue knee-length skirt that showed off her long waist. Brushing his teeth, he imagined what she'd been thinking of at the banquet, through the endless speeches and the dishes being cleared off, the waiters pouring more water. He saw her skirt hiked around her waist and her knees drawn up, her calves wrapped around the small of another man's back. All spring she'd been sick, her paychecks small. He held his tie as he spat, wiped his mouth with a towel.

She'd said six and it was five after. He turned on the porch light for her and saw that Donna hadn't come back. He set the andirons down on the front hall rug, checked his hair and the fit of his jacket in the mirror and sat on the couch, then jumped up again, ran upstairs and got Scott's messages. Vicki had forgotten her deodorant, and he grabbed that too, slipped it like a flask into his jacket. He needed a drink, which made him think of Donna alone in the house tonight, her dependence on Fred. He had beer on his list when they'd gone to Wegman's, but hadn't bought it because of her. His father would serve scotch and talk about the region it hailed from before sipping it appreciatively. In the cupboard, all Larry had was rum. He un-screwed the cap and waved the bottle under his nose. He'd poured a shot and steeled himself for the burn when he heard the Ruster crunch over the drive. He emptied the glass down the sink and ran water over his hands.

Vicki didn't get out of the car. She waited with the lights blazing while he locked the front door and, when he got in, apologized for being late. He told her it was no problem and placed the andirons on the floor, trusting it wasn't dirty. Scott sat between them on the hump, his clip-on tie cocked sideways. His hair wasn't quite dry, and Larry patted down a cowlick. Vicki had a suede jacket on over her outfit—a turtleneck and a wool skirt and cowboy boots. He didn't recognize her earrings, two tiny gold hoops.

"You look nice," Larry tried.

"Think your father will approve?" she said, and he could see she was going to make an effort.

"New earrings?"

"Yes," she said, as if impressed. "You look very handsome yourself."

The heater didn't work, and as they picked up speed, cold leaked in through the vents. Scott pressed the buttons of the radio, changing stations, until Larry stopped his hand and held on to it. His fingers were icy, and Larry rubbed them between his palms. Vicki glanced over to see what they were doing and gave him a resigned smile, then went back to driving.

"So I guess you've talked with him," Larry asked.

"Some."

"And?"

"Later." She nodded toward Scott.

"Anything I need to know about?"

"Let's just have a nice night. We can talk tomorrow."

"I wish I knew what you're thinking," he said, keeping his voice calm so as not to alarm Scott. "Because it's an utter mystery to me."

"I know," she said, as if she were sorry, but didn't go on. She made it sound as if one day he would understand everything. He wanted to pursue it now but was afraid to. He'd believed her the other day when she said she loved him; that wasn't the reason she was leaving. He tried to imagine what this other man could do for her, what new future she saw in him. In his most selfish moments Larry pictured a life with Donna, but it seemed flimsy and untested, wishful at best. It frightened him that Vicki might be sure.

"Red light," Scott said. "Stop."

Larry remembered the deodorant and pulled it out. "Here," he said.

She thanked him and reached over and stuck it in the glove compartment.

"How are you doing without a car?" she asked. "I can use my mom's if you need it."

"I'm okay," Larry said.

"I didn't know the buses would go on strike."

"Donna's been giving me a ride."

"I know," Vicki said. "She says you two have been carpooling."

"Green light," Scott said. "Go."

"My father actually gave me a ride home twice last week," Larry said, hoping she'd follow the change of subject.

"How's the old boat?"

"Just had her tuned up," he mimicked, and Scott's giant eye searched Larry's face for the origin of the new voice. "He didn't look good. He seemed tired."

"He's old," Vicki said. "He should have retired five years ago. He's like my dad; he'll quit when they put him in a box."

"He'd be bored. He wouldn't have anything to do."

"He likes to fish."

"He'd drive Mrs. R. up the wall." It was an old conversation, safe, and they played it out slowly, made it last until they were down the hill and in town.

The gaslight in his father's yard was on, the drive empty. Vicki pulled up to the double garage, the headlights reflecting off the door. Larry expected the five of spades stuck in a window, which was silly. His father had once been ripped off for drugs and had had a professional system installed; an ankle-high sign on the lawn advertised it. Still, this was Creeley. Larry couldn't decide if he was being paranoid.

It was warmer here in town. Larry held his door open, but Scott got out on Vicki's side. Larry tucked the kindling under one arm and lifted the andirons, lugged them like dumbbells. A hedge ran along the flagstone path to the front porch, and he peered into the yard beyond, searching for movement. They kept Scott between them, Vicki parting his hair with her fingers. The porch light came on automatically and they clumped up the stairs. Scott was fascinated by the leaded glass of the front door; he stuck his face against it to look through the beveled edges. They let him ring the buzzer and stood back. After a minute Larry told him to do it again.

Mrs. Railsbeck rippled across the glass, wiping her hands on her apron. "Hello," she called from inside, still fiddling with the lock, then came out into the cold to greet them. She was red-faced and heavier than in the spring, her hair so white it must have just been done. Her bifocals hung from a bead chain around her neck, and when she hugged Scott, they disappeared into her front.

"Look at my big boy," she said, and held Scott by the shoulders, as if inspecting him.

She gave Vicki a quick hug and a peck, and when she moved to Larry, he could smell the chemical tang of her Ben-Gay and the dead stench of her Lucky Strikes. "And my other big boy," she said.

She herded them into the warmth of the front hall and helped them with their coats. From the kitchen came the crackle of fat, the heavy scent of meat. Larry looked for a place to put his gifts down—the marble-top table, where they kept their mittens and winter hats and earmuffs—before setting them on the floor.

"Your father's in the den," Mrs. Railsbeck said, and took a drink order before hustling off to check her rump roast.

"She might need help," Vicki said, but halfheartedly, knowing he expected her to say hello first. It was a trick of hers, to hide in the kitchen.

She trailed behind Scott as they passed through the dining room. The lights were off, but Mrs. Railsbeck had done up the table—thick linen napkins and the cut-glass water pitcher. He used to help her count the silver after Thanksgiving, fitting the pieces into a chest lined with blue crushed velvet. The inside was like the box for his father's medals, hidden deep in the bottom drawer of his desk. He had three—a Purple Heart and two Bronze Stars. As a child, he'd wanted to hear how his father had won them; now, with a box of his own, Larry understood his silence.

The door of the den was closed but they could hear the evening news. He and Susan had not been allowed in it, and those afternoons when he was supposed to be playing outside, he would sneak in the back and sift through the big desk like a spy, going through his father's private files. He coveted the decoys on the mantel and the horse tack hanging by the fireplace, the paintings and cast statues of ranchhands. Like his father, the den was a mystery, but one he loved. It was dark and cluttered, unlike the rest of the house, which he considered his mother's. Over the years nothing had changed; his father's Remingtons were still sequestered, his mother's delicate watercolors showcased in the living room. Larry turned and smoothed Scott's hair, fixed his tie while Vicki waited, looking around the dark walls as if for a clock, an exit. He loved all three of them, he thought; then why was it always so difficult?

His father was asleep on the sofa, sitting upright, wearing his reading glasses, a book in his hand. He had his work clothes on, the hospital nametag still clipped to one lapel of his jacket. On the end table sat a tumbler of neat scotch and a tall glass of ice water. There was a fire going and the TV blared. Vicki and Scott stayed by the door while Larry woke him.

"I'm fine," his father said. "Had a long day, that's all." He tried to push himself up but didn't make it, then shooed Larry when he tried to help.

They wished him a happy birthday. He nodded as if it wasn't his fault. He shook Scott's hand, took Vicki's and kissed her cheek. "You're all looking well."

"So are you," Vicki said.

"Have a seat," his father offered, and Larry eased back into the couch beside him.

"I'm going to see if she needs a hand with those drinks," Vicki said, and left.

"Duck," Scott said, pointing. His father wouldn't let him play with them, which bothered Vicki. In the past, when Scott worked himself into a tantrum, his father would leave the room, and sometimes she'd give his departing back a cutting glance.

"What does the duck say?" Larry asked.

"Quack quack."

"How about a coloring book?" his father said, and showed Larry where they were. Scott got down on the floor to do it, pausing every so often to stare at the fire.

"So how are things?" his father asked, which didn't take long. They never had much to say for themselves. His mother could talk on the phone for hours, so could Vicki, but after a few minutes with anybody, Larry's interest in his own life waned. His father did not want to hear about his job and rarely talked about the hospital. They gave up, satisfied that things were fine, and watched the news. St. Louis had thrown a parade for the Cardinals. Larry had completely forgotten about the series and really didn't care. The next clip was violent and he couldn't look at it, instead watched Scott making purple tornadoes, ignoring the lines. When he looked up, they were still showing it—a shallow grave in El Salvador, a priest's wrists wired behind his back. The newscaster said something about the CIA.

"I think I might have one of your old patients in my group," Larry said. "Ronald Creeley?"

"I knew a Matt Creeley," his father said. "Little younger than I was. Marine. Killed in Korea if I remember."

"This might be his son. He went into the Navy about the time I went."

"Nope," his father said, and shook his head as if Creeley didn't exist. "Korea though, they say that was the worst. Worse than Vietnam, worse than the islands. Temperature got down to thirty below. Human waves, outfits getting completely overrun, no survivors at all. A friend of mine in the Marines said you wanted to be captured by the Chinese because the North Koreans would kill you."

"Worse than the islands," Larry said. He'd never heard his father talk like this, and wanted him to go on.

"They weren't so bad. We griped about the weather and the bugs, but I hear it was worse where you were."

"The rains," Larry said, "they were bad."

Vicki came in with a tray of drinks and handed them around, warning

Scott to be careful with his tippy cup; it was for toddlers and had a rounded bottom and a smiling bear on the side. "We'll do the presents in about five minutes," she said, and left, giving Larry a sympathetic smirk.

"Creeley, you said."

"Ronald Creeley," Larry said.

"Could be his son."

"He lived over on East Buffalo."

"That's where they lived. Big house. I remember his mother because she had problems after Matt died. She had problems to begin with. She was in a private hospital for a while. That must be their boy."

"You don't remember him."

"No," his father said. He squinted as if to see something in the past, then shook his head. He took a sip of scotch, then a sip of water. "But Korea, they say that was the worst—worse than Vietnam. The temperature got down to thirty below. A Marine friend of mine says you wanted to be captured by the Chinese—"

"Because the North Koreans would kill you," Larry finished.

"Compared to that, I guess the islands weren't so bad," his father said, and told him again about the bugs and the heat. Larry sipped his beer and glanced at his father's scotch—he'd barely dented it.

"The rains were bad," Larry admitted.

They did the presents in the living room. The couch was the same one he'd shared with his mother, but reupholstered in faux-needlepoint roses, its familiarity somehow destroyed by the repair. Her huge console radio still stood in the corner, unused, the top crowded with photos. His father let Scott rip the paper off the andirons; Vicki had to help him. He said he could use another pair and admired the horses, rubbing their noses for luck. He sniffed the kindling and passed around a stick. Mrs. Railsbeck had gotten him a seat cover made of wooden beads that were supposed to massage his back while he drove. It didn't seem like him, but his father thanked her with a kiss on the cheek. Vicki checked Larry's reaction, which annoyed him. Scott stuffed the wrapping paper in a garbage bag.

"Five minutes," Mrs. Railsbeck said, and asked Larry if he would come pour the water. In the pantry she put a hand on his arm and asked if she could talk to him.

"I'm afraid your father's slipping a little," she said as if he might dispute her. "He forgets things or gets them mixed up. It's been getting worse and I don't know what to do about it. He gets angry when I try to say anything, and then he won't talk to me. Sometimes he says things. It's very frightening. I thought I should tell you."

"You're right," he said. "I've noticed."

"I want him to see someone at the hospital. Maybe you can talk to him."

"I can try."

"Not tonight," she said.

"Soon," Larry agreed.

She thanked him as if it were a great favor.

At the table, Scott struggled with his rump roast. Vicki cut it for him, but he couldn't keep the pieces on his fork. The tablecloth around his plate was spotted with gravy. Both Larry and Vicki apologized; Mrs. Railsbeck said it had to be washed anyway. His father finished and refolded his napkin, sipped his red wine. He seemed fine, fully recovered, and Larry wondered if he knew, if he'd been trying to hide it. They talked about Halloween. Mrs. Railsbeck couldn't justify buying candy; she was going to make cookies and write a note so the parents would know who they were from. Vicki said that Scott had a party at school to go to.

For dessert, Mrs. Railsbeck had made his father's favorite—lemon meringue pie. While she and Vicki were cutting slices and pouring coffee in the pantry, Scott announced that he had to go to the bathroom. Larry took him to the half bath off the mudroom. On his way through the den he passed the desk and wondered if Creeley might still be in his files. It was likely; his father was meticulous. He told Scott he'd be right back.

He knew where the records were from long afternoons of snooping, but when he opened the drawer and began to dig through the Cs, he thought he'd made a mistake. From above it looked neat and orderly but shoved between the file folders were broken pencils and crumpled envelopes, used tissues and twisted paper clips, the greening crust of a sandwich.

Scott called from the bathroom.

Larry found the file. It was thin; he half expected the five of spades. It was a single sheet, a carbon of the one Julian had dug up. If nothing else, it was verification. Larry replaced it, quietly shut the drawer and went to tend Scott.

They took their coffee to the living room. Vicki sat beside him, though they didn't touch each other. It was one of her complaints, that he never doted on her in public. Larry wanted to take her hand now but didn't dare. She finished her cup and took it into the kitchen, and when she came back, said it was past Scott's bedtime, which was true. He was still working at the coloring book; his father said he could take it home with him.

They all walked to the front hall, stuffed and sleepy. Mrs. Railsbeck passed them their coats. Vicki had her keys out. She helped Scott button up and say good night and headed out the door, Mrs. Railsbeck trailing them onto the cold porch. They made straight for the Ruster.

Larry took his father's hand and shook it firmly, held on to it as he'd been taught. Behind him, Vicki started the car.

"Happy birthday, Dad," he said.

His father thanked him, then asked, "Creeley."

"Ronald Creeley."

"His father was a nice fellow, handsome too—beautiful blue eyes. A real shame." He kept Larry's hand, his lips trembling, as if he'd forgotten what he wanted to say. "That Korea, they say it was the worst," he said, and Larry could not stop him from telling him the rest.

SIX

The VC didn't just kill Leonard Dawson. They gagged him and tied him to a tree and beat him with the butts of their guns and then slit his throat. They cut his dick off and stuck it in his mouth like a cigar. They folded his broken glasses and shoved them up his ass. Then they went away, drifted into the jungle and dissipated like mist.

The platoon saw all of it after the fact. Larry did not want to look but stared at the bloody trousers and the offset jaw. They all did, gathered as if at an accident, as if to prove it had actually happened. Finally Carl Metcalf covered him up, but still they didn't leave. They squatted and knelt about the body, gnawing their thumbnails, looking to the lieutenant. Bates sat in the grass, holding Leonard's hand, twisting his ring around and around.

The next day they cleared the nearest village and called in air. Bogut honked up a FAC named Tony D on his handset, and they watched as the Phantoms dropped everything. The huts went up, the animal pens, the trees. They went in on line, their boots leaving prints in the charred dirt. A singed duck hobbled around blindly, bleating, until Smart Andy stomped on its neck. The residents waited sullenly at the edge of a meadow, farmers squatting with their hoes, children clutching bundles. One old woman held a bright red umbrella to keep her out of the sun, and as the column passed, Nate grabbed it from her and threw it on the ground in front of Bates. He stepped around it.

"Goddamn, Norman," Nate said, and tromped it himself.

They were extracted the next day, and Bates asked the lieutenant if he could police Leonard Dawson's gear. For close to a week he wrote a letter to Leonard's good-looking sister and sent her picture back with it. He boxed up Leonard's comic books and his diary and the suit they'd bought together in Hong Kong. "I'm done," he announced to the hootch, and they divided the rest.

They waited for him to change. You watch, they said, and when he began wearing Leonard's ring on a bootlace around his neck, they nodded sagely. Happen every time, they said. Never fail.

The lieutenant came to Larry and asked if Bates had talked to him. Fred the Head had gotten into the habit, telling him about his failed marriage and his little girl, and sometimes Dumb Andy walked back from chow with Larry and admitted he missed Milwaukee and, incidentally, his mother. But Bates hadn't wanted anything from him lately except foot powder.

"When he does," the lieutenant said, "you keep me abreast."

On patrol, Bates was right behind him with the thumper, and now Larry found himself checking to see how far back he was, where he was looking. Magoo, who followed Bates, had noticeably dropped off the pace, gave him room to fuck up, and Larry thought that was smart. When they stopped for water, Carl Metcalf made a point of sitting with Bates, and though they joked, it was too much like Carl Metcalf to do that, and made the rest of them worry about him even more.

He was quiet now, and kept to himself, reading the afternoon away in the high grass beyond the connex box, sitting atop the sandbagged bunkers at sunset with a warm beer and a cigarette, gazing down the valley. He had kept Leonard's deck of cards; Smart Andy said he'd seen him lay them out as if he were playing solitaire. He continued to write to Leonard's family, though they had not written him back. He read in the latrine, and at chow, and went to bed early. These were all signs, they said.

And yet every other night he still played bridge with the lieutenant and Bogut and Carl Metcalf. When they scrimmaged with third platoon, he scored two touchdowns and took out Redmond with a vicious blindside hit, and afterward went down the hill and got laid by the whore with the trick armpit and came back laughing. For months he and Leonard had been saving their candy from their Sunday packages, and on Halloween he passed it out to the children of the village, dipping into his helmet and strewing whole handfuls of Juicy Fruit and Mars bars over the crowd like Johnny Appleseed. He put money on Hubert Humphrey and dared them to cover it.

One afternoon when Bates was on latrine detail, Pony brought it up for discussion. "I mean, the man cannot be right," he said, and pointed to his temple. "Something like that happens, I know I'd be all fucked up."

"He's going to explode on someone," Nate agreed.

Magoo thought it was shock and appealed to Larry, who just shrugged. Smart Andy said he was repressing his feelings. Bogut and the lieutenant didn't have an opinion.

"It's religion," the Martian said, and went back to his book.

"Listen to him," Nate scoffed.

"Watch him at chow," the Martian said, without rolling over.

"What's he talking about?" Pony asked, and the lieutenant explained that Buddhists didn't eat meat.

"All that makes him is a vegetable," Magoo said.

The Martian got up, dug a dwindling toilet roll from his pack, and, without a word, walked through them and out of the hootch with his book.

"Well," Magoo said, "that proves it."

They watched Bates at lunch, and sure enough, he skipped the chipped beef and doubled up on the creamed corn. He'd brought his book; it was from in-country or possibly China, pocket-sized, the pages onionskin. He hunched over his tray, reading as he spooned up the wet mess. He had a pencil behind his ear, and several times he stopped eating to underline something.

"Good book?" Pony asked, and Bates nodded with his mouth full and flashed him the cover—*The Teachings of Lao Tse*.

"If it works," Fred the Head said later, "I don't see what harm it does."

"I think it's helping," Carl Metcalf seconded.

Nate shook his head with his eyes closed, as if painfully disappointed in them. "You saw my man Leonard there, that's all I'm gonna say."

Larry was surprised that he agreed with him. He didn't know if his opinion counted yet, so all he said was "Yeah," and was embarrassed when everyone looked to him.

A few days later a padre came out on a chopper to do a memorial service. A magic show, they called it, but when they stood formation, everyone snapped to attention. The padre's fatigues were clean. He had a cap that he folded into his back pocket before he put his sash on. A rifle driven bayonet-first into the dirt symbolized Leonard. An empty pair of boots stood at the base, a helmet resting atop the butt. None of the gear was Leonard's; the company kept several spare sets just for this purpose.

Bates stood beside Larry, mumbling along with the Lord's Prayer. When they had finished, they could hear the faint rush of an invisible jet high above them. The padre gave a sermon about sacrifice that Larry wanted to believe, and then an honor guard stepped forward and fired off a volley, the shots echoing.

Afterward, the padre handed out St. Michael medallions to anyone who'd been through jump school. Bates got in line and thanked him and slipped the silver chain over his head and headed back to the hootch with the rest of them, all but Magoo, who stayed behind to take a picture. Larry needed some hydrogen peroxide and gauze from supply, and when he crossed the compound on his way back, the clerk came with him to retrieve the rifle and the boots and the helmet. The padre's chopper lifted off and tilted, turned down the valley. The magic show was over. Leonard Dawson had completely disappeared.

Bates began to lose weight. You could see it in the mornings, before he put his T-shirt on. He was a big man, but not fat, and now his body was dark with hollows. In the village he found a terra-cotta Buddha the size of a teapot and set it at the head of his rack. Several times a day he burned joss sticks before it, the ashes dropping into a thin wooden dish. Ranked in front of the Buddha stood a picture of his mother and father and one of Leonard Dawson wearing the beautiful Hong Kong suit. Because they had rats, the lieutenant wouldn't let him leave offerings of B-ration crackers, so instead he left salt and tobacco. He knelt on a reed mat beside his rack and bowed to the Buddha, his elbows out, palms pressed together, fingertips just under his chin. His face was a picture of bliss.

"Dude is looking solid," Magoo marveled.

"Higher you fly," Nate said, "the faster you fall."

They were supposed to go out on night ambush in the same area where Leonard had been killed, and the lieutenant came to Larry and asked if he had a problem with writing Bates up so they could leave him behind.

"What should I write?"

"FUO," the lieutenant said. "Fever of unknown origin."

"Sure," Larry said, but in a few minutes the lieutenant came back and said it wasn't necessary.

It was sprinkling when they reached their night position. They went on another two hundred meters to let dusk gather before backtracking and setting up a perimeter and laying out their claymores. Intelligence said the main-force VC in the area were showing a lot of activity—bicycle supply convoys, a district chief and a schoolteacher killed in front of their village. These were the men who had tortured Leonard Dawson, and even the Martian had some ideas about how to set up the killing zone. The lieutenant gave Bates rear security along with Carl Metcalf, where he'd be out of the action, yet he didn't complain. Everyone got comfortable and they settled in to wait.

They had been there only a few hours when Fred the Head patted Larry's arm. His finger was on the trigger guard, and the touch almost startled him into firing. Through the patter of the rain on the canopy came a padding of feet, and clinking. He was supposed to wait until the lieutenant blew the claymores and then rake the trail directly in front of him—nothing else. The clinking seemed to be on top of them, yet he couldn't see anything, only the silhouettes of the trees. A man stifled a cough and another laughed. Skin smacked skin. To Larry's left a black shape moved, flowing through the lighter shadows behind it. The cushion of leaves gave under the man's sandals. A second man came, and a third, left to right in front of them, until all three were deep in the killing zone. Still the lieutenant waited, as if there were more. Larry kept his sights on the trail, ankle high. The first man walked past so close he could have spit on him.

The claymores roared, and for an instant the VC and the jungle were suddenly there. Larry jerked the trigger and the muzzle flash blinded him. Pony's sixty clattered. Larry emptied his magazine and waited for the noise to stop. "Check fire," Bogut was yelling.

No one moved or said anything. A man on the trail moaned. The air smelled burnt, sour, metallic. The rain came down.

"Okay," the lieutenant said, and they got up to see what was left of the VC.

Nate brought out his red-lens flashlight and shined it on the trail. All three men had taken the claymores across the waist. Shreds of their black pajamas clung to the wounds. One man was still alive, his stomach a puddle. Larry squatted beside him. His eyes were fixed. His mouth opened and closed as if he were trying to say one last thing, but only a low moan came out.

"Any chance?" the lieutenant said.

"No."

The lieutenant gave him his .45. Larry laid down his rifle and his hand touched blood. The pistol's safety was off, a round in the chamber.

"Quickly is best," the lieutenant said.

"Give it to Bates," someone to the rear said—Dumb Andy maybe.

"Bates?" the lieutenant said.

"That's all right," Bates said.

They waited, as if he might reconsider. He didn't.

"Come on," the lieutenant said. "We can't stay around here."

"Gotta get wet sometime," Nate said.

"Hold it away from you," Pony instructed.

Larry pressed the muzzle under the man's chin and saw his lips move. He paused, thinking Carl Metcalf would save him.

"For Christ's sake," Smart Andy said. "Shoot the fucking thing."

Larry closed his eyes and fired, splattering the leaves. The rain came down. He turned away and handed the pistol back butt first, as if the lieutenant could kill him now.

"It's better to keep them open," the lieutenant said.

Larry said nothing. He remembered his weapon and turned to look for it, but Pony was already wiping the barrel down with a towel.

"Don't mean a thing," Pony said.

"That's right," Magoo said. "Just another day at the war."

The man had a grease gun, which they offered Larry. He didn't want it; the Martian did. Smart Andy pulled the pin on a grenade and gently slipped it under the body, and they moved out.

Back at Odin, the helplessness and anger Larry had felt at that moment didn't lift. He washed a Seconal down with a warm beer before he slept, but woke up knowing what he'd done. No one else seemed bothered by it. He supposed that in the end it was the humane thing to do—a hard thing, but the right thing, and important to learn. Then why didn't he write about it in his letters, why didn't he want to talk about it? It was part of his job, nothing more. And so when everyone wondered why Bates hadn't accepted the pistol, Larry shook his head as if he really didn't know.

Bates was building a spirit house out of raw boards taken from ammo crates. Brightly painted and mounted head-high on a pole, it reminded Larry of his mother's martin house in the backyard. The lieutenant said he couldn't put it in front of the hootch, so Bates dragged it up the hill past the connex box. He burned incense and left crackers in it to honor the spirits. He said there were ghosts everywhere—*ma*, they were called—and one had to be in harmony with them. That was one reason why you couldn't eat meat; the *ma* of all those animals would bother you. Chicken *ma*, cow *ma*. The same went for men, Bates said, and Larry thought it made sense.

Bates exercised up there now, waking before reveille and practicing a series of slow-motion karate moves he called tai chi in just his skivvies. Some days he sat for hours in the lotus position, turning with the sun, skipping chow. His ribs showed through, and the lieutenant ordered him to submit to a physical; Larry admitted that except for the weight loss, he seemed fine. He'd quit smoking, he said, and everyone realized that they hadn't seen him light up in weeks.

"He ain't quit that whacky tobaccky though," Magoo said. "Dude is eight miles high."

"That's scary shit, man," Fred the Head said, "what your brain can do to you."

THEY WERE RUNNING a patrol near Stupidville when they took some fast fire from the right. Everybody hit it and answered back.

"Damn," Bates said behind him, "I'm hit," and Larry turned on his belly like an alligator and crawled to him.

"Look at that," Bates said.

He'd taken a round through the calf, a clean wound, an easy one for Larry. He located the exit; it had taken some muscle but not much.

"How you doin'?" Larry asked, remembering what his father said about shock.

"Okay," Bates said, looking around as if there were something more interesting going on. "It's not bad."

"No," Larry agreed.

As he bandaged him, rounds hummed and snapped above their heads, showering down leaves. Carl Metcalf crawled over and Bates gave him his thumper. Bogut checked the frequency inked on the thigh of his trousers and called for a dust-off. The firing slowed and then ceased. The sniper had packed up. The lieutenant decided not to send anyone after him.

Bates wanted to stand, but Larry made him lie there while they fixed a litter.

"I'm not going to argue with you," Bates said. He seemed vaguely amused by the whole thing, patient, as if it were an inconvenience—a long line at the bank. He refused a cigarette with a smile. They got him onto his poncho and lifted the four corners.

"Jesus," Dumb Andy said, "you still weigh a ton."

"It's all that heavy thinking he's been doing," Pony said.

They carted him to an overgrown meadow and waited for the thupping of the blades, then popped smoke and hefted him onboard. He sat up on the floor and waved as it lifted off, grinning at his bad luck.

"You knew it," Pony said. "Just a matter of time."

"See him smiling?" Nate said. "That is one fucked-up individual."

"Thing like that'll mess with your mind," Fred the Head said.

"I don't know," the Martian said. It took them a second to locate him, though he was standing right there. "Maybe he's happy."

They thought about this for a minute.

Finally Carl Metcalf said, "Then he is fucked up."

IT RAINED. It rained at dusk and all through the night and the next day and the next. It rained when the sun was shining. The mess tent flooded; the bulldozer sank tread-deep in the muck. Early one morning, a thunderstorm set off some claymores, waking them. They waited for the monsoon to move south, which would be at least a month, the LT said. They bailed out the bunkers and hung up their socks and, when cloud cover grounded their resupply, ate C-rations for a week. Even when it lifted and they went out, the jungle was dripping, and after half a klick their fatigues were soaked and every step chafed. Their pack straps dug into their skin, wore sores onto which Larry had to dab ointment.

Because the days were the same, they told time by who died. Remember, they'd say, that was right after Sally, or Leonard Dawson—somewhere in there. They remembered holidays, but it took someone like Dumb Andy to get excited about them. As Fred the Head said, it wasn't like they got a day off.

The news from home interested them less and less. The announcers on Armed Forces Radio made everything sound important, but they didn't care about the Dow Jones or the space race or the movies they would never see. They all knew Dr. King and Bobby were dead and never coming back. *Stars and Stripes* was full of homecoming photos of West Point—floats and football and girls in shoulderless dresses. Carl Metcalf brought it over to show Larry. "Imagine," he said, pointing to the background, "what those trees look like right now."

Larry did not need to be reminded of Ithaca. Nightly he visited the city, wandering the downtown—cruising through the carnival of Woolworth's, catching a matinee at the Strand. He had stored his Fairlane in a friend's barn, battened a tarp over it to keep off the pigeon shit, but there it was at the curb, tanked up and gleaming. Vicki waited for him on her porch, her diaphragm hidden in her bag. They drove up the lake to the state park and sat on a picnic table at the end of the marina, huddled against the wind, sipping sweet wine and watching the whitecaps.

He wrote her a letter every day when they were not in the field, and each time they got pony, he received two or three, the envelopes damp and cool with perfume. She was going with her girlfriend Cheryl to the fall formal and would wear a red carnation to remember him. She missed his arms, she said, and his smell. His mother wasn't doing so good though; had his father written him?

Larry immediately wanted to call him, but calmed himself and drafted a letter. It would be at least three weeks before he heard back.

Bates sent a letter from the 95th Evac Hospital in Da Nang. He was doing fine, he said, and expected to be back by Thanksgiving. Larry wondered what the doctors thought of his job, but after Salazar and Leonard Dawson, it was enough that Bates was well. His handwriting was elegant, perfectly slanted. He thanked them all for helping him, as did his ancestors. He wished them peace.

"Loony Tunes," Magoo said. "Fucking Merrie Melodies."

The platoon's scrapes and sprains kept Larry busy. They all had patches of jungle rot and sores from bamboo thorns and various stages of immersion foot. The whore with the trick armpit picked up lice, and the entire platoon came down with an infestation; Fred the Head said he'd rather have them than let Pony cut his hair and rinsed his head with a dipper of kerosene. Larry kept after them to take their pills and brush their teeth. Mother hen, they teased him, Mother Skull.

Because he and Redmond were new, they were assigned to run a medcap in the village. Redmond still had a shiner from his fight, but said he was getting along. He'd seen fire and set a broken leg.

"All right," Larry said, and he could see Redmond was proud.

They humped down the hill with an escort and, using a Vietnamese doctor as an interpreter, taught the local reaction force the basics of first aid, then saw as many children as they could before the sun set. In line the kids stood on tiptoes, jumped up, trying to see what Larry was doing. They were so small, so skinny, that he couldn't tell what age they were. The girls and the boys wore earrings, their mothers accompanying them. He recognized the circular welts on their scalps as ringworm and handed out his entire supply of pills. Some of the women had the wet, hollow cough of TB, and Redmond suspected several boys with yellowed eyes had contracted hepatitis. A lot of the kids didn't have anything wrong with them; they just wanted the attention of the American *bac-si*. They sat in Larry's lap and rubbed his whiskers. Leaving, Larry thought that he would have to come back.

"Where's your gun?" Redmond asked him on the way up.

Larry stuck a thumb at his aid bag.

"I heard you had to use it."

Larry stopped walking. "That's right—I had to."

Redmond stood with him. "I don't know if I could."

"You won't because you don't have one."

"But if I had to," Redmond said.

"You could," Larry said, and started walking, unconcerned if it was the truth or not, and Redmond followed him.

They'd gotten pony while Larry was out; a letter from Susan was on his cot. She was supposed to be in Albany, at law school, but the return address was their house in Ithaca. The letter explained that their mother had had a stroke and was paralyzed on her right side. Susan had come home to help out. Their father did not want her in the hospital. Don't tell him, she wrote, but I think he's being unrealistic. They had argued, but inconclusively.

She was weak. She couldn't eat or clean herself, and when she did speak, it was a whisper from one side of her mouth. She lay in her bedroom upstairs while Susan read to her. She was constantly tired and mixed up her words. Get me a dalmatian, she said, I need to blow my nose. When she slept, Susan drew the blinds and sat there watching her breathe. It's horrible, she wrote, and Larry thought it should have been himself there, that the two of them were used to spending time in silence. It was unfair; all through high school Susan had strained to leave, hated Ithaca and sometimes them with the same cultivated impatience he saw in his father. She could have *him*, Larry thought.

Then his father was right, he had abandoned her.

He went to the lieutenant to see if he could get emergency leave.

The lieutenant said he was sorry and had him sit on his cot. They talked for a little. The odds weren't good, but he could try. The lieutenant would make sure they expedited the papers.

Larry went up behind the connex box to Bates's spirit house and squatted there in the mud, looking down the valley, the letter still in his hand. It was almost dark, bats fluttering above the jungle. The 105s were putting out night defensive fire; he could hear it hit miles away. In Ithaca they would just be waking up, Mrs. Railsbeck padding downstairs in her quilted robe to light the stove and put on coffee. In their separate rooms, his mother and father and Susan slept, or maybe lay silent, watching the minute hand tick, the sky lighten.

In the west, the mountains turned purple. The arty stopped, replaced by tiny voices, laughter, the chime of spent shell casings. Larry heard a scrap of windblown music, the percussion of some well-known Motown tune. It always astonished him that the radio could reach them even here, as if everywhere the air were filled with spirits.

Bates's house was empty, the inside black in the dusk. He'd painted the window frames, the bricks in the chimney, even the shingles. The sheer detail impressed Larry. It seemed a sign of Bates's faith, and though Larry didn't know if his devotion was born of belief or need, he thought it would be wrong to question it. He looked at his sister's handwriting and the address he'd known so long and tore off the corner. He lifted it to his lips and kissed it, reached up and fit it through the door.

NIXON WON, though only Bogut really cared. They all hated Johnson. He called a stop to the bombing, and the supply lines from the north flooded with equipment. Now they were rocketed more often. Word from down the valley was that patrols were running into company-, even battalion-sized elements of NVA regulars. Division moved the 1st Brigade north, and the skies filled with fast movers. The slow time was over.

Now Echo went out in Shithooks to the plains around Hue or deeper into the valley. They seemed to be needed everywhere. The local VC were getting ballsy, popping away at them all day, then making a stand in the long shadows of afternoon when they knew their air support had to be back. In an abandoned village they came across warm coals, a panic of footprints ending at the well. They ran a full battalion sweep with a lieutenant colonel in a C-and-C chopper calling the shots and captured twenty enemy, stringing them together by the necks with det cord.

They started running into some weird shit. On patrol, they stumbled over a mile-long tunnel filled with American equipment, the limestone rooms piled with helmets and ponchos and canteens, all of it brand-new issue; after they made sure the gear wasn't booby-trapped, they traded in their old fatigues. The jackets all had the name JOHNSON above the breast pocket, and for a few days they called to each other, "Yo, Johnson," and "Hey, J."

At dusk the Psy-Ops planes flew low over the jungle, broadcasting a tape of broken music and ghostly moans, an old woman jabbering in Vietnamese. Operation Wandering Soul, the program was called. The VC were supposed to think it was the voices of disappointed ancestors and surrender; instead, they sent up streams of green tracers.

It was hard to come up with anything scarier than the land—the misted hills and unplumbed caves—but the enemy succeeded. In one dense section of the valley, the Martian slowed and raised a fist in the air to stop the column. On the trail ahead stood three empty sets of boots. The trees on both sides were hung with ornaments; from nylon line dangled a toothbrush, an afro pick, a ballpoint pen. Pony refused to go any farther, and the lieutenant said fuck it and turned them around. The next day Magoo had his glasses shot off, and Smart Andy's hair began to fall out in clumps again.

Bates came back, delivered to them by resupply chopper east of Stupidville. He looked skinnier and didn't ask Carl Metcalf for his thumper. They gave him shit about his Purple Heart and made jokes about the *head* nurse. Bates grinned but didn't laugh. His pack was chunky with books, and when they stopped for coffee, he offered Larry a tea bag. He fit himself into his regular place in the column as if nothing had changed, but they watched him.

"Gotta make sure he's a Johnson," Nate said.

"What can happen after a guy gets hit," Dumb Andy explained, "is he gets gun-shy," and so they waited to see what he'd do when they made contact.

A few days later they were moving through a paddy when they took some fire from a friendly village. No one was hit, but they all dropped into the water behind a dike. It was a lone VC with an old carbine—an M-2, Fred the Head guessed. Rounds whirred high above them. "Just pathetic," Magoo said. Beside Larry, Bates poked his head up and ducked down again. Carl Metcalf let loose, and Magoo, blindly. Larry mimicked him, holding his rifle above the dike, fighting the recoil with his forearms. When he changed magazines, Bates still hadn't moved.

While they searched the hootches, Carl Metcalf asked Larry how Bates had made out, and Larry told him.

"But he looked," Carl Metcalf asked, as if it were evidence. "He stuck his head up."

They didn't give Bates shit about it or ask to see his scar. Larry was unsure whether they were concerned or just being polite. He'd never had someone come back before.

After finding a cache of mortar rounds and five hundred pounds of dried rats, they earned a two-day stand-down. With the piasters from the dead VC, Bogut had finagled a pallet of *Ba-Moui-Ba* beer from down south. He'd gone to a lot of trouble arranging it and was hurt when they asked him what else had been available. Bammy-bam, they called it, or just "33." It was the Vietnamese answer to Budweiser and tasted like formaldehyde; panther piss, they called it, but they drank it until it was gone and thanked Bogut.

They slept and read and got laid in the village. Bates fashioned a staff out of bamboo and every morning practiced slow-motion turns up beyond the connex box. He'd missed the lice but had Pony shave his head smooth. He arranged an audience with the priest of the village temple and came back with two new books and a flowing purple robe, which he wore the next morning for his exercises and then did not take off until he went to bed. People gawked at him as he crossed the compound. Larry thought the lieutenant would come down on him, but he didn't.

Though Bates ate seconds of beans and peas and rice, his ribs and hip bones showed, and again the lieutenant came to Larry and asked him to do a physical. Larry took Bates behind the lieutenant's mosquito netting. His robe smelled of cloves and incense. "I'm fine," he protested, and other than his gums bleeding, he was.

"So he's gone native," Smart Andy said, accepting it.

"I thought we were done with this shit," Nate said.

"Just keep an eye on him," the lieutenant asked Carl Metcalf, who then deputized Larry and Magoo.

It wouldn't take long. They were making contact every other day now, just skirmishes of a minute or so, but the feeling around Odin was that by Thanksgiving they would hit the shit. You could hear it in the quiet in the mess tent, in the constant artillery. A football game between second and third platoon turned into hand-to-hand, and while trying to break it up, Dumb Andy took an elbow to the nose. It wasn't bad, he said, and Larry packed it with gauze, but the next day he woke up with two black eyes. Larry taped it and, before they went out, painted the white square with camo grease.

It was a night sweep. Echo was the anvil. Before dawn, they set up outside of Duc Pao, at the edge of a pepper field, the river at their back. They stayed the day under strict noise discipline, eating cold Cs and pissing where they lay. That night the rest of the battalion was inserted above the village, rolled down the mountainside and drew a cordon. As they tightened it, a gunship dropped several basketball flares to make sure no VC could break through. Echo saw all this from a distance. They heard bursts of gunfire, heavy weapons, and minutes later a platoon of NVA came tearing across the field, their pith helmets bobbing.

Larry lay in the dirt, his eye to the sight of his rifle, listening to his own breathing and the rustle of the leaves. There must have been thirty of them, and Echo was stretched out one deep. The ground beneath him trembled as they closed on the woodline. Carl Metcalf was supposed to start and they would all follow, but he held off. The enemy were so close Larry could hear their gear rattling, their grunts and curses. He trained his rifle on the bushy end of a row. A pair of canvas boots churned the dirt, headed directly for him, and finally Carl Metcalf let loose, and then the rest of the platoon. The man fell but the rest kept coming. A number swerved and broke the line of Delta company farther up, and the lieutenant had them turn and pursue the enemy through the woods.

A few were in the river, trying to swim for the other side, but with the monsoons, the water was high and swept them downstream, right in front of first platoon. Larry stood on the bank, Bates beside him. The NVA were spent from the run; only their heads were visible in the silver light of the flares. They floated on the water like buoys cut adrift, occasionally a hand flailing. The platoon hesitated, gauged the current and the angle of the bank as if solving a physics problem. Someone opened up on the man nearest shore, walking a splashing line of fire across the water until it hit him, bursting his head like a pumpkin. Now Pony had the big gun going, and the others were pitching in. The river seethed.

Larry waited for Bates. Neither had taken aim yet, and he knew people would be looking. Toward the far shore a man slid by in their line of fire. Bates lifted his rifle to his eye and a tracer blazed from the muzzle, the red line streaking into the far bank. He was not off by much but didn't compensate, because the next tracer ripped into the same spot, and the next, and then the two in a row that signaled the end of the magazine. Behind him, Carl Metcalf glared at his back, then spat.

Above Leonard Dawson's ring, Bates's face was placid, blank, as if he'd forgotten what they'd done to his friend, or forgiven them. Larry met his eyes to let him know that he'd seen him, then turned and, as his father had taught him, sighted on the man's head. He had a second to contemplate what he was doing and why. Later he would think that while Bates had been strong enough to give himself a choice, it was one he made only for himself, while Larry's was against his own heart and for the people he loved—for Leonard Dawson and Salazar and the rest of them it was his job to keep alive, whatever the means. The man floated downstream; the flare dimmed and faded. Larry fixed his breathing and stuck his first round dead on target.

He looked to Bates but he'd turned his face away, as had Carl Metcalf.

"Skull's fucking hard, man," Fred the Head said back at Odin the next morning. He was high and philosophizing. "One shot—bing! It's like him and Bates traded places—fucking spooky shit."

"Stone killer," Magoo seconded.

"See?" Nate said. "Get wet, it's just a matter of time. Ain't that right, Skull?"

In his bunk Larry said nothing.

"Jesus Christ," Nate said. "Everyone's gettin' sensitive all of a sudden. It's a fucking war."

Larry got up and went outside and climbed the hill past the connex box. Bates sat cross-legged beneath his spirit house, his robe flapping in the wind. Larry hesitated, but Bates waved him on and he couldn't escape.

"I saw what you left," Bates said.

"I can take it out."

"It's okay." Bates grinned as if nothing was wrong.

Larry felt strange standing, exposed, and squatted down beside him, one hand on the ground for balance. "What happened yesterday—" he began, hoping Bates would finish for him. When he didn't, Larry had to start again. "I'm sorry about what happened yesterday."

"Why," Bates said. "You did what you thought was right."

"I'm not sure," Larry said. "I don't know why I did it. I didn't think everything out. It had something to do with Leonard—with everything, I guess."

"I understand," Bates said, but he couldn't have, because Larry hadn't been able to explain it correctly. As he squatted there with the wind making the flags snap, he thought that maybe he never would.

"There are no accidents," Bates said. "What you think becomes what you do, which is who you are. Everything begins inside and goes outward."

Larry wanted to ask if this applied to Leonard Dawson, but kept silent, nodded as Bates explained how karma worked. The mosquitoes had been bad by the river, and he clawed at the bumps on his arms. Bates seemed unconcerned with the dead man, the way his head caved in like a rotten pumpkin. Good deeds were rewarded with good karma. He made it sound like a form of currency. After a point Larry quit listening. He'd thought that talking with Bates would help, that this was something between them, but when he walked down the hill, Larry understood it was his alone.

That afternoon the resupply chopper brought ice cream. It was soup by the time the mess let them in. The platoon passed Larry to the front of the line, and he knew why.

"You like strawberry?" the lieutenant said, too enthusiastic.

"Yessir," Larry said, though he didn't. He finished his first and sat there scratching.

The itching kept him from sleep. In the morning the scabs caught in his fingernails and he bled. He dabbed on antiseptic and bandaged them, pulled his sleeves to his wrists.

"Don't second-guess yourself," Carl Metcalf said. "You did the right thing. Let him slide and we have to come back and get him the hard way."

"I know," Larry said, because that wasn't it.

"The guys need to be sure of you," Carl Metcalf said. "We've got enough problems with Bates freaking out."

"I'm okay," Larry said.

"No," Carl said, "but it's normal. It's no different for anybody else."

"That's good," Larry said, and added a laugh so he would leave him alone.

They didn't have time to baby him. The NVA were pouring into the valley from Laos. Intelligence had sightings of truck convoys creeping south at night, but in the morning all they found were oil spots, tracks with no beginning or end. The Marines had nicknamed the major highway down the valley the Yellow Brick Road. "Follow, follow, follow, follow," Fred the Head sang in the liftship.

The damp of the jungle softened Larry's scabs; he peeled them off, leaving pink spots in his tan. They worked the high ground, humping ridges and crossing rocky saddles, their only contact an occasional Montagnard village. Yards, Pony said; tough little fuckers, hunt every day of their lives. They made false insertions to confuse the enemy, dropping into LZs and hovering as if letting men off. The Air Force had provided them with a selection, dropping bombs called daisy cutters; they were the size of Volkswagens and flattened everything for a fifty-meter radius.

Their third day out they found a tiger that had triggered a mine. It had bled to death from a neck wound, and Dumb Andy wanted to skin it, but the underside was thick with leeches.

A few hours later, third platoon made contact with a bunker and called in napalm. By the time the Phantoms arrived, first platoon had taken a blocking position in case the NVA ran. Flames rolled over the jungle, left them breathless, their cheeks stinging. Leaves crackled and soared, borne by the heat. People were screaming but not in the bunker. In the trees behind it a colony of monkeys raced flickering through the branches, shrieking, their skin blistered.

Carl Metcalf fired first. Larry had promised himself not to use his weapon again unless he was threatened but couldn't listen to them. Only Bates didn't pitch in; he was still standing there with his rifle slung when they finished.

"Bad fucking karma, huh?" Nate asked, and walked away.

It was the only time Larry noticed any real anger toward him. For the most part, the platoon pitied him, treated him like a touched uncle, someone who'd once been well but was now beyond recovery. It wasn't a mystery; they'd all seen Leonard Dawson. It was sad that he'd snapped, but nothing to hold against him, though they were tired of his ramblings on Nirvana. Dumb Andy inherited his thumper, and on patrol it fell to Magoo to make sure he had good cover. Because he would not fire, they expected he'd be killed, when logically, Smart Andy said, it didn't change the odds.

"He's already dead," Pony observed, and no one argued with him.

Some of them asked the lieutenant to get rid of the dud—for his own good—but they were so undermanned he couldn't; he was hoping Bates would snap out of it. He'd seen it before, he said, and they had enough faith in him to wait and see.

They ran patrols and night ambushes and slow, painstaking cordons in the rain. They hadn't taken fire for a while, which made them nervous. They were tired, and little shit started happening. The Martian stepped in a hidden punji pit but came away with just a sprained ankle; Larry wrapped it in an Ace bandage, and for two jittery days they humped the jungle with Nate on point. While Bogut was eating a can of pears, a wasp stung him on the lip; it blew up as if he'd been in a fistfight, a node hard as a marble. A wait-a-minute vine pulled the pin out of a smoke canister on Fred the Head's web gear; a lavender plume went up, burning his ear and dyeing his hair purple.

"Get your heads out of your asses," the lieutenant shouted. He'd called a special meeting and stalked between the cots like a coach giving his team a pep talk. "Because you know and I know that pretty soon this shit is going to stop being funny."

Larry wanted to argue with him. It wasn't that they weren't concentrating, just waiting for something bigger.

Susan wrote and apologized for their father. He would write when he was able, she said. Their mother was in the hospital and doing better there. Nothing had happened, they just decided it was best, meaning Susan had gotten through to him. It was a gift Larry didn't have. Their father had taken a few days off. If it weren't for the way Mrs. Railsbeck takes care of him, she said. It was almost funny; Larry couldn't believe she didn't know. She'd been gone so long, and before then all she thought about was herself. Maybe it was because it was so obvious that she'd missed it—how she fixed his hair before letting him go out, the way he wanted them to call her Maddy.

The letter was three weeks old. Larry meant to write back immediately, but they went out. The real monsoon season was here, the lieutenant said, as if the last two months had been a tune-up. It was cold now, the sky the depressing gray of March in Ithaca. Streams surged brown down the mountains, sweeping along debris. Only their faces poked out of the olive ponchos; Pony had trouble keeping his cigar lit. Larry kept his writing kit in a plastic baggie tucked inside the webbing of his helmet liner, but the weather never broke, and it stayed there.

In the middle of all this came Thanksgiving dinner and a chopper full of reporters. Echo had just begun a four-day patrol when—as if someone had called a time-out—they were extracted by liftship to Odin. They were glad but confused. They'd gotten pony but there was nothing for Larry. The lieutenant called him in behind the netting and let him know his request for emergency leave had been turned down. Larry had expected it, but still it hurt.

"Should I write up another?" the lieutenant asked.

"No," Larry said, then, "yes," and thanked him.

A blond-bearded photographer stood behind the serving line in the mess tent, snapping away as the cooks ladled stringy turkey and powdered potatoes on their trays, then went around to the tables. Bates wouldn't touch the stuffing because it had giblets in it. The food was hot and there was pumpkin pie for dessert, but after a few bites Larry felt sick.

"Come on," Nate said. "It's your favorite."

The photographer came to their table and asked how they were doing.

"Okay," Bogut said, but the Martian gave him the finger and wouldn't put it down, and the photographer moved off.

"Real nice," Pony said. "I bet your folks are proud."

Back at the hootch, Larry wrote to his father and then Susan. *I'm fine*, he said. *Please let me know what's going on there. I'm doing everything I can here to get home.* He wrote FREE where the stamp was supposed to go and sealed them, wondering if what he'd said was true or if his father had been right. In a way it was easier to be here.

The rain kept them in for a day, but when the ceiling lifted to a few hundred feet, they went out, looking for a Shithook that had crashed. The slicks put them down in a Montagnard meadow and they raced for the treeline. Carl Metcalf hit a patch of water buffalo shit and wrenched his knee; it blew up like a softball but he refused to be medevac'ed. Larry wrapped it tight, gave him two Darvon and all day watched him hobble. The trees dripped leeches like worms; they stopped to burn them off with bug juice and cigarettes.

As the gray of afternoon dimmed into evening, they came upon the remains of the chopper. It lay on its side in a clearing, saplings bent beneath it. They secured the area while the Martian climbed in to look for survivors. It hadn't burned but the fuselage was twisted like a beer can, the skin stitched with silver cracks. An arc of bullet holes ran along the belly, chips of OD paint still clinging to the punctures. The Martian crawled out holding a soaked *Playboy*; they passed it around while he explained the situation. The copilot was dead, still strapped in his seat, a real mess. There was no other gear, nothing.

"The others got out," he said, "or someone got them out."

"Must have been in a hurry," Magoo said, and showed them the centerfold.

"Maybe the Yards got them," Smart Andy said.

"Let's hope so," the lieutenant said. He and the Martian checked the acetate map and they headed for the village. It was coming down harder now. To save time they could take a trail, but the lieutenant decided to play it safe and they dug in for the night. Bates couldn't pull watch, and, sitting in the rain with a bag of grenades in his lap, Larry wished him gone.

They ate cold Cs for breakfast and made the village in less than an hour. The Martian brought them in slowly, keeping to the treeline. The huts weren't burned but the place was deserted, no motion whatsoever. Larry had only seen a few Montagnard villages before but thought it strange there were no lice-ridden chickens rooting around. All they could hear was the rain and the buzz of insects.

"Something's fucked up," Pony said.

They smelled it as they neared the first hut, the same stench of rendered fat Larry remembered from the Arc Light strike. Inside lay three Yards—a man, a woman and a little boy. The boy's feet had been shot off. His parents were bound with wire, one on each side of him; though Larry didn't see an entry wound, the backs of their heads were gone.

"In the mouth," Magoo explained.

"Fuckers," Bates said. He was breathing hard through his teeth, and Magoo gave Larry a worried look, shrugged as if he didn't know what was up.

"Gotta be VC," Smart Andy said. "The NVA don't pull this kind of shit."

Fred the Head bet him ten dollars.

The man in the next hut had been decapitated. His heart had been chopped out and stuck on the sharp end of his neck.

"Hey, Skull," Dumb Andy called. "We got us a head amputee here."

"You're okay," Nate said, imitating Larry. He patted the body on the shoulder. "I seen guys a lot worse."

Next was a pregnant woman, gutted and hung by the heels from the rafters. The killers had severed one breast and shoved it in the mouth of the fetus. Muttering, Bates cut her down with his K-bar; the rest of them left.

In the main hut in the middle of the village, they found the pilot and the crew chief and a heap of Montagnards. The fliers were buried upside-down at the waist, their bruised legs jutting from the earth, ankles staked far apart. They'd been raped and beaten; their scrotums had swollen to the size of canteloupes. Flies lifted from them in clouds, then resettled. While the lieutenant called in, a few men unfolded their entrenching tools and began digging them out. When Bates returned from the hut, he had his weapon at the ready.

"You watch him," Carl Metcalf whispered to Larry, then went to Magoo, who nodded.

They tracked the VC all day, staying fifteen meters off a high-speed trail, cutting through the brush. When the Martian's arms got tired, he traded the machete with Nate and they kept on. They were making too much noise, and the lieutenant told them to slow down. No one seemed to care; they wanted contact. Larry was undecided. He wanted to kill someone but kept seeing the man in the river. If they really hit the shit, he'd have to get to the wounded; he probably wouldn't have time to fire. Behind him, Bates scanned the jungle on both sides without turning his head.

The ridgeline narrowed and they came to a bamboo footbridge over a steep ravine. Below, a stream leaped and shattered on black rocks. It was a natural spot to leave a rear guard, the lieutenant said, but the Martian argued him into letting him go over. The rest of the platoon would provide cover fire. Even Larry could see it was dumb.

The Martian made it, slowly, checking for wires, and then Nate, protecting his midsection like a scatback. Pony went over, lugging the big gun, with Smart Andy right behind, using him as a shield. The lieutenant busted it across, and they all laughed. It was a stupid thing to try, but to actually have it work was ridiculous, as if both the rules of the universe and everything they knew were worthless.

Bogut was in the center of the bridge when a round hit him in the canteen. Larry hadn't seen a muzzle flash. Beside him, Bates let go a burst of six. Larry followed his tracers into the brush and, without thinking, laid a stream of suppressing fire on top of them. Carl Metcalf blooped in a white phosphorous grenade; it exploded like a Roman candle, and the men on the other side poured rounds into the smoke. Bogut was running with his head down, his antenna jerking, slapping his calves. He threw himself on the ground, and Dumb Andy took off across. Larry left his position and crouched by the near end as Carl Metcalf dashed over, then got a grip on his sixteen and tore for the other side, the bridge swinging like a funhouse floor beneath his feet. He sprinted past Carl Metcalf and hit the mud, clicked his safety off and emptied a magazine into the treeline.

When they were all across, the lieutenant called for them to check fire. A bird chirped; the stream rushed over the rocks below. They covered the Martian and Nate into the trees while Larry checked out Bogut. The round had punched a hole in the canteen; his hip bone showed a new bruise but otherwise he was unhurt. His legs were wet; at first Larry thought Bogut had just pissed his pants, which he had, but some of it was dark—cherry Kool-Aid, he said. The canteen rattled. Larry unscrewed the cap and handed the wet slug to him. Bogut held it between his fingers like a pearl but said nothing, and Larry checked him for shock. He was all right, just frightened. The lieutenant pulled a flask out of his pack and gave him a sip of whiskey.

From the woods Nate called for them to come see. The sniper's chest was mush. His papers said he was Le Tranh Nguyen, main-force VC. Bates ran over to him, shouted "Fuck you!" into his face and kicked him in the head. Blood splashed over Magoo's boots.

"Hey, Johnson," Pony said, hard, as if to stop him, then softened. "Good to have you back."

They radioed in the contact and re-formed, mirroring the trail. A cliff ran alongside them, the drop visible whenever the land narrowed. Larry kept looking back at Bates. He had been right to fire this time, yet it still bothered him, which made him angry with himself. He was angry with Bates too—but again, for no reason he could think of.

Ahead, the trail intersected the cliff briefly and they had to walk along it. Larry ignored the view, tracking Carl Metcalf's footsteps.

Ahead, Bogut tripped, said, "Shit," and dove for cover. Dumb Andy hesitated, and then a deafening flash lifted him into the air and flung him over Carl Metcalf. Larry turned and began to run after him, as if to catch a pass well overthrown. A dark object shot by and struck Bates in the head. Bates dropped his weapon and grabbed his face with both hands, but Larry could not stop.

The mine had blown Dumb Andy's poncho off and most of his clothes. His right leg was gone above the knee, the stump gushing into the dirt. The bone was shiny white, the end jagged as a snapped branch. Larry whipped his belt off and knotted it tightly, cutting off some of the flow, but not enough.

"Skull," Dumb Andy said. "How'm I doin'?" The tape on his nose was untouched.

"Doin' all right," Larry said, and dug through his bag for a dressing. He packed the big bleeders, and still it came, pulsing.

"How'm I doin'?" Dumb Andy said sleepily.

"All right," Larry said.

He didn't ask again.

Larry moved to Bates, who was still clutching his face, rocking back and forth. Blood poured through his fingers, ran down his arms. "Oh Jesus," he repeated.

"Let me see," Larry ordered, and yanked his wrists apart.

A flap of scalp hung down over his eyes like a caul, the skull clean beneath it. The wound was bloody but superficial. His pupils were two different sizes. Larry was sure it hurt, but because of the concussion couldn't give him morphine. He dusted the wound with antibiotics, fit the lips together and gently pressed a dressing over it, then wrapped a bandage around his ears and under his jaw.

"It hurts," Bates groaned.

"You're all right," Larry said, and squeezed his bicep so he could feel it. "You're okay."

Pony showed him Dumb Andy's leg, still in the boot. It was what had hit Bates, the bone laying him open. Pony handed it to Larry as if it belonged to him. In a way it did, and Larry took it over to where Dumb Andy lay under someone's poncho and put it where it was supposed to go.

The lieutenant asked Larry to come over and look at Bogut, who was still sitting on the ground. His eyes were dilated and his pulse thumping; he was in shock. All Larry could do for him was give him a drink and tell the lieutenant to put away the flask.

While the lieutenant searched for the right frequency, Larry uncoupled his helmet and liner and scooped up enough water from puddles to wash the blood from his hands. It would not come off. When he held them under, a filmy veil rose from one palm. A shallow gash sliced across his lifeline. He'd taken a piece of shrapnel or cut it on something. As he bandaged himself, he realized it must have been on the stub of Dumb Andy's femur.

The dust-off couldn't land on the ridge so they had to hump Dumb Andy back to the village, taking turns shouldering the ends of the pole. He was wet and heavy and swung with their rhythm, and the bamboo dug into their skin.

In the village they put out security. The lieutenant stayed with Bates and Bogut and left Larry to bag the effects of the dead. All Dumb Andy had on was one boot and his flak jacket; in the pocket over his heart Larry found a toy soldier, a cheap one made of green plastic. The soldier was marching with his rifle slung, completely unprepared. He had a helmet and a pack and a canteen, even a piece of green ground that kept him upright. Larry turned it in his fingers. It had a vague face, and on the bottom said MADE IN HONG KONG. The thought that this was a toy for children mystified him. He put it and the St. Michael medal into a plastic bag and tied it around Dumb Andy's wrist, then wrote up a tag with the how and when and where and wired it to his one remaining button.

The lieutenant said Bogut was feeling better, and it was true, his pulse was back to normal, his pupils the right size. Bates had gone silent, the blood seeping through the seams of Larry's bandages. The dust-off came in, skimming water off the puddles, and they loaded the two on and watched it away.

"Nothing you could do," Carl Metcalf told Bogut.

"Yeah," Fred the Head said, but unconvincingly, and in the slick on the way back to Odin, Bogut sat hunched over, staring at the floor.

"Here we go again," Nate said, and Pony punched him hard in the arm and waited for him to say something else.

That evening, battalion threw them a barbecue, complete with potato salad and cold beer. It was spitting, the smoke of the hamburgers seasoning the air. After the blessing, the artillery started. Only the lieutenant and Bogut didn't come, though no one mentioned them. The whole thing seemed inappropriate to Larry—his fingernails were dark with congealed blood—but after his fifth Miller High Life he didn't give a shit. The burgers were delicious; he had three.

IT DIDN'T FEEL like Christmas, because the rains had ended, gave way to muggy heat. The cooks made fake eggnog and decorated a pine outside the wire, but by midday their clothes were soaked and flies landed in their hair. Both sides called a truce neither believed in. The platoon hadn't seen contact in weeks. They ran day patrols and came back covered with red dust. Christmas dinner was the same as Thanksgiving, just a different group of newsmen.

Vicki asked why he hadn't written in so long. She sent him a box of crushed Toll House cookies; he shared it, and while they were chowing down, Fred the Head bit into a ring. It was a plain silver band with their names engraved inside, and XMAS 68. Larry had lost weight and it was too big for everything but his thumb. All he'd sent her were two rolls of film he'd had Magoo shoot. He wrapped adhesive tape around the ring until it fit and wrote her a long letter.

Susan had mailed his gifts on time but they didn't arrive until New Year's —paperbacks and socks and Johnson's Baby Powder. He'd asked for a better pair of tweezers, and his father sent him a zippered leather kit with six different sizes; they were old, the steel gone dusky, the name of the company German. Mrs. Railsbeck made fudge for him; it had melted and reformed, taking on the shape of the box. There was nothing from his mother.

She would be home for Christmas, Susan wrote, and indefinitely after that. The hospital was too noisy for her, too confusing. She seemed the same but no worse. She would never be able to read again. Susan would stay and look after her, take her old room; why not, she said, the year was shot anyway. Their father needed her. Mrs. Railsbeck was upset; one afternoon Susan found her sobbing on the floor of the pantry. Everything was falling apart, she wrote; she wished he were there. They were all worried about him. They needed to hear from him, so could he please, please write them a letter?

Larry added the fudge to the untouched boxes on the table—the gluey peanut brittle from Pony's aunts and the Santa Claus cookies from Dumb Andy's mother. She had sent a tape, which the lieutenant listened to before writing her the letter. Dead Andy, they called him now, though not in front of Bogut.

A third-grade class from Carl Metcalf's old school in Syracuse sent him a batch of letters. Everyone but the Martian took a few to answer. *I hope you win*, one of Larry's said, *because you are very brave. Do you shoot people?* The boy had drawn a soldier firing a revolver, a dotted line following the bullet.

Thank you for your letter, Larry printed neatly. As he lingered over the next sentence, unsure how much he should explain, he realized no one else had asked him this question yet and that he could not answer it. *I am from Ithaca*, he wrote: *I miss the snow*.

Bates came back with his forehead stitched like a baseball, his hair bristly. His eyes were sunken, his cheekbones flared. He said hello and checked in with the lieutenant, put his robe on and climbed the hill.

"Tell you," Magoo said, "that dude's giving the skipper a serious case of the ass."

The next day the company received a warning order for a mission farther down the valley, reopening an abandoned firebase.

"You know what that means," Nate said glumly.

"More Tinker Toys," Fred the Head said.

"What happened to old Mr. Gung Ho?" Smart Andy said.

"Hey, I'll play hide-and-seek with the motherfuckers anytime," Nate said. "It's this Easter egg hunt shit that pisses me off."

Carl Metcalf said the VC would have definitely booby-trapped the helipad and the bunkers. He took Larry around the side of the tent and showed him how the VC stuck a grenade between two sandbags. A full fuse gave you enough time to swat it away before it blew; if they filed them down, you were screwed. He showed Larry how to find them with a bayonet, what they sounded like.

"Should I practice some?" Larry asked.

"Why?" Carl Metcalf said. "We're going to be doing it all day tomorrow."

That night the lieutenant threw up in his bunk. Against his own advice to them, he'd eaten in the village, at a roadside stand they called HoJo's. He'd split a whole fish steamed in a banana leaf and a bowl of rice smothered in *nuoc mam* sauce with the district chief, and now he couldn't keep anything down. Larry stayed up with him, patting his back and emptying the bucket, giving him Lomatil and sips of water.

The next morning he was still spitting when the liftships came in, and though Carl Metcalf said he could take them, the lieutenant climbed on. It was cool in the Hueys, and Larry thought that might help. He had learned to distrust the beauty of the jungle and watched it flow beneath them, unimpressed. Smart Andy was playing a miniature pinball machine he'd received for Christmas, the BB bouncing out of the plastic scoring brackets; he sighed and frisbeed it out the door. As they spiraled in, no one looked at each other. Bates fastened his chinstrap. Bogut gnawed his lower lip.

The birds hovered and they piled off. Second platoon was already down and fanned out for security. Redmond knelt beside the radioman, empty-handed. The base was smaller than Odin, a maze of bunkers and sandbagged revetments atop a narrow ridge. Battalion had sent three combat engineers to sweep the area; they wore headsets and ran metal detectors over the dirt, holding up a gloved hand when they found something. One did nothing but the helipad; he found a signal and cordoned it off with white engineer tape. They did the bunkers and the gun emplacements while the rest of them checked the sandbags along the perimeter.

The platoon stood clear while Carl Metcalf did one first. He slid the bayonet in, cocked his head as if listening. "The idea," he explained, "is to knock it into the wire where it can't hurt anyone. Get a good grip on the bag and lift it, then sweep the grenade away from you with your right hand— lefties turn it around. Think of a bat hitting a ball."

He knelt by the wall and signaled them to get down. He picked a bag on the top, laid his hand on it and yanked it up. There was nothing, but he swung his other hand through and then hugged the dirt. "Okay?" he said, and when no one answered, assigned them sections of the wall. The lieutenant was missing; without him, Bogut seemed defenseless.

Larry stalled, taking off his aid bag so he could swing freely. Nate was on one side of him, Smart Andy on the other. The first explosions startled them, and they laughed.

"This is the kind of shit I really hate," Nate said.

Smart Andy squeezed his hands together, flexed his fingers like a magician before a trick.

Larry fit his bayonet into the crack between the top two bags and listened for the clink. There was nothing, but he sheathed the bayonet anyway. He grabbed the bag and lifted—it was heavier than he'd thought, waterlogged— and swept his hand across the top. Though he didn't hit anything, a whimper escaped his lips. He unsheathed the bayonet.

"Got one here," Nate said. He waved Larry back and, on his far side, Bogut. He pulled the bag away and whacked the grenade into the dirt berm. Larry followed it like a batted ball, almost forgetting to duck before it went off. It was a smooth-skinned M-26—U.S. issue.

"How you like that?" Nate asked.

Larry turned to him, about to say "Just like your buddy Curt Flood," with just enough sarcasm, when a second grenade went off at Nate's feet.

For an instant, Larry didn't move, as if it were a trick, a joke he was supposed to fall for. Nate ran from the blast, one boot flopping like a horse's snapped foreleg. He staggered through the smoke a few steps before Bogut tackled him.

Larry grabbed his aid bag and raced to them. Nate kept trying to get up; Bogut had to hold him by the shoulders. The foot dangled by a tendon. Larry checked for shock and got some morphine into Nate, and he relaxed. The blood wasn't as bad as Dumb Andy. He tied him off with his belt and sprinkled the stump with antibiotics.

"I fucked up, Skull," Nate said.

"It's nothing," Larry said. "You'll be back in a month, two months tops."

Nate smiled, his eyes glazed. "I didn't think it was gonna be like this." He laughed. "A fuckin' foot, that's funny, huh?"

"You're gonna be all right."

"A fuckin' foot."

Larry looked up to see if Bogut was on the horn yet.

"Goddamn stupid," Nate said, and began to cry.

The lieutenant came over to see how he was, and Carl Metcalf, who patted him on the shoulder. Grenades blew in the wire, making Larry flinch.

The dust-off only took a few minutes, but as it came in, the jungle below the base crackled with AK fire and everyone except the stretcher bearers hit it. Green tracers flitted overhead.

Larry and Pony and Bates and Carl Metcalf hoisted Nate onto the floor of the chopper and bailed. A round struck a hydraulic line, spattering them with greasy fluid. The engine shuddered and smoked. The bird dipped its nose and went into a tight climbing turn, chased by a swarm of fire. It rose steadily and then wobbled, stalled, the tail boom swinging. The platoon was returning fire now, using the sandbags as cover. A rocket screamed past, its fins slowly spinning. It struck with a flash below the rotor, and the bird yawed crazily, tipping the litter out the door.

Nate fell with his arms flailing, as if trying to fly, followed by the chopper, dropping sideways. The rotors snapped on impact, fragments pinwheeling through the air. The fuselage seemed to bounce when it hit, exploded and rose into the air again, then settled and burned.

They didn't find Nate and they had no way of putting out the flames, so the lieutenant told Larry and Carl Metcalf to secure the area and stand clear till it burned itself out. Larry thought Carl would have something to say, but they just looked at each other as if one of them should start.

"There it is," Carl Metcalf said, meaning they would not talk, that words were useless now.

"Guy was going home. I had him fixed up."

"Never happen."

"Story of my life," Larry said. It was easier this way, not really thinking.

Later, when the wreckage had cooled, they got the bodies. The pilot's visor had melted onto his skin. His arm had burst open like a charred hot dog.

"You're going to have a lot of fun getting the effects off these guys," Carl said.

"These guys aren't mine."

"Who's going to do it then?"

"Beats me," Larry said. "Not my job." He could do this all day.

They found Nate under the rotor housing. His lips had burned off and his tongue was black. Carl Metcalf went to get a bag and Larry sat down.

"This is the kind of shit I really hate," he said, but Nate didn't laugh.

Carl came sprinting back, waving, and Larry got up. "The old man says they need you over there. Third platoon got into it."

He ran across the compound, sure it was Redmond who'd been hit.

Bogut pointed Larry down the maze of revetments. A path cleared for him. A private from third platoon was waiting at the perimeter. They clawed through the wire and slid down the hill into the jungle, ducked through the brush. A clump of men were milling around, smoking. The air stank of cordite. At the base of a tree, Redmond knelt over someone, the wounded man's boots kicking feebly.

Larry slid in on the other side. Redmond looked to him as if for a second opinion. Larry didn't recognize the man. He'd taken several rounds to the chest and one in the throat. Redmond had done a tracheostomy and stuck an airway in, but the man's eyes were rolled back. He had a lung full of blood.

"The kicking's not real," Larry said.

"I know," Redmond said, and Larry understood what he wanted.

"No," Larry said.

"He's dead."

"You get him ready to go," Larry ordered him, then turned and walked through the man's friends and up the hill.

Carl Metcalf already had Nate in the bag.

"What's up?" he asked.

"Nothing," Larry said, "same-same," and picked up one end. The lightness surprised him, and Larry thought it was all psychological. They weren't that heavy once you got used to them.

SEVEN

Only one of Ida Sizemore's neighbors remembered her; the rest had either died or moved away. She was in a retirement home. The man didn't open the screen door for Larry. His head was mottled with age spots; flesh-colored hearing aids filled his ears. He crossed his arms and pinched his lips together, trying to bring back the name of the place.

"It's not Lakeview but something just like that—Hillview or Cityview, I don't know. One of the ones up by the hospital. She's been there for years. It's a shame, she didn't have any family. Crestview?"

"Did she ever mention a grandson?" Larry asked.

"The one in the war. She had a big picture of him on the TV. Good-looking kid, smart too. It just broke her heart. She didn't have anyone then. By the end we couldn't watch her anymore. The fire department was over there every other day. She had the Meals on Wheels, and Lena would look in on her, but . . . Cayuga View—that's it."

"You're sure?"

"Cayuga View," the man said. "Don't know how I forgot it so quick. I remembered it right off for that fellow the other day."

Larry did a sloppy job at the 7-Eleven in Varna and at the pay phone outside looked the place up. He blew off his stops in town, caught the light at the Octopus and gunned Number 1 uphill. He turned the radio off so he could think.

He didn't know what he should ask Ida Sizemore—about Creeley's childhood maybe, or where he might go to hole up, where his favorite places were. Larry knew it wouldn't be that simple. You couldn't come at someone like Creeley head-on. It was like trying to find the enemy. You had to sneak up on him, see him before he saw you, then ambush the motherfucker. It took someone with the inhuman cool of the Martian, the saint's patience of Carl Metcalf. Larry wasn't sure he could do it. The detective was a kind of point man; he was supposed to step lightly and find clues. Clines hadn't done squat yet, but he was a professional; his questions led somewhere, made you think of a bigger picture. So far all Larry had come up with were scattered bits of information, cards Creeley had forced into his hands.

He knew Cayuga View. He'd passed the sign for years, barely noting the low motel-like complex, the concrete walks between the wings. The bus stop out front was empty. It was warm today, and the groundskeepers were taking advantage of the weather, guiding their riding mowers over the grass one last time. Otherwise there was no one outside. Larry had the run of the parking lot.

He stepped on the rubber mat and the front doors swung open. Inside, the air was stifling with flowers. The carpet gave under his feet. The lobby reminded him of a hotel—gilded mirrors and wingback chairs, a dried flower arrangement on a drop-leaf table. A receptionist sat behind a plexiglas window with a hole cut in it, as if selling tickets. Larry gave her the name.

"Are you family?"

"Yes," Larry said. He had his Hostess uniform on, but she didn't seem interested. She gave him the room number, stuck her hand through the hole and pointed.

He turned down one wing and the carpeting gave way to linoleum, a hall like a hospital's—open doors and low fluorescents, walls the color of vanilla pudding. A tepid heat closed over him, and a chorus of TVs all tuned to the same soap opera. Against the wall, a balding woman dozed in her wheelchair, a plastic tag about her wrist. Farther on, at the nurse's station, three orderlies gathered around a chocolate sheet cake, laughing. As Larry passed one room, a man groaned, "My ass, my ass," as if he'd been hit. Only the decor reminded Larry of the ward. There his men had to battle for their dignity; here the patients were helpless. He gave the orderlies a hard look as he passed, and they broke up, hustled off on their crepe soles.

Ida Sizemore's name hung from the door on green construction paper, as well as another woman's. A curtain separated the two beds, the TV jutting from the wall on an arm so both women could see, though it played without sound. The ceiling light was off but the sun cut through the Venetian blinds. Ida's name was on the far closet in the same oversized print Scott's teachers used. The woman nearest the door slept with her mouth open; Larry could not stop himself from picturing her dead.

Behind the curtain, Ida lay supine, wearing a hospital gown, sunken into her pillow. Her eyes noted Larry and wandered back to the TV. Veins moved blue beneath the translucent skin of her forehead. One eyelid drooped, and her chin was white with stubble, her teeth dirt brown at the roots. On the wall hung a bulletin board covered with curling pictures. Larry took a chair and pulled it up next to her head; her eyes shifted to the movement, stayed on his face.

He said her name.

"Yes," she whispered, and swallowed.

"My name is Larry Markham."

"Doctor," she said. "How is Ellen?"

His mother's name was Helen. "She's fine."

"She didn't like that place." She caught her breath, her tongue darting in and out like the head of a turtle. "Matt asked about you."

"What did Matt say?"

"I mean Ellen," she said, and coughed wetly. A thin, institutional box of tissues sat on her nightstand beside a plastic picture cube, but she didn't reach for it.

"Ellen," Larry reminded her.

"You used to have that car," she said. "Ellen loved that car. You were so good to her." Her eyes slid to the TV again. "Matt's dead."

"Yes," Larry said, trying to remember what his father was driving back then.

"He said you would take care of her."

"Yes."

"Thank God," she said. "Thank God." On screen, a burglar with a mask and a flashlight rummaged through a dresser, catching her attention.

Larry twisted in the chair and looked up at the pictures—a rheumy-eyed dachshund, Ida with two heavy women, then a row from the fifties of a young woman and a boy. They stood by a fat rocket of a Ford, holding hands. The boy wore a cowboy hat and chaps, a gunbelt slung low on his hips. The woman had long dark hair and the high cheeks of a model. She was leggy; in another shot she teased the photographer with the slit of her skirt.

"Where is Ellen now?" Larry asked.

"She did it. She said she would. I knew it wasn't your fault. Everybody knew. I had the hardest time after that."

"After Ellen died."

"I know that was hard for you too, with her gone." She coughed. "It was a hard time for all of us."

"What about Ronnie?"

"He was just here the other day. We talked about you. You looked after him before all of that happened. I know she's mine and I love her, but it was unfair, that. But you know, don't you?"

"Yes," Larry said.

"Oh, that was a hard time."

"Where is Ronnie?"

"Ronnie," she said, as if he'd just brought him up. "Ronnie's dead—or Matt. Matt's dead. I know one of them is because one of them was just here. I remember that. Ronnie. He asked about you. He always loved that car of yours, same as Ellen. They were so much alike. How I worried about him that way. The fits he had—exactly like his mother. Exactly. They said he was dead but I knew. All the time I knew. It wasn't like Matt because they never sent anything home."

"Do you know where Ronnie is?"

"He said he was going to talk to you. I told him about Helen. We're all so sorry."

"Thank you," Larry said. He wasn't sure that he needed or even wanted to know more, and got up.

"That car," she said, "do you still have it?"

"The Packard," Larry said, surprising himself. It was maroon and huge, the grille intricate.

"That car was something. I remember Ellen getting dressed up special for it. She was a beautiful girl, wasn't she?"

"Yes," Larry said.

She coughed and brought something up and reached for the tissues. The bones of her hand stood out plain beneath the skin. Larry hoped she could pluck the Kleenex from the box, if only so he wouldn't have to pity her, but after two futile swipes, he moved around the bed and pulled one out for her. As she dabbed at the bedspread, he snuck a look at the picture cube. A teenaged Creeley in Navy whites smiled back at him. She was occupied, and Larry turned the cube. The next face held the six of spades.

The cube would fit in his pocket, but as he palmed it, someone knocked on the door. He replaced it and pulled back his hand. A maid in a powder-blue uniform wheeled a long rack of clothing over to the closet. The clothes all had tags with the owner's name sewn into them.

The woman said hello to Larry, slid Ida's side open, and hung up two jogging suits. "How we doing today, Ida?"

"Good."

"That's good. Excited about Halloween?"

"Yes."

"All right," she said, and wheeled the rack out again.

Ida drifted back to the TV as if Larry weren't there. He reached for a Kleenex to see if she'd notice, and when her eyes stayed on the screen, he draped the tissue over the cube and jammed it into his pocket. She didn't see him leave.

"Do you have a bathroom?" Larry asked a nurse picking crumbs from the aluminum foil.

A sign said it was for residents only; he hesitated but went in anyway. An enema bag hung from a chrome hook, the tube dangling, subtly curled. Larry popped the cube open and pinched out the card and the picture of Creeley. Across the six of spades, Creeley had written: *Vicki loves Alan.*

CLINES HAD FOUND the file Julian left open for him. He let Larry know he was pissed at him for going to Ida's alone, but slipped the six into a baggie and added it to the pile. He centered the shot of the young Creeley on his blotter and took a sip of Diet Pepsi, waiting for Larry to explain.

"Vicki is my wife."

"I figured that."

Larry searched for a respectable way to say that she had left him and realized that other than Donna, he'd told no one. This made it official. Down the hall, a copier clicked.

"We recently separated."

"And this Alan," Clines asked.

"I don't know him," Larry said.

"Never heard of him before."

"No."

"But it's possible our friend knows what he's talking about."

"Yes," Larry said.

"Still nothing personal, huh?" He dug a manila envelope out of a drawer. "Let me show you what we came up with."

He spilled a single glossy photo on the desk and turned it toward Larry—a hole in the ground surrounded by plaques fixed in cement, each attended by a tiny American flag.

"It's his father's," Clines said, "over at Pleasant Grove. It happened sometime Tuesday night. And we've got more on the mother. She was in and out of sanitariums from the late fifties on. She was in Auburn State Hospital when she finally killed herself—this is August '69, about the time our friend is listed KIA. Also right around the time you were hurt." He looked to Larry as if he needed to answer this.

"If I ever worked on him, I don't remember it."

Clines gave him time to say more, then relented. "Okay. What did you get out of the grandmother?"

Larry pictured his father and Ellen Creeley laughing in the backseat of the Packard, their shoes off, shirts unbuttoned. She would have been a patient of his, a young mother. As a child he'd feared the hospital in Auburn; it stood beside the state prison at the weedy edge of town, surrounded by a high brick wall, its smokestacks chuffing out soot. He thought of his father making the long drive up the lake to visit her, what he would say, and then the ride back in silence.

"Nothing firm," Larry said.

He tried the name on Donna. It was late; they'd put the dishes away. They were watching PBS—something about eye surgery, which Larry could not bear. She'd made popcorn, the kernels bursting like small-arms fire. She seemed quiet tonight, and he was careful not to rub up against her. Her feet were cold; she had red wool socks on, her feet tucked under. From the mantel, Brian and Chris looked down.

"His name is Alan," Larry said, seeing if she'd blink.

Donna kept her eyes on the set and dug another handful. "Where'd you hear this?"

"A friend."

"It helps to have a name," she said. "I don't know why. Wade's was Beverly. At least that's what he told me, who knows what it really was. He called last night."

"How are the boys?"

"They miss me," she said. "He misses me, at least he says he does. He says he's sorry."

"I'm sure he is."

"I don't know why. It was my fault. It doesn't really matter, I suppose."

"No," Larry agreed.

"He wants me to fly out so we can start over. He's sending me a ticket." She smirked to let him know it was ridiculous. "He's like you, he needs someone to cook him dinner. The sad thing is, I'd do it if I thought it might work."

"It wouldn't," Larry asked, hoping she'd agree.

"It might for a while, then I'd lose it again and he wouldn't know what to do. He was probably right to take the boys away, I scare the hell out of them." She pulled back an arm of her sweater and showed him the white inside of a bicep, a long scar running up toward her armpit. "I did that with a filleting knife—why, I have no idea. I'd taken my medication; I wasn't drinking. I was working in the kitchen one minute and the next thing I was in the car bleeding on the seats. Chris showed the police how I did it."

"But you're better now."

"You're not listening to me," she said. "I'm telling you that I'm not right."

"And I am," Larry said.

"It's not the same at all. Why do you say shit like that? It doesn't help." She pushed the bowl off her lap and onto the coffee table.

"I guess it doesn't matter what his name is."

"Can we just watch TV? I'm sick of talking about them."

"How about us?" Larry dared.

She sighed, tired of the question. "I don't love you."

"You don't have to."

"I'm just warning you now," Donna said, "so there's no misunderstanding later. I might say that I do later, but I don't. I still love him, even if he doesn't want me."

"It's okay," Larry said, and took her hand and kissed it.

She turned it over and laid her soft palm against his cheek. "Just remember what I said."

When he leaned in to kiss her, she turned her face away.

"Not yet," she said.

She let him keep her hand but turned back to the show, and Larry thought she was right, that the whole thing was hopeless and probably harmful. They watched without talking. A long pledge break came on, and he said he should be getting to bed.

At the door, she apologized and held him and he smelled her hair, felt the press of her chest against his. "Go slow," she said. "I'm not that strong."

HE DREAMED of Fred the Head reading on his cot, his transistor by his ear, and then his daughter wandering a jungle trail in the dress she wore in the picture. Larry knew the dream and how the pieces would fly into the banana tree. The dress had a bow in the back, and the girl wore a string of pearls. She paused to consider the leaves as if they were flowers, her shiny Mary Janes and white kneesocks inching toward the nylon line of the tripwire. She had just touched it, pulling the grenade out of the empty beer can, when Larry came awake.

Scott's machine clicked in the other room. Probably Rudy wondering why he hadn't gotten back to him; the kid didn't have his time zones straight. Larry swung himself out of bed. The ceiling light blinded him; his tongue was dry from the furnace, his knees creaky from yesterday's run.

The miniature tape was still rolling. He turned the volume up to see who had ruined his sleep.

"I wish I could promise you that," a man said, "but I can't."

"So what am I supposed to do?" Vicki asked.

"I told you not to, I don't know why you didn't listen to me."

"I can't live there anymore," she said. "I have to lie all the time and I can't see you. I feel sick when he touches me."

Larry sat down on Scott's bed and stared at the machine.

"That's not good," the man said. His voice reminded him of Gregory Peck —older, with a touch of breeding.

"I can't help it. I want *you*. I'm sick of all this running around, it makes me feel cheap."

"I'm sick of it too, but . . ."

"But what?" Vicki said. "I'm ready. Isn't this what we talked about?"

"Yes," he conceded.

"I love you, Alan."

"I know."

"You know I'll do anything for you."

"You've already done it," he said. "It's up to me now."

Vicki didn't return. A patch of static rustled, then a click.

"Skull," Creeley greeted him. The name stung Larry, as if he'd been caught doing something. It was an effort for Creeley, and Larry wondered what he'd substituted for the Dilaudid. "Listen." He ripped a piece of paper. "Seven of spades."

Before Larry thought to open the microphone, the machine clicked and rewound. When it was done, Larry stood over it, a finger above the play button, then decided he'd heard enough.

The next morning Vicki called while he was getting his lunch ready and asked if he wanted to see Scott that weekend. She offered quickly, impatient with him, as if she might rescind it. He thought it was wrong; he'd done nothing.

"Sure," he said. "When?"

"Saturday."

"Fine," he said, and waited for her to say good-bye.

"Are you all right?" she finally asked.

"What do you care?" he said, and hung up.

As he turned for the kitchen, the phone rang. He chopped an egg on top of his tuna fish, spooned in a glob of mayo and mixed it all together. Every ring made him want to throw the bowl against the wall, but he laid out the rye bread Donna had recommended and, when he was done, rinsed the bowl in the sink. He left the answering machine off, and thought it would be a good policy from now on.

"Is that your phone?" Donna asked as he lowered himself in.

"The machine'll get it," he said.

When he punched in, Marv said he had a call in the office, and Larry decided that that was it, he'd tried to be nice. He picked up, ready to shame Vicki with everything he knew.

"Mr. Markham," an operator he recognized said, "please hold for Dr. Downs," and then another woman came on.

"I'm afraid your father's been in an accident," she said. "A fairly serious one."

MRS. RAILSBECK SAW him get off the elevator and stood up, clutching her purse. She wore his father's green-and-black mackinaw over a pink sweater and tight white polyester pants. Out of the house, she seemed old and helpless, a joke. She had a tissue balled in one hand but wasn't crying. She took a few steps toward Larry as if he'd rescued her and fixed a dry kiss on his cheek. He lightly returned her hug.

"They say he's going to be all right," she said.

"What happened?"

"He was driving when he shouldn't have been. It was just an accident. They told me but I don't remember."

"It's okay," Larry said, but for some reason he was angry with her. She didn't want a coffee. The elevator silently opened and closed. They stood against the wall while traffic passed, and finally Dr. Downs came out.

He was in recovery, she said. She was a colleague, a short woman with plucked eyebrows and expensive heels under her labcoat. It wasn't as bad as they'd thought, just a cracked kneecap, some facial lacerations, possibly a concussion. Larry asked her what had happened.

"It was at the Octopus," she explained. "The officer said your father ran the light and hit a woman in a van."

"How is she?"

"A little shaken up but otherwise fine. The police said both cars were pretty well totaled. Your father's probably saved him. I'm sorry if my call alarmed you, but at first it appeared he had a serious head injury. People at the scene said he didn't know what was going on, but he seems fine now. It was probably just a bump."

Mrs. Railsbeck took his wrist as if for balance.

"He's been having trouble with his memory lately," Larry said. "More than normal."

"If you'd like, we can run some tests while he's in."

Mrs. Railsbeck left it up to him.

"That would be good," Larry said, and though he knew it was right, he felt he'd betrayed him.

From recovery they would move him into a private room. Larry and Mrs. Railsbeck caught the elevator and got there before the orderly finished making the bed. Mrs. Railsbeck inspected the bathroom, then took a seat in the corner. The window looked out on the water, the hills of the far shore ablaze. It was too cold for boats. He knew the view from the ward; Cartwright always complained that he didn't give two shits about trees, he wanted to see people. Secretly, Larry disagreed. Growing up, he'd learned to treasure stillness, to husband it, and even now he could retreat to those afternoons in the living room, the Sunday mornings with his unopened foot locker. Vicki was right when she said that sometimes he just wasn't there, but never asked where Larry went, or why. It was a temptation he had to resist now, to withdraw into the fixed brilliance of the season.

"How are you doing?" he asked Mrs. Railsbeck.

"Not so good." She filled the chair. She still had her coat on, her purse in her lap. "It's my fault, I think."

"He'll be fine," Larry said. She began to weep without sound, dabbing at the tears. "He will," Larry repeated, and when she didn't stop, squatted down and held her in the chair, but stiffly. Her body hitched with sobs; he thought of piloting Number 1 through the bright countryside, the radio playing, all of this gone. His own coldness shamed him, and he realized he was no comfort to her, that something would always keep him at a distance —his mother, perhaps, or his wish for all of his father's love. With his arms around her, he understood what Vicki had said, that touching him made her sick and that she had no control over it, and Larry wondered how long ago she'd left him.

"I'm sorry," Mrs. Railsbeck said, and crushed a tissue to her nose, and they parted. "Last night I was going to call you, he was so bad. He was screaming and yelling about something, I don't know what. He thought I was your mother, he kept calling me Helen and saying these awful things. I locked myself in my room I was so frightened. Then this morning he seemed fine.

He ate his breakfast and I got his hat for him, and everything was fine, and then at the door he called me Helen. I knew something like this was going to happen, but I didn't know what to do."

"He's all right," Larry said. "They'll do the tests and we'll see. Maybe they can give him something."

"I hope so. You've never seen him when he gets like that. The way he looks at you, it's like he doesn't know you. I don't know what to do anymore."

"He doesn't hurt you," Larry asked.

"He doesn't mean to. It's not him then, it's someone else."

"Physically," Larry said, and she looked at him as if giving him time to withdraw the question.

"I know it's not him."

Larry didn't know what to ask next.

She rolled up one sleeve of the mackinaw and showed him her wrist—bruised the color of grape juice beneath the skin.

Larry examined it, contemplating the force needed to do that to her.

"I know I should have told someone." She fingered the fraying handles of her purse. "But when you get to be my age, everyone's dead. I don't have anyone else."

"You can't let him do that to you," Larry began.

"Nobody," she said. "I'm not like you or Susan. Your father's all I've got."

Behind him, an orderly peeked through the door, and Mrs. Railsbeck snorted into a Kleenex. Two men rolled in the gurney, a plastic IV bag swinging. Larry moved to the window to give them room.

His father was awake, his head swaddled in bandages, eyes dilated, waning. They'd shaved one eyebrow to stitch him up, and he had a rash of scratches on his nose from the windshield. Without his glasses, he seemed defenseless.

"I'm all right," he slurred. His head rolled on the flat pillow.

"Oh, he's a tough guy, this one," the bigger of the orderlies said. "He wanted to take the stairs."

Mrs. Railsbeck joined Larry at the window as the orderlies readied to lift his father into bed. They pulled the sheet down; he had a soft cast on his right leg fastened with Velcro straps. They cranked the bed up a touch and hung the IV from a hook on the wall, then dropped the aluminum rail.

"On three," said the big one, and with little effort they laid his father in the middle and pulled the sheet up to his chest. He seemed delicate in their hands, a relic that might crumble to dust.

"All right now," the other said to his father, as if he'd helped them, and they whisked the gurney away, one wheel shimmying. Larry closed the door behind them.

Mrs. Railsbeck leaned over his father, stroking his jaw. His lip had puffed up, and somewhere they'd lost his teeth. The bottom of his face seemed to have collapsed, his nose almost touching his chin.

"Maddy," he said.

"Shhh. Larry's here." She moved aside so he could see.

Larry raised a hand, as if to be counted. "Hey."

His father said his name, then to both of them or no one, "I'm tired."

"Of course," Mrs. Railsbeck said.

Larry turned off the light and drew the curtains. Mrs. Railsbeck pulled her chair to the bedside and took his father's hand. Larry stood above him on the other side, watching the sheet lift with his breathing. His father had been a large man; now some of him seemed missing. He lay drugged under the blankets like a child, his mouth open, and Larry thought of Scott, how sometimes when he looked in on him at night, his flashlight was on under the covers, still in his hand, and Larry had to fight the unbearable rush of tenderness that ended with the fact that his son would always be like this and that it was his fault, and though he wanted to, they could not trade places. Watching his father, Larry wondered what had gone wrong. So often his own life seemed worthless, unconnected to the world and the people he loved.

A nurse knocked and came in with a plastic bin of his father's property—his polished oxfords and black socks; his belt; a matching pen and mechanical pencil Susan had given him; his Elgin watch and Cornell ring and wedding band; his car keys, the Chrysler star faintly outlined in dried blood. His billfold had fifty or sixty dollars in it, and all his credit cards; he didn't carry pictures. He was wearing a suit, the nurse said, but they couldn't save it.

"Not even the pants?" Mrs. Railsbeck asked. "And what happened to his briefcase?"

The nurse said it might still be in the car. She'd see if she could find a number for the police, and in a minute came back with a slip of paper. Larry thanked her and said he'd go right over.

"I'll be here," Mrs. Railsbeck said. She still had his father's hand, rubbing the back of it with a thumb. His eyes shifted beneath his lids, his jugular pulsed. He would be fine, but still Larry laid a hand on his shoulder, as if a touch could heal him. For so long he'd seen his father as an unforgiving judge, yet now when the evidence seemed overwhelming, he could not hold it against him.

"You go," she said.

At the door, Larry hesitated, looked back to make sure he was safe.

She waved him out, making fun of his dramatics, and he thought it was strange how they'd changed places. She believed his father would be all right.

THE PROPERTY OFFICER was expecting him; he gave Larry the briefcase and led him outside. The impounded cars sat in a fenced dirt lot behind the police garage, some burned and rusted. Vines twined around the barbed wire. Larry carried a box from Number 1 he'd emptied of Ding Dongs. The officer left the key in the lock so he could close up when he was done.

His first look at the New Yorker shocked him more than his father in the hospital. The face of the car was unfamiliar, its headlights wall-eyed, the hood a tent. Antifreeze dripped into the mud. The impact had pushed the grille into the radiator and flattened the front tires. The windshield was the old kind, the glass deep green, and instead of shattering into cubes, it had cracked, the bright lines converging above the steering wheel. Larry was prepared to see blood. His first summer back, he'd tried being an EMT, but he had trouble with the smell and the screaming and the children, and after three months he quit. He was glad for the breeze today, the bracing chill of the month's end.

The door was unlocked. Blood darkened the seat, the mat, the carpeted hump, spattered the beaded backrest Mrs. Railsbeck had given him. A wad of gauze lay among the shards, an envelope for a compress. His father's hat rested in the far footwell, and Larry walked around and opened the passenger door. The brim held a fang of glass, otherwise it was untouched; he set it in the box and popped the dash.

His father still had the owner's manual, the maintenance charts religiously ticked off. A map of Ithaca, the registration and insurance, carbons from a muffler shop. He kept a miniature flashlight and a pack of matches in case of an emergency, several stubby golf pencils, some peppermints from restaurants. Larry tossed it all in the box.

The trunk was just as empty—some flares, which he left, and an old blanket folded neatly by the spare. In the back sat a cheap, telescoping umbrella Larry had bought him one Christmas; under the front seats he found a combination brush-and-scraper, the bristles a ridiculous blue.

His father's teeth hid beneath the pedals, but only the lower plate. Tiny pebbles and flecks of crushed leaves clung to the pink imitation gum. Larry wiped it clean with his shirt tail, then groped behind the brake for the upper, running a hand over the rough pile of the carpet. He checked the trough between the seat and the door on both sides, and the crack of the seat itself, but came up with nothing but pennies. He studied the back, imagining a ricochet, a crazy angle. He did the footwells again, ducking under the steering wheel till he could see the color-coded wiring.

As he searched the top of the dash, he noticed a card hanging from the rearview mirror. If it was the eight of spades, he swore he would kill Creeley without remorse. He snatched it down and saw it was his father's parking pass for the hospital lot.

"I'll kill him anyway," Larry said.

He thumped all four doors shut and took the box from the roof. For how closely he associated the New Yorker with his father, it held very little of him. Walking away from the car, he thought it was wrong to leave it here, that his father would want him to rescue it somehow. Larry closed the fence and snaked the chain through, clicked the lock and removed the key.

He asked the property officer if he thought it was totaled.

"Oh yeah," he said.

"So what's the best thing to do?"

"Donate it to the fire department. They come and pick it up and you get to write it off."

"What do they do with them?" Larry asked.

"Practice," the man said.

MARV PROMISED he could have Number 1 all day, but his father was still asleep and the bus was just as easy. Larry said he didn't know if he'd be in tomorrow. Not a problem, Marv said. Derek offered to do his route.

Mrs. Railsbeck hadn't moved. She had her coat off now, her purse on the windowsill. Larry told her to get some lunch. She didn't argue, but took her time leaving. His father lay on his side in the dark, his hair mussed, the sheets tucked under one arm. Mrs. Railsbeck's chair was warm. Larry looked at the dead TV, the call button on the wall. He went to the window and tipped a slat of the blinds up with a finger—the perfect blue of afternoon. His father took them walking on days like this, the leaves dropping into streams, pooling at the bottom of Buttermilk Falls. At home, their mother slept. She came down for dinner on an escalator seat that followed the stairs on a rail; they were forbidden to play with it. You could hear the motor throughout the house, and sometimes when he heard the whirring, he crept through the kitchen and slipped out the back door into a day like today, knowing she'd be waiting for him, eyes closed, conducting Brahms with a tilt of her chin. He pulled back his finger and the slat dropped, the room surrounded him.

When Mrs. Railsbeck returned from the cafeteria, he called Susan at her office. He had to get the number from information.

"And whom should I say is calling?" her secretary said. She seemed surprised that Susan had a brother and made him wait.

Susan apologized, but carelessly, as if it were understandable.

"It's Dad," Larry said. "He's had an accident."

"Is he all right?" she said, and he recognized the calm of his father. They were not equals; the years between them would never mend.

"He's resting."

"Do I need to come out there?"

"No," he said. "Let me tell you what happened."

She didn't interrupt. He told her about everything except Mrs. R.'s bruises. When he was done, she asked if there was anything else she needed to know, and he thought of Ellen Creeley.

"I don't think so," Larry said.

"If I can get a late flight I'll be there tonight, if not, then tomorrow early. You don't have to pick me up, I'll rent a car."

"You don't have to come out," Larry said. "He's fine."

"What's his room number, in case no one's home."

Larry gave it to her.

"And how are you?" Susan asked. She was serious, taking things in order of importance. She was a listmaker, someone who knew where she'd be for the holidays.

"I'm fine," he said.

When she'd hung up, he dialed Cornell information and got the number of Donna's department. She picked up on the first ring.

"Oh no," she said. "Oh, Larry."

He said he didn't know how late he'd be tonight, and she told him to come over whenever he got home.

"I love you," he said.

"I know," she said, as if she pitied him, and he thought he should stop, that it just hurt her.

He called Vicki's mother, got the machine and left a message.

Still his father slept. Another orderly brought his dinner in but left the lids on. Mrs. Railsbeck asked a nurse if they should wake him. He would come around soon, she assured them, and opened the blinds. The afternoon was fading, a white moon solidifying. Mrs. Railsbeck turned on the light.

Larry had just put on the national news for her when his father rolled onto his left side. He smacked his lips and groaned, stretched, changed position again. Mrs. Railsbeck told Larry to turn off the TV and shook his father's shoulder.

"Here we are," she said.

"God," his father said, squinting at the light. He touched the stitched eyebrow. He noticed Larry, then turned back to her. "It must be bad if he's here." Without his teeth, he lisped.

"It only looks bad," Larry said. "Except for the kneecap."

His father felt his legs and found the cast. "Great."

"How do you feel?" Mrs. Railsbeck asked.

"Tired."

"Do you remember what happened?" Larry asked.

"Thomeone hit me." It was a question.

"Where?"

His father shook his head.

"The Octopus," Mrs. Railsbeck prodded.

"I don't remember."

"You took a pretty good lick," Larry said. "Dr. Downs said she was going to run some tests."

"To make sure you're all right."

"What kind of tests?" his father asked.

"I don't know," Larry said. "Just tests."

"You should eat something," Mrs. Railsbeck said, and raised the bed and wheeled over the adjustable table. She insisted on feeding him, cutting his chicken into tiny bites he wouldn't have to chew; his father didn't have the strength to refuse. Larry wanted to know about Ellen Creeley and the bruises on Mrs. R.'s wrist, but decided there would be time.

They both stayed till the end of visiting hours. Larry walked her to her car, and she offered him a ride home. He had to adjust the seat to fit in the Rabbit. The season had turned; leaves were falling in the streetlights, a sickle moon raced through the trees.

"I don't think he's well," she said.

"No," Larry agreed.

"I'm glad your sister's coming out."

"So am I," Larry said.

"You're a terrible liar," she said. "Do you know that?"

DONNA CALLED to him from the porch. She stood on one bare foot, the other crossed on top for warmth. She had her glasses on, a Cornell sweatshirt, her hair up in the tortoiseshell clip. Even in jeans she seemed elegant to him; it was her height, how her waist cinched in.

"I made you something," she said, and though he was tired and wanted to be alone, he followed her inside.

A blues tune shuffled from the speakers, the rooster squawk of a harmonica. Incense spiced the air. She was stoned, her eyes rimmed red; a good-sized roach sat in one notch of the ashtray.

"Is that okay for you to be doing?" he asked.

"Technically no," she said. "Do you want a hit?"

"Not right now."

"Probably smart," she said, and did the rest of it.

She'd made ziti with broccoli and pine nuts; she had to reheat it. While he ate, they talked about his father, and hospitals. She'd committed herself once, when she was twenty.

"There were no doors on the bathroom stalls. My father came down in his uniform and told them to let me go. By law they couldn't because I hadn't passed evaluation. Every day for a week he came and told me what a stupid thing I'd done, and every day I tried to explain that I was hearing voices—which he knew I was because I did when I was little. I'm sure Wade told you all about it."

"No," Larry said.

"Voices aren't so bad. Most of them you can just ignore." She took his plate and fixed him with a look. "I'm kidding."

"I never know when you are."

"That's because you don't know me," she said, and kissed him, tasting of dope, then spun away, headed for the kitchen.

"What was that?" he asked when she came back.

"What?" She gave him her mouth again. "That?" She took her clip off, and her hair spread.

"I don't understand."

"Larry," she said. "I trust you. I think you'll be good to me. I don't think I'm wrong about that."

"What about everything else?" He nodded toward the picture of the boys.

"I don't know about everything else. I'm tired of thinking about everything else."

"I thought you wanted to go slow."

"Aren't we?" she said.

"Yes," he said, but defensively.

"Oh God." She picked the clip off the coffee table and held it in her teeth while she pulled her hair up with both hands.

"Donna," he tried to apologize.

"I don't need this," she said. "I thought you loved me."

"I do."

"Then why don't you act like it?"

"I don't know," he said, truthfully. He leaned over to hold her, and she stood.

She turned off the stereo.

"I'm going to ask you one thing," she said. "Answer me truthfully. Do you want me?"

"Yes," Larry said.

She pulled off her sweatshirt and the T-shirt beneath it and let them fall to the hardwood floor. She unzipped her jeans and seesawed them over her slim hips, stood before him, utterly revealed.

He went to her on his knees, bowed his forehead until it touched the cold bones of her feet.

They never made it upstairs. He left the one sock on. Her tan had faded, and the color of her thrilled him, her white bottom and dark hair, the extreme pink. Everything was different with her, everything was a surprise. She was smaller inside, a soft, hot pocket; the end of him grazed her, a ship easing into port. She threw her head back, her neck flushed with blood. "Give it," she urged, and when they were done, still connected, asked tearily, "Do you really love me?" and held him to her, her breath warm in his ear. "You're not lying?" she said. "You wouldn't lie to me?"

In the morning his knees were raw, the crust on the brushburns sticky. Crossing the yard, he was aware of his silhouette, the possibility Creeley was hidden in the trees. Susan was coming, and he needed to call Vicki. He gave the cows, the fields, all of Ithaca the finger.

The house shamed him—Vicki's curtains, the needlepoint samplers on the walls, Scott's Charlie Brown bedspread. Waiting for the shower to warm, he smelled Donna on him, a dried, perfumed brine; when he toweled off, it was gone, and he thought he'd lost something. He decided to call Vicki from the hospital and clicked the answering machine on.

In the car, he sat on the hump, a hand on Donna's leg. She covered it at the lights but was quiet, and he asked what was wrong.

"You're not worried?" she said.

"I am," he said, but couldn't stop smiling.

"It's wrong."

"I know," he said, "but I love you."

"That doesn't matter. Jesus, haven't you been listening to me at all?"

"I have."

"Then what are we doing?" Donna said. "Tell me, because I really don't know."

He retracted his hand. He couldn't accuse her of changing her mind, and she'd already taken away his only defense, so they rode along, a silence growing between them.

"I don't know," he finally admitted.

"When *will* you know?" she said viciously, her eyes on the road, and he wished he had never fallen for her, which was foolish. All he had to do was look at her now—her hair up in the clip, her delicate wrists, the slope of her nose—and he was completely hers. In Vietnam, the greatest fear among the platoon was being captured, and here Larry had surrendered willingly. He would again, he thought, but only to her, no one else. She would be the last. He would spend everything on her, lose all he knew and have nothing left in the end. When this did happen, he'd think back, like a man crippled in an accident, trying to remember what his life had been like before her, and he would honestly not be able to.

SUSAN WAS IN Mrs. Railsbeck's chair, playing cards with her father. All three turned toward the door, noting Larry. Susan got up and met him at the foot of the bed. She wore new hornrims, and her hair was subtly hennaed, her bangs cropped in a neat line; her navy-blue pantsuit was freshly pressed, as if she had a court date later. She moved like a politician, rigid and assured; he could never muster the respect her posture demanded. She gave him a grandmother's kiss on the cheek. She smelled of talc and dried violets.

"You didn't have to come," he said, holding her a moment, trying to be private.

"But you're glad I did."

She knew how to silence him, the limits of his bitterness. She would always be stronger.

"We'll talk later," she said, and pushed off, a hand on his chest.

They were playing gin, their father was winning. One cheek had gone livid, a dark like rot below the bone; he still didn't have a set of uppers, and when he smiled at a card, a black slot showed. Susan tallied the score and shuffled.

"He's still tired," Mrs. Railsbeck whispered. She'd brought a book, a cheap mystery with a skull on the cover. She loved the game shows and soap operas but kept the set off in deference to his father.

"Would you like to play?" Susan asked, and Larry took her place. She went out into the hall.

"You saw the car," his father asked hopefully.

"It's bad."

"Any chance of repairing it?"

"No," Larry said.

"Well hell," his father said, and fanned his cards, "I got my money out of it."

"Feeling better?" Larry asked.

"It just stings." He pointed to the stitches. "I haven't tried to use the knee. I'm sure Nancy did a good job. I'm hoping to get out of here tomorrow."

"I think she wanted to run some tests," Larry said.

"I'm fine."

"That's what the tests are supposed to tell us."

"Look," his father said, "I'm only staying today because your sister came all the way out here. The knee's a simple thing, just a couple of screws. I don't want to be in here any longer than I have to."

"It's not your knee we're worried about," Larry said. "I don't see why you're so upset about these tests."

"I am not upset!" his father said, and threw his cards down. "I do not need a test to tell me I'm fine. I want to go home and get back to work. I'm busy, or maybe you don't understand that, driving your little Twinkie truck around all day."

He went on. Larry just stared, his cards still in his hand. Mrs. Railsbeck wedged herself between them, stroking his father's arm to calm him.

"And you," his father accused, "you're just like her. You're not even a woman anymore. I don't know what you are, just some kind of thing." He shrugged her hand off and she shied back. "There's nothing wrong with me." He pushed the table and the pitcher toppled, spilling water over the cards and onto his lap, an ice cube clinking against the rail before it hit the floor.

The catastrophe silenced him. He sat propped up, drained, dumbly pondering the sopping cards. Larry recovered the pitcher while Mrs. Railsbeck grabbed a fistful of paper towels from the bathroom. She balled the towels and lifted the sheets and stuck her hand under, and his father looked to the window.

"I'm not going to do them."

"You're going to do them," Larry said, but his father pretended not to listen. "Is this the way he is?"

Mrs. Railsbeck looked to his father as if for permission, then nodded. "And worse."

His father didn't argue.

Susan opened the door and still he didn't move. The big orderly from the other day followed her in, rolling a folded cot. She pointed to a corner and he left it there and closed the door behind him.

"What happened here?" she asked.

"Just a little spill," Mrs. Railsbeck said. Their father was still fixed on the window.

"Dad?" Susan said.

"I want to go home."

She went to him and laid a hand on the back of his neck. "You will."

"Today."

She glanced at Larry, who shook his head faintly, as if bidding.

"Soon," she said, and checked with Larry. "I promise."

"I don't want to take any more tests."

"Why do they want to do tests?"

"Because that's how they operate now. They don't try to figure out what's wrong with you, they don't even know who you are."

"What do they think is wrong with you?"

"I'm old," their father said. "That's what's wrong with me."

"That's why you don't want to take the tests, because they're for older people."

"No," he said, but didn't go on.

"You're going to pass the tests," she asked.

"I don't know."

"That sounds like a good reason to take them."

"No," he said, but without conviction, as if she'd broken him.

"Who's your doctor?" she asked.

"I don't have one."

She looked to Larry as if it were his fault.

"What the hell has been going on here?" she asked in the empty lounge. "He doesn't have a doctor, he's been having spells. How come I'm just learning this? I'm glad I didn't listen to you and stay home. Jesus, Larry, really!"

"It's new to me too," he said, but it was no defense.

"I'm going to stay until they figure out what's going on. If it's bad, we'll have to decide what to do. It's obvious Mrs. R. can't take care of him."

"I can take care of him," Larry said.

"When?" she said. "After work? On the weekends? He's not like a kid, you can't send him to school. You know Vicki's not going to watch him. We'll have to get a nurse. God knows what that'll cost."

"He's not going in a home."

"We'll have to see what our options are."

"That's not an option," Larry said, ready to hold his position.

"It's too early to tell anything," she said, retreating, denying him victory.

Afterward, he wished that, like Creeley, he'd gotten her betrayal on tape. Though she'd convinced his father to do what Larry wanted, he could not forgive her for succeeding where he'd failed—and effortlessly, by her mere presence. She was the favorite, the one who carried their parents' dreams. On the bus home, he wondered why he thought things would be different; all that had changed was time, which he knew from experience softened nothing, only showed his faults in deeper relief.

DONNA WAS SORRY she'd gotten weird on him this morning. They lay on the couch under an afghan, her feet in his hands. The TV was on— something dumb, the volume muted. He was memorizing her face, the stubble on her calves.

"Just guilt," she admitted.

"I haven't called Vicki yet for the same reason."

"You should."

"I don't feel like it."

"That's good," Donna said, "I think."

The mantel was bare. He asked what had happened to the pictures.

"They flipped me out a little this morning."

He was falling in love with her clothes, her earrings, the tough skin of her heels. He could not look at her enough, astonished she was his, if only momentarily. If this was wrong—which it was—he'd take the blame. He wanted to think of them in a distant city, innocent, living in a walk-up, waking late and drinking coffee, the ships calling from the bay. He wanted the rights of a lover, the envy of other men. He wanted her to tell her friends that this was the one, finally.

"Stop," she said. "You're making me self-conscious."

He ducked under the afghan and clumsily switched positions, lying on top of her. "I'm not crushing you?"

"No," she squeezed out.

He did not have to make love with her, but she turned off the TV and took him upstairs. She'd cleaned her bedroom, the closets closed, the one ashtray rinsed. She unplugged the phone. A crack wandered across the ceiling like a great river; a candle flared on the dresser. She turned down the comforter and took her socks off, pulled the clip out of her hair and laid it on a table. They watched each other slip into the cool linen. The smell of her skin welcomed him, the fit of her hips.

"Talk to me," she said, taking him in. "Tell me what you want to do to me."

He turned her over and ran his nails down the long muscles of her back. His hands were dark on her bottom; her hair covered her face. She moved to meet him, breasts swinging, then dropped her arms and buried her face in the pillows. A faint glaze of sweat glistened between her shoulders; he bit her there and tasted it, pressed his chest against her, their fingers meshed at the edge of the mattress.

"This is what I want," he said.

"Are you sure?" she asked afterwards, under the covers.

"I'm sure."

"It must be nice."

"It is," he said. "It's a little scary too. Because of everything."

"I know. I tried to warn you."

"It's all right. I love you."

"I believe you," Donna said. "Otherwise you wouldn't be here."

She wanted him to stay. She had ice cream—Purity chocolate almond; it was his favorite, Vicki always bought it for his birthday. Larry was pleased she'd noticed.

"You'd be surprised," Donna said, "what I know about you."

"Like what?" he asked, but she was making it a game.

She lent him a flowered housedress and they went downstairs to the kitchen. The floor chilled him. She only took one bowl from the cupboard; she put on water for herself. He watched her body move under her robe, her tiny feet in slippers scuffing the tile. On the refrigerator, under a daisy-shaped magnet, hung an envelope from American Airlines.

"I take it that's from Wade," Larry said, pointing with his spoon.

"Yes."

"Are you going to go?"

"Don't ask me that," she said. "Not now."

"I'd like to know if you are."

"I'll tell you as soon as I know myself."

"You asked me to tell you the truth."

"Why would I lie to you," she said, as if he were interrogating her, and he couldn't answer. He'd thought the ticket was proof.

They fought without talking, rolling away from each other in bed, but later he woke to Donna nibbling him. He turned her around and brought her warmth down to his mouth. It was not forgiveness on his part, more an acknowledgment that he was wrong, expecting her to need him equally. He was lucky to be with her, he had to remember that; if it was true they had no future, he could still be proud of what he meant to her now.

"Make love to me," she said, and he did, hoping he could show her how he felt—the strength and helplessness she inspired in him. Filling her, it seemed simple and right, but later, cooling in the sheets, Larry saw only complications, disaster. She returned to sleep while he lay staring at the unfamiliar room.

The ice cream had given him a headache, and, careful not to wake Donna, he climbed out of bed and padded down the hall. An orange night-light glowed over the sink. He creaked the mirror open but couldn't make out the aspirin among all the bottles. He grasped the chain of the overhead light, closed his eyes and pulled.

He found a bright red bottle of Tylenol and knocked two of the chalky tablets back, then stood there, examining the cabinet, checking for evidence of Wade. There was none—no shaving cream or razors or lime-scented deodorant. A line of cider-colored vials cluttered one shelf. They were all for

Donna, all current, prescribed by the same doctor. Stickers warned her not to take this medication with alcohol. Larry turned them to read the labels—Tofranil, Loxitane, Desyrel. They were antidepressants. He recognized the names from Cartwright's chart. They were supposed to keep him from seeing Mobley.

Larry rinsed his sticky chin and made his way back to bed. She was asleep, her hair shading her face. He rubbed his hands on his thighs to warm them, slipped in and tucked his knees behind hers. He kissed the knob at the top of her spine and smelled her on his breath. He told her what she didn't need to hear.

IN THE MORNING Donna was warm and he didn't want to get out of bed. It was strange waking up with another woman. He had no place in her routine and kept getting in the way. She kissed him and told him to go home.

Vicki was on the machine. She said she'd tried him at the hospital and gotten his sister. She was sorry this had to happen now. She wanted to make sure Saturday was still on with Scott. Scott missed him. She missed him too.

"My ass," Larry said, and wondered if he had lost the right to shame her.

He called Susan and said he'd be in after work. She feigned surprise, giving him a hard time.

"Don't worry," she said. "I'll take care of everything."

In the car, Donna said, "So what did she say?"

"Who?"

"Don't be dumb," she said.

They didn't kiss good-bye. She liked her privacy, she said; she didn't want people to talk, for his sake, and he grudgingly agreed.

Marv said he didn't have to come back so soon, but Larry knew he didn't mean it. The deliveries were running two days behind. Yesterday Derek had done the route, leaving the counter to Marv, and the register tapes were a mess.

Larry needed a regular day. He checked his invoices and loaded up Number 1. The sky was gray, the streetlights on, rain over the lake. A day for Bach, his mother would say, and as Larry climbed South Hill in the mist, one of the English Suites came on, Glenn Gould humming above the keys. They would have heard it together then, in the still living room, the heat of the reading lamp over his shoulder while they struggled with the puzzle from the Sunday *Times*. Two or three spaces in the corners eluded them each week, nagged at her like missed stitches. She asked him to bring the dictionary in from the study, and they leafed through it, cheating. When his father returned from church lugging the new paper, Mrs. Railsbeck checked with her before throwing the old one away. Larry could not bear to see their efforts wasted and catalogued them in a looseleaf binder, grading each as if it were a test. He imagined the album was somewhere in the attic now, the pages brittle with acid. Glenn Gould plunged through a run of triplets, played peekaboo with a developing theme. He was too showy for his mother. "He's Canadian," she said, as if it were an explanation, but he had lasted, Larry thought. The Bach had lasted, and the weather; everything else was gone.

At his first stop he bought a pint of milk and broke open a box of crumb cakes, and by midmorning he'd recovered, dropped into a rhythm. He would see Donna in six hours, and tomorrow he'd spend the afternoon with Scott. Susan would make sure his father got tested. Vicki said she missed him. It was Friday; all along his route people wished him a good weekend, and, answering them, Larry thought it was more than courtesy. He *would* have a good weekend. He would make love to a beautiful woman and throw a football with his son and pound down a cold Genesee and see the leaves—everything he'd dreamed of in Vietnam. He was alive, and to forget that, to live as if this world were something other than a paradise, would be to dishonor the memory of his friends.

He caught himself whistling one of Salazar's tunes at the Sunoco on Meadow Street—"Whistle While You Work." Sally knew hundreds of them. He lived in West Hollywood and his mother was a dancer. "Remember those Cuban movies," he'd ask, "where Cesar Romero is the gambler in the white suit?" For months after the medevac lifted him out, they sat around the hootch trying to come up with a list of his songs. The lieutenant had an old-fashioned tremolo perfect for ballads; they'd all stop to listen to "The Very Thought of You" or "Some Night a Stranger" and then give him a hand. Like everything else of importance, the list had passed to Larry, lurked upstairs in his foot locker.

"Have a good weekend," Larry told the clerk.

"You too now," the man said.

Outside, Number 1 wasn't where he'd left it, and Larry stopped whistling. He was sure he'd parked under the gas pump overhang to stay out of the rain, and now the truck sat in the corner of the lot, by the pay phone. Larry scanned the pumps. Just customers—some workmen's pick-ups, a few college students in old Toyotas. Traffic on Meadow was steady. Across the street the lot of Chef Peking was empty save a blue dumpster.

Larry had the key on the ring at his waist; at most he'd forgotten to lock his door. That was all the opening Creeley needed. He'd probably taken off already. He was like the VC, always playing games, little hit-and-run shit. Still, Larry snuck up on Number 1, keeping to the driver's blind spot, hunched as if protecting a weapon. In Saigon, they'd pull the pin of a grenade, then wrap a rubber band around the spoon and drop it into a deuce and a half's gas tank; after a week or so, the gas ate enough of the rubber away and someone's motor pool would go up.

Larry reached the back of the truck. He used it for cover, peeking at the mirrors, then ducked and spun around the passenger side, stopped, crouched by the door. He checked underneath as if he and Creeley were playing tag. If he was still around, he'd be in the driver's seat; the back was a trap. Larry grasped the door handle and counted to three.

He pulled and in the same instant felt the tug of the tripwire, heard the fuse pop and begin to sizzle. He dove away from Number 1, covering his head, one elbow landing hard on the concrete. He pushed his face into the wet grit, ready to feel the hot metal rip through his uniform, burn into his skin, but there was no explosion, only a familiar, powdery smell. When he looked up, a gush of red smoke was pouring out of the door. A farmer filling his Ranchero stared.

It was a common trick to toss a smoke grenade in a bunker first so the enemy couldn't grab the real frag and throw it back. Larry counted off another five-second fuse, then covered his face with his jacket and opened the driver's side so the smoke would dissipate quicker. It rolled out in clouds, thick enough to cover a magician's disappearance, floated over traffic into the rain, calling for an invisible chopper. A small crowd had gathered; people stopped at the light gawked.

The clerk came out of the store and asked Larry if he was okay. "I looked out, I thought you'd caught fire."

"Kids probably," Larry explained. "It's almost Halloween."

They watched it like a house burning down. In seconds, the canister sputtered, then quit, the wind lifting the last tatters over Chef Peking. The clerk accompanied Larry to the door.

Everything was popsicle red, as if spray-painted—the ceiling, the windows, the gearshift. Cartwright's K-bar stuck from the driver's seat, a plastic bag hanging from the blade.

"What is it?" the clerk said.

Larry told him to go call the police, and when the door of the Sunoco closed, he tore the bag from the blade. Red dust clung to his fingers; he wiped his hands on his pants before spilling the contents onto the pay phone's metal shelf.

He expected the nine of spades, but along with the card was a photograph of a couple making love, the man behind. The picture was dark and taken from far off, grainy as a surveillance camera. Larry's red fingerprints made it hard to see what was going on. He cleaned the picture with a sleeve and tilted it to the rainy light, trying to remember which way the window in Donna's bedroom faced.

He was relieved to see that the man's head was cropped. It was not necessarily him raised up on his knees, his hands on her waist, just someone with his build. As evidence, it was inconclusive—in fact, in his defense, because it was not Donna's dresser in the background, but a light-colored one. He wiped his sleeve across the picture and tilted it again. No, it was not her dresser, because there was a mirror, and Larry saw that the woman, her face turned to see what was happening behind her, was not Donna but Vicki, and that the man had a watch on, and was therefore not him.

On the nine of spades, Creeley had written: *Red means hot.*

When Clines showed up, Larry only showed him the card.

AT THE HOSPITAL, he could not concentrate on what Susan said about the tests. Later, in bed, Donna asked what was wrong.

"You're seeing Scott tomorrow," she answered herself, and convinced him to go along with it, but as they were making love he pictured Vicki beneath Alan, her breath pressed out in gasps.

"Talk to me," Donna said. "Tell me."

He'd hidden the photograph in the attic, but the next morning, waiting for Vicki to show up, he took it out again. Alan reared. Vicki looked back, her teeth showing, as if she were saying something, and Larry wondered if it was different with him. He sat on the unused bed in his windbreaker, looking out at the cows, the barn, the trees. He knew she was making love to Alan, yet this evidence stunned him. He wanted to argue with it, refute it somehow, but there the man was, bucking, reaching deep into her.

Outside, the Ruster crunched into the drive and waited, idling. Larry looked at her face in the picture, the subtle turn of her nose, the generous lower lip. He wondered if she and Alan had done everything. Why wouldn't they? They were in love. He understood what it meant, to irreversibly turn to another; Donna had taught him how a life could change in a couple of days. He was not sure he believed it. Lately he felt more lost than exalted, as if all this were tenuous, doomed, and he was just going along with it. The Ruster honked, and Larry slipped the picture into his pocket like a revolver.

In the car, he kept his hand on it, as if to pull it at the first sign of trouble. Vicki didn't kiss him. Her hair was mussed and her lipstick made her seem pale. She had on her mother's quilted jacket and no socks, and he wondered if she'd been sleeping. She asked after his dad and then Susan and apologized again.

"You don't like them anyway," he said.

"I'd like to be there for you though."

She was sincere, and besides, it was too early to use the picture. It was cloudy; leaves vaulted the hood, stuck in the wipers. He sat against the locked door, arms folded, daring her to start a conversation. She drove with her mouth closed, frowning at the traffic, the lights that went against her. Waiting at the Octopus, she looked at him as if to say something, then changed her mind, grimaced as if they both knew it wouldn't do any good and she was sorry for that too.

"At least say something," he said as they passed Vinegar Hill.

"I'm tired of talking about it."

"You've hardly talked to me all week."

"I know," Vicki said, then, "I don't know." She sighed as if tired but didn't elaborate, drove as if he were no longer there. Below, the lake was a muddy green. They passed the hospital and headed out into the country. The last of the corn was in, the cribs filled. In the fields, machinery rusted, sea gulls huddled in the furrows.

"I'm doing what I said I would," Vicki said when they were almost to Trumansburg. Her voice was flat, drained of affect, like someone resigning under pressure, unexpectedly defeated. "I'm trying to figure out what's best for me. And for Scott."

"Scott shouldn't come into it."

"But he does," she said. "You know he does."

"You know I'll take him."

"It just may take a while," she said, as if she really hadn't decided, hadn't already left. "I don't know how long."

If it was an act, he could not tell. Though he no longer trusted her, he had to fight the instinct to comfort her, to tell her everything would be fine, that he still loved her. He fingered the glossy surface of the picture to recover himself.

At her mother's, she showed him to the den, then disappeared into the back bedroom. Mrs. Honness and Scott were playing Sorry, the light right down on the board. Scott greeted him by rocking in his chair, and Larry kissed him on the cheek. They had to play the game to the end, otherwise Scott would cry. Larry watched them, aware of his jacket hanging in the front hall closet. Mrs. Honness reminded Scott to roll the die easily. He hurled it across the board, toppling pieces; it leapt off the table to the floor. "Three," Larry said, and handed it back along with the top of the box. Scott moved his piece excruciatingly, finally setting it down on the wrong square. His arms were pudgy, soft as an infant's. Mrs. Honness cleared her throat and knocked him back one.

They played all the games on the shelf, shuffling the boxes like cards. Above Mrs. Honness hung a clock fashioned from a shellacked cross-section of driftwood, and as the day waned, Larry tried not to check the progress of its gilded hands. He listened for Vicki. The TV hadn't come on in the living room; maybe she was just sick.

"It's been a long week for everyone," Mrs. Honness said, and asked after his father.

Scott fell hopelessly behind in Candyland and lost interest, then refused to take his turn. With one sweep of his arm he scattered the pieces.

"What was that?" Larry scolded, and Scott rocked.

"Well," Mrs. Honness said, "I've had enough for one day." She told them to go play outside and she'd have warm cider ready when they came back in. The Nerf ball was in the closet, right beneath his windbreaker. Larry had Scott cover his eye with a hand and tugged a sweater over his head, then slid the patio door open.

"Don't you want a coat?" Mrs. Honness asked.

Scott couldn't catch, he would never learn. Larry stood a few feet from him and underhanded the ball so it hit him softly in the stomach, where his padding was thickest. The ball seemed to stick to him for a second, then dropped. Scott's arms closed. When he saw that he'd missed, he collapsed on the ball as if it were a fumble and rolled in the grass. Larry swiped at his hands, trying to strip it, but Scott held on.

"Touchdown!" Larry signaled, and they did it again.

Scott was tireless. Grass covered his sweater, stuck in his hair. Larry tossed the ball as if it were made of crystal. When Scott was a baby, Larry had thrown a green plastic ring he'd dropped out of his crib back to him— nonchalantly, a flick of the wrist; he watched it arc through the air toward Scott, who stood peeking over the rail. It struck him in the middle of the forehead and caromed off, knocking him on his bottom. He sobbed long after Larry picked him up. At dinner the red dent was still there, and Vicki didn't speak to Larry until he'd done the dishes. It had been an accident but he'd been careful since then. Scott didn't run, but anytime he descended the stairs, Larry was there to catch him. He took his hand crossing the street, helped him over curbs. Larry knew it wasn't healthy, that it was exactly what the Special Children's Center preached against, but he could not stop himself. He tossed the ball short rather than risk hitting him in the face.

Mrs. Honness called them in and helped Scott off with his sweater. Larry put the ball back in the closet. They sat at the counter between the living room and the kitchen, perched on barstools. A clotted island of cinnamon swirled on top of the steaming cider. It was sweet and made Larry's teeth hurt. Scott took a few sips and wandered over to the couch, sat as if watching the dark TV. The clock on the stove said it was time for Larry to go.

Vicki still hadn't come out of the back bedroom. In the hall sat a heaping basket of laundry, mostly Scott's, a sock on the floor.

"I'll take you," Mrs. Honness said, but he knew she could barely see to drive in the daytime.

"I can take the bus," Larry said, and assured her it was all right.

"I just don't want to wake her," she said. "She hasn't been having the easiest time."

"I know," he said, unsure what to hope for.

Scott didn't want him to go. "Dad," he called in alarm and grabbed at his jacket.

"It's okay, champ," Larry said. He kept a hand in the one pocket like a plug while Mrs. Honness peeled Scott's fingers off. The storm door banged shut behind him, and Scott slapped at the window. Larry waved.

The hippies were working on their van by flashlight, kneeling in the leaves. He passed the black hedges, the yellow windows. People were making dinner, watching the late game. Downtown a crowd milled outside of the Rongo; otherwise it was quiet, the T-burg Diner closed, its chairs up for the night, the Greek portico and steeple of the church where they were married spotlit. Waiting at the bus stop, Larry looked around and took out the picture. In the dull glare of the streetlight, he could not make out her face, only a white blur, and though for his own sake he could not forgive Vicki, he realized that it was unfair, that the face could just as easily be his.

AFTER THEY made love, the covers flung off, Donna talked about Wade and her infidelities. He had been her only real love, she said; the others were mistakes, bastards. One had raped her when she told him she was leaving— an older man at the university, well known in his field. Another still called when his wife was out of town. Wade knew about some of them, not all. He had left because of it, she was sure. She didn't understand why they wanted her. She wasn't attractive, not really; her chest was slight, her calves athletic. Men couldn't see what she did. She never fell for them, or only after the fact, and then they hurt her.

"I told you I wasn't stable," she said, and Larry could only hold her and tell her it was not true.

They talked all morning and made lunch naked, the blinds drawn. Her slippers scuffed the floor. She ate an apple on the couch, her hair over her breasts. The cold shriveled him and she led him upstairs again. In the shower, she soaped him with both hands, lathered his back.

"You do love me," she asked afterward. "You won't abandon me."

Jane
805-383-6282
760-310-7617
cell

He promised, and meant it, afraid he might be lying.

She took her pills with dinner, a line of five on the placemat, and again at breakfast, chasing them with coffee. He was sore. She patted his lap in the car, cooed to him, stroked his jaw. Dropping him off, she kept his hand a second.

"I've got group later," he reminded her.

"I'll make something light," she said.

He waited to wave to her, then watched the Monte Carlo away, and when it had disappeared into traffic, the normal world returned, indifferent to him. Larry sighed and headed for the door.

Number 1 was clean, the seat fixed with a strip of silver duct tape. Marv said he had messages—a bunch from the police and one from Julian.

Clines said the smoke grenade was from Holley's Surplus. He'd talked with Holley and taken a description, but it didn't fit Creeley. He was looking into the possibility of tracking both Larry's and Creeley's movements in-country through the papers in the Vietnam War Collection in Washington.

"He's Phoenix," Larry reminded him. "He won't be there."

"I can't wait for you to remember," Clines said.

"What am I supposed to remember? You have any idea the number of guys I worked on—and the conditions? I'm lucky I can remember my buddies."

"That's another thing," Clines said. "I've been trying to find some of your buddies."

"Yeah?" Larry said.

"You don't have any. Everyone I talk to says you were a good medic but you didn't have much to do with them."

"Who did you talk to?"

Clines gave him a list of names he didn't remember.

"When were they there?" Larry asked.

"June of sixty-nine, July, August."

"They were just new guys."

"Who *should* I be talking to?" Clines asked. "Give me something here, anything."

Larry thought of his father, of Ellen Creeley stretched out on his leather examining table.

"Talk to Creeley," he said.

Julian would have the Pentagon report by next week at the latest. Burt was in the system but having trouble finding Creeley's file. He had three friends from the Synchrotron working on the problem.

"Is this going to cost me extra?" Larry asked.

"Come on," Julian said, "this is fun for us. Fifty should do it."

It was cool and the damned Scandinavians came on around two, summoning the clouds. At each stop, he locked his doors, did a quick recon of the lot. Derek had done some of his convenience stores; the Donettes were way past their expiration date. He boxed his returns for the outlet to sell at half price and tidied the shelves. "Monday," the owners said, as if it explained the weather, the lack of customers. At the Food Giant in King's Ferry, all the Halloween candy was on sale. It was six days away, and the shelves were ravaged—only six-packs of Mallo Cups left—but in the back a stockboy was razoring open a shipment of mini Snickers bars. Larry bought enough for the ward and Scott's party and a few to hand out at home. He was done early. Closing up Number 1, he touched the duct tape as if it were a scar, as if to say he was sorry.

The bus up the hill passed Cayuga View, leveled off after the crest and gave them the lake, the lights defining the shore. Larry sat in back, over the warm engine, the Snickers vibrating on the seat beside him. He thought of Donna waiting for him, her girlish arms. She needed to know about Creeley; she would sense it anyway.

He decided to tell his father, but in the room with Susan and Mrs. Railsbeck, Larry didn't have the chance. The gin game continued. The tests so far were inconclusive; they needed to be repeated over the course of a week.

"It's all very demeaning," their father said. "They give you this children's puzzle—all different shapes—and you have to build a square while they time you. And words, they give you this huge list and see how many you can remember day to day. Honestly, I don't think they really know what they're doing."

Larry could only stay a few minutes.

"He seems better," he told Susan in the hall.

"I've been talking with Mrs. R.," she said. "It sounds like he's been having these episodes for a while." She looked to him as if he might have a different opinion.

"It's possible," Larry said.

"Dr. Downs thinks it may be the beginnings of Parkinson's disease, or Alzheimer's. I'd like to take him to Boston and have someone at Mass General look at him."

They would say the same thing there, Larry thought, but didn't argue with her logic. His silence seemed to make her reconsider.

"They might be able to do *something* for him," she said.

"He'd never go," he said.

She bitterly agreed. "I don't know what else to do though." She waited for him to suggest something, hung on his next sentence, and Larry understood she was equally helpless in this.

"He'll be all right."

"I don't think so," she said. "And I think he knows it."

She walked Larry to the elevator and, saying good-bye, surprised him by holding him close. Going down, he could not remember how long it had been, and it worried him.

On the ward, the party had already started. They gave him shit for being late. The tape player was going, the Spinners with "I'll Be Around," and streamers hung from the lights. Johnny Johnson was wrapped in toilet paper to look like the Mummy. Trayner had fangs, Sponge was a pirate, Cartwright a football star; they were all stoned and dancing stiffly, a hint of whiskey on their lips. Larry dumped a bag of Snickers bars into a mixing bowl full of popcorn balls and candy corn, and Meredith scooped a few up. He was an angel, his halo a coat hanger covered with tinfoil.

"Who are you supposed to be?" Mel White asked Larry. He had turned his chair into a Formula 1 car, complete with a cardboard spoiler, and Larry felt he had let them down.

"So what's up with our boy Creeley?" Mel asked.

"Yeah," Rinehart seconded.

Trayner turned down the music, and Larry told them about the smoke and Cartwright's knife.

"You said the nine," Sponge said. "What happened to the six, seven and eight?"

"Why doesn't he just grease your sorry ass already?" Cartwright said.

" 'Cause the dude is a fruit loop," Sponge said. "I seen it a million times. He's got to get to the ace."

"He's still got my bread," Cartwright complained.

"He's still got my gun," said Meredith.

Mel White rubbed one eyebrow with a finger. He was the thinker; even Sponge wouldn't play Othello with him. "He's doing things now," he finally said. "He's probing you, seeing where your weakness is."

Again, Larry thought of Donna, that he had left her unprotected.

"He delivers the ace in person," Sponge predicted. "That's how it ends."

"Don't joke," Mel White scolded. "The guy is fucking dangerous."

The two of them traded looks, standing their ground. Johnny Johnson laughed, and the rest of them were nervous enough to join him.

"Okay," Larry said. "Enough. Who's got a ghost story for us? The weirdest thing I saw in Vietnam."

"You kiddin'?" Cartwright said. "That's everything, the whole goddamn country."

"I got one," Sponge said.

"Not you again," Larry said, but no one else volunteered.

They turned out the overhead fluorescents and formed a circle around the bowl, dipping in, the candy corn clinking against the metal. Trayner had a red-lens flashlight that he gave to Sponge, who turned it up beneath his chin, making his nostrils glow.

"There was this cook for this ROK outfit," Sponge started, and they all groaned. It was a liver story, how the Koreans cut them out of the VC and ate them so the dead wouldn't enter the Buddhist equivalent of heaven.

"Nirvana," Mel White offered.

"Whatever," Sponge said. He handed the flashlight to Larry.

"Okay, who's got a good one?"

"The weirdest thing," Rinehart repeated, stumped.

"You guys should have tons of these. Meredith?"

"It's the wrong war for it. It was all weird."

"Dig," Cartwright said. "You don't get any of those haunted bombers or castles—all of that heroic crap you see in the comic books. I mean, the jungle's some scary shit, but it's not ghost scary, it's cut-your-nuts-off scary, get-blown-into-a-piece-of-gristle scary."

"Anybody?" Larry said.

A piece of candy corn clinked.

"I've got one," Mel White said from his chair, and Larry passed the flashlight along. Mel White turned it off so only the red exit sign glowed.

"It's not really a ghost story," he said. "It was sixty-seven 'cause I was nineteen—a young nineteen. It was off in the rubber country. We were running a sweep through this plantation laid out by the French. If you've ever been, you don't forget it—you're hacking through jungle and all of a sudden you step clear of it and the trees are laid out in rows, spaced just so. I mean, they're so even you can't see—turn one way it's like you're looking down a hall, turn the other it's the same thing. It's like a maze except there aren't any walls to guide you through it. And completely open, you can see a hundred, two hundred meters, so you know you're exposed. Every tree's got a little bucket, and the rubber's dripping—tip-tap, tip-tap. At first you can't hear it, but after a few steps it's like a fucking drum. So now you can't hear and you can't see shit and you're basically at the mercy of anybody hanging around.

"We were running sweeps through this place at the request of the owner. He was this old Frenchman, he'd been there sixty, seventy years, he knew everyone in Saigon. In the middle of these trees he's got this chateau, there's no other way to say it. It's got stained glass windows and this mile-long cobblestone drive, and right in front of the entrance he's got this old Sherman tank, the star still on the side, with this huge fucking Nung in tiger stripes behind the fifty. In the garage he's got this thirty-foot Daimler touring car, all black. He's got horses, he's got wine, he's got a swimming pool. He's got his own militia of Nungs, but the VC are picking them off one by one and it's getting expensive, so he calls Saigon and Saigon calls Higher and we ruck up and hump it out there, and there's the old guy on this Appaloosa with a sword hanging off his belt like Robert E. Lee and shit. He wants to go out on recon with us.

"The captain calls in and Higher says to take care of the man. Intel says there isn't much activity—a tax collector who comes around once a month, but no serious cadre. Our second day out we find a base plate for a mortar. We bring in a dog and he tracks whoever's using it to a well with a tunnel, and in this tunnel there's this fully equipped operating room, everything brand new from East Germany, stuff still in boxes. So the engineers wire it up to this hell box—I mean, straight out of Bugs Bunny, the plunger and everything—and the captain has the old guy blow it.

"The old guy gets off on it. I don't know if it's the France-Germany thing or what, but he's happy as shit, he can't stop talking about his *amis* the

Americans. We do two or three more days mopping up the eastern edge of the place and then it's time to motate.

"The night before we leave, the old guy invites us all to the chateau for dinner, and we know it's big because Higher flies out our class A's. The rumor goes around they'll be ladies there. The captain has us stand inspection before we go over, and damned if his clerk doesn't hand out bouquets to every one of us. We get a lecture on representing our country, and then everyone climbs in the six-bys and we roll over there.

"The place is lit up like a premiere, little bags with candles in them all along the drive. You can hear a piano through the trees. The rumors are getting better; guys are saying it's round-eye waiting for us, and champagne, all kind of ridiculous food. At the same time we're thinking it's a set-up, that we should have brought our guns.

"We pull in and the Nung behind the fifty has a tuxedo on. The old man's in tails, waving a bottle of champagne around. The captain gets out first and salutes him and the old man kisses his cheeks—it's like we've liberated Paris. He kisses everybody as they go in, and inside, it's true, there are women decked out in gowns, their hair done up fancy.

"But the bouquets aren't for them. The old man takes us right past them and into a room where the piano is, and there, playing what we heard coming up the drive, is this little girl with white hair. White as sugar, honest to God, and her skin's the same. First look you'd swear she's a ghost. She's an albino, her eyes are pink like a rabbit's. She can't be more than ten, and she's got on this frilly white dress with these puffy sleeves. She's got white tights on and white patent leather shoes.

" 'Genevieve,' the old man says, and she finds a place to stop the song. She puts on these long gloves like ladies wear to church and gets up from the bench. And the captain, they must have explained this to him, because he goes to her on one knee and offers her the bouquet.

" 'Merci,' she says, and takes it and curtsies.

"Everybody does this. It takes forever. Then we go into dinner, and she sits right beside the old man. She's obviously the granddaughter, but where her parents are is a mystery. By that time they've got us sitting boy-girl all the way around, and I'm losing interest in her. There's candles and everything is silver; the knives are heavy. One of the servants rings a bell for quiet and the girl stands up in her white dress and says grace in French and we all say amen. The food comes and for a minute we forget about the ladies.

"There's duck and lobster and more wine. For dessert we have Bananas Foster. The servants come around and pour brandy on top of bananas and brown sugar and then light it on fire right in the pan. While we're having coffee, the servant rings the bell for quiet and the girl gets up again.

" 'Good night,' she says in French, and all the ladies and servants and the old man answer her.

" 'Good night,' she says in English, and we all say, 'Good night, Genevieve,' and the servant takes her away by the hand.

"It's a wild night, let me just leave it at that.

"Five months later—"

"Whoa, whoa, whoa," Sponge protested.

"No, 'cause this is the story," Mel said, and the bowl clinked. "Five months later it's Tet and we get overrun and the captain is killed. We get our shit together and the first place they send us is this plantation, to see if anything's left.

"We lose two guys just busting jungle to get there, and when we step clear it's the same feeling—those trees standing there in rows, the drip-drip, drip-drip. It's a hundred-something degrees and the trigger's slippery and you feel about fifteen feet wide.

"We come in from behind the chateau, figuring they'll defend the front. Our probes don't draw fire, but we take our time, we make sure. We fuck mud through the formal gardens, bees all over the place. The outside looks okay, not even a window broken. The stable's empty. The pool filter's running, the water's blue.

"Inside, nothing has been touched. There's the banquet hall, there's the piano. We check the place room by room. No bodies, no blood, nothing. In front, the tank's gone; you can see tread marks going over the curb.

"We're standing around trying to figure out what's up when our doc points to the roof. There's a white flag up there on top of a chimney.

"No one can believe it, a guy like that giving up. Everyone's bumming, thinking about the guy on his horse, all the years he'd stuck it out there. The new captain says it's time to saddle up, but nobody listens to him. It's like the old man was family, someone who opened his home to us, but the captain's new and doesn't understand. Finally someone explains it to him and he sends somebody up to get the flag. We watch him walk across the peak of the roof to it, his arms out for balance, and all of a sudden he stops and goes to his hands and knees.

" 'What's the trouble?' the captain hollers up. A West Pointer, an utter fucking jerk.

"The guy on the roof crawls to the chimney and lifts the flag off the lightning rod and starts heading back with it.

" 'Throw it down!' the captain says, but the guy acts like he doesn't hear him.

" 'Throw the goddamn thing down!' the captain orders, so finally the guy does. He balls it up but still it doesn't throw so good. It lands on the roof and slides down the tiles and floats over the gutter and down toward us, and about the second floor we see it's not a sheet or a pillowcase. It's the little girl's dress."

Someone across the circle let out their breath; someone else whistled in appreciation.

"True story," Mel White said.

"Fuck," Cartwright said, and chuckled. "Think I believe that shit?"

"I don't know if it's true," Sponge said, "but it's a good one."

It was the best they'd get. Sponge told one about a chopper crew who'd stuck a pair of enemy heads on the tips of their skids and then another about an ARVN interrogator firing a flare up some spy's cunt, but it was average stuff and he knew it. They turned the lights on and cranked the Motown until Shaun rolled through the doors.

They showed Larry their lists. Only Johnny Johnson didn't have one, and Trayner said his family was putting one together from his letters. Mel White's was the longest because he'd served three tours. Rinehart's had one name. Most of the names were useless—Tennessee and Cream and Grizzly, Johnny Dog, the Hurt, Cleanhead. Larry said they had two weeks to finish them.

"So you're going," Meredith asked, and they all watched him.

"What am I supposed to do," Larry said, "say no?"

On the bus home, the girl's dress troubled him, the empty chateau. He would tell Donna about Creeley, see if Clines could spare a man to watch the house, though it would complicate things. Larry was almost relieved

Creeley was up to the ten; it meant there were only five to go. In his footlocker in the attic he still had his .45, the slide rusty from the damp. He would clean it and take it to a range.

He debated this all through town, his Snickers bouncing with the potholes, the roar of the diesel warming his seat. Of everything in the trunk, Larry feared the pistol most. He would not touch the blued steel or feel the grip in his hand. It stayed snapped in its holster, under the rubberbanded stacks of Magoo's pictures. To get it back to the States he'd given a corpsman at the 95th Evac his new watch. His first months he carried the gun everywhere, but gradually he had come to trust again, not fully but enough to venture out unprotected. Now he thought that it was not a question of trust; he was under siege. He'd kill to protect Donna or Scott, he knew that; it didn't trouble him. Still, he couldn't imagine picking up the .45 again and firing it at someone.

The bus labored up East Hill, dropping off college students until he was the only one left. The streetlights stopped and the overgrown fields and ranch houses slid by, a barn with a chore light over an empty pen. He thought of the little girl's dress again, and Donna alone in the house, and he was angry with himself and with Wade for leaving her.

The driver was the woman from the other night. "Take care now," she said.

The wind was up and he couldn't hear anything but leaves. Her lights were on. So were his, top and bottom.

He was sure he'd turned them off this morning. He crouched, keeping the Monte Carlo between himself and the house, peering through the fogged, frosted windows. When he reached the back bumper, he saw the Ruster in the drive.

He thought of Vicki and, instantly, Creeley. He was only supposed to be on the ten.

He hugged Donna's car, made his way to the front fender. The porch light was on, frosting the dewed grass. He laid the bag of Snickers bars on the ground. If it really was Vicki, he wondered if she'd come to talk or just to pick up some things. He wondered if this was it, if Alan had kept his part of the bargain, and discovered he was strangely disinterested, that he was hoping only that she would be happy. He could not tell if it was selfish. Next door, Donna was watching TV, the front window aglow.

Far off, a car approached, the drone of its tires closing. As it passed, Larry dashed across the lawn to the cover of the bushes. He inched to the foot of the front steps and inspected them for tripwires; they were clean. The porch offered no shadows, no concealment. He gripped the rail with one hand and swung himself up, crept from step to step, easing his weight from one foot to the other, keeping his eyes on the windows.

The door was unlocked. Her purse hung from the newel post. In back, the kitchen light was on.

"Vicki?" he called.

Overhead, feet padded down the hall, stopping near the top of the stairs; he recognized her step.

"I'm up here," she whispered, as if he should be quiet, but didn't come down. Her footsteps retreated to their bedroom.

Climbing the stairs, he wondered if Creeley could do voices, but at the top the hall was empty.

Scott slept, his covers up to his neck, his eye moonlike. Vicki was in their bedroom, filling the dresser with piles of folded shirts, jeans, underwear. Her bags lay on the floor, deflated. She wouldn't look at him until she was done. She threw the bags in the closet and rolled the door closed, then sat on the end of the bed.

He watched her pull off her shoes.

She looked to him, waiting for a response, but he could not think.

"Come on," she said. "At least pretend like you're happy to see me."

EIGHT

In the dry season the farmers burned their fields and smoke floated down the valley as if from a battle. Carl Metcalf's sketches showed the women brandishing torches, bandanas over their noses. The village was busy. The market stalls were sparse, prices rising. The madame of the whorehouse bought a turquoise-and-cream Honda scooter. Saigon replaced the district chief with someone's disgraced brother-in-law; he was a Catholic, and the lieutenant expected trouble. He liked the old one, had become used to his cheating at bridge, his warm beer and disgusting cigarettes. They were both tired, glad for the company; it was not a war for old men.

Tet was coming. The Year of the Monkey was nearly over. It would not be like last year. A crew of engineers flew in and stoked up the bulldozer and knocked down another hundred meters of jungle. For a week after they left, Echo strung wire and rigged tripflares. The Martian and a guy named Boat in second platoon mixed a barrel of foo gas and fixed it in the hillside. It was a fifty-five-gallon drum filled with gas and liquid soap, a charge of C-4 and two white phosphorous grenades attached to the bottom. The C-4 would launch it into the air, where the phosphorous would ignite the contents, showering the enemy with homemade napalm. If that didn't work, artillery could level their 105s at the wire and let off beehive rounds, each releasing thousands of flechette darts the size of ten-penny nails. A buddy of Fred the Head had seen one last Tet; it pinned guns to people, people to trees. The name came not from being stung but the noise made by the swarm of flechettes.

"That is one sound," Fred said, "you definitely do not want to hear."

They finished the wire and reinforced the guard bunkers, a skycrane lifting in sections of perforated steel plate, kicking up dust. They filled sandbags and hauled logs, dug the grenade sumps deeper. They landscaped the apron to provide cleaner fields of fire. When they were finished, battalion sent a few Special Forces boys to show a film and lecture them on hand-to-hand combat.

"Now I feel safe," Smart Andy said.

Larry and Redmond ran extra medcaps in the village, which was suddenly off limits. The madame buzzed up and down the road on her Honda, scattering geese, impressing the children. Her girls leaned in the door of the club, brushing each other's hair and dancing to tinny Vietnamese pop—covers of the Beatles and Animals, the Electric Prunes.

"*Bac-si,*" they called to Larry, kissing the air. "I love you too much, okay?"

His mother was dying. Susan wrote every day now, quoting their father. Larry ordered her letters by the date on the postmark and tore through them, reading only the first words, then going back. Their mother returned to the hospital; it was shocking how quickly she'd deteriorated. The treatments made her lose weight. She complained that nothing tasted right. It's always too cold for her, Susan wrote. There was nothing to operate on, no space-age procedure. Only Vicki said it directly: it was just a matter of time. It was funny, Larry thought, how long his mother had believed the exact same thing.

Tet was a week away. At night, Odin went on 50 percent alert. Higher ordered more day patrols, and now Echo ranged far into the A Shau. The column was smaller; replacements still hadn't come. Bates's hair closed over the scar and he asked for his thumper back. Carl Metcalf gladly relinquished it and moved up to take Nate's old position at slack, leaving Larry right behind Bogut and his antenna.

They humped the jungle, chasing the 23rd VC Battalion. By lunch the temperature was in the hundreds. Every twenty minutes they stopped for water, filled their canteens from streams, and still the lieutenant passed out, Bogut fanning him with his towel. His face turned white, his lips cracked and bled. Back at Odin he sacked out after chow, snoring wetly behind the mosquito netting.

They went back to Stupidville and found the same women, the kids playing with the deflated ball. Third platoon flushed two suspects from a pineapple field; they knelt by the well, their eyes and mouths sealed with green duct tape. Magoo pushed over a basket of yams and marrows and found a handful of rounds underneath. The straw in a pigsty hid a typewriter. Echo herded the residents out of the village. While they waited, Larry inoculated the children for smallpox and cholera. The hootches gave off a gray smoke, the women jabbered, and soon a pair of Shithooks came down and took Stupidville away again.

The holiday cease-fire went into effect the day Bogut and the Martian left for R&R in Sydney. Odin stood 100 percent alert and dug in for the night. For the first time since Christmas the big guns were quiet. Larry shared a bunker with Fred the Head, who had taken three Dexedrine and wouldn't stop talking.

"You like applesauce?" he said.

"No," Larry said, and scanned the perimeter.

"I'm talking about real applesauce. My granny makes this applesauce, it's not sweet at all. It won a prize once. You'd like it."

"I hate applesauce," Larry said.

"How about corn relish?" Fred said. "My auntie makes great corn relish."

When the wind shifted, they could hear the snap of firecrackers from the village, the gleeful shrieks of children up way too late.

"Hey," Fred said, suddenly reminded, "Happy New Year."

"Yeah," Larry said. "Happy New Year to you too."

In the morning the platoon climbed out of their bunkers and shrugged at each other, spat in the dust. The cease-fire expired and guns started up. Patrols went out and made contact or didn't, and the war went on. In the village, the madame's Honda leaned on its kickstand; her girls beckoned from the door.

When Bogut and the Martian came back, they were disappointed they hadn't missed anything. Bogut had a shark's jaw he hung over his bunk; the Martian had a stack of paperbacks. The women were beautiful, they said, and the beaches, but neither of them told stories.

"You're next," the lieutenant told Larry, and showed him the orders. He would leave in two weeks. "Where do you want to go?"

He had a choice of Sydney, Bangkok, Hong Kong or Taipei; Hawaii was reserved for married people. They gave him advice. What did he want to do, they asked. Did he want to go surfing or buy a stereo? Did he want round-eye tail or some wild shit?

They debated it, laid down ground rules for the perfect R&R.

"You mean I&I," Magoo said. "Intercourse and intoxication."

"What you don't want to do is get shit-faced your first night," Pony warned. "You spend half your time recovering."

"Yeah," Smart Andy agreed, "slow and steady wins the race."

"What you really want to do," Carl Metcalf said, "is sleep and eat, and the place for both of those is Hong Kong."

"Sleep is about all you do there," Magoo ridiculed. "Now Bangkok, there is the fucking capital of the world."

"Australia's got women," Fred said. "All you get in Bangkok is little girls."

Their enthusiasm amused Larry; he didn't care where he went. Lately Susan's letters said less and less. The lieutenant said the Army would arrange for Larry to call Ithaca on a MARS line while he was waiting to fly out of Da Nang, and this excited him more than the prospect of a week alone in a place he didn't know.

He began to count the days, at night writing down what he would say to his mother, his father, Vicki, Susan. It was clear now how deeply he cared for them. He wanted to apologize for his shortcomings and pledge to do better, guarantee that he'd see them all again, yet even as he thought this, he knew it was untrue, that simple wishes were not enough for any of them, least of all himself.

On patrol his mind drifted back to Ithaca, traded the suffocating heat for a foot of snow. His father laid a blanket over the New Yorker's engine block, checked his antifreeze weekly. The waterfalls hardened, the snowmen turned brittle as glass. On the lake, leftover geese rode the ice floes. He remembered himself and Susan at the breakfast table listening to the school closings, nodding with the rhythm of the alphabetical list, their eyes locked, fingers crossed. "You still have to eat," Mrs. R. would say to calm them.

He went back to elementary school and walked the rows, naming everybody. He followed his old paper route, chucking tomahawks, slipping a copy inside the screen door for a tip. He picked up Vicki in his Fairlane and drove up the iced-over lake, ate lunch at the Glenwood Pines—a Tullyburger and fries, a bowl of chili and a pair of Schaefers in thick mugs.

"Skull," Magoo had to say, "watch where you're fucking going."

Three days before Larry was scheduled to leave for R&R, they stopped to eat lunch in a graveyard outside of Phong Thua. The lieutenant conferred with the Martian about the spot. The grave mounds were good cover if they had to defend themselves. They unassed their rucksacks and settled in. It was too hot to cook; they undid their canteens before breaking out their C-rats and P-38s, their sporks stolen from the mess tent.

Fred the Head wandered among them, holding up a can of turkey loaf.

"What am I bid?" he asked. "Serious offers only. No ham and mothers, no ham and eggs."

"Beanies and weenies," Bogut offered.

"Fuck you very much," Fred said, winding through the mounds. "What am I bid?"

"Fruitcake," Pony joked, digging into his spaghetti and meatballs.

"Do I hear pears? Pineapple chunks?"

"Pound cake," the Martian called, and Fred turned.

"What else?"

"Straight up." The Martian had his arm cocked as if to throw it to him.

"Can I get a butt on top of it?"

The Martian lowered his arm.

"Okay," Fred the Head said, "I'm not here to make a profit." He tossed the turkey loaf to him and held up his hand.

The Martian flipped him the pound cake. While it was still in midair, a single round cracked and caught Fred the Head in the chest and blew him against a tombstone. The can landed where he'd been standing.

Larry grabbed his aid bag and started for him, but Carl Metcalf dragged him down with one arm. It was enough time for the others to open up, pouring fire into the hedgerow. Carl let go and Larry ran behind their cover.

The Martian was already there but had done nothing, just stared at the mess. Larry ripped Fred's T-shirt down the front. The entry pulsed just off the heart, bubbled—a lung shot. Larry rolled him over and checked for the exit. It was fist-sized. He covered it with the dressing in his helmet band and

laid Fred on his back. The Martian hunched in close, saying "Shit. Goddamn it, shit."

"Get the fuck out of my way," Larry said.

The entry hissed and wheezed under his fingers. He shoved a dressing in
but still the blood came, bright with oxygen.

"Skull," Fred said.

"Don't mean nothin'," Larry said. "It's just one."

"Aw, man," the Martian said over his shoulder.

"Get the fuck away from me," Larry whispered.

"Truth, Skull," Fred the Head said, and Larry had to lie. He used all the
blood expander in his bag. In the hedgerow Pony found one spent shell,
nothing else.

Fred was still breathing when they lifted him onto the chopper. The
rotors chirped, the pilot pulled pitch and the bird rocketed off, leaving them
to finish lunch. Smart Andy kicked dust over the blood, and they sat back
against the mounds.

The Martian hadn't opened his turkey loaf; now he contemplated the
olive-drab can, the pound cake still lying on the ground. He stood and
walked over to it and traded the two, sat down again and opened the pound
cake.

There was not enough water to wash Larry's hands, so he shook more hot
sauce on his ham and eggs and couldn't smell anything else. As he was
eating, a voice over Bogut's radio changed the urgent dust-off to a routine
one.

"Our Whiskey Indigo Alpha now one Kilo Indigo Alpha," the man said.

They finished eating and policed the area. Nobody touched the turkey
loaf. Then they moved out, Magoo walking a cautious slack, Carl Metcalf
coming back to take drag. Larry kept a healthy interval with Bogut, his
hands sticky on the pistol grip. In Ithaca, students were traying on Libe
Slope, kids sailing over the snow on silver disks. In three days, he kept
thinking, in three days I will not be here.

HE CAUGHT the afternoon log ship to battalion at Phong Dien and then a
deuce and a half to Phu Bai, where they put him on a C-130 to Da Nang.
He'd thought that once out of the jungle he might relax, but the traffic and

270

the sheer number of people made him reach instinctively for the .45 in his bag. It was gone, confiscated back at Odin. Though he'd left only hours ago, he wondered how the platoon was doing. He'd told Redmond to take care of them, but now Larry thought it was wrong, that he should not have left them.

In Da Nang, everyone on base was clean shaven, their fatigues pressed, their boots new. Civilians worked inside the wire, and Larry found himself crossing the street to avoid them. At the transient point, a PFC searched his bag for contraband, supply items; he found only the hundred dollars Smart Andy had given Larry to buy Italian shoes, which was completely legal.

He went to the PX and bought a pair of underwear, a sport shirt and some chinos. In the transient barracks he shaved and took an hour-long shower, his body whittling the soap to a sliver. His cuts stung, his fingers burned. He pulled on his new clothes and wrapped a fresh piece of adhesive tape around Vicki's ring. He brushed his teeth. This simple regimen hid a luxury. In the mirror, he looked tanned and fit, like someone back from vacation.

He wasn't sure how the MARS thing worked or what the time difference was. He hoped they'd be home. The room the MP pointed him to was carpeted and bright as a library, the air-conditioning too high. Behind the sign-in desk, the clerk wore a T-shirt under his fatigues. A row of numbered booths separated by frosted-glass partitions ran the length of one wall, some with dark shapes inside. He would be in eight, the clerk said, and explained that he had ten minutes. All he had to do was pick up the phone; a relay station in Guam would patch it through to a stateside operator, who would dial whatever number Larry wanted. At the end of ten minutes, the line automatically cut off.

The clerk gave him a key with an oversized plastic tag, like that for a gas station bathroom.

"I can make more than one," Larry checked.

"Yes, but remember you only have ten minutes. And don't forget to say 'over.' Otherwise you end up wasting time."

The walls of the booth were lined with perforated ceiling tile, like a radio station; he could no longer hear the air-conditioning. A plain table held a phone with no dial, a blank legal pad and some nubby pencils. The air reeked of cigarettes. The phone was bolted down.

Larry unfolded the list of things he wanted to say and smoothed it with a hand. It was not long. He wanted to thank Susan for taking care of their parents, Vicki for loving him, his father for all he'd taught him. He did not have anything specific for his mother, only that he loved her very much and wished he were there with her. When he had written these things down, they seemed powerful, great gifts he was unworthy of; he'd been moved, but now, in the silent booth, the receiver under his clammy hand, his sentiments seemed bland as a store-bought card, and though he still felt them, he suspected he was being melodramatic, overwrought. He did not want to alarm them.

There was no dial tone but an immediate hiss, a clicking. He looked to his wrist to time himself, but his watch was gone; he'd have to buy one in Hong Kong. Ghosts of other calls drifted through an electronic fog, the nattering of faraway conversations, and then the line cleared and an operator came on. She was the first American woman he'd heard in months, her voice stirring and alien.

He knew the numbers by heart, even the hospital. He decided he should talk to his mother first, in case.

The girl at the switchboard had an Upstate accent, flattening her vowels, hitting her r's hard. She said they didn't have a number for a Helen Markham, and, panicked, Larry asked for his father's office. He hunched over the phone, listening to it ring, wishing he knew what time it was there, what day. It was March, the rest escaped him.

"I'm sorry, sir," the girl said, "he's not picking up."

"Do you have another you'd like to try?" the operator prompted, and Larry gave her his home number.

His father answered.

"Dad," Larry said, his head bent, his nose inches from the table.

"Larry," his father said, then called to someone, "Larry's on the phone!"

The operator reminded them to say "over."

"How's Mother?" Larry asked. "Over."

"She's here. Would you like to talk with her?"

"Yes," Larry said.

"Hold on. Let me run upstairs." The phone clonked and his father hollered something else.

"Larry," Susan said. "Are you okay?"

"I'm fine," he said. "I'm really doing okay. How's Mother doing?"

Upstairs their father picked up.

"I'll talk to you after you talk to her," Susan said, and clicked off.

"She's going to be a little tired," his father warned.

"What time is it there?" Larry asked.

No one answered, and then his mother said softly, "Larry?" He had to stick a finger in his ear to hear her, and then she didn't say anything.

"You're home," he said loudly, as if she might follow his lead. "How are you feeling?"

"I'm tired, dear." Her voice was thick, the words imperfectly formed, the gummed speech of a retarded child.

"Susan says you didn't like the hospital."

"No."

"But you feel a little better now?"

"Yes," she conceded.

"I'm glad you're home. I miss you very much."

"I miss you too."

"My tour's half done. I'm going to Hong Kong tonight for R&R."

"You be careful."

"I will."

"Over," the operator coaxed.

"Who is that?" his mother asked, and he explained, wondering how much time he had left.

"What are you listening to?" he asked, expecting something heavy—Bach's Mass in B minor or Brahms's German Requiem.

"Nothing," she said, and apologized. "I don't have the energy."

"That's all right," Larry said.

"You should talk with your father."

"I love you," Larry said before she could hand him off.

"I love you too, dear. You come home soon."

"I will," Larry promised.

"So," his father came on, "I think Susan wants to talk to you."

"How is Mother?" Larry asked him.

"Good," he said, but didn't go on. He was in the room with her. "Let me get Susan for you."

The phone clunked again. It was all taking too long; he still needed to call Vicki.

"Okay," Susan yelled, and the upstairs phone clicked off.

"Tell me what's happening," Larry demanded. "Why isn't she in the hospital?"

"She wants it this way. We all do."

"Is it that bad?"

"Dad thinks another month or two."

"I've applied for emergency leave but they keep turning me down."

"I know," she said, as if it were not his fault.

She told him to keep his head down and gave him back to their father.

"So how are you?" his father asked, and Larry thought of Fred the Head and Nate and Dumb Andy and Leonard Dawson and Salazar. He thought of the platoon out somewhere now without him and the clean sheets of the hotel room.

"I'm okay," Larry said.

After they hung up, the operator said he had one minute left, and Larry wondered where the time had gone; he hadn't said anything.

Vicki's mother answered and said she was out.

"What day is it there?" Larry asked. "What time?"

"It's Sunday," Mrs. Honness said. "It's about nine-thirty. She has a food drive at church she's working on. She's going to be really teed off she missed you. What should I tell her?"

"Ten seconds," the operator announced.

He looked at the list, at everything he hadn't said.

"Tell her I'm all right," Larry said. "Tell her I love her."

"Anything else?" Mrs. Honness asked, and the line clicked, then like a trapdoor gave way to charged, hissing space, an endless fall.

Larry placed the receiver back in the cradle and straightened up in the chair. His back hurt and one ear was hot and tender. He crumpled the list into a ball, but there was no wastebasket under the table.

He opened the door and the hum of the air conditioner filled the room.

"You got a garbage can back there?" Larry asked, returning the key.

"Sure," the clerk said, and held out his hand.

HIS FIRST NIGHT in Hong Kong, Larry locked the door and sat on the balcony overlooking the harbor in the dark, eating room-service burgers and drinking warm Carlsberg. The hotel was the Hilton, the marble fountain in the lobby plashing. He wanted to throw a penny in, but the doorman waved him away. "Bad *feng shui*," he said. "Bring trouble to the young sir's house."

The room had two beds. Both the cabbie and the bellboy had offered him women, and now he wished he'd gone along with it, if only to have someone to talk to. Below, the neon streets glowed. So far up, the night was quiet. The corners of high-rises blazed, warning planes away. In all the city, he knew no one. The TV was in English, *Rowan and Martin's Laugh-In*.

He woke up naked, under the bed. Light poured through the sliding doors; freighters dotted the harbor. In the hall a vacuum roared. He sat on the john, then took a shower, going through the tiny soaps. He put on the stiff bathrobe and stood at the rail of the balcony, looking down at the warehouses and cranes of the dockyard. He thought he'd finished the six-pack, but there was one left, the bottle hot in the carton. He checked his wallet, then sat on the unused bed and read the brunch menu, the impossible prices. He had five more days here.

"Mr. Markham," the desk clerk addressed him.

"Sir," the doorman said, and bowed, letting him out.

On the street, he felt giant. All the people were Chinese; his eyes searched for a white or black face, blond hair, a bold 'fro. The sidewalks reminded him of his class trip to New York—crowds bunching up at corners, ignoring traffic. There was no grass; everything was paved or trampled to dust. The narrow streets buzzed with Vespas and Lambrettas, cyclos and old-style rickshaws, a rare ancient Chevy, all on the wrong side of the road. The fact registered, yet the first time Larry stepped off the curb, only a restraining hand on his belt saved him from being hit. The man responsible jabbed a cigarette at the oncoming traffic as if Larry were a moron. He was a business-man, his black coat folded over his arm.

"Thank you," Larry said, almost in apology, and the man nodded harshly, then refused to look at him.

The streets were steep, sloping down to the harbor. Overhead, advertising signs linked the buildings, their Chinese characters obscuring the view. Ivory, jade, pickled snakes. Some streets sold only one thing—Egg Street, Cloth Street. He bought a map and some fish and chips cradled in newspaper and wandered through the electronics district. The windows were full of cameras and tape players, the prices in both Hong Kong dollars and pounds. Whores in hot pants and halter tops and glossy kneeboots leaned in the entries of Love Hotels like bored cheerleaders. In the distance a cannon sounded and Larry ducked. The whores giggled; it was the Noon-Day gun, a British tradition. The discotheques were already open, Creedence or the Stones pouring from the doors, the bouncers dressed as if for a wedding. He had Smart Andy's money in his sock; in the humidity it stuck to his calf like a bandage.

It was an island, the city built straight up, yet he was terrified of becoming lost, wandering the clogged streets. He followed Jubilee down to the harbor, where double-decker trams plied the wide boulevards, and took a Star ferry across to Kowloon, feeding the last of his chips to the sea gulls. The water was crowded with sampans and oceangoing junks, their sails sectioned like fans, spirit eyes painted on their prows to guide the way. At the airfield jutting from the far shore, jets landed and took off. He wondered how much the cheapest ticket cost. He had his military ID, Vicki's ring. His father would forgive him.

On the map he found the street Smart Andy had written down. He'd given Larry a list of what he wanted; their feet were the same. The owner welcomed him at the door, took him inside by the arm. He was old and thin, his cheeks collapsed, a mouthful of brown teeth. Behind the counter a nightingale whistled in a cage.

The man had one pair of each shoe from which he made copies. Even the boxes looked expensive, the cardboard sturdy, the designs staid. He had Larry smell the leather, run his fingers over the stitching.

"You come from the war," the man asked, fitting a pair of oxfords on.

"Yes," Larry said, wondering if he could be a spy.

"War is lousy, I know myself." His hands flew over the laces; he pressed a thumb against the tip to locate Larry's big toe. "Stand up," he said. "Walk."

"They feel good."

"I make for you," the man said. "You come back tomorrow, they be ready."

Larry ordered four pairs for Smart Andy and one for himself, thinking he could find a watch cheap. At the door they shook hands.

"I wish you luck," the old man said. "In war it is the best thing."

Larry figured he said this to everyone but wished him the same, not wanting to jinx himself.

He took the ferry back toward the white skyline. On his way up Jubilee, he stopped at a jeweler's and looked at a copy of his father's Hamilton. At that price it had to be a fake, but Larry knew the square face too well—and the demands of coincidence—to leave it in the case. With the money he saved he went to a steakhouse and had a filet the size of a brick; his stomach was unaccustomed to red meat, and he spent part of the night on the john.

He was ready for the Noon-Day gun. When he picked up the shoes the store was busy, the nightingale silent. The old man wished a pair of sailors luck. It was a kindness, Larry thought; they all needed it.

He had nothing left to do. Mornings he lay in bed, his feet plumbing the covers for cool spots. His money was all right. He ate lunch at cafés, poring over the *South China Morning Post*, then walked the streets, following along on the map. High up the slopes, the apartment buildings bristled with bamboo poles festooned with drying laundry. The great villas and their gardens ended and the city petered out in tin shanties and ditches used for sewers. On the docks, whores gave dollar blowjobs to sailors in the public toilets. The kiosks sold condoms and lottery tickets, packets of firecrackers. Children pointed at him, and sometimes women stared. His clothes were wrong; he went days without speaking. The Noon-Day gun boomed. Though he was getting used to the city, its odd contrast of languor and industry, he wanted to leave. There were places he would never belong.

His last night he packed his bag and laid out his clothes for the morning, then sat on the balcony, watching the lights of the airfield on the Kowloon side. The ferries plowed the dark waters. It seemed he had been in this city for months yet knew nothing of its mysteries, its real life. He drained his last Carlsberg and checked the empty carton. His father's watch said it was time for bed.

In the morning he went through the empty drawers again, riffled the pages of the Bible. He stole the envelopes and the paper with the Hilton letterhead, the tiny soaps, the pen. He tipped the bellboy and paid his bill and had enough left to splurge on a rickshaw to the docks. From the rail of the ferry, he watched the skyline diminish, still gleaming, untouched by his absence.

The airport was uglier in the daytime. The United schedule advertised a flight to Hawaii, another to Tokyo. At the gate everyone was his age, their clothes new, ill-fitting. A few were still drunk; one had no shirt. Larry wondered if Loomis might show up; he would have been due for R&R at the same time. When the sergeant at the desk announced the flight, Larry thought it meant nothing that he wasn't there. Loomis seemed more of the Bangkok type.

They boarded by rows. The seat beside Larry was empty, as was half the cabin. He didn't know what it meant. The stewardess said there would be limited beverage service but no one complained. Leaving Da Nang, they had cheered; now the only sound was the engines, the thud of the gear retracting as they banked over the harbor. He leaned his face to the window to watch it go.

So, they would say, how was it?

And he would say, Crazy.

Yeah?

Insane, he would say, and it would not be a lie, because that was how he felt.

NO ONE met him at Odin. He came in on the log ship with a crate of grenades and a bag of pony. The heat made it hard to breathe; the dust stuck to his skin. The private from supply who unloaded them stank. The compound was deserted, no one throwing a ball around. As Larry passed the empty mess tent a 155 let go and he bit his tongue. He didn't think he would miss Hong Kong so quickly.

They were out on patrol. The hootch hadn't changed; everyone's gear was there, the pictures and knickknacks. The air was musty with old sweat and curdled foot powder strong as Parmesan cheese. He put Smart Andy's shoes on his cot, and an envelope with his change and the receipt. As he was filling his footlocker, the company clerk came by with their mail; Larry walked between the bunks, handing it out. Susan had sent the letter two weeks before they talked on the phone. It didn't say anything different. He went outside to wait for them, sitting on an ammo crate in the shade of the tent, flipping through Magoo's Hot Rod.

Around chow they called in and then came through the wire, the Martian leading. Larry stood and counted them as they navigated the maze of tanglefoot. They were all there, covered in mud from the waist down. The stench made him squint.

"What the fuck are you smiling at?" Pony asked, and smeared a handful on Larry's T-shirt. Smart Andy and Bates did the same, and Larry thought that soon he would be used to the smell again.

Smart Andy didn't try on the shoes for fear of getting them dirty. He said Larry could have kept the change.

They wanted stories, souvenirs of Hong Kong. Larry just shrugged. "I took it pretty easy," he said. "It was nice."

"He didn't get laid," Magoo complained. "Dude goes to Hong Kong and doesn't get laid."

He'd missed some big shit. Twenty klicks north of Firebase Blaze, Delta Company had ambushed what they thought was a squad of VC. They blew claymores on them, turned them to spaghetti. A minute later they engaged a reinforced battalion of regular NVA.

"Motherfuckers were wiped out," Magoo said.

"Most of 'em shot once in the forehead," Pony added.

"You can bet something heavy's going down at division," Carl Metcalf said.

Bogut was on the net. "We're going north," he guessed. "Two, three weeks tops."

"Two," the Martian said from his bunk, and though they scoffed, they believed him.

Spring training came with its split squads and meaningless games—the Cubs and the Athletics, the Dodgers and White Sox—but Nate was gone and the box scores in *Stars and Stripes* went unread. Mail came for Fred the Head and Dumb Andy, which the lieutenant marked SEARCH FOR and returned to the company clerk. At dawn Bates climbed the hill to do his tai chi. Pony smoked his stogies. Carl Metcalf sketched. *What a day this has been*, Larry found himself whistling. *What a rare mood I'm in. Why it's, almost like being in love.*

Days they ran local patrols, nights they cleaned their weapons, passing the LSA bunk to bunk. Battalion promised replacements again, but they didn't expect any. The company was down to sixty-two men.

The Martian was wrong. Two weeks passed, then three.

"I wish they'd just send us," Smart Andy said one night, and the next day without warning a flock of Shithooks took them to Blaze to prep for a combat assault. The NVA had some 2nd Cav pinned down on top of a mountain.

"You know what?" Pony hollered, hanging on to the wall webbing.

"What?" Smart Andy said.

"You're not so fucking smart."

The rest of the battalion was waiting at Blaze, a platoon of Hueys spread out across the compound, turbines winding up. The lieutenant joined the captain at the command post, then came back and filled them in. The NVA had shot down two choppers and when the Cav went in to get their men, the enemy let them unass the liftships and then tore into them. The Cav circled the wagons and called in artillery on top of their perimeter. That was five hours ago. So far no one had come out.

It was late in the day, the sun bloody over the mountains. Larry's new watch said it would be dark in an hour.

"This is fucking nuts," Magoo said, and Larry agreed.

They would carry only web gear. They drew fresh ammo and extra frags and boarded the liftships. Carl Metcalf passed around sticks of Juicy Fruit. It was chilly, and no one spoke. Below, the river interrupted the jungle, cut the valley in half.

In minutes the radio filled with calls for dust-offs. Artillery screamed overhead, prepping the LZ. A pair of Cobras shot rockets into the mountainside; the hulk of another bird lay charred in the brush. They could see the fighting beneath them, muzzle flashes through the trees.

"She's gonna be hot," the crew chief warned as they spiraled down. Slugs thumped underneath their feet, and he gestured that they would not stand on the skids but go on his signal. The other door gunner sprayed the woodline in sweeping bursts, stopping only when the crew chief whacked him on the back.

"Go, go!" Bates yelled, and they piled through the doors into a sloping field of scrub and dashed for cover. Larry and Carl Metcalf ducked behind a log. Below, the Cav had dug into the hillside, repulsing the NVA with sixties salvaged from the downed choppers. Echo scrambled across the field on their elbows and knees, mortars rushing in on top of them. They crowded into the Cav's shallow fighting holes and laid down fire for the rest of the liftships. A mortar knocked one into the woods, its rotor clacking, the tail boom jackknifing around a banyan tree, snapping like a bent antenna. Above, the Cobras heeled for home; artillery walked in on the enemy position, felling trees, the shocks running through Larry's arms. A lump of shrapnel landed behind Pony; they handed it around, still warm.

Everyone was down now, and the light had begun to fail, the day to cool. The NVA had pulled back, satisfied to wait for the dark. Echo broke out their e-tools and dug in on the left flank; the ground was rocky, but they knew they would be mortared during the night and bent their backs to it. The lieutenant needed one volunteer for a two-man listening post; the Martian nodded and walked off. Scraping stone, Larry thought of him and the other guy out there in the dark by themselves, unable to make a sound, the enemy creeping through the brush on all sides.

"The dude is hard," Magoo said. "Give him that."

The sky deepened as they ate their cold Cs. Far below on the valley floor, an enemy convoy snaked along Highway 548. They stood 100 percent alert, shoulder to shoulder in their holes, grenades ready.

The first probes tried the right side of the line. Echo didn't turn to look, discounted the sound, the glow of the tracers. The firing quieted, then died. From below came the thup of a mortar tube; they searched for the red flash before covering up. The shell was well short, and the enemy corrected. The center of the line threw back another probe. The mortars were zeroed in on them now, making the ground jump.

From above came the drone of a heavy prop plane, growing as it approached until it seemed to be stopped right on top of them. With an electric screech a red beam of light connected it with the hillside, a curtain of fiery streamers.

"Spooky," Magoo explained, shaking his head in admiration. Its miniguns shrieked like a band saw chewing through steel pipe. It loitered overhead at low speed, expending every round. The light stopped first, retracting into the earth, then the noise; the plane thrummed away, leaving darkness again, silence.

The mortar thupped, and Larry buried his head in his arms, willed himself into the earth. He waited for the scream to tell him it would sail over, that it wasn't close, but heard nothing.

It hit to their right with a flash, knocking Magoo into him. Dirt showered down.

"Skull!" Smart Andy shouted.

"Skull!" Pony called.

As he was running, Larry heard the tube again. This one screamed and he didn't stop.

It was Bogut and the lieutenant's hole. Bogut had taken most of it; his shoulder was missing, his radio smashed. The lieutenant was unconscious, bleeding from the ears. It was hard to see in the dark. Larry undid Bogut's chinstrap and pulled his helmet off; the top of his head came with it, neatly as an egg.

"Shit," Larry said. He fit the helmet back on and checked the lieutenant.

His eyes were rolled back but his pulse was strong. Larry snapped an ampule of smelling salts under his nose, then another, and the lieutenant weakly pushed his hand away, muttered as if dreaming.

"You're okay," Larry said. He gestured to Pony and Smart Andy to move Bogut before the lieutenant came to. Smart Andy took his ankles; Pony swore and grabbed him by the fatigue jacket, one hand on top of his pot. Larry found his code book and tossed the remains of his radio into the grass.

"Come on, Skip," he said. The barrage continued, a shell dropping into the middle of the line; someone screamed for a medic. As he shook the lieutenant, Larry thought of the view from the balcony, the blue harbor and the white high-rises of Kowloon.

AT DAYBREAK, Phantoms ran an airstrike on the enemy position, setting off secondary explosions—boiling orange columns of flame. Artillery followed, softening them up for an assault downhill. Echo had the high ground and the firepower, but the enemy were dug into bunkers, firing from inch-wide slits. For three days the Phantoms pounded them. Arty from Maureen and Pepper and Airborne put steel on target round the clock, and still the enemy probed them at night, the convoys flickered in the valley.

On the fourth day, the enemy broke. The bunkers were full of smoking NVA, ownerless pith helmets. The complex was large and switchbacked down the mountain, connected by tunnels now clogged with rubble. For the next five days the battalion mopped up snipers and catalogued arms caches.

They piled the NVA dead on cargo nets for a Skycrane to take away, the big chopper shuttling between the field and Blaze. Occasionally a body slipped off, crunched when it landed. Magoo hadn't brought his camera; he pointed and sighed and said, "Did you see that?"

Without Bogut they didn't know what was happening. The lieutenant made Smart Andy his new radioman, but they had no radio. Third platoon's RTO came over to tell them they were being lifted back to Camp Evans to be briefed on a new operation. An hour later they were inbound.

THERE WERE no rumors this time. The entire battalion knew where they were going—back into the A Shau to take on the NVA. They sat in rows in the dim hanger while Colonel Honeycutt paced in front of a screen with a rubber-tipped pointer, his assistant at an overhead projector as if they were in grade school. Operation Apache Snow, the cover sheet said.

"Whip it on me, Jim," Magoo whispered.

The colonel called the operation a recon in force. Besides the 3/187th, the division was sending the 1/506th and 2/501st as well as two ARVN battalions. They would make a combat assault into the northern end of the valley to locate and disrupt the enemy's supply lines from Laos. The 3/187th would be responsible for securing Dong Ap Bia, a hill believed to be a way station between a nearby base camp and the network of trails along the valley floor. The colonel pointed to a topographical map; an octagon marked their LZ. The assistant changed transparencies, the new one with an arrow signifying the battalion headed east, pointing toward the west face of the mountain.

Beside Larry, the Martian shook his head as if it were an obvious mistake.

"Talk about a cowboy operation," Pony said when they'd been dismissed. "He's hoping we'll hit that base camp and get him a fat body count."

"It's nice of him to invite us," Smart Andy said, "but I think we already have plans."

"Gotta be easier than Dong Ngai," Magoo said, but nobody agreed.

They went back to Blaze, where their gear was waiting for them, piled in a field outside the perimeter; it would be the staging area. Supply had coughed up a new Prick-25; Smart Andy extended the antenna, fiddled with the knobs and strapped it on his back.

"One Adam Twelve," he said. "See the man—drunk."

They humped into the hills above the LZ and made camp. Carl Metcalf fashioned a C-rat stew in his pot, stirring it with his K-bar. Afterward, they played bridge, Larry ineptly filling in, trading places with the others so he would be the dummy. The lieutenant failed to make his two no trump and reminded them that H-hour was 0710 and sacked out. The night was cold; all across the hills, fires burned. There were only seven of them left, small enough for a circle. Everyone except Bates wanted some of Larry's coffee.

"You finish all your books," Carl Metcalf asked the Martian, "or are you just being sociable?"

"I heard the Kit Carson with Bravo got himself arrested."

"Yeah," Smart Andy verified. "He said he wasn't going into the valley again, that there was some bad shit waiting for us. They thought he was just fucking with them, then he gets busted inside the wire with a bag of grass."

"Don't tell me this shit," Pony said.

"It gets worse," Smart Andy said. "Last night Alpha's *chieu hoi* went over the hill. Guy was a family man too."

"Say what you like," Magoo said. "These people love their country."

"No one's beat the NVA there," the Martian said.

"Outside of us, you mean," Carl Metcalf said.

They pondered this, sipping. The lieutenant cleared his throat and Carl Metcalf checked his watch.

"It's that time, gentlemen," he said.

THE OPERATION started the same as all the others Larry had been on; the only difference was the size of it. Five full battalions waited at the staging area, scuffing the dust, playing grabass. They cheered as a forward air controller buzzed over in a single-engine plane. A Shithook dropped its ramp and unloaded some heavy-weapons crews toting recoilless rifles and boxes of ammunition, and they too drew applause.

"It's a fucking pep rally," Magoo said.

Finally a squadron of liftships came in and they rucked up and piled on. The weather was suffocating; everything was on schedule. Larry leaned an ear to his father's watch but couldn't hear it. Magoo took a picture of him picking his nose.

The rumor went that Echo's LZ would be hot, but it wasn't. As they spiraled in, the door gunners peppered the treeline for form's sake. They hit the ground and spread out security, then when everyone was down, formed a column and headed for their objective, first platoon on point.

The jungle closed over them, the air sticky. They stayed off the high-speed trails, shadowed them in the heavy brush. Smart Andy was taller than Bogut, a better target; his radio nodded in front of Larry, tucked under a poncho. Behind him, Bates walked drag; the lieutenant had asked Magoo to be Pony's AG and Carl Metcalf to take the Martian's slack. That was it, the eight of them. They'd given up on replacements.

While they were stopped for water at a stream, a miniature red deer broke from a thicket of bamboo and bolted away, yipping like a dog. Bates emptied his canteen back into the creek.

"It's like a black cat," he explained.

"Great," Pony said.

When they crossed the path of the deer, Smart Andy took an exaggerated step backwards, then went on. It doesn't work like that, Larry thought.

Farther on, the Martian held up an open hand and the column halted. They waited, frozen in their intervals. Birds chirped, ferns shivered. The Martian dropped his hand and they continued, and soon Larry saw what they had stopped for—a packed-dirt road wide enough for a truck, a natural tunnel of canopy above. They followed it east, where it intersected a slow, shallow river. In a bend stood an L-shaped hootch with six blue hammocks, a pen of chickens cackling in back. The hearth was warm, the broom on it new. They searched the place briefly, turning up one sock and the cap to a ballpoint pen. In the distance, small arms crackled. They got on the road and beat feet.

They reached a knoll at the base of Dong Ap Bia before 1500, which pleased the colonel, hovering above in a C-and-C bird. They established a perimeter around a clearing, and he landed and set up a temporary command post. He conferred with the captain; the captain spoke with his lieutenants.

"We're going up," the old man said.

It was a good deal; instead of busting their humps the next three weeks, Echo would pull security for the real CP on top of the hill. The palace guard, they called it.

"Black cat, huh?" Magoo said. "More like a white fucking pussy."

They started up a ridge, winding with a narrow trail. It was a wash, the red dirt stepped and channeled like a riverbed, dams of dried leaves caught behind rocks and fallen logs. Tangle shouldered in on both sides; in front of Larry, Smart Andy ducked to keep his antenna clear of the vines. The brush was thick, the air dim and fetid under the canopy. The Martian disappeared around a bend, then Carl Metcalf. Since this morning they'd humped at least five klicks, and Larry's thighs burned. His picture of Vicki was back at Odin. He tried not to see it as a sign. He kept both hands on his weapon, his helmet backwards to see better. He concentrated on Smart Andy's feet, placing his own perfectly over his bootprints, listening to the murmur of the jungle. The palm fronds parted, then swung back and joined like a door. Behind him he could see Bates, no one else.

The trail narrowed and rose, cut steeply up a gully. Smart Andy went to his hands and knees and Larry did the same. They stopped and waited; Smart Andy looked back and shrugged. A mosquito landed on Larry's face and he rubbed it into his cheek. Somewhere above the canopy a chopper paddled the air. He turned to check on Bates when a rocket grenade erupted up the trail.

He could not see it through the trees. An AK chattered, drowned by return fire. Another rocket crashed, followed by a cluster of grenades, more small arms. Smart Andy bent over his handset, calling the contact in, then scuttled on his elbows for the lieutenant. He signaled for Larry to move up. Bates was right behind him, his ruck already off.

Ahead, several men lay across the trail, others taking cover in the brush. From behind a downed tree, Pony and Magoo put out fire, shredding leaves, splintering a stand of bamboo. While they changed belts, an NVA soldier popped from a hole in the ground and emptied his clip at them, the bullets slapping the trunk. Larry answered, but the man had ducked. Beside him, Bates thumbed a round into his blooper. As he brought his eye to the sight, a rocket sailed down the trail and caught Pony in the neck, disintegrating him from the waist up, bathing Magoo.

Bates missed. The man popped up again; Smart Andy put a burst through his neck yet he kept firing, the clip cooking off before he pitched over. Bark and twigs rained from the trees. Another rocket whooshed through, exploding behind them. Third platoon was on-line now, pouring fire into the enemy. Carl Metcalf used it as cover; he chucked a grenade and ran across the trail to the bodies, dragged the top one into the brush. He did this three times, finally taking a round high in the arm, a mist of blood puffing over his shoulder.

Larry started for him but the lieutenant grabbed his leg. Carl Metcalf swung the body partly off the trail and dove after it. The man was missing his helmet. It was the Martian.

"They're calling in air," Smart Andy said. "We gotta get the fuck out of here."

They retreated behind third platoon's suppressing fire, lugging the dead in ponchos, the wounded on makeshift litters. Magoo had a concussion; his glasses were cracked. He cradled his head and groaned. When Larry tried to look at Carl Metcalf's bicep, he yanked his arm away. "I'm all right," he said. Only later, when they'd established an LZ for a dust-off, did the lieutenant order him to let Larry bandage it. Third platoon was all chopped up; Larry helped Redmond stabilize the wounded. The dead lay on the far side of the clearing, untended.

A single-prop job dropped a white phosphorous rocket to mark the target. Two Phantoms made a run with their cannons, circled and delivered some heavy shit, making the IVs jiggle.

It was too late in the day for a recon. The dust-offs came and took the Martian and Pony's legs away, and they set up a night position and ate a cold supper. No one said anything about Bates's black cat.

Smart Andy knew they were watching him.

"I seen guys worse," he said, then, softly, "At least it was quick."

Larry nodded, waiting for the lieutenant or Carl Metcalf to say something that would make sense. They were drinking cold, strong coffee, eating the desserts from the dead men's Cs.

"The poor fucker," the lieutenant said.

Magoo didn't want to talk; his head still hurt.

"And the Martian," Bates said. "I never thought he'd get it."

"Nope," Smart Andy admitted.

There just wasn't much to say. They kept looking around as if the rest of the platoon would join them. The bridge deck stayed in its plastic wrap. Larry checked Magoo's pupils by flashlight and gave him three aspirin for the headache, feeling useless.

They stood 50 percent alert, pulling three-hour watches. Larry blew into his hands and thought of his mother in her room, the morning light through the curtains, the glass of water on the nightstand. He needed to write her, though he doubted he would be able to say how he felt. He tried, gazing out at the quiet night, but could not concentrate.

He'd had to tag Pony, wiring the cause of death to a belt loop, and now all he could see was how his torso stopped, the nub of his spine. He had a half-smoked cigar in his pocket, and a small box of Rosebud matches, both soaked.

The Martian had taken a round in the chin and one behind the temple; he was missing an eye and his nose swung unattached. Larry went through his pack for personals and found a bad sci-fi paperback with the bookmark twenty pages from the end; on the cover a woman with unbelievable cleavage leveled a raygun at a two-headed monster. No one was interested in it. Larry stuck the book in his own pack, knowing he'd never read it. He wired the tag around a button on the Martian's fatigue jacket and covered him again with the poncho. Then he walked across the clearing and ate supper.

The radio played empty space. Someone in third platoon snored; another got up and stumbled into the brush to take a piss. Larry had expected mortars but apparently none were coming. When Smart Andy relieved him, he curled up in his poncho liner, hugging his ruck to his cheek. He touched the pocket over his heart where Vicki's picture should have been and, though he knew he would not sleep, whispered good night to her.

In the morning the sky was undecided and Carl Metcalf's bandage was wet. Magoo hadn't been able to sleep; his eyes were dilated and bloodshot.

Echo ran a recon of the enemy position, third platoon on point. The bend still stank of cordite. The airstrike had leveled a stretch of jungle. Light poured down, uprooted trees leaned precariously over the trail. The column stopped while third hauled dead NVA from the rubble.

The captain called an interpreter forward to examine their papers. Larry knelt on the trail, scanning the woods for movement, then continued up the ridge, passing the enemy dead. Their uniforms were new, stripped of unit insignia, their pith helmets and weapons already gone to souvenir hunters. Smart Andy stepped on one's ankle and spat in his face.

The jungle returned, and the damp. The trail twisted down a saddle and up the other side. Farther on, they came across a bundle of commo wire disguised with vines running uphill. Smart Andy pointed and shook his head incredulously. The column slowed, then went to their bellies. Larry clicked his sixteen to full auto and decided which way he'd dive when third platoon hit the shit.

It didn't take long. Up the slope, rifle fire snapped, a rocket crashed. Smart Andy rolled to his right and crawled to the lieutenant. As Larry followed, a man from third sprinted down the trail the other way, untouched yet weaponless.

"You see that chickenshit?" Smart Andy said while the lieutenant called in a sitrep.

The enemy were in the trees, in zigzag trenches and bunkers above them. Third platoon had men down. Again, Echo withdrew behind suppressing fire, carrying their dead and wounded. Larry looked for Redmond, then figured he was busy. They tromped through the wreckage of the airstrike and down the gully, halting at the steepest parts to pass the litters hand to hand.

The CP was strewn with wounded when they got there. Two of their own gunbirds had strafed it by mistake.

"What else can go wrong?" the lieutenant said.

He released Larry to work at the LZ, evacuating casualties. One man had been blinded and lost both arms to a Chicom grenade. His head was a ball of gauze, his collar hung with bent morphine syrettes. He waved his bandaged stumps as if fighting off someone in a dream. There wasn't enough room, and they had to stack the dead, their boots sticking out of the door. Climbing, the Huey dripped like a clogged downspout.

Redmond showed up, the sleeves of his fatigue jacket rolled to his elbows, his arms crusted with blood.

"You're alive," Larry joked.

"Now tell me the good news," Redmond said.

The rumor was that they were up against the 29th NVA regiment, the pride of Ho Chi Minh; their orders from Hanoi were to stand their ground and kick some butt.

"They'll turn tail," the lieutenant assured them. "It's just a matter of when."

That night they were mortared until Spooky droned over, drilling its red beam into the hillside. In the morning two pairs of Skyraiders made runs against the bunkers, the blasts echoing down the valley.

This time they went up with just their web gear. The airstrikes had torn more gaps in the canopy. They crossed the saddle, hiked through the blackened patch, vaulted the toppled trees. The point deployed short of the bunkers. A heavy-weapons team brought up a recoilless rifle and fired a high-explosive round into a gunport; it caved the roof in. As the team rigged its second shot, a rocket struck the log it was balanced on and knocked all three men down the trail. On cue, the bunkers opened up, and the trees. Machine-gun fire stripped leaves from branches, kicked up sprays of dirt. The clatter rose to a plateau, a steady, deafening rain. There wasn't enough cover to return fire, and wisely they retreated.

"Ever see so many of them?" Magoo asked that night.

"Don't worry," Smart Andy said. "Honeycutt'll call in the heavy hitters on their asses—guaranteed. This nickel-and-dime shit's making Blackjack look bad."

The next day they trudged up the ridge into position, then waited while a pair of Phantoms hammered the bunkers. It was drizzling, mud heavy between the cleats of their boots. When the smoke cleared and they moved in to do a recon, the NVA blew huge claymores attached to the trees.

The lieutenant flew off the trail, his helmet spinning into the brush. He was dead when Larry got to him, a hot rock of shrapnel behind an ear. A knifelike piece of steel jutted from his cheek. An RPD cranked up and though there was no reason, Larry shielded him with his body.

Carl Metcalf helped him carry the skipper down. The trail was slick, and as they crossed the saddle, Carl slipped, and the lieutenant dropped facefirst into the mud. It stuck in his hair. Carl lifted him again, glaring as if it were Larry's fault.

The lieutenant had two combs in his back pocket, the rest was personal, to be expected. Magoo took his Winstons and offered one to Bates, who gave in and lit up. The platoon watched as Larry tied the plastic bag to the lieutenant's wrist and closed the poncho. They waited till all the other bodies were on, then laid him on top, facing the ceiling. The chopper rose and nosed over, turned and climbed into the drizzle until it disappeared behind the canopy.

There was nothing to talk about. The rain weighted their fatigues. They dug through their rucks for heat tabs and cooked up some Cs, boiled water for coffee in Larry's pot. Magoo snapped pieces off a chocolate bar and passed them around. It was stale, like the gum his father left for months in his glove compartment.

"The first thing I'm gonna eat when I get home," Smart Andy said, "is a chicken pot pie. I love those little fuckers."

"Prime rib," Carl Metcalf said. "And a baked potato with sour cream on top."

"Fish fry," Magoo said.

They looked to Larry. He thought of what his mother would make, but everything was Mrs. R.'s. He saw the kitchen, the little rose soaps in the dish above the sink. On weekends his father got up early and thumped down the stairs, stood at the stove in his bathrobe. Larry set the table, pouring juice for his mother and Susan. The bottle was heavy, and when he spilled, his father didn't yell at him like she did. Larry had to understand, she was sick, she needed quiet.

"Pancakes," he said. "And bacon."

"What about you?" they asked Bates.

"I'm not hungry," he said.

At daybreak rain bubbled in the puddles, ran soupy over their boots as they climbed the trail. Honeycutt was through fucking around; he assigned Charlie Company to assault the bunkers, Echo to serve as their stretcher bearers. The Phantoms ran sorties, arty screamed for fifteen minutes and Charlie started up the muddy slope. The NVA had reseeded the trees with claymores and now they detonated them, followed with a barrage of rocket grenades. The bunkers' gunports blazed. A burst tore the stuffing out of one man's flak jacket, and Larry thought it was the same as yesterday, only worse. Three times they re-formed and waded uphill toward the enemy. From behind his tree, he wanted to call them back, tell them to stay down.

At dusk they withdrew in disarray. The litter blistered Larry's hands; on the other end, Smart Andy turned around so he wouldn't have to look at the wounded. They took the dead last, then went back for weapons. The survivors carried four or five rifles, stacks of helmets, muddied, unused bandoliers. What they couldn't hump down the mountain—the boots and rucksacks, the ponchos and bandages—they piled in a bonfire, two scouts staying behind to make sure it all burned.

It rained and their holes filled with mud. At night they were mortared.

Charlie went up again and dug in; the fast movers flew over, bringing down heat while they huddled, rucksacks held over their heads. They splashed through the craters and dug in again, waited for gunships to work over the bunkers. The snipers cracked in the trees.

"I didn't sign up for this shit," Magoo said. "This is like the fucking Marines."

Larry thought of Tarawa, the tide burying bodies in the sand. If this was what his father had been through, he understood why he didn't tell war stories—he'd lived it, he didn't need words to remember. Words weren't good enough. Nothing was. It wasn't a story anyway.

Larry pulled double duty, helping at the LZ. The stretcher bearers laid the wounded in the rain. A man with no hands apologized for getting hit. "Sorry," he kept saying, even after Larry had gone on to the next man. The dying cried for their mothers, the dead relieved themselves. Larry told everyone that they would be okay, then when that proved untrue, took an end of the poncho and dragged them across the slick grass to the far side of the field. The angle hurt his back; it was easier when a chopper brought in a load of real bags.

"Finally," Redmond said.

"No shit," Larry said.

The nights were cold, then by midmorning the LZ reeked of blood. The Phantoms rolled in; the top of the hill was bald. At dusk they could see the enemy's rice fires spread across the face of the mountain. Around midnight a Shadow gunship buzzed over, training its spotlight on the bunkers, laying out red lines of fire. In the morning assault, Charlie Company made it thirty meters and ran into new claymores. Their dead looked like the LT, their faces studded with nails and washers, rusty ball bearings. Officers squabbled openly over the net.

"This is stupid," Carl Metcalf said. "We're fighting a regiment with a battalion."

"I'm telling you," Smart Andy said, "it's Blackjack. He's a little MacArthur."

"We should throw an Arc Light on the motherfuckers and walk away," Magoo said.

Bates smoked. Larry stirred the coffee with his bayonet.

"Tomorrow makes a week," Carl Metcalf complained.

What a difference a day makes, Smart Andy whistled. *Twenty-four little hours.*

"Shut the fuck up," Carl Metcalf said, then tossed his coffee into the mud and battened himself inside his poncho hootch. The rest of them slowly followed suit.

Explosions woke them. "Sappers!" Magoo shouted, and kicked Larry through his hootch. Larry struggled with the zipper of his sleeping bag. They were all hugging mud. Carl Metcalf clutched a sack of grenades, Bates his thumper. It sounded like the left flank was under attack. They waited for the perimeter to open up. A few frags crashed, that was all. Bates broke the thumper over his arm and plucked the shell out; Carl Metcalf replaced the safety clip on his grenade. Larry looked to his watch but it wasn't a radium dial.

"What time is it?" he asked.

"Way too late for this shit," Magoo said.

In the morning the sky was low and Bates couldn't keep a match lit. The trees thrashed, empty C-rat boxes cartwheeled across the LZ.

"Looks like we're going to get some weather," Carl Metcalf said, buckling his chin strap. Charlie humped up the ridge, Echo lugging their metal ammo cans. The trail was wide as a street now, the brush flattened on both sides. Artillery had taken down the big teak trees. The canopy no longer existed here, the jungle smashed stumps, blackened craters. Mist lingered on the hilltop—just mud, bunkers, leafless trees.

Phantoms came in beneath the clouds and the napalm canisters tumbled. Arty started. The enemy's fire discipline was impeccable; they waited until Charlie had broken into the open, then pinned them to the hillside and lobbed in grenades. The wind picked up and the rain came down, the trail a sluice. Lightning split the sky, thunder crunched. Charlie held their position, waiting for the downpour to end, but it didn't. Anyone who tried to crawl forward slid downhill. The enemy rested, dry inside the bunkers. To the rear, Echo moved out the initial casualties, mud sucking at their boots. The rain dripped off Larry's chin. The gully was awash, and they had to hand the wounded down.

"This is stupid," Smart Andy said.

In a draw south of Charlie's position, Bravo hit the shit. The LZ was packed with their casualties. Redmond knelt in the mud, tending to a man whose legs were sheared at midcalf. Carl Metcalf said Larry could stay.

The first man Larry treated was tall and gutshot, his intestines visible, bluish. His veins had collapsed, and Larry couldn't get an IV in, and he died. It was triage, Larry thought, and got up, looking for someone he could save. The dust-offs came in despite the rain. Across the field, Graves Registration had set up a card table.

They did not stop for lunch. A man with a belly wound wouldn't stay down for Larry, and Redmond hustled over and pinned him, a forearm across his throat.

"Some pacifist," Larry said.

"Hey," Redmond said, as if to refute this, and then his forehead burst, gushed, and he toppled over.

Behind him in the middle of the wounded stood an NVA struggling with the bolt of his AK. Larry rolled, shoved his hand in his bag, pulled out the .45 and fired blindly. The man dropped his weapon and fell, clutching his ribs. He lay on the ground, curled around the pain. Larry ran over to him and jammed the barrel in the man's ear and fired, then spun around on one knee, looking for more.

The guy from Graves ran over with a sixteen while Larry was kicking the dead man's head in.

"What the fuck?" he said.

"He killed my friend," Larry said, and continued with the job, swinging his heel down into the cheek, feeling the bones of the nose give. "You fucking bastard," Larry said. "You fucking scum."

The guy from Graves helped him get Redmond into a bag, and together they dragged him across the field.

"I'll tag him," the guy said, and Larry thanked him.

When Magoo and Smart Andy brought the next load down, they asked where Redmond went.

"They killed him," Larry said.

"Where?" Smart Andy said. "How?"

"Right here," Larry said. "Right in front of me."

"No shit," Magoo said. "No fucking shit."

"This guy," Larry said, and pointed to the dead NVA.

"Looks like someone punched his ticket good."

"Me," Larry said.

"Jesus," Magoo said. "What the fuck is going on around here?"

Bates and Carl Metcalf had a man with a sucking chest wound, and Larry was glad to work. The man died, and kneeling there, Larry noticed his own boots were coated with the NVA's brains. He ran to the edge of the wounded and threw up.

That night they were considerate of him. Bates made the coffee, and Smart Andy laid off the jokes. Larry's socks were wet; his fatigues made him shiver.

"It won't be long now," Magoo said. "Another two hundred meters."

"You saw how far they got today," Carl Metcalf said.

"That was the rain."

"You think it's gonna stop?"

It did. The next day arty dropped in CS gas and they wore their masks. Charlie assaulted the lowest row of bunkers, fighting in close and taking heavy casualties again. They stuck a beehive round through a gunport and advanced fifty meters up the slope, digging in behind the lip of the bunker while two Skyraiders made a run on the next complex. The hill shook, dirt spewed into the air, splinters drifted down. They fought all afternoon to a draw. Journalists in ridiculous utilities waited at the bottom of the gully. Carl Metcalf bumped one off the trail, daring him.

"Fucking leeches," Magoo said, "rooting for us to lose."

"We're gonna take it," Bates said, as if someone might argue with him.

"Tomorrow," Smart Andy said. "Day after at the latest."

The airstrikes began at 0800, followed by arty, gas, then more arty. Smoke poured from the bunkers. Charlie assaulted up the open slope, and the enemy shredded them.

Echo moved in to reinforce their old positions and clean out the bunkers they'd overrun. Carl Metcalf led them in with a flashlight. It was dim, the air heavy with piss and gunpowder and flesh. The supports were simple A-frames of bamboo, the earthworks ten feet thick. The fighting above them trickled in faintly through the gunports. Spent cartridges clinked underfoot. Larry tiptoed over fallen beams, empty ammo cans. The enemy had taken their dead with them, leaving nothing but trash.

The passage narrowed and turned. They had to wait while Carl lay down and poked his head around the corner. He signaled to Bates and they moved on. Ahead, the roof had caved in, admitting a sudden, dazzling light. They passed back into the minelike darkness, the flashlight picking out shattered helmets, soiled bandages. Black water streamed down the walls, pooled on the floor. Their footsteps echoed. They were inside the mountain now, the only light a jiggling circle.

Carl Metcalf stopped and lay down on the ground and they waited, a draft flowing over their faces. He waved Bates on.

The bright lines of tracers deafened them, illuminating the room. One caught Bates at the waist, his thumper blowing up in his hands. The flash tossed him against the wall. Shrapnel splashed back at them; Smart Andy grunted and swore. The tunnel went black, then roared orange as Carl Metcalf's frag searched for the gunner. He threw two more to be sure.

The dead man was chained to a support. He had already lost a leg before the grenades hit him; the bandages were dirty.

Bates's front was mush, his thumper wrecked. The four of them hefted him by the arms and legs and carried him outside. It was raining again. His lips were blue. While the engineers laid det cord to blow the bunker, Smart Andy keyed the handset and called in Bates's initials and the last four digits of his serial number.

"Fucking Norman, man," Magoo said, and pulled the LT's Winstons out of Bates's helmet liner and lit one up. Above them, the backblast of a recoilless rifle cracked and boomed. Charlie was taking it to the enemy.

At the LZ, a new crew of medics was performing triage. Larry led the way to Graves. The field between the two was littered with dressings and empty syrettes. Larry looped the bootlace with Leonard Dawson's ring over Bates's head and added it to the bag he knotted around his wrist. The guy who'd helped him with Redmond unzipped the flat rubber sack and guided Bates's feet in.

He was too big. They pulled his boots off and still it wouldn't close. They tried bending him at the waist, Larry and Smart Andy pushing as if on a stubborn duffel while the man from Graves forced the zipper, but he was just too tall. Carl Metcalf stood in the rain shaking his head; Magoo couldn't resist a picture. Finally they turned him around so only his feet were sticking out, the tongue of the zipper at his shins. He had a bad case of immersion foot, his skin peeling and soft as cheese. Larry wished he had a dry pair of socks to put on him, but didn't, and they walked across the field and through the screams of the wounded and back up the gully.

The next morning, between the tac air and the arty, Smart Andy saw a flock of birds flying in the shape of an H.

"So what?" Magoo said.

"It's a sign," Smart Andy said.

"There's no one left with an H," Magoo said, and Larry thought of his mother.

It would take another day. Charlie had sixty meters to go; Bravo and Delta were mopping up bunkers. The enemy booby-trapped the dead, and souvenir hunters turned up at the LZ in shock and missing hands. At nightfall a cloudburst sent flash floods rushing down the mountain.

"Tomorrow," Carl Metcalf said, and they nodded as if it were in their power to take the hill themselves.

They went up behind Charlie Company. The morning was cloudy but dry, the footing good. Above them, bodies draped the craters, the hillside spiked with stripped, twisted trees. The flanks brought up the recoilless and hit the gunslits with HE and then flechette rounds. They poured on rocket grenades, laid a base of fire and assaulted on-line, and, as the LT predicted, the NVA finally ran.

Bravo was waiting for them on the far side of the hill. From the top, Larry could hear them ambushing the survivors, the sixties chugging out rounds.

"Man, that sounds so sweet," Magoo said, cupping an ear. "I gotta get that record."

They secured the hilltop and did a recon. In the bunkers they found more men chained to the supports, some crushed to death, folded backwards at the waist, heads between their canvas boots. Magoo clicked away. The engineers planted charges and rolled out det cord and the smoke mushroomed. Echo pulled body detail, evacuating the friendly dead, digging them from the mud. Some had been there since the first assault, and Larry's sleeves were covered with blood and maggots. It had taken ten days. On a charred tree stump near the entrance of the gully, someone had nailed up the bottom of a C-rat carton; on it was written: HAMBURGER HILL. Underneath, someone else had asked, *Was it worth it?*

THAT AFTERNOON Division lifted them to Eagle Beach on the South China Sea for some in-country R&R. The green waves ran in, the palms lolled. They shed their wet fatigues and took showers, came out in OD T-shirts and shorts, cheap foam rubber sandals in candy colors. Beer cooled in a fifty-five-gallon drum brimming with ice; aproned cooks were flipping burgers at a grill. The four of them went through the line and walked down to the water. They sat in the hot sand, chewing, the surf rushing over their toes, burying their ankles. The saltwater burned. Larry took his first gulp of beer too fast and got the hiccups; Carl Metcalf pounded him on the back. The sea splashed and hushed. They went up for seconds, sliding extra beers in their pockets, the metal freezing against their thighs.

Smart Andy said he was going for a stroll and got up and walked down the beach until they couldn't see him.

Carl Metcalf lay back and balanced his can on his chest. "This is good," he said. "We need something like this."

Larry didn't have an opinion. He went back for a third burger and two more beers, and as he was eating, watching the waves break and the far calm of the horizon, he thought it was just like Hong Kong—that either he or the world was unreal. But here was the burger, still steaming, the beer bubbly on his tongue. He did not want to be ungrateful. He drained his other two and went back until he could no longer walk.

The sea woke him the next day, splashing cold over his legs. He remembered digging a hole to puke in, smoothing it over with his hands. He lay in the sun until he couldn't stand it and waded into the waves. The water was warm, not at all medicinal. He fueled up on barbecue for lunch, ignoring the bones, then took pictures of Magoo playing volleyball. Tomorrow they would go back to Odin.

In the morning they blearily stood formation and were issued new fatigues. His aid bag was still damp. On the Shithook the four of them sat together, leaning back into the wall webbing. Magoo asked someone in third platoon to shoot them. They yoked their arms over each other's shoulders.

"Say 'Pepsi, please,'" the man said, and blinded them.

The ride only took fifty minutes. From the air, Odin looked tiny, a raft on a sea of green. The captain and his clerk waited at the helipad, saluted as they came in. They tromped down the ramp and across the compound.

The hootch smelled of dust and stale sweat. The place seemed big with just the four of them. Piles of mail rested on the bunks—Bogut's and Pony's, the Martian's and the LT's—and Larry thought with annoyance that the company should have already policed their gear.

On his cot he went through the envelopes, ordering the important ones by the postmark. Near the bottom was a telegram from the Red Cross. He tore it open.

They had okayed his emergency leave.

"Hey!" he said, "I'm going home!"

"That's great," said Carl Metcalf.

Beneath the last *National Geographic* was another wire with the same return address. It had arrived three days ago, and though it was impossible to remember now, Larry feared it was the day of the H. He plucked out the yellow slip and found himself on the wrong end of a scene he'd imagined since receiving his induction notice. It was just as he'd predicted, only the players had changed. She was supposed to read the telegram. He was supposed to be dead.

NINE

The week of Halloween the weather turned, the garden frosted at dawn. Larry pretended to sleep. Vicki left their bed before the alarm went off and showered first. She covered herself with a towel, waited until he was in the bathroom to get dressed. He double-knotted his Nikes and jogged past Donna's, searching the windows, knowing Vicki was glad to be alone. His splits were fast but she didn't ask him how he'd done. The bathmat was wet. In the shower, he bent his head beneath the stream and frowned.

They made love once, the second night, brilliantly, but he could hear Donna urging him on. He was used to her now; he missed the fit and the heat of her, her words. With Vicki, it was more reflex than desire. She closed her eyes, and Larry thought she was where he was, with someone else. When he came, immediately he wanted to retract it. They didn't try again.

Why was she back? What had happened?

She didn't want to talk about it, and so they argued.

"Tell me his name," he said, trying to summon rage. It was expected, this interest, though what he felt was indifference, futility, at best confusion. He imagined it was the same for her.

"I can't," she said. "Please."

"Why can't you?"

He didn't know which of them was being cruel, which was suffering.

Sometimes it was funny, but only for a second, then it was dumb, a melodrama not worth watching.

He hid the picture in the attic, interrogating it a moment before tucking it into a rip in the silver insulation above the rafters. Her hair and her breasts hung plumb. She looked back at Alan, smiling, maybe saying something. He thought it should hurt more; instead, it made him want Donna. It was foolish, none of them were happy. They went to bed with headaches, argued in the dark—long, bitter silences.

Vicki was thinner, her jeans gapped at the waist, her Photo USA top baggy. She cooked breakfast and picked at her eggs, popping the yolk, letting it run then stiffen. Her hair was dark from the shower, her eyes tired. Scott gnawed the crusts of his toast, his juice leaving a purple mustache, and Larry thought of his father fresh from seeing Ellen Creeley. They kept the radio on to fill the silence; the Wall was behind schedule and drawing critics. Vicki scraped the plates into the garbage with a sigh, piled the dishes in the sink and ran water on them, leaning against the counter as if exhausted.

In the car she smoked, flicking the butts out the window. Scott sat between them, his lunch in his lap. There was no reason to go in with Donna, no convenient excuse. They backed out past the Monte Carlo, the transmission shuddering. On Q104 all the songs were about lost love. In town, porches were decorated with gauze stretched to imitate cobwebs, spiders the size of dogs. Dropping him off, Vicki didn't wave.

He called Donna from work, from roadside phonebooths, from the Great American in Groton. He drove up the lake to meet her for lunch, waited in parking lots, Number 1 giving him away. They ate at the state parks, conscious of the time, the police cruising through. Gulls faced into the wind on picnic tables, puffed for warmth. He slipped a hand down her blouse and she rose against his palm, arched, gave him her throat. She wanted to make love but not in the car. They did anyway, his feet searching the door for leverage. He held her hand while she smoked, staring through the windshield as if at a drive-in. The waves were gray and pitching; no boats were out.

"What are we going to do?" she asked.

"Tell her."

"No," she said, as if he'd misunderstood, and pulled her hand away. "Don't you ever listen to me?"

"You keep saying that."

"Because it's true," she said. "I can't do this, Larry. We've got to stop."

He didn't have to ask why. It had been wrong from the start. She laid out her plan like a judge. Her logic was flawless, childlike. They would not see each other for a week. Larry thought that if it were true—if she could do it—then he would have to, for her sake.

"We've got to try," she said, and though it angered him, he agreed.

"Here," he said, "a week from today." He kissed her so she'd know he didn't think it would work, then got in Number 1 and followed her down the lake and into town.

They split at Meadow and State, where Creeley had ambushed him. Waiting for the next light to change, Larry wished he'd fought with her, begged. Why be proud now? He stopped at the Mobil and cleaned himself with paper towels in the cold restroom, droplets wetting his pants. In the mirror he resembled a street person, a murderer, someone lost and unafraid of it. He bought a coffee and, though he'd just eaten, dug up a box of crumb cakes.

It was a luxury to drive below the speed limit, the heater on. The hills outside Danby were gloomy, clouds scudding low over the muddy fields. The pumpkin cupcakes were breaking records. He appreciated the Scandinavians, wallowed in their hopelessness. It was a confirmation; he expected misery from love. All these years, nothing had changed.

He took the bus home and had to walk past her car. Her windows were empty, the Ruster sitting in the drive, on the porch an uncut pumpkin. Vicki didn't kiss him. Scott wanted to carve it now, before dinner, and Larry was glad to be out of the house. He laid down pages from a week-old *Journal* and cut the top off. At first Scott was afraid of the guts, but soon he was squishing fistfuls, wiping it on his thighs.

"What kind of face should we make?" Larry asked.

Scott got a marker and a piece of paper and concentrated, nodding. He gave it round eyes and a moonlike smile with one tooth. Larry raided the knifeblock and copied the design. Vicki came to the door to look.

"What do you think?" Larry said.

"It looks very happy," she said, as if that were wrong, then amended, "It looks fine."

They baked the seeds on tinfoil, shook salt over the bowl. Dinner was frozen ravioli.

"What did you do today?" she said.

"Same old," he said. "How about you?"

In the past she told stories about weird shots people brought in to be developed—S&M parties, dead pets—but today was dull. She would get paid tomorrow, which he already knew.

"Great," he said cheerily, and the table went silent again.

She escaped upstairs while he did the dishes. When he went to use the bathroom, she was lying on the bed, reading the new Stephen King, and didn't look up. Scott watched cartoons until bathtime. Larry peeked in and asked if he could do him.

"Knock yourself out," she said.

He would do stories too, fitting himself onto the small bed so Scott could read along. He picked out *Curious George Goes to the Hospital* and *The Little Engine That Could.* Larry knew them intimately, yet now they seemed to be talking about him, mocking the foolishness of his situation, their morals bald, obvious. Curious George was a greedy idiot, the Little Engine a soft-headed optimist. Scott pointed to the pictures, stopped Larry from turning the page, then, as if he'd processed everything, let him.

"The end," Larry said, and tucked him in. He brought him water and kissed him. Larry still had three hours before he could go to bed, and then it would be with her.

She read while he watched TV. It was a long book, the cover glossy. She sat Indian-style with it in her lap and leaned over the pages, picking at her nails. Occasionally she released a surprised "Hmm," as if pleased with some insight.

"Good book?"

"It's okay," she said guardedly, as if she'd written it.

On *Hill Street Blues,* the sergeant had fallen in love; it was supposed to be funny. Vicki didn't notice.

"Do you want something to drink?" she said, pausing on her way to the kitchen.

"No thanks."

M*A*S*H played back-to-back after the news, and he had to turn. Lately she'd been reading late, staying downstairs while he brushed his teeth. She studied the novel as if she had a test on it tomorrow. Johnny Carson was on, flipping his pencil.

"I'm going up," he said.

"I think I'll read a little, if you don't mind."

She did not expect an answer; he didn't offer one. From the landing window he could see Donna's lights were out, and he thought that merely by sleeping he might join her. Scott was long gone; Larry fixed his blankets. He sat on the closed toilet lid and rubbed lanolin into his transition, hoping it wouldn't be too cold to run tomorrow.

It would be a shitty day. After dinner he had to see Susan about his father. He was out of the hospital and back at home with Mrs. R. His knee hurt, and from what Susan said, he was growing more confused. They fought often. The tests were inconclusive. The scabs had come off, leaving pink spots; they'd taken out his stitches, only a faint boxer's scar on his eyebrow. Susan would want to talk about what they were going to do.

He crawled in bed with the light on and thought of Donna's skin, the freckles on her arms. In the Monte Carlo, suction stuck their chests together; she had laughed at the sound, meaning he could. It was hot, and she killed the heater. As she raised an arm above her head to roll down the window, she elbowed him in the nose.

"God," she said, "are you all right?" He held the bridge, stunned, the blood coming, and she began to cry, covering her face. "I always do stupid things like that," she accused.

"No," he said, "it's all right, I'm fine," but it just made her sob harder.

"I'm so fucked up," she said. He was sure it was his fault that he didn't know what was wrong. He held her close, staring over her shoulder at the floor mat, the worn pedals. The blood ran thick down the back of his throat.

"I don't think anyone can help me," she said, and he thought that while it might be true, he at least needed to try.

Downstairs, Vicki went into the kitchen to check the back door. The light switches clicked, the pullchain of the lamp jangled. The steps creaked under her feet. He curled up facing the edge of the bed and closed his eyes. She paused to look in on Scott before continuing down the hall. She turned off the overhead light, went into the bathroom and closed the door. A minute later he heard a page rattle. He wasn't sleeping when she got into bed, and even after she'd drifted off, he lay awake listening to the wind and the plumbing's uneasy digestion. He hadn't seen Donna in twelve hours.

He dreamed about her shoulders and then Carl Metcalf and woke to the black room, jerking up like a gassy corpse. Vicki slept, her back to him. He went downstairs and checked the doors again, the windows. Outside, bare branches waved beneath the streetlight. Scott's pumpkin sat on the porch rail, watching the yard. In the drive the Ruster glinted, across from it the Monte Carlo, the interior shadowed. Clines had been threatening to stake out the house. Larry fixed his field of vision, expecting movement, but there was none, only leaves skipping over the yellow line.

"Paranoid," he said, and let the curtains close again.

In the dream, Carl Metcalf had hands. He staggered toward Larry, his fatigues burned off. "I know you're in maintenance," he said, and fell to the ground.

Larry puzzled over it while running. Frost starred the windshields. Once the two houses were out of sight, he fell into his rhythm. The sky was clear, his fingers freezing. He spat at the crows and waved to the cows and imagined running coast to coast to benefit the Vet Centers, running away from here. It had rained late in the night; the leaves left prints on the road. Larry no longer trusted the answers he conjured up alone. He outran thoughts of Donna, of Vicki and Scott, his father, Creeley. It was a relief not to think. His first split time was quick, the roof of his mouth dry. In a month the snows would come.

He was so used to the route that its very familiarity surprised him; after weeks of not seeing anything, he might remark on a rusting culvert, a rubber-smudged guardrail, the filmy streamers of a wasted cassette tape. Once he'd seen a box turtle crossing the road with a plastic six-pack ring around its neck, but mostly the scenery was dull, just crows picking at roadkill, garbage tossed from cars.

Today he noticed the highway department had been out. A wavy line of fluorescent red spray paint ran along the shoulder, as if to mark the limits of some new improvement. Beside it were lopsided crosses, each with its own mysterious number. The line wandered over stones, across small washes in the dirt berm. It swerved then looped back, hugged the white line. Larry could see it turn the curve ahead and wondered how far it went. When he was a boy, sometimes vandals would steal a can of paint and drip an inter-mittent line along the sidewalk; he remembered the thrill of searching for the next thread, rooting for it to go on and on, not really caring where it took him.

The line was on the other side of the road as well. Maybe they'd widen it to include another lane; it was something the town always wanted from the state. A string of cars rushed past, the last nosing out to slingshot by. He was nearly to the bridge over Six Mile Creek, his halfway point; he thought this split would be just as fast.

The bridge was white, made of poured concrete. In the middle, the red line cut across the road and started back on the other side—exactly as Larry did each morning. He crossed the double yellow line and checked his watch. On the road, in fluorescent numbers beside a tiny cross, was his normal time, twenty-seven minutes.

The line ran ahead of him in the dirt. Larry's first thought was of the smoke grenade, how easily Creeley had gotten it. He crossed back, staying in the lane, keeping to the asphalt. Pines rose on both sides, boulders and brush providing cover. Creeley would be an expert with any weapon. By the time Larry hopped the guardrail it would be too late. He could feel the crosshairs on him, which he knew Creeley wanted him to, but kept chugging, pumping his arms. He realized he was running too fast, leaning forward, his breath hot in his throat, and slowed.

Ahead, the red line on the other side stopped. Closer, he saw that it turned into the dirt drive of a hunting camp. A chain dipped between two rotted posts. Larry jogged in place a moment. Trees overhung the drive, brush shouldering the ruts. The line disappeared behind a bend.

His watch peeped as he turned it off. He looked both ways and crossed the road. The dirt was soft from last night's rain and gave beneath his feet. Creeley had left prints—tennis shoes—meaning he'd been there this morning. The prints only went in.

Larry stepped over the chain, careful not to disturb anything. Though he wanted to walk in Creeley's tracks, he kept to the weedy hump. The brush was still, insectless, the high grasses white. Pinecones lay in the ruts. The light sliced through the trees, leaving patches on the forest floor. A perfect day for hunting, his father would say.

The line led him around the bend, then suddenly disappeared, a clot of red like a period in the dirt. Creeley's prints vanished.

Larry stopped and crouched, afraid of his next step. Already the sweat had gone cold on him, his shirt sticking to his shoulders. The camp was in sight, an old Airstream trailer on cinder blocks in a clearing, a woodpile butted up against one end. He listened, expecting the clack of a bolt jacked home, but there was only the trees. He focused on the brush as if it were jungle—dead tangle, dried vines, the dark clumps of nests. It was easier here, he thought.

The Airstream had one curtained window beside the door. Larry came at it from the woodpile, keeping low. The grass in the shadows wet his Nikes. He let his hand lead, probing in front of his feet; he would not be fooled again by a wire. In the dirt beneath the trailer were spiderwebs and rust-eaten beer cans. As he inched toward the door, the sun coming off the silver skin warmed him.

He turned the creaking handle, listened a moment, then threw the door open and rolled away. It crashed against the trailer and slammed shut again.

He lay in the cold grass, waiting for Creeley to move, for the springs to squeak, but nothing happened. He pushed himself up and crept to the door again and opened it, letting out the smell of dust. Inside was a screen door, also on a spring. He inspected it for wires, then kicked it with his new foot. It banged a counter and rebounded, its frame shaking.

He checked the clearing behind him again and stepped inside, ready to flee. The kitchen was neat, the counters and the fold-down table bare, the sink tiny. He noted the one cupboard that might hide a man.

He moved down the hall as if he held a gun, protecting it with his back, as if when he turned the corner he would level it at someone. Though there was no point in subtlety, he went to his knees like Carl Metcalf to poke his head into the next room.

In a recliner sat a skeleton in fatigues, complete with a boonie hat and new boots. It appeared to be real, the skull the color of diseased teeth. It held a pistol to its temple. Larry recognized the pearl grips of Meredith's antique. With its other hand, it flashed the ten of spades like a badge. CREELEY, the name above the breast pocket read.

"Who else?" Larry said.

He got up and crossed the room in two steps. He plucked the card from the skeleton's hand, and the pistol fired.

The shot sounded like a bomb had gone off. It blew the skull to pieces, a chip blinding Larry as he dove for the floor. A bitter cloud of dust and gunsmoke filled the room. His cheeks were bleeding, a finger stoved from stopping his fall.

He lay still, afraid it was only the beginning. The skull crumbled, bits ticking against the linoleum. He touched a fingertip to his eye and it came away specked with grit. He blinked, letting the tears collect in his lashes until he could see again.

The fatigues slumped headless in the recliner. The recoil had snapped the hand clean at the wrist; it still held the pistol. Larry crawled to it. The hand was glued on, a piece of nylon line looped through the tip of the trigger finger. Larry popped the clip out. It was empty.

He slid open the window to clear the air, then inspected the ten. It was glued. He didn't touch it this time.

THE CHILD IS THE FATHER, it said.

He left everything and walked down the drive and along the road until he came to a trailer with a car in the yard and white smoke chuffing from a stovepipe. A woman in a gas company uniform answered the door and let him in to use the phone.

Technically, the police operator said, the crime had taken place outside the town of Ithaca; what Larry wanted was the county sheriff's department.

Larry tried to reason with her a minute, then asked for Clines.

He wasn't in yet; she expected him at eight.

"I'll call back then," Larry said, and walked home, poking at his bad eye, his cheeks stinging.

Vicki didn't understand what was happening. She dabbed Mercurochrome on his cuts, holding his chin like a corner man while Scott splashed at his Lucky Charms. Larry gave her the basics—that Creeley had escaped and harbored some grudge against him. It was easier not to mention his father and Ellen Creeley, though now he was sure that was the connection and not the war. It made sense; in a way they were brothers.

"When is this Vietnam crap going to be over?" Vicki said.

She did not want an answer, and he did not justify the question by providing one. Though he had no evidence, he thought that Donna would understand.

Vicki said she could come back after dropping off Scott, but Larry said he didn't know how long the police would need him. He'd just take the bus.

"You be careful," she said, and gave him a lipless kiss. The Monte Carlo was gone. He watched the Ruster back out and rumble away, then went into the kitchen and poured himself a bowl of cereal, glad to be alone, if only for a few minutes. He didn't taste the Lucky Charms, and he thought that his symptoms were clinical, that like Donna, he had begun to see himself as fucked up. It was only his second day away from her. He wanted to stick a note under her door but decided that if she was trying, so should he. He didn't believe his reasoning. He didn't like to think her plan might work.

Marv was not pleased. "First the truck and now this," he said. "I got cakes. I got bread that needs to go out."

"Hey," Larry said, "I'm sorry."

Clines was on time. He told Larry he'd be right out, and in minutes a blue LTD pulled into the drive. Clines wore an olive trenchcoat over a blue suit and brown shoes; his hair was just as desperate. The interior of the car was spotless, a garbage bag hanging from the cigarette lighter, a pine air freshener from the mirror. Clines squinted at the cuts on Larry's face. Larry showed him which way to go. Clines drove like an old man, one hand at the bottom of the wheel.

"Why'd you say you touched the card again?" Clines asked, as if he'd really forgotten.

"I know it was dumb, I should've just left it alone."

"Next time," Clines reminded him. "This guy's obviously thinking, so you've got to too."

"There," Larry said, and pointed to the wandering red line.

Clines checked his mirror and slowed. In the trunk he had a suitcase full of camera equipment, plastic baggies and rubber gloves. He took several extra shots to be sure.

At the gate they parked facing the wrong way and stepped over the chain, Clines carrying the suitcase. Larry wondered if he had a gun in a shoulder holster, but didn't see a bulge. He half expected the trailer to be gone, yet there it was, the door ajar, the window open. Clines knocked on the screen before going in.

"All the way to the right," Larry said.

Everything was as he'd left it, the steely smell of the round lingering. Slivers of bone flecked the recliner; larger shards littered the floor. Clines tiptoed close and leaned in to see the ten, then backed up and flashed away. He pointed to the ceiling above the chair, where the curled ends of nylon line dangled from a pair of eyehooks. His finger traced an invisible path, following the pulley's geometry.

"That your buddy's gun?" Clines said. He crunched over the splinters and took a close-up of the jaw. He picked it up and inspected the molars' silver fillings. "I'd be surprised if this really was his father."

"Yeah," Larry agreed, but only because he hadn't thought of it.

"You can get this stuff anywhere," Clines said, rubbing a thumb over Creeley's name. He patted the pocket underneath and felt a lump, took a pencil and poked around inside. He reached his hand in and pulled out a miniature Snickers bar.

"What's this?"

"A joke," Larry said.

"Is it funny?"

"Actually it's a threat."

They sat in the stale air of the kitchenette while Clines took his statement. The worst Creeley could be charged with was reckless endangerment, maybe a weapons violation. Clines was assigning someone to watch Larry's house until they found Creeley. Larry imagined it would make seeing Donna harder, but said nothing. What was the difference—he wasn't seeing her anyway.

Clines could give him a ride in. They stopped at the house to get his lunch from the fridge.

"We picked up something on the mother," Clines said as they passed East Hill Plaza. "You might be interested in it."

He waited, made Larry ask what.

"She was a patient of your father's."

"Creeley's mother," Larry asked.

"Since she was a teenager. Your father was responsible for signing her in and out of a whole slew of places, including Auburn, where she died."

"So?" Larry said.

"The personal thing," Clines said. "It's coming together. He's a kook but he knows what he's doing. And he's doing it to you. My question is, why aren't you helping me stop him?"

Larry tried silence rather than a lie.

"See," Clines said. "I can't do anything with that."

"I never met the man."

"Look. You can ask your father about her or I can. I think I'm being pretty nice here. Normally I wouldn't give you the choice, but I know he just got out of the hospital."

310

"I'll ask him."

"Today," Clines said.

"Tonight," Larry conceded, and it wasn't a bluff. He'd do it because he knew he wouldn't get anything.

"I'm also having someone take a look at your father's car."

"Why?" Larry asked, but it was just reflex. He knew.

THE DAY was almost half over. Marv wanted him to do Tops and Wegmans, and at both places Larry had to wait behind the Frito-Lay guy. At Tops his shelves were a mess; at Wegmans they were completely empty, not even the dessert cups left. It had to be Creeley but there was no jack, no note, only the bare metal.

When he got off the bus, the Monte Carlo wasn't there.

"How was work?" Vicki asked, as if she were interested.

"Okay."

She came in from the kitchen and gave him a real kiss, which he wasn't prepared for, her tongue insistent. She smelled of perfume and cigarettes and the developer they used at her work. She inspected his cheeks, looking concerned. He wondered out loud why she was so happy to see him.

"Do I need a reason?"

"I guess not."

Scott came over to join in the hug, clinging to their legs.

"Can you watch him a minute?" she asked. "I've got to run out for some milk for dinner."

"Sure," Larry said, and waited for her to leave. She borrowed a five and kissed him again. When she was finally gone, he sat on the couch, looking out at Donna's yard. It seemed he was never alone anymore, and then when he was, he couldn't think. On the rug, Scott smashed his Matchbox cars together, making wet sound effects.

"Let's play nice," Larry said, apparently too hard, because Scott stopped as if hit and began to sob.

"It's all right," Larry said, and got down on the floor and patted his back, but nothing comforted him.

"I want Mommy," he cried, heaving. "I want Mommy."

"Mommy's not here," Larry explained.

"I want Mommy," he whined, turning it into a chant.

He repeated this long after Larry had gone upstairs. He closed the bathroom door but he could still hear Scott droning, tireless as cicadas on a summer day. Larry rubbed his eyes with the heels of his hands. "Please shut up," he said.

He heard the Ruster pull in and yanked up his pants and headed downstairs. On the landing, he saw it was the Monte Carlo.

Donna walked across her yard without looking up. She had her tweed suit on, her hair in the tortoiseshell clip. His breath fogged the window and he wiped it with a hand. She disappeared beneath the porch roof, and he bounded downstairs, cracking his knee against an endtable, just in time to see the storm door close.

He swore, and Scott stared at him.

"You stopped," Larry said. "Good."

The phone tempted him but Vicki would show up any minute.

She didn't come back with the milk until six. The checkers in the P&C were slow, which was true, yet he didn't fully believe her. He imagined her calling Alan, setting up a meeting. In some ways he no longer cared. If Donna hadn't asked him to stop, they would be doing the same thing—but they weren't. He wanted credit for it.

He cut Scott's hot dog and bun into pieces, spread the macaroni around to cool. Vicki held the ketchup upside-down over the lip of his plate.

"Take a drink of milk while you're waiting," Larry prompted, and Scott pouted.

"You guys have a tough time without me," she asked.

He wanted to confess, to say that he loved Donna to her face and make them even. He wanted to tell her what he knew, that she was not fooling anyone.

"We were fine," he said.

"I'm sorry I got angry this morning," she said. "What did the detective say?"

They were careful not to be too polite or too quiet, too happy or annoyed. They faked everything; he did the dishes, thinking that tomorrow they would just be dirty again. He had to break out of this paralysis, but the only way he could see was the most painful. He wished he were ruthless, or stupid, able to blame his mistakes on fate—or better, that he might take off in the car, drive away with a change of clothes and half the savings account. He wanted to believe those stories about the husband going to the corner for cigarettes, but for him they were untrue, useless. He'd always been the one that stayed.

He was supposed to be at his father's around seven. Susan had called a meeting. He borrowed the keys from Vicki, kissed her and then Scott good night and went out to the Ruster.

On the far shoulder sat a black-and-white, a uniformed officer at the wheel. Larry waved, and the man held a gloved hand up.

The steering wheel was cold. Donna's living room window flashed blue with the TV. While the engine warmed, he watched her curtains, alert yet expecting nothing. He checked the brakes—they were okay. The transmission clunked into reverse, then drive, and soon he was gliding through the night to Schubert. It was the Unfinished Symphony, the performance a childhood friend—Toscanini and the NBC—yet after a minute he clicked it off.

Branches flew beneath the streetlights; the moon shone bright and high. In the valley, the city glowed. Clines was being unfair, making him ask his father a question he himself had yet to answer truthfully. In one sense it was simple, in another impossibly complex. Do you love her? Do you love him? Do you love me? Larry thought that he would make a lousy detective. He didn't want to know everything.

Mrs. Railsbeck let him in, the wind whisking leaves through the vestibule. She had missed her hair appointment; patches of the spun white had faded to gray. In the living room the TV played to an empty couch.

"Look at your face," she said.

"Work," he explained.

"Your father's much better," she said, without waiting for him to ask. She took his coat and hung it up, talking the whole time. "Your sister doesn't think so, but I know your father, and I think he's fine now. She thinks I'm not capable of taking care of him, which is asinine if you ask me. What does she think I've been doing the last twenty years? I wish you'd talk to her."

"I will," Larry said, and they started down the hall. The house was warm, the air close; he could smell the meat from dinner.

"I'm serious. She's talking about a rest home. I don't want to see him in a rest home."

He thought of Cayuga View, the attendants scarfing the crumbs of the sheet cake. "I don't either."

Mrs. Railsbeck stopped at the bottom of the stairs. "She's in your mother's room."

"You're not coming up?"

"I don't think I'm invited."

"Oh, I'm sure you are," he said, trying to keep things light.

"No," she said, definite, and he didn't push it.

The climb reminded him of all those nights after dinner, going up to kiss his mother, the light already out, the radio on her night table turned so low you had to close your eyes, hold your breath a second. Somewhere a record turned, a pianist laid his hands to the keys.

"Do you know who this is?" she'd ask, and Larry did. Gottschalk, Cherubini, Sweelinck. She said he had a gift for it; he thought it a logical product of their afternoons together. It was remarkable when he missed one. Even now when he flipped through the dial he identified everything, like a student, someone on a quiz show. It was like training a dog, he thought—impressive but of little significance.

Susan was working on papers at their mother's desk, her back to the door. She wore a dark suit but no shoes, her feet crossed at the ankles beneath the chair. With her bobbed hair and military posture, she looked nothing like their mother. Her first and now third husband, Grant, was a systems salesman with Digital, gone for months at a time, and Larry was tempted to see her as lonely, spinsterish, when it was not true. Her life was not here, continued invisibly beyond his imagination. She would leave. It was the weapon he needed, one he possessed to a fault already—the grunt's dumb patience.

"Hey," he said, poking his head in.

She held up a finger and finished what she was writing, as if this were her office. None of the furniture had changed, the paint, the drapes, the light fixtures. The wind rattled the glass.

"Sorry I'm late."

"You're not late." She remarked on his cheeks, and he lied. The only place for him was the edge of the bed. She turned the chair to face him and crossed her legs. When she took her glasses off, her eyes were tired, the skin of the lids crinkly. "I want to talk about Dad."

"How is he?"

"The same, I'm afraid—inconsistent. It's been hard." She touched the papers on the desk behind her. "I want to talk about his will."

"He's not *dying*," Larry said, trying to make it a joke. His father was probably somewhere between what Susan and Mrs. Railsbeck said.

"No, but legally he may not be able to change it later. He may not want to, who knows. He's not as sound as he should be right now. I just thought it might be a good time to finalize some things."

"Like what?"

"Right now I'm listed as the executor. I'm thinking it might make more sense if you were, being here."

"Sure," he said, and instead of his father's death seeming unreal, Larry himself did—his words, what he would have to do. "You'll come back and help me with the details."

"You'd want an accountant, actually."

"But you'll be here," he said.

"After the last few days, I really don't know. I understand that he's not well, but he's said some things I don't think I can forgive. Ugly, hurtful things."

"So that's what this is about."

"Not completely. I do think it's better that you do it."

"What did he say?" Larry asked.

"Things I won't repeat."

"About you."

"About Mother and Mrs. R. and Grant. Some things about you. I know that he's sick but I can't stop myself from reacting to them. I can't stay in the room with him anymore."

"Mrs. R. said you were making noise about a nursing home."

"I was upset. I know you don't want him in one of those places, I understand that at least." She pinched the bridge of her nose between a finger and thumb as if to stave off a headache, then held her forehead in her hand. "It's me. I can't take it. I should be able to but I can't."

"He'll get better."

"He's not going to get better. That's another thing I wanted to talk to you about. They say he could be like this a long time. You haven't seen him—it's not that, I know you've been busy. I just don't want you to be shocked."

"I don't think that's possible."

With her glasses off she looked frail and defenseless. "He's bad, Larry. Maybe it's because I remember Mother being like this, I don't know. I just can't deal with him."

"But you'd come," Larry said, and she gave him a puzzled look. "To the funeral."

"Of course," she said. "I didn't mean that."

"*That* would shock me."

"It's honestly been that bad."

"I believe you."

"God, I hate coming back here," she said, but mockingly, poking fun at her own intolerance for the place.

"I know."

"I wish I was more like you that way. You've always fit in."

"Not always," Larry said, relieved to be done with the interview.

"It's true. I start seeing the signs on eighty-one and my head shuts down, my stomach hurts."

"I'm glad you came. Mrs. R. is too, she's just intimidated."

"I could stay, that's the problem. Grant's in Thailand. I don't really have to be back for anything. I know I'll just mope around the house and think about what a terrible daughter I am."

"You came. You didn't have to."

"Do you remember the last time I was here?"

"Yes," he said, though in truth he didn't.

She smiled at the lie. "It was right after Scott was born. The time before that was your wedding and the time before that was for Mother."

"So you don't like it here," he admitted.

"It's more than that. I think something's wrong with me. When I think of us—when all four of us were here—I don't remember anything good. I just remember wanting to leave. I still feel that way when I'm in the house, like it's squeezing me. I'm thirty-eight years old, for Christ's sake."

"Have you told Dad you're going to leave?"

"I will tomorrow. I'm sure I can get a ticket out of Syracuse whenever I want. I just need to take care of some things first. And I wanted to talk to you." She looked to Larry as if asking his permission. He thought it was not his place, but she needed an answer.

"I think it's the right thing," he said.

She nodded sadly, as if it were beyond her control. "Anyway, you should see him before he's down for the night." She reached across the space between them and touched his knee. "I'm sorry."

"It's okay," he said, taking her hand. He didn't know what to do with it, and stood. They both let go. She didn't see him to the door, but didn't turn the chair toward the desk either.

"Don't talk to him too long," Susan warned. "He gets tired."

He left her door open. In the hall, he wondered why his entire life he'd thought of her as too strong to need his help. Now that she'd asked for it, it was too late.

Outside, wind moaned in the eaves, as if the house were a ship at sea. His old room was dark, a picture on the dresser flashing a scrap of streetlight. It would be him in uniform before shipping out, the background a neutral blue like sky. The bathroom had a new shower stall, new matching towels and bathmats. It was the only room that had changed; Larry still did not accept it, still pictured the clawfooted tub with its greening mineral deposits.

Thirty-eight, she'd said, as if age made a difference.

His father's room was at the top of the back stairs. The door was closed, a skirt of light sneaking out from underneath. He knocked with the back of a hand and looked in.

His father was propped up in bed, reading. He waved Larry in and set the book on his nightstand, toppling a vial of pills. Only the one lamp was on, the corners of the room dark.

"I was wondering when you'd come by," he chided.

"How are you doing?" Larry asked.

"Good," he said, but Larry had discounted his answer in advance.

A chair sat beside the bed, angled as if in conversation with him. His eyebrow was closing nicely. Larry replaced the vial—Ceclor for infection—and noticed the book was the same as Vicki's, the new Stephen King.

"What happened to you?" his father asked, tilting his head to get a better look at Larry's face.

"I got ambushed," Larry said, and told him the whole story. He waited for his father to respond to Creeley's name.

"Very strange. You don't know this man at all?"

"No," Larry said. "You do though. At least you told me you did."

"A patient of mine?"

"His mother was too. Ellen Creeley?"

His father said nothing.

"You knew her," Larry asked. "Tall, dark-haired."

When he still would not answer him, Larry added, "She was your patient most of her life. She was mentally ill. You signed her into Auburn."

"Why are you asking me if you know everything already?" He said it calmly, as if found out, resigned, tired of lying.

"I don't know everything. I need to find out why he's after me—and you too. The police think he may have done something to your car."

Larry waited, then said, "The detective said I could talk to you or he could talk to you. I'll tell him you'd rather talk to him."

They looked at each other, and Larry thought it had always been like this, that this scene repeated again and again between them and they never got any better at it. He stood up to leave.

His father sighed, lifted his chin and looked to the ceiling, then dropped it again. "I was always good to his mother. Always."

"Then why is he after me?" Larry said. He sat down again, prepared to hear anything—that they were brothers, Creeley the bastard, deprived of his birthright; that his father had fallen in love with Ellen Creeley when she was thirteen and couldn't help himself, took her then and there on the leather examination table. His father seemed a stranger now, capable of anything, and Larry thought how little he really knew him. He could not say whose fault it was, though he was ready to take the blame.

"Because I lied for her," his father said. "I knew what she was doing, but I didn't want her to lose him. He was all she had. I didn't think she could take it. And I was right, that was what finally happened."

"What did you lie about?"

"She hurt him. When she wasn't right, she would hurt him. Then she'd bring him to me."

"And you didn't report it."

"Things were different back then. Now I'd be obligated by law, but back then you tried to keep the family together."

"That's it?" Larry asked. "There was nothing else between you two."

"She was a patient. She didn't have anyone else to turn to. I'm sure there were rumors, but they're not true. She was devoted to her husband's memory. It was very sad. When she was right, she was a wonderful girl. That's probably why I couldn't turn her in. I tried to get her help."

"What about him?"

"Ronnie. When you said his name, I couldn't believe it. He was a good kid. I always felt sorry for him. He loved her despite everything. I'm sure he hated her too. It's hard to tell what that does to a person. He was quiet. After a while he didn't even cry. She'd bring him in and he'd sit there on the table. He wouldn't say a word, and she'd be going a mile a minute apologizing, begging me not to tell anyone. Very sad."

"Why didn't you tell me this before?" Larry asked.

"I didn't think it was anybody's business," his father said. "I still don't, but it sounds like it's not my choice anymore. They said he was dead. I guess I was foolish to believe them."

"Who?"

"The Navy. They sent her a telegram. She was in Auburn then. She drank a bottle of floor stripper, it was awful. I had to drive her mother up to identify her, and her mother couldn't believe it. She looked right at her and said, 'No, that's not her.' And there she was, right in front of us. The stripper had burned her lips but otherwise she was fine, still striking. She was a beautiful, beautiful woman. And I said, yes, that was Ellen, and her mother started to argue with me. That was terribly hard. I was almost glad that everything was over for her. When you told me Ronnie was alive, I didn't know if I wanted to believe it or not."

"Why couldn't you just tell me this when I asked you the first time?"

"Respect for the dead, I suppose. It's not something I like to remember."

"So you lied to me."

"Maybe. I don't remember you asking. I honestly can't sometimes. Or things are confused. I see the wrong people in the wrong places."

"Can you still remember the war?" Larry said, hoping his father would not stop.

"Every day," his father said.

"Me too," Larry said.

The wind shivered the panes. His father gestured to a glass of water, and Larry handed it to him, then placed it back on the nightstand.

"What did your sister tell you?"

Larry hesitated, and his father laughed. "Now look who's squirming," he said.

Leaving, Larry shifted into reverse and nothing happened. The transmission clunked, fumbled among the gears. Mrs. Railsbeck had turned off the porch light, and the house loomed huge and dark between the trees, only a frame of light sneaking out behind the blinds of his mother's room. His father had not cut the grass or the hedges, and Mrs. R. was too busy to remember a pumpkin. Larry thought that if it looked like this Sunday night, the littler kids would hide behind the bushes, daring each other to go first, convincing themselves that the owners weren't home, that they were on vacation or didn't celebrate the holiday, when by then it would be obvious even to the smallest that the place was haunted.

WHEN HE pulled in, the cop was still there but the Monte Carlo was gone. It was nearly ten and not her meeting night. He waved, then felt watched as he crossed the yard, a target. Vicki was reading with the TV on; she didn't get up. He couldn't ask her what time Donna had left, and it made him impatient with her, as if it were her fault—which it was, ultimately.

"Someone called for you," she said.

It was Julian. Larry got his machine. "Jackstraw from Wichita," the Grateful Dead played, and the beep beeped. He'd have to catch him tomorrow.

"How's your father?" Vicki asked. She kept a finger on the sentence she was reading.

"It's hard to tell," Larry said, and gave her a few details to let her know he appreciated her interest. "Did Scott get down all right?" he asked, and received the same. They had nothing to say about themselves.

Dynasty was over, Barbara Walters interviewing celebrities about their private lives. He could hear cars passing outside. He watched the window beside the TV, waiting for the lights of the Monte Carlo to swing across the yard, but no one slowed. Vicki made hot chocolate and flipped the pages. The news trailer ran—firemen dousing flames, a running back diving for a score.

"I'm going up," he said.

"I'm going to read a little."

It was a dance, its subtleties rigid.

Brushing his teeth, he checked the drive one last time, looking down from Scott's window, then went into the bathroom and spat. In bed, he pictured Donna on top of him in the car, her buttons undone, her bra hiked above her breasts. He was still hard when Vicki got into bed. He rolled away from her, she threw an arm over him, and soon it was not a problem.

In the dream, Magoo was squeezing his hand, his fingers slick with blood. It could have been real; he was missing his glasses and half his ear. His grip weakened. When he stopped, he would be dead. "Don't let me go," he cried, as if Larry had. He faltered, then went still, and Larry woke up, a fist still clenching.

Vicki murmured as he swung himself out. He left the light off and crept into Scott's room. Below, Donna's car sat in the drive, the cop across the road. He lay down again. The clock said three-fifteen, then three-forty, then four twenty-five. It surprised him; he'd thought knowing she was home would help him sleep. It had been three days—less, really. If nothing else, he was getting used to the dark.

He didn't feel like running. At breakfast, Vicki commented on it, and he answered her truthfully. He expected the Monte Carlo to be parked wrong, the fenders ragged, blood on the bumper, but there it was, perfectly straight in the ruts. He couldn't get Scott buckled in and turned in the seat to do it, his knee squishing his lunch. He swore at no one in particular, then closed his eyes, waiting for his anger to bleed away. Vicki clicked on the news to cover the silence. After dropping off Scott, she asked what was wrong.

"What are we doing?" he asked her.

"What do you mean?"

"Are you happy?"

"Yes," she said, but too quickly.

"You don't act it. All you do anymore is read that goddamn book."

"What do you want me to do?"

"I don't know," he said. "What do you and Alan do when you're together?"

She drove as if she hadn't heard him, her eyes on the road. Finally she said, "We don't have to do anything."

"Why did you come back?" Larry asked. "One day you say you need time to think and the next you're back to stay. What happened?"

"We talked, and Alan thought this would be the best for everyone. He knew I didn't want to take Scott away from you and he didn't think he could leave his wife."

Larry thought he should have seen it earlier. "That's great," he said. "That's so stupid."

"He's right though," she said, as if Larry would come to understand.

"Of course he is," Larry said. "He's Alan."

They turned into the outlet and Vicki pulled up beside Number 1. She smiled at him sadly, as if to say they would continue this later. He could see she wanted him to leave, that it would be cruel to go any further.

"Are you still seeing him?"

"No," she said, but her eyes slid off his.

"Jesus Christ," he said, and pushed out of the door.

"Larry," she said, "I love you."

"Lare," she called after him.

Inside, as he was punching in, Marv stuck his head out of his office. "We gonna get a full day out of you today?"

"Fuck you," Larry said to the picture in his locker, then sat on the bench and stared at his unlaced boots. After a while, he tied them and buttoned up his top. When he went out to Number 1, Vicki was gone. It was a bad sign. He thought she'd at least fight for him.

He took it out on the truck, shifting late, taking the corners hard, a loose pen rattling across the dash. "You," he said to a Cordoba taking forever to turn, "are an asshole." At the Common's Market downtown, his shelves were empty again.

He called Julian and woke him up.

"We got everything," Julian said. "Burt did. You won't believe it, it's only four pages."

"Don't move," Larry said. "I'll be right there."

He parked across from the Chapterhouse. The stairway smelled of beer and wet newspapers. Julian had left the door open. He was in the kitchen, eating cereal from a plastic cup with Darth Vader on it. The apartment was too hot, a radiator hissing; he was wearing only gym trunks. He handed Larry the pages and kept eating.

Most of it Larry knew—Creeley's background, his date of induction, stateside training. He had processed through Cam Ranh Bay in December of '68. The file mentioned several operations Larry had heard of near his AO— Dewey Canyon I, Massachusetts Striker—but nothing of the Ruff Puffs Creeley would have commanded. He was into August '69 and beginning to think it was another cover when he hit a line that made him stop.

Reported MIA, it said, and below, at a later date, *Identified POW*. In January '73 he'd been released and admitted to the neurological ward at Bethesda, where he was still receiving treatment for Gun Shot Wound, Head. After the admissions date ran a long list of citations.

"Does that help you at all?" Julian asked.

"I'm not sure," Larry said.

"I hope so, 'cause that's all there is. We checked everything." He balanced the cup on the pile already in the sink.

"How much do I owe you?" Larry said, digging his wallet from his back pocket.

"Forget it."

"Seriously."

"Seriously," Julian said. "I'm going back home to work for my brother."

"When?" Larry asked, and they chatted a moment before he had to leave. "You take care," he said at the door. They shook hands, Julian giving him a soul grip.

He'd gotten to the top of the stairs when Julian called, "Hey, Larry."

"What?"

"You never told me any of your war stories."

"I don't have any."

"Bullshit," Julian said, and saluted him.

At the A&P in the Triphammer Mall, he called Clines with the news.

"Officially I didn't hear that," Clines said. "But it makes sense. The last after-action report I've got on him is July, in the Rao Lao Valley. Guess who else was there."

Larry said nothing, remembering the shallow brown river, the sandbars and snags of driftwood. He recalled floating Smart Andy across on Carl Metcalf's air mattress, joking that they'd tip him over.

"Me," Larry said.

"Good guess," Clines said. "Now guess who that was with us in the trailer yesterday."

"It *was* him then."

"Face it, the guy's not right. We thought all he had was his headstone. Did you see our man outside your house this morning?"

"No," Larry said.

"Good. He saw you."

Larry hadn't checked but still he was disappointed. He had to be sharper, and not only for Creeley. If the man was hidden in the trees, Larry thought he could cut through the backyard without being seen and meet Donna at her cellar door. By the time Clines hung up, Larry had settled on it.

He tried her at work, telling himself he would give it two rings. If she was at her desk, she'd pick up immediately.

The phone never rang. "Plant Pathology," she said, and he could talk or hang up.

Beside him a woman lifted a toddler into a shopping cart and fit its legs through the child seat.

"Hello?" Donna said. "Plant Pathology."

She sounded fine, and he wondered if she'd seen Fred last night, if by calling he was just making things harder for her. He needed to know, which was selfish.

"Hello?" she said.

"It's me," Larry said.

"Larry," she whispered, as if someone might overhear her. "Where are you? What are the cops doing outside your house?"

He told her the truth.

"Bizarre," she said.

"Your car was gone last night," he said. "I was worried."

"I had to do some shopping. Brian's birthday is coming up. How are you?"

"Shitty. I miss you. How are *you* doing?"

"I'm okay," she said.

"Are you?"

"I don't know."

"I'd like to see you."

"Larry," she said, tired, as if they'd gone over this before.

He waited, the phone pressed against his ear. If she said no, it would be fine, he would still feel the same for her. It was wrong of him to call when she was trying so hard. It was not her fault he'd lost his heart to her.

"Where?" Donna asked, as if that mattered.

They met for lunch at the Treman Marina. The parking lot was matted with leaves. She stepped out of the Monte Carlo and they kissed. She wore an orange sweater that darkened her hair, her purse over her shoulder. He started to talk but she put two fingers to her lips and then to his. The slips were empty, geese plucking at the yellowed grass. They walked away from the lot and past the cement-block restrooms and over a rise where a bench looked across the inlet to the meager lighthouses, the blue table of the lake. The wind lifted her hair. Neither of them had brought anything to eat. He traced the curve of her ear, laid a hand on her throat. She was right, it was better not to talk.

"Tomorrow," she said back at the car, and he kissed her through the open window, then followed her out.

For once the Scandinavians weren't playing but Erik Satie, who fit the day, the simple blue of afternoon. The sun was warm and he didn't need the heater. He drove slowly between stops, as if to apologize for this morning. He didn't need to eat, and thought that tomorrow he'd run. He paid extra attention to his shelves, whistling when they were empty. Even Creeley couldn't discourage him. In the hills around Mecklenburg, starlings burst across the sky like shot. He kept checking his watch, seeing how many hours it would be till he'd see her again.

He dreaded going home, but strangely it was easier to be there now. Vicki was busy with dinner, ignoring him or possibly contrite. He grabbed a cold Genesee and a sweater and threw the football in the yard with Scott.

"Why are *you* in such a good mood?" Vicki joked when he came up from behind and kissed her.

The dishes took fifteen minutes, Scott's bath another twenty. Larry read *Lyle, Lyle Crocodile* and *Harry the Dirty Dog*. While the TV ate up the half hours, Vicki sewed Superman's cape to a blue T-shirt, doubling the stitches. She finished well before the news but didn't pick up her Stephen King.

"Go ahead," Larry encouraged her.

"That's all right."

"It's not the book."

"I know," she said.

He thought he should tell her now, if not to absolve her then to join his guilt to hers, but because it was Donna, Vicki would not see it that way, and so instead he said, "I'm sorry."

"Why?" she said. "It's my fault."

"It's mine too."

"Did Donna tell you? I'll bet Donna told you."

"The police did. They've been watching the house for a while now."

"I want to stop, do you understand that? But I can't. I can't, Larry."

"Don't cry," he said, rubbing her back, and felt heartless for not wanting her confessions. He did not deserve to forgive her. "It's all right," he said to quiet her. "It's okay."

They made love as if to recapture the last year, their entire past. Her head and shoulders hung off the edge of the bed, her hair swinging; she had to drop her hands to the rug, giving him the white undersides of her breasts. She laughed and he bit her and she shrieked. "Darling," she called him afterward, as she had when they were young, then gently pinched his earlobe, something she'd never done. It was too hot; their knees made a tent of the sheets. Before rolling over, she kissed him and said, "I love you," leaving him no choice but to echo her. The clock said he would see Donna in less than twelve hours. He felt like an assassin awaiting the chosen moment. Until he kept his appointment, the world did not exist, was ground to dust between his guilt and desire. It was dumb.

The next day she was waiting for him, the Monte Carlo running. She wore her tweed skirt with nothing underneath. In her purse were green grapes and a block of sharp cheese, a knife in plastic wrap. It was Friday; they took their time parting, lingered in last kisses. His eyes were soft from staying closed so long. As they left the lot, Beethoven's Seventh came on.

The holiday was nearly upon them. The woman in the 7-Eleven had a white fright wig and a foam rubber nose. Scott tried on his tights; they bagged at the ankles. He wanted *The Snowy Day*. Downstairs, Vicki closed in on the end of her book.

In the morning Susan stopped on her way to Syracuse, tucking a big rented Lincoln behind the Ruster. She was late and wore her jewelry, drank her coffee standing up. Their father was the same. "You look good," she told Vicki. Scott took a break from his cartoons to get a hug. Larry thanked her for coming.

"Maybe he's all right," she said. "I just can't put up with him very long."

She finished the cup and checked her watch. They went out on the porch to see her off, Scott protesting the cold.

Susan hugged him close. "He's yours now," she whispered, and let him go.

"Next time stay longer," Vicki said, kissing her stiffly.

"I will," she promised.

The tailpipe smoked in the cold. She pointed the car north and accelerated away. Vicki took Scott in, leaving Larry to watch the Lincoln dwindle. He had not thought he'd missed Susan so much, or that he would now. Soon they would be all that was left of the family, linked only by the telephone. He considered what she'd said, and it was true; he never thought of all four of them together, just one by one, isolated like stars. His own family seemed to be disintegrating in the same way, yet he had no plans, not even the faintest inclination to prevent it. He understood why Vicki couldn't stop. He couldn't imagine what he and Donna had begun ever ending.

In the mail they got a postcard from Wade with a statue of a bronc rider, one bronze hand flailing higher than its kicking hooves.

That's right, guys, it said. *We're getting back on that horse. Maybe we'll have better luck in the Wild West. Thanks for everything you've done for both of us. I know you guys were worried. Hope to see you soon and take care. All best, Wade.*

Larry read it again, hoping it was a joke, Wade's thinking wishful, pathetic. He'd had his chance.

"What's he got to say for himself now?" Vicki asked, and Larry handed her the card.

"No," she said twice, as if the news was too good. "I didn't know this. Did you know this?" She looked to him hopefully, to see if he was happy, and Larry mustered a grin. She handed him the card as if it were a gift. "So it can happen."

Though he could not picture them the way they'd been, he wanted to believe it was true, so it was not a lie when he said yes.

"I've got to talk to her," Vicki said, already leaving. "Can you watch Scott?"

"Sure," he called after her, as if he had a choice. He read the card one more time, then fastened it to the fridge with a magnet shaped like a halved apple. Everything was a symbol to Larry now, every song part of their sound-track.

He walked around the downstairs, straightening things. He put away the dishes and tossed the dead leftovers in the garbage. Finally he bundled up Scott and they raked the backyard, the tines tearing at the grass, ripping divots. Scott's was plastic, fluorescent red. The sandbox was gray with rain, Vicki's garden overgrown. Larry brought out a radio to listen to the IC game so he wouldn't have to think; he set a Genesee next to it on the back steps. The beer seemed warm, but it was a trick. He built a leaf mound for Scott to dive in. At the Jamesway Vicki had bought a trash bag printed like a jack-o'-lantern; they stuffed it and Larry dragged it around front. When he'd bagged what was left, he opened the gate and did Donna's yard. The kitchen window glowed. He expected shouts any minute, screaming, but there was nothing; the Bombers were running the score up on someone. The light was weak, the color of sherry; he hadn't noticed the days growing shorter. Scott wanted hot chocolate, and Larry put the rakes away and collected his empties.

"I'm sorry," Vicki said when she came in, "but that woman is just too weird for me. You'd think she'd be excited about seeing him. All she did was talk about the kids. Brian this and Chris that. When I tried to talk about Wade she just ignored me. I don't know. I couldn't tell if she was drinking or not."

"I think she's stopped," Larry said, then worried that his defense of her was too quick.

"Anyway, they're really going to do it. She's supposed to leave next week. He sent her a ticket and everything. I think it's great."

She waited for him to second her opinion; it was like being a cheerleader.

"We'll see if it works," he said.

After dinner, Scott asked if he could go right to bed, as if in the morning they would be waiting downstairs with candy.

It always rained on Halloween—it was an Ithaca tradition—and when the clouds moved in around lunchtime, Larry was secretly pleased. In the afternoon the rooms grew dark; Vicki had to put a light on to read. Larry set Scott's pumpkin out early, reaching the kitchen match in and singeing the hair on the back of his hands. Scott stared at it as if it might speak. The wind picked up and the candle flickered, making the face change. Drops speckled the walk, beaded on the Ruster. The cows wandered toward the barn, then stood there lowing, waiting for someone to let them in.

Clines called to let him know a man would be there all night.

"Even if it pours," he assured Larry. "I'd be real surprised if he doesn't try something."

"Because of the day."

"Because he's a showy bastard," Clines said. "I'll have someone good on the job."

They were too far out of town to get many kids, usually just Brian and Chris and those classmates whose parents drove them. Each year Scott's school threw a party in the cafeteria, which Larry and Vicki helped chaperone. Scott's tights still bagged around the ankles, but the cape and the shorts looked good; Vicki sprayed black dye on his hair, shielding his eyes with a hand.

"Look, up in the sky," Vicki said. "It's a bird, it's a plane, it's—Christopher Reeve."

It was a local joke, he'd gone to Cornell. He was supposed to be a really nice guy.

Scott laughed asthmatically. "No," he said. "Superman."

He didn't want to wear a coat over his costume but Vicki insisted. It was only spitting, the road almost dry again. They left a bowl of Snickers miniatures on the porch and moved the pumpkin to the bottom of the steps in case it tipped. It was not quite dusk, the sky blushing. Larry picked the man out of the trees easily. He buckled Scott in, then did himself. Donna's porch was bare, her windows black; even if she was really leaving, it was wrong of him to keep abandoning her like this. They waited for the transmission to kick in.

"I finished my book," Vicki said on the way down the hill.

"Was it scary?"

"It wasn't as good as the last one. I think he's losing it."

"You always say that."

"I don't know what it is. He just doesn't do it for me any more."

"Kind of like me," Larry said.

She weighed it. "No, that's never been our problem."

329

"What do you think is?"

"I don't know, Larry." She sighed, tired of his questions. "Me. I'm our problem. Is that what you want?"

"No," he said, gently disagreeing, but she was done discussing it.

In town it was fully dark. The bars on Aurora overflowed with college students in elaborate costumes—rabbits, Frankensteins, a lobster. Wet toilet paper hung from the trees. The sidestreets teemed, parents carrying umbrellas. Already someone had smashed a pumpkin in the road. Tomorrow there would be candy wrappers among the leaves.

Vicki let Larry and Scott off by the door and went to look for a spot. Inside, the hallway smelled of paste; disco thumped from the cafeteria. The children had decorated the walls with pictures made from dried beans and macaroni; Larry could make out flowers and houses, a sun.

"Where's yours?" he asked, though it was right in front of him, and Scott searched the board with a finger.

"Mine," he said, holding a corner.

It was haphazard, mostly pinto beans with a few wagon wheels scattered along the bottom. His best guess was a plane crash.

"My race car," Scott managed.

"Look at that," Larry said.

He recognized most of the children and some of the parents, nodding as they passed. They seemed good people to him, while he was a monster, thinking of Donna and the car, the vinyl seat squeaking under his knees.

Finally Vicki backed through the door, shutting her umbrella. She gave Larry a look as she took off Scott's coat, as if he were supposed to do it. She hiked up Scott's shorts so his tights wouldn't sag and straightened his cape.

"What does Superman say?" she asked him.

"Up, up, up!" Scott said, giving them the Black Power salute.

She'd brought their camera and clicked away.

"How about one with all of us," she said, and convinced another mother to shoot them. They knelt on either side of him, their arms crossed over his shoulders. Larry imagined that eventually it would be used as evidence.

"Smile," Vicki ordered.

"I am smiling."

"With your teeth," she said. "Pretend you're having a good time."

The modular tables of the cafeteria stood folded in one corner like machinery, the steamtables unplugged and rolled against the wall. Twisted crêpe paper festooned the game booths—Sponge Toss and Mini-Golf, the Grab Bag, the Lollipop Tree. A clown in red Chuck Taylors handed out balloons, talking through a kazoo like a duck. There was a table with baked goods and a punchbowl that Vicki had signed them up to proctor for an hour. They let Scott go off with his friends—an aluminum foil C3PO and a werewolf in corduroys—occasionally asking each other, "Do you see him? Do you have him?"

Later the children bobbed for apples, taking turns kneeling at a zinc tub. Most came up sputtering; a few cried. The apples were big, but it was not impossible; the boy before Scott pinned one against the bottom and emerged sopping and victorious, holding it aloft like a medal.

When the applause had died down, Scott followed him, dunking his face into the tub. Vicki had moved into position with the camera. He had no chance yet Larry rooted for him, hoping that by some luck he would come up with one, that this once fate would let him win.

As Scott flung his head back, Vicki took his picture. His mouth was empty, but the hair dye had run, the black bleeding down his face. The crowd had to laugh. Scott looked around, shivering, unsure what was going on. He smiled and they laughed harder. Larry shouldered through the ring around the tub and got to him just as another father draped a towel over his shoulders. Vicki was right behind him, her camera poking him in the ribs. The crowd was clapping now, forgiving themselves.

"Dint win," Scott said.

"But you tried," Larry said, "right?"

He nodded, unconvinced.

"Was it fun?" Vicki asked.

"Yes," Scott admitted. "Yes," he said again, and they led him away, Larry rubbing his hair with the towel, wondering how he could ever leave them.

At the end of the night, the children each received a goodie bag on their way out. In the Ruster, Scott dug through it, showing his trophies to Larry.

"Zagnut," Larry said.

"Yuck," Vicki said. "Give me something good."

Packs of older kids were still out, filling pillow cases. Vicki cursed the heater and they climbed the hill. Larry crunched a Tootsie Roll Pop and asked for another, but Scott was asleep. Larry tapped Vicki on the shoulder and pointed.

"Think he had a good time?" she whispered.

The Monte Carlo was still there, the right lights on. He'd been busy some of the evening and had forgotten Donna; now he silently apologized. The trees dripped, leaves reflecting the streetlight. Larry imagined the man on stakeout damning Clines.

Vicki got the Ruster into park and killed the engine. Larry cradled Scott, twisting to lift him through the door. The dye had dried in a line on his forehead like the edge of a mask. Vicki led them up the walk, the key out. The jack-o'-lantern was upright but dead. Vicki leaned over to glance in the bowl, then picked it up and showed it to Larry.

The Snickers were all gone; in the bottom rested one half of the jack of spades. In the shadowed light, he couldn't read what Creeley had written.

"Hold on," he said, and inspected the storm door. "Okay. Be careful."

Vicki touched the door and it swung open. Inside, a trail of mini Snickers bars crossed the carpet and headed up the stairs.

"What the hell is this?" Vicki said, and started to follow them.

"Wait," Larry warned. He knelt and laid Scott on the couch.

"This is that guy," Vicki whispered, and he nodded to let her know it was serious.

It was a suicide jack; on the sword, Creeley had written: LIKE FATHER. Larry squatted and tilted his head, trying to catch any wires in the hall light.

"I'll call the police," Vicki said.

"There's a guy across the street," Larry said, and started up, sidestepping the Snickers bars.

"Don't go up there."

"He's probably gone," Larry said. "That's how he works."

"Wait for the guy at least. Please?"

He hesitated, and she ran out the door onto the porch. "Hey!" she called, "hey!" waving her hands over her head as if flagging a train.

She opened the storm door. "He's coming."

It was Clines, swimming in a cheap parka, the hood lined with dirty fur. He had a flashlight instead of a gun and held it up in greeting. He stared at the candy bars. Larry handed him the half of the jack.

"Son of a bitch," Clines said.

Larry leaned against the railing to let him past. Below, at the newel post, Vicki motioned that she'd watch Scott.

"What happened?" Larry asked upstairs.

"Hey," Clines said, and shrugged. "The guy's good."

The trail ran down the hall toward the bedroom, then turned and stopped by the attic door.

"What's up there?" Clines said.

Larry thought of the picture and told him about the trunk.

Clines had him stand back. He reached inside his parka and drew out a small revolver, holding it at arm's length as if it might explode. He leaned against the wall and backhanded the doorknob and slowly opened it.

"Looks okay," Larry said.

Clines crouched beside the frame like Carl Metcalf, then spun through, following the gun. He flipped the light on and waved Larry in behind him. They went up together, watching the opening above, squishing the Snickers underfoot. Larry was careful to leave a few steps between them. At the top, Clines stopped and swiveled the gun around, holding it with both hands.

"Goddamn," he said, astonished, and stood, the gun by his side. "Look at this."

Larry rumbled up the stairs.

The walls were shingled with Magoo's pictures, festooned with souvenir flags. Larry's class A's hung from the rafters, its limbs stuffed like a scarecrow's. At the far end, the top of the footlocker stood open like the lid of a coffin. It was empty, the pistol missing; taped to the bottom was the other half of the jack. LIKE SON, it said.

TEN

The honor guard couldn't find the funeral. All five of them were from the area, loosely, but none close enough to know the roads. The Army had a black LTD waiting for them at the Elmira airport, and now the sergeant gunned it up and down the hills, slowing at crossroads. It was trout country, full of hunting camps and roadhouses; the motels advertised electric heat. They didn't have a map. The guy riding shotgun had a case of Stoney's between his feet, handing cans into the back, where Larry sat, cramped on the hump. The time difference was twelve hours; he didn't have to change his watch. It was almost noon, meaning he'd been awake for two days. The beer took the edge off but nothing more. They tossed the empties out the window, twisted to watch them cartwheel and hop in their wake.

The Martian's home was Wellsboro, Pennsylvania; his name was David Purifoy. Larry had orders never to leave the body, like a secret agent hand-cuffed to a briefcase. He'd flown over the Pacific, knowing the aluminum casket was below in the hold; at San Francisco he'd followed as a Spec 4 rolled it through a cold, echoing warehouse. He'd cheated once, at the PX at Travis, buying a diamond ring to give Vicki. He wore his class A's out of respect; in the airports, people stared. He'd been going so long his body didn't know what to do; when he went to the lavatory, nothing happened. He peered out the window of the DC-9, the tame land flowing beneath—the ballfields and parking lots of factories, the farms and subdivisions. Roads stretched everywhere, dead-ended in the middle of the woods in mounds of trash and outworn appliances. It was a country without mystery, neat, predictable. Though he wanted to, Larry no longer belonged to it.

Finally in Elmira he signed the Martian over to the funeral home and met the rest of the guard by the information desk. The sergeant carried a quilted gun case; he laid it in the trunk as if it were a baby. It was cold for late May, rain clouds caught in the mountains, the wipers clearing the windshield. Their first stop in Pennsylvania was a drive-thru beer distributorship; the owner insisted on shaking their hands. "God bless you, boys," he said, and sold them the case at wholesale though it was well before noon and at least three of them were underage.

Larry was the only one who knew the Martian and the only one currently serving in Vietnam. The sergeant was a lifer from Fort Drum finishing up his stint on permanent honor guard; the other three were on funeral detail from a reserve unit in Binghamton. None of them talked about the dead.

"The Nam," they said, as if they knew something of it. "That's a bitch."

"It's all right," Larry said, and they didn't mention it again. He surprised himself by not telling them it was his friend they were burying, as if denying them his grief, keeping it all for himself.

A rusted sign flashed past, the paint faded from the sun.

"What'd it say?" the sergeant asked, but they were busy with their beers. He screeched to a stop and backed up, weaving, making Larry's stomach jump.

GRAND ARMY OF THE REPUBLIC HIGHWAY, it said.

"That's helpful," the sergeant said, and mashed the gas.

They wound through the glens, past fake Swiss chalets and taxidermy shops, rusted trailers and A-frames facing wide, stony creeks. Larry imagined breaking into a rickety cabin and living there the summer, waking at noon to fish the shadows, never going back, never going home. He thought of Carl Metcalf and Smart Andy and Magoo maybe right now out on night ambush, and these men he didn't know, the big sedan, the town he would never visit again—everything seemed unreal. He was tired, he wanted to stop. In Ithaca his mother lay in a refrigerated basement, waiting for him, the telegram packed in his bag like an invitation.

He would see Vicki, if only for a few hours. His father. Susan. It was almost not worth it for so short a time, yet he'd accept anything now, he'd take what they gave him.

Finally they came upon another sign; the sergeant slowed.

MANSFIELD 4, it said, WELLSBORO 21. They had twenty-five minutes until the service. The private riding shotgun turned up the radio—the Temptations, "Papa Was a Rolling Stone." The guy on Larry's right took the bass part, singing into his beer can like a mike. The sergeant cut the corners; the Ford slewed over the double yellow line. A tight turn threw them into the doors, and the guy on his left spilled his beer on Larry. He sleepily brushed at his pants with a hand, wiped it on the carpet, thinking he'd smell. The Martian wouldn't care, but still Larry was sorry.

The signs said twelve, nine, one, and the speed limit dropped to thirty-five. A tree of signs for the Moose and the Lions and the Rotary passed, another with a Bible verse sponsored by a local church—FEAR OF THE LORD IS THE BEGINNING OF WISDOM—and they crossed the city limits.

Wellsboro was only a sooty block of shops on each side of a stoplight, several storefronts empty, including the long face of a McCrory's. It was an old oil town built on a hill; on the high side of Main a cracked retaining wall ran along a frost-heaved sidewalk, a pipe railing separating it from the street. The bank was black with rain, its clock stuck at a quarter past eleven. There was no one on the street, not a car moving—as in a dream—and Larry asked what day it was.

"Wednesday," the guy to his right said.

"May something," he checked.

"Twenty-sixth."

At the end of town the sergeant turned left past a Foodland and over a green steel bridge. The high school football field and its cinder track glistened in the rain. Behind a rusting cyclone fence rose a small refinery, a pair of riveted tanks. They bumped over a railroad crossing and climbed into the hills.

"Three minutes," the guy riding shotgun said.

"We'll get there," the sergeant promised.

The chapel was only another mile, hidden in the pines, the parking lot overflowing, well-kept Plymouths and fifties' pick-ups listing in the ditches. Larry had seen the Good Samaritan Church of the Brethren before, on the roads outside of Ithaca, its congregation farm families, salt miners for Cargill. The building itself was a peeling clapboard box, the window frames off square. Beside it sprawled a graveyard alive with wildflowers, guarded by a wrought-iron archway. A hearse lurked outside the gate as if the Martian and not Larry were due for another funeral. Before they got out, the sergeant passed a Binaca squirter around; Larry gave the wet spot on his pants two cool shots, then sniffed at the fabric. They all hauled their dress gloves on. The sergeant had them fall out beside the LTD to make sure they were strak, then led them inside.

The preacher and the director from the funeral home wore the same dark suit. They both spoke briefly with the sergeant and shook his hand. The pews were full, the air warm with tallow and perfume and food. Someone solemnly played a march on a piano—American, Larry thought, nineteenth century. The preacher led them up the aisle, at the head of which rested the coffin, shrouded with an American flag. The parishioners whispered or sat in silence, musing soberly; they were older for the most part, matron ladies with cracked, rouged faces, gaunt men in threadbare suits, shoulders flecked with dandruff. A few young couples grappled with children. Along one wall stood a long folding table laden with Saran-wrapped bowls and casserole dishes, their lids steamed. A link of velvet rope marked off the first pew on both sides of the aisle. The funeral director thumbed back the clasp and the honor guard filed in and sat down. The sergeant checked his watch and gave them the thumbs-up.

The preacher stood beside the casket, hands folded over his crotch. The piano stopped and the church went silent. Across from them, the front pew was empty, as if awaiting the arrival of the bride's family.

The piano struck up an anthem—English, seventeenth century, Larry couldn't place the name—and the congregation stood and turned their eyes to the rear. The Martian's family entered, the mother in front. Larry expected her to be decrepit and veiled, but her hair was black, her face tanned and rugged, drawn as if with hunger; she dragged a toddler by the hand. Behind her came a girl Vicki's age with the same squinty eyes and foreshortened chin, leading three more children. A frail couple trailed them, the woman relying on the man's arm and an aluminum cane. The crowd turned as they passed. Once they were seated, the piano stopped and everyone settled.

"Welcome," the preacher said, holding his arms high and wide, and someone coughed. "Before we get started with the service," he said, "I'd like to take care of some business." He announced an upcoming bake sale and reminded them of the registration date for this summer's vacation Bible school. Larry interrogated the coffin; it was blond with copper handles. He remembered the Martian's nose hanging by a flap and how he lay all day on his rack reading, and he thought for someone he had trusted daily with his life, how little he had actually known him. It didn't matter. Larry had trusted him and the Martian had repaid that trust. In that way they knew each other deeply.

The piano crashed and everyone stood, the preacher leading the song, his hymnal raised. The man beside Larry hiccupped with his mouth closed, his shoulders suddenly jumping. The next man laughed.

Larry reached across the first man and snatched the other's tie, yanking his face close to his own. "You don't laugh," Larry said, and he was glad that the man was scared. The man with the hiccups did nothing. The sergeant leaned over, and Larry let go of the other's tie. The preacher glanced at them, then kept singing.

They knelt and prayed, stood and sang again. Larry followed along in the hymnal; he wanted to yawn, to stretch out on the pew and close his eyes. The pianist was terrible. Finally the preacher asked them to sit and stationed himself in front of the coffin and unfolded a sheet of paper. He took a pair of half-glasses from inside his jacket and put them on. Before starting, he nodded to the Martian's family. All but the mother acknowledged him; throughout the eulogy, she stared at him as if bored, waiting for him to finish.

"Is there anybody here who *didn't* know David Purifoy?" the preacher asked. "Is there anybody who never heard him sing right here where I'm standing? When someone older passes on, sometimes I have to ask people who knew him what that man's life was like, but sadly that's not the case today. We all knew David. We knew he was a good son to Amelia here and on top of that a good Christian and a good American. Most of us knew David more than anything from his singing, so with Peggy's help we're going to hear some of that right now."

He gestured to the woman at the piano. She sat on the end of the bench now, lifting the needle of a phonograph like the ones Larry knew from grade school, a gray case, the corners reinforced with steel like a footlocker's. She turned up the volume and a scratch orbited, blipping. A piano laid down the first chords of "Amazing Grace," a song so overused it irritated Larry.

The voice was a boy's, a thin soprano too pure to be really pleasing. His mother had never liked the style, preferring sickly divas; the song itself called for a hint of suffering, not the earnest clarity of the choir. Larry tried to match the child to the man he'd known; those rare times the Martian had spoken he'd betrayed nothing about himself. Whether he was ashamed or merely private, disgusted or amused, Larry couldn't say. For him, that was the Martian, that was what he knew, the limits he accepted.

"I'd like us to all join David," the preacher said, and the congregation rose and followed him in song. In seconds, their voices closed over the Martian's, drowning him out. Larry listened for the boy but he was gone.

When the song was done, they remained standing. The pianist lifted the needle and positioned herself on the bench again. The preacher nodded to the sergeant, who led them into the aisle. He and the private riding shotgun folded the flag into a fat triangle, then with a simple tilt of his head directed each man to the proper handle.

The piano began, and the preacher started down the aisle; the sergeant nodded again, and they lifted the coffin off the gurney. The weight of it tugged like a bucket of water. Larry had imagined the Martian dried like a husk, but the box was heavy, and not simply because he was tired. His palm was sweaty on the metal handle; people were watching and he couldn't adjust his grip. "Shall we gather at the river," the congregation sang. He remembered carrying the Martian down Hamburger Hill with Smart Andy; he'd been heavy then, and slippery, swinging as they navigated the mud. He was chinless, missing an eye, and Larry thought that it wasn't him, just his body. Like they said, he was meat.

Outside, it was still spitting, drops ticking against the roofs of parked cars. The breeze revived him. They were careful on the stairs. The sergeant went around to the trunk of the LTD while they followed the preacher through the archway. The grave gaped; burlap covered a mound of dirt. They laid the coffin on a brace of four-by-fours and stood back. Inside, the recessional thundered to a close. The sergeant hustled through the stones lugging the gun case. He passed it to the private riding shotgun, who took up a position on a slight rise beyond the next row and unzipped the rifle, an old M-1 from his father's war.

The Martian's family emerged first, then the rest of the congregation, louder now that they were outside. The children skipped. The last person out was the pianist; she closed the doors against the cold.

The preacher read the same verses as the padre at Leonard Dawson's memorial service. Ashes to ashes. It was a gyp, Larry thought, just another magic show. The man who had laughed bowed his head; the other solemnly hiccupped. Raindrops darkened the flag. The preacher finished and stood by the Martian's mother, who held the little girl's hand. Her face hadn't changed, though somewhere in the crowd another woman wept, sniffing wetly.

Beyond them, the private fit his eye to the sight, and Larry braced himself. The man fired three rounds, the reports echoing briefly. With each shot, Larry's heart spiked; when it was over, he was wide awake, ready to drive.

Beside him, the sergeant took a measured step forward and crisply faced right. He marched to where the Martian's mother stood and pivoted to face her, then, bowing like a servant, offered her the flag.

She glanced down at the triangle but made no move to take it. She looked at the sergeant a long moment, still holding the girl's hand. He stayed there as if she might reconsider. She kept her eyes on his, and he stepped back.

He tried the sister. She shook her head and looked at the grass.

Finally the old man accepted it, tucking it under one arm like a newspaper.

The private joined the four of them at attention and the preacher dismissed them, the congregation filing through the archway, headed back to the church for the pot-luck supper. The preacher apologized to the sergeant and said they were welcome to stay, then when the sergeant declined, shook their hands again.

The sergeant packed up his gun while they piled in. They stripped their gloves off and tugged at the knots of their ties.

"Man, you see that?" someone said. "She wasn't buying that flag shit for a minute."

Larry could just see over the wall. In the grass, boys dirtied the knees of their good pants searching for the spent casings. The Martian's coffin lay on the braces, beaded with rain, forgotten.

There it is, Larry thought.

The sergeant got in and thunked the door shut.

"What happened there, Top?" someone asked from the back.

"Nothing new, that's the truth."

When they were out of range, the private riding shotgun passed around the beers. They were warm but Larry didn't care. On the way back to Elmira, the sergeant stopped at the same distributor. When he dropped Larry off at the Trailways station, he gave him a few cold ones for the road.

"Good luck over there," he said.

"Yeah," someone seconded. "Kick some ass."

"All right," Larry said, hoping they would just leave, but when they did, he felt even more alone. Already he was forgetting the church and the three-bean salad, the graveyard daisies, the roots intruding on the Martian's hole. He had to see his mother now, and home, and then he would have to leave again, when all he wanted to do was stop, sleep, let this end.

The service was at three-thirty and the bus left at two. He bought a ticket and called his father to let him know when he'd get in.

"That's cutting it close," his father said, as if Larry had any control over the schedule. "We'll have to leave from there, which means I'll have to go pick up Vicki right now."

"Fine," Larry said. He didn't need the details, just results. The beer had given him a headache, and he needed to pee.

"So how does it feel?" his father asked.

"What?"

"To be back."

"I don't know," Larry said. "I'm not really back yet."

After he hung up, he went to the men's room, where someone had scratched a giant peace sign among the phone numbers and disembodied pricks. He dried his hands on the endless towel, then sat across from his gate, fiddling with the little pay TV on the arm, drinking a Coke to stay awake.

The bus was empty, for which he was grateful. The windows were tinted green, air-conditioning leaking from the honeycombed frame. He was afraid of falling asleep and missing his stop. Outside, the rainy country slid by like a terrarium—the familiar hills and rotting barns, corn just coming up. Larry knew the sideroads, the best places to make out. He leaned his seat back and dreamed of Vicki, only minutes away now. He wished they could spend the night together, but he'd be expected to stay home; tomorrow he would leave again, waste another two days getting back. They would make love to night, that was enough. There was no need to be greedy.

They climbed through Newfield, on a level stretch glimpsing a blue arm of the lake before descending the long hill into the valley. He knew the homemade signs advertising honey, the deserted farmstands and ugly motels, the black creeks with their crumbling bridges. He bent close to the window, astonished at how much he'd forgotten.

They passed Buttermilk Falls and the city limits and cruised through the built-up strip on 13—the Burger Chef and the Carvel and the used car lots, the Manos diner, where he and Vicki ate breakfast drunk at one in the morning and the waitress named Ruby had a rose tattoo on her boob. It was so dark the streetlights were on, the fluorescents of the Hess station. They made the turn onto Fulton and passed beneath the Agway's grain elevator, a flock of pigeons sitting on the tin roof. The light at State Street was red; in the lot of the bus station sat his father's New Yorker.

Vicki was with him, standing under the clock, her hair pulled back in a ponytail. She had on a straight black dress under a puffy jacket. His father wore a dark suit but no hat. Larry grabbed his bag and made his way up the aisle, moving seat back to seat back. The bus pulled in and stopped, the brakes chuffing, and the driver opened the door.

Larry dropped his bag to pick Vicki up and crushed her to him. He kissed her neck and smelled her hair, kissed her on the cheek and then the mouth, their teeth clicking. She held his face in her hands and looked at him as if to make sure he was real.

"Okay, okay," his father said. "Save some for later." He gave Larry his hand and then held him a moment, patting his back. "We've got to catch up with your sister and Maddy. They're probably there already."

On the way to the car, Larry grabbed a soft handful of Vicki's ass; instead of batting his hand away, she leaned into him and looped her arms about his waist.

All three of them fit easily into the front, Larry in the middle. His father pushed the seat back to make room for his legs.

"You're so tan," Vicki said, touching one cheek. "And so skinny." She squeezed his hand and kissed it, then looked at the mass of cuts across the back. "What happened to you?"

"Nothing," he said. "It's just scrapes."

"Look at this," she told his father, and showed him the hand.

"It's infected," his father said.

"It's the dampness," Larry explained. "There's nothing you can do about it."

"I'll put something on it when we get home."

"It's fine."

"It doesn't look fine to me," Vicki said, inspecting his wrist, and he thought of pulling the black velvet box from his pocket, if only to distract her. He would find the right time tonight, the right place—just before they made love, or maybe after, probably here in his father's car, parked above the lake, the heater whirring. He would not make promises, he'd just offer her the ring. If he didn't come back, at least she'd have that.

"So," his father said, and gripped Larry's thigh, "how are you?"

"I'm okay," Larry said. "I'm sorry I wasn't here."

"It's been hard. Susan's been a help." His father looked to him for agreement, and Larry nodded thoughtfully. After all the unsatisfying letters and halting phone calls, now he had nothing to say to him.

They seemed to be hitting every red light. Outside, the wet street reflected the marquee of the State Theatre, the neon of the Chanticleer. Nothing had changed except him, and suddenly he wished he hadn't come back, that they could have buried her without him. Larry wondered if that had been his plan all along, if a year ago his father had seen it clearly.

"You said you went to Hong Kong," his father asked. "How was it?"

"Beautiful," Larry said. "Busy."

"Where did you stay?"

"One of the big hotels." He remembered a fountain, a balcony, ships on the blue, blue bay. He saw Pony's legs laid out on a poncho and his own hands emptying his pockets, bagging the soaked matchbox and the cigar. He shook his head as if the name escaped him.

"You must be tired."

"I am," Larry said, relieved, and sat back, holding Vicki's hand and watching the scenery pass. The gutters were running. He wanted to ask his father if they could have some heat, but they were only a block from St. John's. The clock on the dash said twenty past three—0320 there. In the hootch, Magoo, Smart Andy and Carl Metcalf slept. A loom round went out, silvering the jungle.

The parking meters along Buffalo had black bags over their heads, printed with the name of the funeral home. Behind the church, a more formal sign reserved a spot for his father. The hearse was a brand-new Cadillac with gray curtains. Vicki left her coat in the car; her dress had gauzy arms with ruffled cuffs. Larry took her hand.

They came through the back way, past the darkened kitchen. The organ reached them—Bach, one of the chorale preludes. In the vestry, husbands were fitting hangers into coats. His father acknowledged them but didn't stop. He led them downstairs and through the Sunday school rooms and up again, past a door in which two altar boys were struggling into black robes. Larry was lost but trusted him. The fatigue made him simple, disinterested; he was just going. They followed a long hall, the organ growing closer, and finally emerged in a niche beside the pulpit. The sudden result pleased him like a disappearing trick.

The casket sat where the Martian's had, at the head of the aisle. It was closed, which disappointed Larry. He'd thought it would be open, his mother's face waxy, her makeup severe, unreal. He thought he'd have a chance to say good-bye.

In the front row sat Susan and, farther down, as if with another family, Mrs. Railsbeck.

"It's good to see you," Susan said, holding him.

"How are you?" Mrs. Railsbeck said, then quickly let go.

His father sat on the aisle, Susan next to him, then himself and Vicki, and finally Mrs. Railsbeck. It was bright and warm, the altar crowded with flowers, tapers burning. His mother's name in the program seemed final, a release. Larry couldn't get comfortable in the pew; he was jumpy from being awake so long. He checked his watch—it was time. He sat up straight and rubbed the back of his neck, and Vicki glanced at him to see if he was all right. He mustered a smile and she patted his hand. The Bach pealed, the lower registers shivering the floorboards. He concentrated on the play of the contrapuntal runs, the two themes of the fugue racing then twining around each other, resolving briefly at a plateau of minor chords before darting off again. He closed his eyes to listen. His mother would be pleased. She'd wanted this to be simple and dignified, a tribute to her good taste. For twenty years she'd picked the music, those long afternoons. "I wouldn't mind that," she'd say after a Handel anthem, and hum the passage that had struck her, testing Larry's reaction. "Don't you think that might be nice to have?"

He was aware that he was asleep before Vicki nudged him, the organ suddenly deafening, an explosion. He was in Ithaca, at his mother's funeral.

"Sorry," he said. He was fine, he repeated, though he knew she didn't believe him. His eyes were burning, his head empty. He should have eaten something in Elmira, then slept on the bus.

The service was longer than the Martian's. The organist played Purcell's funeral music, one of her favorites. Larry read along with the reverend—the Prayers for the People, the Confession, the Peace. He thought of Bates and his Spirit House, how he'd wanted to believe, how he didn't now. Why? he wondered. Nothing had changed.

He and his father and Susan received the guests in the parish hall, where the church held fellowship suppers and the Christmas bazaar. Mrs. R. wasn't part of the line. There was no one under fifty. They were his father's patients; Larry knew their illnesses, their operations. His mother always said she didn't have any friends. They were all very sorry, they said, and shook his hand. They'd heard he was in the service; how was he finding it? He was tired of standing and being pleasant, repeating the same bland thanks; he needed something to eat. He expected at least one of them to cry, but none did. In the car, Larry remembered—*he* was supposed to.

The burial was private. The reverend and a driver from the funeral home met them at the cemetery. The driver waited in the road while they walked across the grass. There was no stone. The five of them faced the reverend over the hole. He still had his robes on. While he recited, traffic moved in the distance, trees dripped. It seemed quick to Larry, as if he'd skipped something. As they walked away, he glanced back at the casket, hoping a last look would make sense of everything, then when it didn't, accused himself of wanting too much. Never happen, Carl Metcalf would say. He had to learn when to give up.

At home, he found the last Stoney's the sergeant had given him, now warm, and fit it into the door of the refrigerator. He changed in his old room while Mrs. R. made dinner. His jeans bagged; his red-and-black-checked flannel billowed around him. In his closet, board games filled the shelves. He'd written his name on one as a child, the K backward. He could not remember doing it, and though it had been years ago, it seemed proof that he had become someone else, that this new person did not belong here.

He could not rid himself of the feeling. At dinner, they caught him up on what was happening around town, but none of it mattered to him. He regained his strength, taking seconds of Mrs. R.'s stroganoff. He told them about the flight over and even some of the ride to Wellsboro, yet he balked at any mention of the Martian, made it seem as if he were chosen because of his destination. Susan was going to summer school, Mrs. R.'s cousin coming over for Memorial Day. It was fine, Larry thought; he didn't want to talk either.

His father took him into the den to inspect his hands. He offered him a scotch but Larry said he'd better not if he was going to take the car. His father bent the desk lamp over the blotter and clicked it on. The scabs on Larry's knuckles were cracked, crusted with amber pus.

"Looks familiar," his father said, and dug a tube of ointment from a drawer. He squeezed a cool blob on and gently rubbed it in.

"How's your outfit?" his father asked. "You taking good care of them?"

"I try."

"That's all you can do."

While it was true, Larry thought it wasn't enough. After the Japanese, his father had to know that.

"Can I give you some advice?" his father asked. "As a doctor."

"Sure."

"Treat it like a job. Don't take any of it personally."

"Is that what you do?"

"Not here, no. But there I think you have to. I wish I had."

"I'll try," Larry said, when of course it was too late.

Even Susan came down from her room to see him off. The box was a lump in his pocket. His father made a production of giving him the keys and twenty dollars. Larry had never driven the New Yorker before, had never asked; his father came down off the porch to help him find the lights. On his way out, Larry honked.

It was easier to be alone. Though the radio said it was fifty, he was freezing. The colleges were out, the bars and laundromats empty. He splashed through the Octopus and up the hill, the lake black, invisible. The waterfalls would be brown, the fish moving. The farmhouses were dark, sometimes one bright square. His lights picked out the reflectors by driveways, on mailboxes. The roadside motels glowed with pink neon. He did not want that to be her memory of him. He thought it should be by the water. He turned the heat up, and the fan, hoping it would reach the backseat. On the dash, the clock's red second hand swept around; he had less than twelve hours, at least half of them sleep, and still he was not sure he could endure it, escape untouched. He felt his pocket for the box.

Vicki was waiting for him, her silhouette in the door. Larry was afraid to swing the big car through the gate and parked it on the street. He checked his hair before going in to see her parents. The yard was spongy, the air heavy with mist. She opened the door, and Jojo scampered out to meet him, leaping at his knees.

Vicki was wearing a skirt to make it easier. She clung to his arm as he shook her father's hand. Her father wore slippers; moles sprouted above his eyebrows. He was older than her mother, retired from the shop floor at Borg-Warner, his hands knotty and scarred. He carried a newspaper everywhere, as if he'd been interrupted.

"How long are you back for?" he asked, and Larry told him. "Well," Mr. Honness said, "you two be careful and have a nice time."

"Call if you're going to be late," her mother said, and kissed Vicki.

"I'm sorry," Vicki said outside.

"For what?" Larry said.

She sat in the middle, pressed against him. In Trumansburg, the pillars of the church were spotlit. They passed the new high school and the fairgrounds and the speed limit changed. The dotted line flew through the headlights. On the radio, Elton John sang, "I sat on the roof and kicked off the moss." She slid her hand in his shirt, her tongue in his ear. He took the turn for Taughannock Falls, hoping the park was open. Last summer they'd made love on the sunny rocks above the rapids, braving the mosquitoes and fishermen, the freezing current.

The chain was up. They sat there with the engine running and then he shut it off.

"The cops won't let us stay here," Vicki said.

"I just want to see the falls."

They could hear it through the trees. A weak streetlight shone over the entrance to the stone steps. They headed down toward the noise. After the first turn they couldn't see a thing and held onto each other. There was no railing; Larry ran his hand along the rock wall. They made the landing, stumbling on an extra, phantom step. The stone bench was cold through his jeans. Across the gorge, a white veil rose from the falling water. The noise was soft yet relentless. Vicki leaned into him for warmth, her arms crossed against her chest. She kissed his neck.

"I wish you didn't have to go back," she said.

"Me too."

"I worry so much about you." She began to cry, and he held her tighter. The falls purled. "I wish you'd talk to me," she said. "I miss that."

"I'm tired."

"I know, and I know you're upset about your mother and everything, but you haven't said anything to me since you got back—nothing. It's like you don't trust me or something."

"I trust you," he said, but it was the wrong thing, because she turned away. He leaned back to fit his hand in his pocket and pulled out the box.

"Larry," she said, as if disappointed. "That's not what I'm talking about."

"It's just strange to be back for one day," he said. "I don't feel like I'm really here."

"Why couldn't you just tell me that?"

"I didn't want to hurt your feelings."

"We're supposed to be able to tell each other anything."

He thought of Leonard Dawson bound to the tree, the gout of blood Salazar coughed into his mouth. He remembered how it felt to kill the man who killed Redmond.

He got down on one knee, the stone cold beneath him. He opened the box and held it out.

"You're changing the subject."

"Vic," he said, "we only have one night." He balanced on his kneecap, waiting for her to give in. The ring was big; he'd blown all of his combat pay.

"All you have to do is tell me how you're feeling. It's not like I'm being unreasonable."

He bowed his head, trying to think of something to placate her—the LT's helmet spinning into the brush, Fred the Head reaching for the can.

"I'm tired," he said, "and I don't want to go back. It's pretty simple."

"Did you have to kill anyone?"

He thought that no one had earned the right to ask him this—not her, not even his father. He waited for her to withdraw the question.

She searched his eyes, then, as if she understood, went to her knees and held him. "I'm sorry," she said. "Of course I will. I love you."

He slid the ring on her finger, and they made love on the cold stone bench, the falls plashing in the background. His jeans bunched around his knees. Her warmth filled him, and for the first time since he'd arrived, Larry was glad to be home. After, he was satisfied and drowsy. She took her panties from her purse and slipped them on.

"It's freezing," she said, and they hurried back to the car. Vicki inspected the diamond under the bubble light. She apologized for asking so many questions; he apologized for not talking. If they could do nothing but make love, he thought, they'd be fine. He drove down the hill to the boat ramp and they did it in the backseat with the heater going, the sweat cold on his back. Vicki ran out of cigarettes. They went to the Antlers to get a pack from a machine and stayed for a beer. When they came out, the clock on the dash said he was almost finished.

Mrs. Honness was waiting for them. They said their good nights in the car and then Larry came in so Vicki could show her the ring.

"That's wonderful," she said, and kissed them both, but let Mr. Honness sleep.

"I'll see you tomorrow," Vicki said.

It was past two when Larry got home. The porch light was on, the house quiet. He packed, knowing he wouldn't have time tomorrow. He was too tired to sleep, his hands cramping. All morning he woke to the clock, as if dreading a test.

Mrs. Railsbeck rose early to make them eggs. Larry had his class A's on again, the ugly green. Susan said good-bye in her nightgown, bleary-eyed, and headed back to bed. His father carried his bag and set it in the backseat. It was the white hour before dawn, bread trucks stocking the supermarkets, route men retrieving yesterday's papers. On the way to Trumansburg they got stuck behind a manure spreader.

"It's going to be close," his father said, as if he hadn't planned to pick up Vicki.

She was standing on the sidewalk. His father didn't notice the ring until Larry pointed it out at a stoplight.

"It's big," he joked, then congratulated them. In silence, they waited for the light to change.

He left the way he'd come, running the gauntlet of Route 13. The day was fair, the cows out. The New Yorker rocketed along. They cleared a rise to find a goose wandering in the middle of the road, the rest of the flock on the berm. His father swerved but struck it with a thump, and Vicki squealed. He slowed and checked his mirror, then went on. In Horseheads, children in sweaters waited for the school bus. His father tried a shortcut but the road was closed, a flagman waving them into a detour.

"I'm sorry," his father said, already conceding defeat.

At the airport, Larry checked the bumper but found nothing. They hustled through the deserted terminal to the United gate. The attendant was just closing the door.

He kissed Vicki. His father hugged him and gave him his bag, and then he was outside, jogging across the tarmac and up the jetway. He waved before ducking his head and entering, and he was alone again, suddenly relieved. The man sitting next to him had been a Marine; he shook Larry's hand. Through the window, all he could see was a slice of wing, a fire hydrant, a baggage tractor. The plane taxied out, bumping, then turned, powered up and shot down the runway, lifted with a jolt into the air. He was getting used to it, he thought.

It was hotter at each stop. In San Francisco, he called Vicki one last time, promising Mrs. Honness to pay all the charges. Martha Raye's band was playing the Honolulu U.S.O. "You'd be so nice to come home to," her understudy sang. "Requests?" she said, but Larry drained his Dr. Pepper and picked up his gear. On Okinawa, they sat on the runway for three hours, then had to abort their approach to Da Nang due to rocket fire. They circled over the sea until it was clear, his sense of direction undone. The steep descent made him yawn and pop his ears; the landing screeched.

The plane rolled to the gate and stopped, the intercom pinging once, dimming the seatbelt sign. He jostled into the aisle, nodded as he passed the stewardess. The heat closed over him like a bath, and he stepped out into blinding sunshine, the familiar stench of charcoal smoke and sewage. A mountain rose above the harbor, crowned with antennas. In the distance, artillery thundered. Larry turned toward it like a farmer worried about his hay, then continued down the stairs. A troop of new recruits bunched up around a sergeant with a clipboard. Though Larry had never come in this way, he walked past them and through the terminal to supply, where the clerk issued him boots and a pair of fatigues. He stuffed the greens into his bag and headed down the road toward Highway 1, looking for a ride home.

SMART ANDY couldn't remember all the FNGs. There were ten, and not all of them had names. One was called Nine, another Ten. Chumley was the fat one, Frankenstein the guy with stitches in his head. The others were hard to tell apart.

"First time out," Magoo said, "you never saw such a cluster fuck. We took them down the hill, and one of them has to break his ankle. And what do they do—they all crowd around him trying to get a better look. Metcalf calls for security and they just look at him. Nobody moves."

" 'Three-sixty!' he's yelling," Smart Andy said.

"Let me tell it," Magoo said. They were perched around his bunk; the rest of the tent could hear but pretended not to. "So he yells, 'Get in a fucking circle!' and they do, except it's about as big around as a kiddie pool. Metcalf doesn't say a word. He grabs one of them by the shoulders and walks him out about twenty meters, comes back and gets another one and walks him out and so on until we've got actual security."

"Tell him the best part," Smart Andy said.

"So the doc fixes this guy up, whatever his name is, and Metcalf wants me and Andrew here to haul his sorry ass back up the hill."

"Which we were not happy about."

"No one was going to fuck with Metcalf at that point. He had this look on him. So we ruck up and hump it."

"It gets around chow—"

"It gets around chow and they're still not back, so we go over to the commo bunker and honk them up."

"And Metcalf answers."

"He says they're making camp there."

"And they did. Stayed there the whole night spread out in that circle."

"I'm sorry," Magoo said. "I love the brother but his shit is flaky."

Larry checked Smart Andy, who nodded. "He's trying to be the LT."

"But see," Magoo said, "the LT let that shit slide, that's why he was the LT."

"He's probably just worried about the new guys," Larry said.

"But you can't do that," Magoo said.

"Yeah," Smart Andy said. "That's not where the smart money is."

One of the new men had stopped polishing his boots to listen.

"What the fuck are you looking at?" Magoo said. "Fucking no-name Chumley motherfucker."

The man turned back to his rag.

"See?" Magoo said. "You can't teach them if they don't want to learn."

The tent was crowded now, the bunks of the dead filled. They still used them for shorthand—the guy in Leonard's rack, the one next to Dumb Andy's.

Carl Metcalf had taken the LT's corner. He used his rickety table to go over duty rosters and warning orders. At night his silhouette flickered on the mosquito netting. He'd stopped drawing, his sketchpad gathering dust under his bunk. He knew everyone's name and where they were going the next day, but his eyes were bloodshot and by lunch he'd be yawning. He'd inherited Fred the Head's transistor radio and startled Larry by tuning in the classical hour on Armed Forces Radio. The DJ had a penchant for the French, the lush, limpid turn of the century—elevator music, his mother would say. One evening, Larry heard a scrap of the Art of Fugue and went back to listen and found Carl Metcalf asleep on an acetate map, his drool a new river. He was reading Clausewitz and an official history of the Vietnamese people. Larry helped him onto his rack and blew out the candle.

Echo was making heavy contact in the Rao Lao Valley. The captain knew they were green and kept them in the middle of the column. The snipers missed, the Phantoms came in, the villages went up. Frankenstein cried and peed his pants.

On days off, they patrolled around Odin, trying to find a point man. The first candidate was a Navajo chosen solely for that fact; he led them into a marsh and sank waist deep in muck before they pulled him out. His new name was Wrong Way. The second and third were small and quick, like the Martian. Carl Metcalf booby-trapped a section of jungle with duds and had them walk through it; both were dead in seconds. He had the rest of the new meat do it. The best was Chumley. He was fatter than Carl Metcalf, but just as neat, his trousers bloused. They made him do it again, and this time he was perfect, even spotting Carl's toe-popper. He was from the suburbs of Atlanta, his eye honed by playing third base.

"Great," Smart Andy said. "At least they won't bunt on us."

Larry kept his spot toward the back of the file. The man in front of him carried a thumper and had a Norwegian flag Magic-Markered on his helmet. His name was Smith, but everyone called him Dizzy because he had a lazy eye. The guy behind him had a summer cold and every morning came to Larry for aspirin. His name was Isley, but no one could remember it. He'd been one of the small guys to try out for point, and his failure clung to him like shame. He kept a perfect interval of ten meters, as if excelling here would make up for it. Larry showed them how to double their magazines and told them to fire low. They listened intensely, as if he were leaking secrets, and Larry thought that Magoo was wrong. They wanted to learn; the problem was the opposite. It was not something that could be taught.

Smart Andy convinced Magoo to play bridge. All four of them were short, though after Salazar, none was dumb enough to tack up a calendar. They were cautious. "Forty-eight and a wake-up," they'd say, but with none of the exuberance of Leonard Dawson or Fred the Head. Under Bates's spirit house, they had quiet beers instead of a DEROS party for Bogut. On Pony's they passed around a cigar Smart Andy had saved. Magoo remembered the rocket grenade headed straight for them, then nothing.

"That was a bad day," Carl Metcalf said, as if it were months ago. It had only been three weeks. They were still getting mail for all of them, extra Sunday packages. In one of Vicki's letters, his mother was still alive.

The new operation was called Montgomery Rendezvous. Carl Metcalf read them the warning order. The battalion would be inserted into the northern end of the A Shau—the Warehouse Area—to neutralize suspected NVA concentrations.

"For you new guys," Magoo said, "that means kill the little fuckers."

They boarded the liftships at dawn and roared up the valley, the sun angling over the ridges, making him squint. Magoo took a picture of Wrong Way vomiting. The slipstream brought it back into the ship, spattering the gunner's helmet. Carl Metcalf checked his watch as if this were Normandy. His pocket bristled with grease pencils; he'd lashed a compass case to his web gear. Beside him, Smart Andy was eating a Milky Way bar and reading one of Leonard Dawson's comics—*The Human Torch*. When he was done, he doubled a rubberband around it and chucked it out the door.

The gunships softened up the LZ and they spiraled in. Larry expected one of the new guys to catch his pack and fall on his face, but none did. They established security, Carl Metcalf checked the map, and Chumley led them into the jungle, his back already black with sweat.

He was slower than the Martian, and kept well off the trails. Light filtered in, dappling the leaves. Monkeys screamed. In front of Larry, Dizzy crept along, swiveling his head, his rifle held across his body, the muzzle skyward. The little guy behind him sniffled and slapped at the insects. Seventy-six and a wake-up, Larry thought; I'll never make it.

Near the river, they intersected a high-speed trail, in the mud the print of a bike tire. They followed along in the brush until they came upon an abandoned camp—a circle of burnt stones, the grass worn in patches. Carl Metcalf had them search the area while Smart Andy called it in. One of the new guys found a cathole with fresh shit in it. Magoo told him to pose.

"Saddle up," Carl Metcalf said, and they moved out again, mirroring the trail along the river. The water was slow and brown, flat as glass. Ahead, a fisherman in a coolie hat was poling a sampan, the current drawing him toward them.

Carl Metcalf stopped and dug a phrasebook out, but before he could wave the man down, Smart Andy shouted something in Vietnamese.

The man cupped his ear.

Smart Andy shouted louder.

The man nodded with his upper body and poled for the bank, the entire platoon covering him.

Someone fired—a single round—and Smart Andy grabbed his shoulder and fell. Larry hit the ground, but Dizzy paused a second, unsure what to do, and a round caught him in the neck, a patch of blood suddenly there. Larry thought the shots had come from behind, but the platoon let loose on the sampan, the man pitching overboard, floating, the boat itself drifting downriver.

"Check fire!" Carl Metcalf yelled. He grabbed the barrel of Wrong Way's sixteen and yanked it out of his hands. "Who told you to fire?"

Dizzy was in shock, gurgling, his carotid artery spurting. He probably wouldn't make it. Dizzy—it was a stupid name.

"Smith," Larry said, "how you doin'?"

The man coughed blood.

"How's Andy?" Larry called.

"Just a shoulder," Magoo said.

Larry cut a hole in the man's throat and thrust an airway in. He taped a pressure dressing on and started a bottle of blood. Smith's eyes were fixed, his breathing quick.

Carl Metcalf ran over to see how he was doing. He was huffing from the contact, his pupils dilated as if he were speeding.

"What's their ETA?" Larry said, and when Carl looked at him blankly, said, "The dust-off, what's their ETA?"

"I don't know."

"Find out," Larry ordered, and Carl scrambled back to Andy. Andy had to help him call it in.

They couldn't transport Smith in an extractor and the only place the chopper could get in was across the river. They did a recon by fire, shredding the jungle, changing magazines until they were sure the sniper was gone. Carl Metcalf and Chumley donated their air mattresses. Smith was unconscious, the airway bubbling. Smart Andy said he didn't feel anything yet, but the joint was a mess, and Larry popped him with morphine.

Just upstream, a trail ran to the river's edge, then picked up on the far side. Stones poked out of the water, catching dark snags of driftwood, clotted froth. Carl Metcalf set out security around the ford. Larry and Magoo eased Smith onto the mattress; already the bandage was wet and falling off. Smart Andy held his breath as they lifted him, then let it out, his lips farting like a balloon. He laughed.

"Shut up or we'll tip you over," Larry said.

"Fuck you," Smart Andy said, his voice thick.

The water was chest deep and warm, faster than it looked, the bottom mud. Larry stayed with Smith, tugging the head of the mattress against the current, careful of every step.

"Man, I can see why people do this shit," Smart Andy said.

In midstream, Larry thought he heard the whopping of a chopper, but it was a trick of the wind, a far-off jet maybe.

A mortar screamed overhead, went silent and landed on the far bank, debris sprinkling the water. One of the new guys with Smart Andy ducked under.

"Keep moving," Larry shouted. "Don't let go!"

He dug his feet in and leaned against the water and pumped his free arm like a skater. Onshore, the grass burned. It wasn't more than fifteen meters.

Another shell crashed, throwing a plume of dirt.

Smith's airway bubbled. Smart Andy slurred something, waving his good arm.

A round landed in the water and knocked Larry off his feet, punched the air from his lungs. He lost his balance and went under and came up to see Smith and Smart Andy and the rafts floating downstream, trailed by a scattering of dead fish.

Though he wanted to swim after them, his legs were strangely weak, drained of muscle. Only the arm he'd been dragging the raft with responded. He flailed, the river sweeping him along. Gradually the feeling returned to his limbs; it was like thawing himself by a radiator after sledding all day. He struggled to the muddy bank and pulled himself up by a root. His arm was bruised blue, his kidneys tender. Downstream, the others were climbing out stiffly. The river slid past. It was stupid to hope, though Larry knew he would.

When the dust-off touched down, the four of them got on. The bruises on the guy called Nine went up to his neck.

"Let me guess," the medic said, and told them exactly what happened. He didn't ask about the two men they'd been sent to pick up, and Larry thought that was good of him, that it was a courtesy he should remember.

While they were at the evac hospital, another chopper brought the bodies in. It didn't have time to settle; the crew chief flipped the bags out onto the pad, and it nosed over and shot off again. An ambulance swung up and two orderlies opened the rear doors. They took their time with the bags, for which Larry silently thanked them. Then they drove away.

Back at Odin, Carl Metcalf apologized, as if it were his fault. On the contour map, he showed Larry and Magoo what they should have done. "I just read about that too," he said, and leafed through a field manual until he found the diagram. The river had waves like smiles. Carl yawned and rubbed one eye with a fist. "I don't know what happened. All of a sudden I couldn't think."

"Nothing you could do," Magoo said, and handed the manual back.

"I should have done *something*," Carl said. He stared at the page as if committing it to memory. On his bunk he'd laid out Smart Andy's gear—the letters and books and writing paper, his fountain pen, the ink refills like vials of blood. A cardboard box waited.

"I don't know," Carl Metcalf said. "Maybe I wasn't supposed to do this."

Both Larry and Magoo protested.

"No," Carl said. "I felt weird out there today. I didn't feel right. I just froze up. That's never happened to me before."

"You're trying to think too much," Larry suggested.

"That's not it. It's like I was green again. I didn't know what to do."

"You've got ten greenies who open up on *papa-san*," Magoo said. "What are you supposed to do with that?"

"I don't know," Carl said, and looked at the floor between them. "The captain said he'd try to get someone but it may take a while."

"Just what these cherries need—some Nestlé's Quik looking for a commission."

"You're a soldier," Larry said. "Just be a soldier and they'll learn how to do things from watching you. That's what I did."

"Yeah," Magoo said, "and look how he turned out." It was a joke, but true too.

"I guess," Carl Metcalf said. "It's not like I have a choice."

After chow, Magoo took Larry up by Bates's house. The sky to the west was smeared, the ridges dark. Behind the mess tent someone was scrubbing pots.

"Is he fucked up or what?" Magoo said.

"He'll be all right."

"You know who called for that dust-off?"

"Andy," Larry admitted.

"Try me. Metcalf gave them the wrong grid."

Larry wanted to refute it but came up with nothing.

"I know, I know," Magoo said. "I don't know what his problem is. I'm not saying I can do any better, but he's the man now. We're not talking Victor Charlie anymore, this is the real deal, and he's got to be solid. These greenies aren't going to do shit."

"So what do we do?" Larry said.

They changed places in the file, boxing Carl in. Magoo took the radio so he'd be close, while Larry dropped back to lead the second fire team. It seemed to work, for a few days at least. Carl was cautious of water, draws—anywhere they'd taken casualties in the past. Often he halted the column to consult the map, conferring with Chumley, Magoo by his side. Carl kept them off trails and streambeds, sticking to the deep brush. They hacked more than they humped, letting the platoon on flank get ahead. Chumley's palms split and bled from the machete. He was too big for the heat and didn't have any wind. Circling above, the lieutenant colonel asked them to pick up the pace. Chumley huffed. When they stopped for water, he barfed up lunch. His lips were white, his skin dry. Larry gave him a double dose of salt pills.

"What's the holdup?" the lieutenant colonel asked.

"No holdup," Carl Metcalf said, and made for the head of the file, as if to lead them himself. Magoo scampered after him, the antenna waving, and stopped him by the arm. They talked, then came back to where Larry was standing.

"Isley," Carl Metcalf said. "Take point."

The little man double-timed it to the front, and they moved out again, Chumley taking his place. Larry glanced behind to see how he was doing. His feet wandered, and once he fell with a grunt, but got up again. He reminded Larry of himself, dogged, a worker. They crossed a dry streambed, the sand channeled, glimpsing the sky for an instant, then plunged deeper into the jungle. To make time, Carl had taken a game trail. Larry was wondering when they'd stop for water when the jungle erupted.

Ahead, dust puffed from the back of Ten, and he flew into the bushes. Larry dove right and rolled and fired toward the noise. A Chicom grenade sailed over him. He swiveled, clicked his sixteen on full auto and finished the magazine, did the flipside, then punched another in. The grenade was a dud, or Larry was too busy to hear it. The sixty was up. Fire rustled the brush, rounds splintering thickets of bamboo, chewing off bark, snapping saplings. The belt finished and it went quiet.

The noise had stopped but hung in his ears, a single piercing tone. He waited for the click of a bolt driven home, the ting of a spoon. Smoke drifted through poles of sunlight, blue and thick as a poolroom. In the dirt by his elbow, a centipede wriggled, tunneling deeper.

"Medic," someone called. The stupid fucks, Larry thought, they hadn't even learned to shut up. He hesitated, giving the enemy a last chance to declare himself before rolling to his knees and scuttling toward the voice.

It was Frankenstein, kneeling by Magoo and Carl Metcalf. Carl didn't appear to be hit, but Magoo had taken a round just below the ear. He lay on the trail, still strapped to the hissing radio. The exit wound was huge, a bloody custard spilled in the dirt.

"I can't help this man," Larry said, angry with Frankenstein.

Carl Metcalf sat in the grass, blinking; his flak jacket was spattered with bits of pink tissue. Larry snapped an ampule under his nose, and Carl pushed his hand away.

"Goddammit," he said when he saw Magoo. "Jesus Christ."

In the thicket they found a few shells from an AK, still warm. Carl Metcalf slipped the radio off Magoo and called in the names and numbers of the dead. "Barclay," he said, and Larry remembered. At the LZ he wired the tag around a button and went through his pockets, tied the plastic bag to his wrist. He did the same for Ten, whose name was Snyder, but he was too new to really count. They rode back to Odin in silence, Isley alone on a bench, staring out the door.

That night Carl Metcalf asked Larry behind the mosquito netting. On his bunk sat Magoo's camera and at least fifteen shoeboxes full of pictures. Carl cleared a spot for Larry to sit and showed him some of the shots. In one, a rat hunched on the chest of a dead boy, gnawing at his chin. There was a whole series of women, corpses pulled from rivers, a man crushed under a pagoda.

"I don't think his family would be interested in these," Carl asked.

"No," Larry agreed.

Carl showed him which boxes he was going to send—the guys smiling, posing barechested with their weapons; sunsets; the hootch. He'd only hold on to these two. Larry said that was fine.

"The reason I'm telling you is that if something happens to me I don't want them to go home."

"Why not just get rid of them?"

"I don't know," Carl Metcalf said. "I think they're important. I was thinking of maybe using them for sketches." He riffled a stack, stopping at the dead NVA under the tree. "Remember him?" He smiled as if it were a joke.

"How are you doing?" Larry asked.

"Okay," Carl said. He waited for Larry to stop staring at him, then looked away, rolling his head on his neck as if it were stiff. "I just got a little startled out there, with everything. I shouldn't have put Isley on point, that was dumb."

"What did Magoo say?"

"He said Isley too. I should have just stuck with Chumley. I should have told the lieutenant colonel to go fly a kite." He passed the stack from hand to hand while he talked, then stopped and fit it into the box. "I can't think," he said. "It's the weirdest thing. I'm not afraid, I just can't think. It's like when you're almost drunk and you think you can do things but you can't. It's messed up."

"You're just new to it," Larry said. "It'll get better."

"I sure hope so."

It did. Chumley went back on point and for a week the patrol didn't hit contact. The days gave Larry hope. Sixty-one, sixty, fifty-nine. Carl Metcalf was a month ahead of him. One of them would go home, he thought, though the odds weren't certain. The heat broke and they played Grease the Pig with a Vaselined football. Nine got drunk at the whorehouse and caught his foreskin in his zipper; Larry had to cut his trousers around it, and he was fine, but his name changed to The Fly. On the Fourth of July, they had cold beer and the artillery put on a show, the ridges shimmering. They sat beneath Bates's house, watching the blossoms jump and die, the embers drift down. "Wow," they said. "Whoa. Man."

Vicki said she'd taken flowers out to his mother's grave and found some from his father. His father said everything was as well as could be expected.

He was back at work, the weather was good, he was hoping to go fishing. Susan wrote a note saying she wished she'd been feeling better when Larry had been there. She missed him. They ought to see more of each other. Larry wrote them each a postcard. *Everything's fine here. Not much going on. We had watermelon on the Fourth. Please don't worry.*

Carl Metcalf was learning. First they blew up the bunkers, then they searched them. They waited for third platoon to hit the village, then moved in. Sometimes the radio didn't pick up the lieutenant colonel. Chumley was losing a pound a day. At night he did sit-ups and chinned himself on the doorframe. Larry briefed the squad on shock and proper brushing technique. He could see which ones were friends, which ones would be hurt. Wrong Way, The Fly, Frankenstein. They were his, yet he had nothing to do with them. He and Carl Metcalf sat behind the mosquito netting and talked like old soldiers, remembering the dead.

They went north again and ran into the rear elements of an NVA battalion—firefights during the day, mortars at night. Chumley got his first kill, a burst taking off the top of the opposite point man's head. They laid it on and ended up with three confirmed and an injured prisoner, whom Carl Metcalf delivered personally to the lieutenant colonel's interrogator. Back at Odin, a pallet of beer was waiting for them.

"Check it out," Isley said. "Some dude walked on the moon."

"Good for him," the Fly said. "That and ten cents will buy him a cup of coffee."

"Let him make his own fucking coffee."

"Probably a zoomie, they always get the soft jobs."

"Let him walk the valley, then we'll see who's the big fucking hero."

Carl Metcalf thought it was good. "It's like *Star Trek*," he said. "It makes you think something better might come along, a better world or something. Maybe I'm too optimistic."

"Not me," Larry said.

"Shoot," Carl Metcalf said, "that's not true and you know it. It's just easy to say."

The next day they were cleaning out bunkers when someone opened up on Chumley from a gunport. He went down. Now Carl didn't have to tell them to hit it and spread out. A solid line of fire poured into the slit. Larry crawled to Chumley; he'd been hit in the tit, right through the nipple, but he was breathing all right. Larry started some blood to stave off shock and had The Fly call him in.

He stayed with Chumley while they worked on the sniper. The guy would wait till the fire died down and then let fly. Isley tried his thumper but couldn't put one on target.

"Forget it," Carl Metcalf said, and called in air.

Larry and Frankenstein dragged Chumley clear, and the rest of them pulled back and established an LZ for the medevac behind a clump of trees. Carl Metcalf stood on a rock ledge well out of range and trained a pair of binoculars on the gunport.

The chopper got there before the jets. The sniper took a single shot at it, and the platoon drowned him in noise. They hefted Chumley on, his pulse surprisingly strong. He waved like Bates.

"It's all that blubber," Wrong Way explained. "It's like shooting a walrus, you need an elephant gun."

The chopper was still climbing when two Phantoms rolled in. They cut across the hills, snapped out of a long, curving turn and angled in for the run, coming from behind Carl Metcalf. He turned to watch them, binoculars at the ready, waved like a fan urging his team on.

The Phantoms dropped their bombs. Larry saw them let go, the noses wobble, then correct. He was walking with the rest of the platoon toward the clump of trees. They screened him for a minute, and then the ledge Carl Metcalf was standing on was lost in a wall of flame.

"Short round," someone said.

They all hesitated a step except Wrong Way. He sprinted through the trees, outdistancing them. The black smoke rolled.

The rock was gone, nothing left but a scorched crater. Carl Metcalf lay in the smoking bowl. Larry tried to slide down the side and fell, jamming his knees. He ran to him.

His face was gone, nothing but a few holes, his tags melted into new skin pink as Spam. His hands were seared into mitts. He was breathing, choking up his lungs.

"You're okay," Larry said.

He reached deep into his aid bag until his hand brushed the milled pistol grip. He kept it in the bag while he racked the slide back, shielded Carl with his body so the others wouldn't see. His hand was steady. He was good at this. It was the one thing he could do.

AT ODIN he spent most of his time up beyond the connex box, gazing down the valley, winging pebbles at the windows of Bates's spirit house. In the hootch they stayed away from him. Skull, they still called him, though they didn't know why. He took the corner, retreating behind the mosquito netting after chow, reading the Martian's awful book. He kept Magoo's shoeboxes under his bunk, and Leonard Dawson's cards. In the middle of the night, they came to him, as Chuck the Duck had predicted. It was strangely comforting. In the morning, Larry missed them. Breakfast was powdered eggs, powdered potatoes, powdered milk. He handed out his pills, rubbed salve into their cut knuckles. The platoon piled onto choppers and went out to find the war.

He was under thirty days. He didn't mention it in his letters. It was like a no-hitter, the slightest acknowledgment would destroy it. He thought it would be hard but there was no one to talk to, nobody to slip up. He watched the sun wink out behind the mountains, then, as if satisfied, stood and walked back down the hill. All night the guns put out fire.

In the dream, he was killing an NVA about to bayonet Carl Metcalf. The scene belonged to his father's war, the palm trees and soft foxholes of the Pacific. Tracers blazed into the man's chest and he lay back in the sand, gushing. Carl thanked Larry with a handshake, and then, like a cardboard target, the NVA popped up again and stuck a round through Carl's mouth.

Twenty-seven, twenty-six. In the mornings he couldn't get out of bed, then after lunch nodded off. He didn't feel like eating. When they stopped for water, he didn't take any. He tucked a salt pill under his tongue and rucked up, sucked it like a breath mint. At dusk he popped a Seconal, followed it with a warm beer and waited for his friends to visit him.

He had seventeen days and a wake-up when they went back to Stupidville. The thatched huts had sprung up again. It was lunchtime; the children carried teapots to women in the fields. The boy with the soccer ball was gone.

Isley was leading the platoon along a hedgerow when someone opened up from behind a dike. At the noise, a heron lifted into the air. Larry planted his foot, hoping to roll right, and a blast sent him flying.

He landed on his back. For an instant he believed it had been a mortar, a grenade, something other than a booby trap. It was dumb. His first thought was how much shit they'd give him. His foot felt like a nail had been driven through it. He sat up to see how bad it was. The toe of his boot was missing, a good chunk of the foot with it, blood pulsing into the dust.

"Fuck," he said calmly, as if he'd misplaced his keys, and lay down again, waiting for the shock to roll over him.

Wrong Way peered into his face as if reading something difficult. "Hang on," he said, and disappeared. The sky was white, the sun hot on his arms.

The doc from third platoon leaned over him. "You're all right," he said. His hands ran down Larry's calf, checking for more damage.

Larry wanted to tell him what was wrong, but his mouth wouldn't work. He tried to sit up and found he couldn't. His limbs were heavy, as if bound down. His body was stiffening from the inside out, setting like ice.

"You're okay," the man said, his voice tiny, as if he were behind a thick window. "You're going to be fine." He uncapped a syrette and plunged it into Larry's arm, and soon it was true—he felt nothing.

They carried him through Stupidville on a litter and out the other side. The shock wore off and he could speak again. He thanked them for taking care of him. He had to swallow to talk, and then couldn't hear himself. At one point he began to cry with gratitude.

"Don't worry about it," they said.

The doc stayed with him until the dust-off came. The noise was enormous, solid as rock. The rotor sprayed his face with grit; his eyelids didn't close quickly enough. They lifted him on and slid him across the floor. Someone patted his shoulder good-bye. In the air, Larry wondered who it had been, then thought it didn't matter. They were all gone. After Carl Metcalf, even he was not really there.

The dust-off medic wore a flight helmet, his visor giving back Larry his own face. The man leaned down and shouted, "Where you from?"

"New York," Larry said. "Ithaca."

"Hey, Ithaca, guess what?"

"What?" Larry said.

"You're going home."

It was a dumb thing to say, something out of a movie, though Larry knew it would be rude to say so. It was not his place. The saved were supposed to be grateful.

ELEVEN

When the photographer was done, Clines gave Larry the okay to clean the attic. The pictures were brittle; the corners tore. Creeley had used a glue gun. The silver paper backing the insulation came off, pink fiberglass poking through the holes. Larry expected to see Alan and Vicki among the torsos and exploded foreheads; he worked his way toward the corner where he'd hidden them. He hadn't seen these pictures in years; some he didn't remember, which he thought heartening. At first he tried to save them all, then gave up and stuffed a garbage bag.

Vicki picked up a handful, then dropped it as if burned. "Oh my God," she said. "Larry, oh my God."

They were Magoo's women, the poses trite, excruciating. He thought of Donna in the park, Wade's postcard.

"These aren't yours," Vicki pleaded, hoping he'd say no.

"They're a friend's," he confessed.

"Then why do *you* have them?"

"He didn't come back."

"So why do you keep them? Why don't you just throw them away?"

She waited for him. Larry didn't have an answer, but he was not getting rid of the pictures. They belonged to him in the same way Magoo was his, and Smart Andy, and Carl Metcalf.

"They're mine now," he said. "They're important to me."

"I don't want them in my house."

Clines knelt by the empty trunk, pretending not to listen.

"You don't have to look at them," Larry said.

"I don't want *you* to look at them. It's been thirteen years, Larry—thirteen years. You've got to stop wallowing in it."

"I don't wallow in it. I don't even look at them."

"You come up here. When we're at church, you come up here and sit in that chair. It's like a religion with you."

"That's crap."

"You torture yourself with it. That's what your group at the hospital's all about—keeping it fresh. God forbid you should talk to me."

"You don't want to hear it," Larry said. "You think if you pretend it doesn't exist I'll forget about it—just like everything else."

"Fuck you," Vicki said, and retreated downstairs to watch Scott.

Clines waited until Larry took a break from ripping down the pictures, then showed him another shot of Magoo's—an old woman floating in a muddy canal, a bird perched on her back.

"Nice friend," Clines said. "Someone I should know?"

"It's not him. This guy's name was Barclay."

Clines pointed at Larry as if he'd said something important. He pulled a notepad from his jacket, licked his thumb and flipped the pages.

"Barclay. Jerome Donald."

"You've got them all there?" Larry asked, and Clines showed him the list.

Nathan Allen Stargell.

Frederick James Parmenter.

Norman Arthur Bates.

Some of the dead he didn't know, but he found all of his. The dates brought back weather.

"Make me a copy," Larry asked.

"I'm not sure if you've seen this," Clines said, and handed him an unmarked envelope.

Inside was the picture of Vicki and Alan. Larry didn't have to take it out.

"So you have," Clines said.

"Where was it?" Larry asked.

367

Clines pointed to the pocket over the scarecrow's heart. Larry looked to him as if to explain, but there was nothing to say.

Clines had the two pieces of the jack in separate baggies. "I'm going to have to talk with your father."

"Good luck," Larry said.

Clines would assign a car to watch the house full-time. As long as possible, he said; the force really couldn't spare a man. He didn't know what else to do, he said, as if admitting he was overmatched. When he was gone, Larry hid the picture in the exact same place. He folded the VC flags and his class A's and banded the surviving pictures together and returned them to the footlocker. He clapped the latches down and lifted it. Carrying it back to its old spot by the chair, he thought that he'd kept very little, then wondered if Vicki was right.

They didn't apologize in bed, slept with a cool gap between them. In the morning he woke to her splashing in the shower. He thought he shouldn't run, to show her he was concerned. At breakfast, the cop from across the road knocked on the door and asked if he could use the bathroom. While he was in it, Vicki made an outraged face at Larry.

"I won't live like this," she said after leaving Scott off.

"What do you want *me* to do about it?" he said.

"Nothing. I'm just telling you I won't live like this."

He drove poorly all morning, cutting corners too short, Number 1 dropping off curbs. Above town, the wind pushed him into the other lane. The Entenmann's guy was ahead of him everywhere. Waiting, Larry thought of what he'd say to Donna. He'd treat the postcard as a joke, and she'd laugh with him.

He met her in the lot of the Glenwood Pines. They still had a banner up from that summer's Bud at the Glen. WELCOME, RACING FANS, it said across a checkered background. Larry recognized the Chevy pick-up of a regular, its locked toolbox. Clouds moved low over the lake. Donna pulled her Monte Carlo in next to him, and he got out.

She had on slacks and flats, her face made up, hair pinned in the clip.

"Big meeting?" he said.

"Not really."

They lingered a second, gazing at the lake, but didn't kiss. She started across the lot and he caught up with her, held the door. They made their way through the pool tables. A waitress led them to a spot in back by the windows; she'd had them before and knew they liked the view. The cold leaked in. Donna took her jacket off, then a minute later slipped it over her shoulders.

"The food'll warm you up," he said. "Are you hungry?"

She barely answered, staring down at her menu. Usually they played footsie or held hands across the table, but today she smoked. She seemed distracted, as if later she were meeting someone more important.

"I got this strange postcard from Wade the other day," he said. "He made it sound like you're going out there."

She looked out the window at the pines and the lake beyond, then turned to him, her eyes downcast, and Larry understood.

"I am," she said.

He laughed as though it were a joke, but her face didn't change. He recovered by reading the menu. Pinesburger, Boburger, Tullyburger. Schaefer, Genesee, Utica Club. She'd warned him, she'd told him the truth all along. Still, he felt cheated. He hadn't done anything to lose her.

"When are you leaving?"

"Don't be angry," she said.

"When did you decide this?"

"What other choice do I have?"

He wanted to ask her to stay, to be his, but she was right. "I'm not angry," he said, "just disappointed."

"When I'm with you I don't miss him, but the rest of the time I can't help it. I'm not happy without him."

"And I'm supposed to be happy without you."

"You'll be all right," she said. "Remember I said I might say I loved you? I do now, honestly." She lay her hand palm-up on the table, and Larry took it in his.

"What good does that do me?"

"None," Donna said. "I just thought you'd want to know."

The waitress came to take their order, and they withdrew their hands. He'd forgotten what he wanted. He needed a drink.

"So when?" he asked when they were alone again.

"Sunday."

"Just for a little while."

"For good," she said. "We're going to start over, if that's possible."

She took his hand again and said she was sorry. There was just too much stuff. Larry thought he'd made it clear he was willing to go through anything for her. The waitress hovered, and they stopped talking. The bread came in a latticed plastic dish, then his beer, the chili, the burgers. He didn't feel like eating, and barely tasted his. He wished he could be angrier with her. He watched her dipping her fries in ketchup and pictured her all those times in her car, in her living room, in her bed. His greatest pleasure had been opening her clothes, listening to her soft talk afterwards. Now he could feel her moving away from him like a missed train.

"I told you I'd fuck you up," she said.

"You did."

It would be the last time, they agreed, though he insisted on driving her to the airport. She was donating her car to AA, taking full blue book as a tax write-off. The house would go on the market in December. She had thought things out—she and Wade had—and he wondered how long she'd known. It didn't change how much of a fool he'd been, and still was. He was not good at stopping.

In the parking lot they kissed primly, and he followed her back to town, the lake flitting in the trees. Everything was for the last time. They split, and he slumped over the wheel, infinitely tired. He could not imagine their time together had come to nothing, but it was true; in a strange way it no longer existed, had never really happened.

All afternoon he thought of how he'd lost her, as if he might come up with a loophole, a solution she'd overlooked. Already he was planning what he would say to her Sunday to make her stay. The flight he couldn't think about; the days and months after that stretched like a desert—a glimpse and he rejected it.

He rode the bus to group, eating Wendy's. Their lists were growing. Trayner asked if Larry could take things for them—boonie hats and medals, patches and armbands. Rinehart wanted him to take a wreath, Cartwright a bracelet made of bootlaces.

"As long as they're not too big," Larry said.

"What are *you* taking?" Sponge asked, and Larry thought of Carl Metcalf's sketches and the battle flags, the list of Salazar's songs.

"Just myself," Larry said.

"Any word from Creeley?" Mel White asked, and Larry lied.

"Who's got a story?" he said, and they formed a circle between the beds. In the middle of Meredith's recon, he drifted, walking with Donna past the empty slips of the marina. Even in Vietnam he wasn't safe.

Vicki made a point of asking how it went, as if to apologize for last night, this morning, the entire year.

"It went fine," he said, hoping that would satisfy her.

"What did you talk about?"

Again, he felt the urge to confess, if only to shame her, throw it in her face, yet instead he told her a shorter version of Meredith's story.

"Hmm," she said at the end, as if she were thinking about it. She was trying. She was his wife.

"And what did *you* do today?" he asked.

Going up, he didn't check to see if Donna's lights were on, but in bed he replayed their lunch again and again, the way she turned from the lake and lowered her eyes, the words she spoke like a verdict. Vicki slung a leg over his, an arm across his chest, and Larry lay still beneath her, wondering if he had squandered everything.

The next day he didn't break for lunch, eating his ham sandwich between stops. It was bright, the leaves whirling down into streams. He was done early and took Number 1 to East Hill Car Wash to do the windows and vacuum the interior. When he rolled into the outlet, Marv had a message for him. It was from Mrs. Railsbeck. His father was missing.

He drove over in Number 1. It was the beginning of dusk, the cautious going to their parking lights, sunset reflected in office windows. Mrs. R. was waiting for him on the porch, her jacket unzipped but her gloves on. She hadn't called the police.

"That detective was just here after lunch," she said, as if there were some connection. His father was supposed to walk a half mile for therapy. She opened the front hall closet and showed Larry an empty hanger. He'd taken his down vest instead of his good coat. His scarf was gone but not his walking stick. He'd left three hours ago.

"Did you see him leave?" Larry asked.

She hesitated, shook her head as if it couldn't possibly make a difference. "No."

"Call the police," he said.

He had her wait for them at the house while he drove around the neighborhood, boxing the blocks. Everyone had left their decorations up; skeletons twisted in the wind. The sun was down now, the sky brilliant above West Hill. Dusk filled the trees. On Utica, kids were playing football, catching passes between the parked cars. They hadn't seen anyone. Larry tried to describe Creeley, sketching a line across his forehead with a finger. While they were talking, the streetlights blinked on.

He cruised past the firehouse with its blue light outside, past the black windows of the Lincoln Street diner. Only the laundromat was open, a few students reading. He asked the room at large; they hardly acknowledged him, went back to their textbooks.

The school playground was vacant, leaves racing over the crosswalks. He turned up Queen Street toward Gun Hill, and the beer signs of the Fall Creek House stopped him. He couldn't picture his father drinking Genny Cream and shooting pool but stuck his head in anyway. The man at the nearest stool wore a baseball cap with a trout's head sticking out of it, a new reel in a box on the bar. Larry asked if he'd come from the falls.

"Sure," the man said, "there's a bunch of them over there."

Outside, Larry could hear the boom and rush of water farther down the street. He jogged to the bridge and held the steel railing, peering up the gorge, the walls on both sides sheer, the falls a white curtain. In the darkness, it gave off a vague light. The wind blew a frigid mist over him. Below, the creek flowed black and high, the riffle purling; it gave him the illusion of movement, as if he were at the stern of a ship. Up the gorge on the far side of the pool, tiny beside the crashing water, stood a single fisherman.

Larry clambered down a set of stairs made from railroad ties and cut through the brush, tromping over the stones and fallen logs beside the creek. The trail ran under the cliff, the sheer slate seeping groundwater. The mist was worse here, the trees dripping with it. Behind him, a car stopped on the bridge, and Larry thought that it was a trap, the gorge a box canyon with nowhere to go. He would find a dummy propped in the water, a charge of C-4 duct-taped to a wooden silhouette. He used a tree as a shield, relying on the darkness. A flash went off in the car, its taillights flared, and it continued on.

He stumbled on a rock, banging his good foot, but stayed up and said nothing. He was still concealed in the brush, close enough to make out the man's shape. He was slim like his father. Larry stepped out onto the wet ledge around the pool, but before he could call out to him, the man lit a cigarette; in the flame of the lighter, Larry could see he had a mustache.

"Excuse me," Larry called. He shouted but the falls drowned him out, the mist soaking his hair. He waved his arms over his head, and still the man didn't notice him. Finally Larry chucked a hunk of slate across the water, and the splash distracted him. Larry had to convince the man to leave his spot, waving him over as if he were in danger.

"What's the trouble?" he said, and Larry explained that his father wasn't right.

"He wasn't having any luck," the man said. "He said he was gonna head further down."

Larry ran back up the railroad ties and across the bridge and downstream along the high school side of the creek. To prevent flooding, the banks were steep, the channel straight as a canal; there was really nowhere to fish, and after he reached Cayuga, he scourged himself for wasting time. His good foot hurt, and he wished he were wearing his Nikes.

The creek ran under Route 13, but to get there Larry had to take Willow in past the city bus yard and the far edge of the golf course. He jolted over the railroad tracks, passed the boats in drydock for the winter. A spotlight was on in the corner of the city lot, the graders and salt trucks throwing shadows; then there was nothing but the dark golf course, the trees, garbage dumped by the roadside. The asphalt turned to mud, and Number 1 bumped through the puddles, its headlights jiggling. He hadn't turned off yet to reach the water when he saw his father.

He was standing at a fence, behind which rose a square cinder-block building. He had his waders on but no rod or tackle box. The building had burned, black swoops of soot licking from the windows. About it rested the charred hulks of cars, some with their roofs sheared off. It was the training ground for the fire department. The fence was topped with barbed wire. His father leaned against it, stared through the diamonds like a child at the zoo. One of the cars was his New Yorker, its headlights wall-eyed.

"Are you okay?" Larry asked.

"That's my car," his father informed him. He clutched his pants pocket. "I can't find my door opener. The thing you put in the hole, the metal thing. I had it right here and now I can't find it."

"Where's your rod?" Larry asked.

His father looked at him as if he'd missed the question. "That's my car," he said. "I can't go anywhere without my car."

"Come on. I can give you a ride in my truck."

"I've got to wait here," his father said. He was breathing hard, as if working himself into a fit. His hands gripped the fence. When Larry tried to take one, his father shouted, "That's my car!"

"I know," Larry said, grappling with him. "We'll get it tomorrow."

"I want my car!" he cried, batting at Larry's hand.

Larry was afraid of hurting him. He tried to grab his wrists. He got one, but his father spun, an elbow catching Larry in the eye. He let go to cover the burn.

His father was running from him, splashing through the puddles.

"That's it," Larry said, and went after him. He closed on him and pinned his arms to his sides.

"I want my car," his father sobbed.

"Stop it," Larry said. "Your car's gone." Larry kept his wrists and marched him to Number 1, buckled him into the seat and locked his door.

"My car," his father lamented.

"Your car is gone," Larry said, trying to be nice, glad that the ride was only a few blocks.

Clines was waiting with Mrs. R.

"So he's okay," Clines said. "What happened to your eye?"

Mrs. R. took his father's scarf off and helped him out of his down vest. She had him sit on a chair and peeled off the waders.

"Where *were* you?" she asked.

"They stole my car," he said, and Larry had to tell her. His father sat dazed as a patient, his hands idle on his thighs. They called Dr. Downs at her office and got a recording. The best thing was rest, they figured, and took him upstairs, Larry steadying his elbow. He'd stopped talking, as if his strength had left him. Mrs. R. began to undo his buttons, and Larry closed the door.

On the porch he apologized to Clines for the false alarm.

"Better safe," Clines said, and got into his LTD.

Larry called Vicki to say he'd be late. Mrs. R. offered him dinner, but he said he really shouldn't. They looked in on his father sleeping.

"He'll be all right," she said. It was a question, and not having an answer, Larry took her in his arms, and this time meant it, as if finally he was ready to share him.

Back at the outlet, he let himself in, hung up the keys to Number 1 and changed in front of his locker, ignoring the shots on the door. He hadn't thought of Donna in hours. Just picturing her car in the drive tired him.

It was there, a monument to his stupidity. Vicki asked him what he was so pissed off about, and he told her what had happened with his father.

"I thought you might still be mad at me," she said.

"For what?" he said, honestly unsure.

"Look," she said bitterly, "I'm trying."

"I know you are," he said. It could have applied to any number of things. It was wise, he'd found lately, to assume the worst.

As if to prove herself earnest, she was too enthusiastic in bed. Though she drained him, it only made him miss Donna more. The infuriating thing about love was that nothing changed. In the morning she asked if he was going to run. It was a show. He was supposed to smile, to like it. She brought home a bottle of wine for dinner, and when Scott was in bed they finished a second and made love on the rug. It had been a long time since anything made sense.

At lunch he cruised through the Treman Marina, searching for the Monte Carlo; the first time, the lot was empty, the next day another couple were parked at the far end. He called Plant Pathology and a different woman answered, her voice tricking him. Donna no longer worked for the department. It was like an execution, the preparations final; there would be no reprieve.

Both porches were lit. He had to walk past her car before crossing the yard. The cop waved. Larry imagined turning early, heading for her door instead, but kept on. They'd had enough chances.

Scott's pumpkin was beginning to rot, its skin going soft, the grin subtly corrupt. Vicki didn't come to the door to greet him. Scott was glued to the TV. Larry checked the kitchen. The stove was bare, which disappointed him; he didn't feel like eating out. He heard footsteps upstairs and a drawer slam shut.

She was in Scott's room, stuffing clothes into two bags on the bed. Larry stopped in the doorway, but she ignored him.

"What's going on?" he said.

She zipped the bags closed and shouldered past him to drop them in the hall, then stalked off to their bedroom. He followed, entering just in time to see her fling a white package at him.

It glanced off his shoulder and slapped the wall. It was an envelope of prints from Photo USA. It had his name on it.

Vicki threw open the closet door, the knob punching the wall, and started tossing dresses on the bed. The hangers clattered.

Larry pulled back the gummed flap and slid the inner envelope out. Taped to the front was the queen of spades. *August 5, 1969*, it said, which meant nothing to Larry.

The first picture showed him kissing Donna on the bench, his hands in her hair. The next was her car parked beside Number 1; there was a series of them, his ass rising and falling in the window. He didn't need to see more and laid them on the dresser.

"It's over," he explained.

"It sure is," Vicki said.

"She's leaving."

"What a coincidence." Vicki moved to the dresser and gathered her underwear. "I can't believe you let me think it was all my fault. She's crazy. I know you've always wanted to fuck her, but Jesus, Larry."

"You left me," he said, but he knew it was a feeble excuse.

"I don't know why I came back. You don't even want me anymore. I don't know what you want."

"I don't either."

"It's the wrong time to start being honest," she said. "And don't bother with the pathetic act. I'm done feeling sorry for you. I've already wasted fourteen years."

"Vicki," he said, but couldn't think of anything else.

She shook her head as if she expected it.

She took the bags downstairs two at a time, piling them by the front door. She didn't want his help. In the living room, Scott was a foot away from the set; Larry moved him to the couch and sat down. Speed Racer pressed a button on his steering wheel and the Mach 5 vaulted over an oil slick. She left the door open to take the bags to the Ruster, the cold reaching in. He'd never been able to stop her; his entire strategy was to be there when she returned.

She came back in and went upstairs to make sure she had everything. He thought of the picture of her and Alan still hidden in the attic, but there was no point in showing her; it would only shame him again. They had lost the power to move each other, like two fighters at the end of a grueling bout, even their desire to win spent.

She had her coat on, and threw Scott's at Larry. The show wasn't over; Scott watched it as Larry fit his arms into the jacket.

In the window beside the set, Vicki climbed Donna's porch and rang the bell. In her other hand were the pictures.

He ran outside and across the yard, bounding up the stairs just as the door opened.

Donna didn't have a chance to say anything. Vicki thrust a picture at her; she had the whole stack out, clutching it like a deck of cards.

"I like this," Vicki said, and threw it in her face. "This is nice. How about this one?"

Donna fended them off, her arms lifted as if she were being stabbed. Before Larry could get between them, she recovered and rushed Vicki, knocking her backwards. The two fell, swinging at each other, the pictures scattering.

Larry wedged a knee between them. He pinned Vicki's arm, and Donna landed a shot to the side of her head. Larry wrestled them apart, pushing Donna to the long end of the porch. He stood between them while they screamed.

"You slut," Vicki said. "You think you know him?"

"You're the slut."

"I can name them," Vicki said, and listed several men he didn't know.

"Larry doesn't care," Donna said.

"Because he doesn't know what you are. Wade knows, that's why he left you."

"That's why he wants me back."

"See?" Vicki said. "She doesn't even want you, she just needed to get laid."

"That's not true," Larry said.

"Do you love him?" Vicki asked.

Donna gave him the same look she had at the Pines. He'd thought he was stronger, that she could not break his heart again.

"There's your answer," Vicki said. "I don't have to ask with Alan." She kicked a picture off the top of the stairs and clomped down, stalked away across the yard.

Donna didn't want him to touch her. She closed the door while he was still apologizing. As he was gathering up the pictures, she turned her light out.

The cop from across the road came over with a long flashlight. "Everything okay here?"

Larry showed him the queen, but couldn't hide all the pictures.

"They're private," Larry said.

"Yes, sir," the man said, and shined the light so he could find them all. He asked what had happened.

"Family stuff," Larry said.

They'd moved to the yard when Vicki came out of the house.

"Are you going to say good-bye to Scott?" she called.

"Where are you going to be, at your mother's?"

The cop looked off down the road as if he weren't listening.

"Where else am I going to go?"

"I don't know," Larry said.

"I don't think his *wife* will let us move in with them."

She went back into the house, and the cop excused himself.

Scott waited in the hall in his hat and mittens. Vicki went out to warm up the Ruster. Larry knelt down and gave him a hug.

"You be good for your mother."

"I will," Scott said, but it was a reflex. His eye wandered as if tracking an insect, and Larry kissed his cheek.

"Okay, champ," he said, and guided him down the stairs. He helped buckle him in.

"I'm not coming back," Vicki warned him.

"I told you it was over."

"Is that why you defended her?" she said, and Larry had no answer. "You're so obvious."

"And you're not."

"Why am I even talking to you?" She stared straight ahead, waiting for him to close the door.

"I'll talk to you soon," he said, made sure Scott was in and thunked it shut. The transmission clunked but refused to catch. Vicki revved the engine as if it would help. It caught and the Ruster leapt backwards into Donna's grille, glass smashing, then fishtailed across the lawn. The cop got out of his car, and Vicki nearly ran him down.

Larry checked to see if he was okay.

"Damn," the cop said, "it's busy tonight."

Inside, Larry thumbed through the pictures. There was a pretty one of Donna at a picnic table, laughing, her eyes closed. They were only a few weeks old, yet Larry couldn't remember how he'd felt then. Now he felt watched, and went through the house, checking the locks.

Clines called to talk about the date on the queen.

"You're still in the Rao Lao then. So's he. I've got an after-action report here says your company skirmished with the enemy throughout the day. Two men died—a Ronald Grossman and an Alvin Harrison; neither of them were from your platoon. Enemy casualties were heavy—twenty-two confirmed, four of them claimed by your platoon. Remember anything?"

"I would have told you if I did. We probably ambushed somebody."

"Could it have been at night?"

"It could have," Larry said, not seeing the difference.

"Because the next day he's listed missing in action."

"That's great, but it doesn't have anything to do with me."

"I talked with your father," Clines said. "I don't think the connection's there. There's something but it's not enough. The guy wants you."

"Why?"

"That's what I want *you* to tell *me*."

When he hung up, the house went quiet. He called Mrs. Honness, who said she'd tell Vicki to call him back, but when the phone rang, it was Clines again.

"The battalion report says your four dead were Viet Cong."

"So?" Larry said.

"The rest were NVA regulars. I thought it might be significant."

"Not anymore."

"I'm going to find it," Clines vowed, and for the first time Larry wondered if he might. While that year had a hold on him that would never let go, there were pieces missing. He hadn't remembered all of Magoo's pictures, even some he'd been in.

He slept with the light on, and still they came. Leonard Dawson was tied to the tree, bleeding cards, Bates trying to push them back into his wounds. Dumb Andy's leg pinwheeled through the air. Larry woke alone, in the center of the bed. He went through the house like a night watchman. The light on Scott's radio glowed. Donna's windows were dark, the cruiser parked on the berm. All Creeley had left was the king; the ace would be his.

The next morning he took the bus, suspicious of the other passengers. At the Price Champion, his shelves hadn't been tampered with. He tried Vicki at her mother's, but Mrs. Honness said she didn't want to talk to him.

After work, he dropped in on his father, who seemed lucid. He'd switched to an electric razor Larry had bought him some long-gone Christmas, and his hair was parted neatly. Mrs. Railsbeck suggested they take a walk, and his father hauled on his coat and tossed his scarf over his shoulder. Larry wanted to help him down the porch stairs but held off.

They strolled toward the falls, leaves crunching underfoot, the rush of the water growing. His father looked to the sky as if it might rain. He had no memory of the other night, and Larry didn't push it.

"Ronald Creeley was a prisoner of war," he mentioned.

"Is that right?"

"I was wondering what that does to you."

"It's like anything else," his father said. "It does different things to different people. I think it made me stronger. I can't speak for anyone else."

"I understand," Larry said.

"You remember a lot. You go over things you've learned or people you know, things you did. You plan what you're going to do when you get out. In some ways I'd imagine it's like any kind of prison. You try to find a place inside yourself no one can get to."

"Then what do you do?"

"You wait," his father said. "You wait for them to come and take it away from you. They'll try but you don't let them. They couldn't take your mother away from me. I knew I had to come back for her."

"What if you don't have anyone like that?"

"There's always something. We'd dream about anything—girls, food. Cigarettes was a big one. One fellow had this dream of seeing the Grand Canyon; he'd never seen it before. He'd imagine what it would be like to ride down to the bottom on a mule. He could go on for hours."

"Did he go?" Larry asked.

"I don't know," his father said. "I suppose he did."

They stopped on the bridge to watch the falls, the mist sprinkling their cheeks.

"What about you?" his father asked. "What did you think of?"

"Here," Larry said. "Vicki. Sometimes you."

"Your mother."

"I tried not to think about her," Larry confessed.

"I'm afraid I did the same. That was a hard time for all of us. Your sister was the one who showed us what to do then."

"I've always been sorry about leaving," Larry said.

"You had to do it. And you came back, that's what counts."

"That place you mentioned," Larry said. "Sometimes I think I'm still there."

"That's the problem," his father said, as if he understood. "You can't get rid of it."

"Never?" Larry said.

"I haven't been able to, *you* should know that."

They watched the falls in silence a moment, their hands in their pockets, then turned for home.

"Vicki left me again," Larry said. "I think for good this time."

"What did you do?"

"I fell in love," Larry said.

His father stopped. "Honestly?"

"Honestly."

"Well," his father said, "that'll do it."

Mrs. Railsbeck invited him to stay for supper. Afterwards the three of them watched *Wheel of Fortune* in the living room. Mrs. R. brought his father a pill and in the middle of *Jeopardy* hinted that it was getting towards his bedtime. They said good night at the door, Larry shaking his father's hand as if they wouldn't see each other for months. Walking to the bus stop,

Larry wished the evening could have gone on and on. He had to go back to the house now.

Donna's car hadn't moved, the glass from the shattered headlight still resting on the bumper. Her windows were lit, but with the cop across the road, Larry thought it better to call. Tomorrow was Friday; in two days she would be gone. He expected her to hang up; when she didn't, he was speechless.

"Are you okay?" he asked.

"I'm not drinking, if that's what you mean."

"Do you still want me to drive you to the airport?"

"If you want to," she said.

"I want to."

She waited for him to say more.

"I love you," he said.

"That doesn't help," she said, and gave him the time of the flight.

Upstairs, he had to pass Scott's room—the Muppet bedspread, the map of the world stippled with pins. In the holder above the sink hung one toothbrush. Her Stephen King still rested on her bedstand, the vacation pictures on the dresser. He would call them tomorrow—every day until he got through.

In the morning, he reached Mrs. Honness. She was sorry, she said, but Vicki didn't want to talk to him, and right now neither did she. He imagined Vicki telling the story of the pictures, and again he thought of the shot of her and Alan, how meaningless it was. They'd gone beyond evidence.

Clines had left a message with Marv. He had proof it was a night ambush.

"So what?" Larry said.

"It says the four VC were unconfirmed."

"That's not unusual."

"How do we know they were VC? What if they're Creeley and his team dressed like VC?"

"And we blow them away," Larry said. He saw a flash of jungle and the night close over it again. "Still, it doesn't explain why he's after me in particular."

"The rest of your platoon's dead."

"No," Larry said. "By then we've got all new people."

"Hey," Clines said, "I'm working on it."

"I've got a feeling he'll tell me when he sees me. You know what's coming up."

"I know," Clines said. "Veterans' Day."

When he got home there was a gray Audi behind Donna's car. Later, a woman in a red trenchcoat came out of the house, lifted a Century 21 sign from the trunk and hammered it into the lawn. When she'd left, Larry went over and knocked on the door.

Donna only opened it a crack. She had a mouse under one eye from the other night, the bruise a lurid purple. He wanted to touch it, but she turned her face. She had a sweater on and no shoes. The couch held a row of boxes, the TV was unplugged.

"So it's official," he said.

"I can't stay here. We both need to do what's right."

"What's right?"

"Don't be stupid," she said.

"That's my problem, I get stupid around you."

She didn't honor it with a response.

"You need any help?" he asked.

"The movers are coming next week. I'm just doing the breakables."

"Well," Larry said, "I ought to let you get back to work."

"Don't be like this. I tried to tell you, didn't I?"

"You did," he said. "I just didn't want to listen."

"I'm trying to do the right thing."

"You are. I'm the one being selfish."

"I'm sorry," she said.

"So am I."

They were done talking but still he waited for her to let him in.

"Go on now," she said, releasing him.

When he looked back, she'd closed the door.

Saturday he took the bus to Trumansburg, hoping to see Scott. Though the Ruster was there, Mrs. Honness said they were gone for the day.

"Where?" he asked.

"I'm not certain."

"How were they getting there?"

"A friend of Vicki's was giving them a ride."

"A friend," said Larry.

"I *will* tell her you came by though."

Larry thanked her and walked around the block and snuck through the backyard and along the side of the house, peering in the windows. The den was dark, a puzzle half done on the card table. She was telling the truth. Walking home from the bus stop, he wondered if the cop knew the whole story.

For supper he had a beef pot pie and two Gennys. Donna called to remind him when they needed to get going in the morning. He thought of asking for one last time, then realized how dumb that was, how anything less than all of her wasn't enough.

"Are you okay?" she asked, and he said he was tired, which was true.

In the middle of the night, Scott's radio woke him. Larry scrambled for a pen and paper, certain it was Creeley and the king—that he was getting off easy—but the Morse code only said hello. It was Rudy, calling across the date line. Larry wrote it down, knowing he'd use it as an excuse to talk to Scott.

Donna came over around eight to make sure he was awake. She gave him the keys, as if she didn't trust herself with them. It was gray and still, the cows clumped by the treeline. She had six bags, which filled the trunk. She'd arranged for Fred to pick up the car later in the day. The title and an extra set of keys were in the glove compartment. She checked the house one last time, then locked up and got in the car.

"Do you have your ticket?" Larry asked, and she patted her jacket.

"Thanks for doing this," she said. "You didn't have to."

"Don't be stupid," he said.

As they backed out, the glass fell clinking from the bumper.

He drove perfectly, like a chauffeur, holding back, drifting into curves. Downtown, the churches were busy, the sidestreets quiet. They took 13 uphill, the lake black beneath them, a V of geese making for the north end. "Pretty," she said. He wanted to remember her voice, the smell of her— things he would need in the coming months. She was taking their days with her, the secret meetings, the luxurious noons. He felt himself emptying out, a stadium after a legendary game.

They were early. The terminal was slow, only the Hertz woman open, a few college students with their carry-ons. Donna's plane sat on the tarmac, an avgas truck filling it through a scuffed yellow hose. He stood with her in line at the ticket counter, herding her bags, then at the last minute stepped aside.

They sat looking out the window, waiting for the boarding call. He took her hand, and she let him keep it. He needed to see her face, to memorize it for later, yet when he looked at her, his throat closed and he began to cry.

"Stay," he said.

"You'll be all right," she said.

He turned away to recover, wiped the tears with a knuckle. No one was looking at them.

"You understand," she asked. "Larry."

"I do," he said, though just now he didn't.

She held out a miniature pack of tissues, and he plucked one to blow his nose.

"Can I call you?" he asked.

"No," she said. "It would be better if we didn't write either. I'm tired of lying all the time."

The announcement came over the PA, and everyone got up. The security guard turned on the conveyor belt and the metal detector.

Larry held her hand until the last student was through. Donna kissed him on the cheek.

"Good-bye," she said. "I do love you, you know."

"I know," Larry said.

"Please don't write."

"I'll try," he said.

Her purse disappeared into the metal detector, and she stepped through the frame; it didn't beep. He went to the window to watch her cross the tarmac. The others were backed up on the jetway. She waved, he waved. They waited, embarrassed at the delay, and then the line moved again, and she was gone.

In the parking lot he stood by the Monte Carlo with the door open. The plane roared and lifted and cleared the terminal. Though he didn't know which side she was on, he waved to the blank windows, hoping she'd see him. He followed its long, curving turn over the lake, heading westward until it was a speck, and even then he caught it and lost it several times, the perspective tricking his eyes. Finally he got in and started her car and drove back home.

Fred came in the middle of the Bills game. He was older, his head too large for his neck, his body withered. Larry gave him the keys and watched him inspect the headlight and then back out, revealing the FOR SALE sign.

After a six-pack, he called Vicki's mother. He got her machine.

"Hello," Larry said. "This is your son-in-law. I would like to see my son sometime if that's not too much trouble. Also his friend Rudy left a message for him. Thank you."

He finished the rest of the beer, then went upstairs and lay down. He came to at four-thirty in the morning, fully dressed, and chewed three aspirin. She would have been there for hours now, probably sleeping beside Wade, her hair spilled over her face.

He thought of calling in sick, but it was Monday and he had group that night. He forced down a heaping bowl of Count Chocula and dragged himself to the bus stop. It was sleeting, the freezing rain ticking on the fallen leaves. The cop's relief came, and he swung up beside Larry and offered him a ride.

Marv had last month's figures. He read them out loud as if Larry and Derek had won something. Larry did his trays, adding an extra box of crumb cakes. The first thing he heard out of the lot was Brahms. At the stoplight by Wegmans, he closed his eyes; when it turned green, the guy behind him honked.

Larry jerked the emergency brake and jumped down from Number 1. The man was going bald and had a mustache; he didn't roll his window down, even after Larry tapped on it. Larry stood there with his arms wide while the other cars honked.

"Who the fuck are you beeping at?" he said, then got back in the truck and drove.

He needed to keep busy, and skipped lunch, finishing early. Marv called him in, and Larry thought he would have to explain his efficiency.

Marv had a message from Mrs. R.

"It's the same as last time. Your father's taken off."

"I'm getting real sick of this," Larry said.

Marv let him take Number 1. The day had warmed, the sleet changed to rain. Everyone had their lights on. He sat high above traffic, listening to the news, the wipers shuttling. He expected his father would be in the same place, gripping the fence. Susan was right; Mrs. Railsbeck was too old to take care of him. Larry thought of Cayuga View, the hush of crepe soles on linoleum, the orderly rolling in the rack of clothes. It was dumb, unnecessary. He was more qualified than any of them.

Mrs. Railsbeck let him in and showed him the closet. He'd taken his down vest again. It had been two hours now.

"I'm sorry," she said, as if she should have prevented it. "Should I call the police?"

"I'll find him," Larry assured her.

The blocks were deserted, a few wet students humping along under backpacks, their hoods pulled tight beneath their chins. He cut across Route 13 and wound past the Montessori school and the bus yard. The drivers were going home, first shift emptying the parking lot; in the glare of the garage, the big diesels were being fixed. He skirted the golf course, squirrels darting over the sodden greens. The road dropped off, turned to mud, and the burned building came into view. There was nothing but puddles, a plastic bag billowing in the barbed wire.

He went on, checking the water's edge. The creek was high and loud, wide as a river, the bank littered with bottles and tennis balls. The mud was deeper here, cut with the tracks of other cars, and he worried about getting stuck. A floral couch faced the water, and a matching easy chair, as if this were someone's living room, but the rain had scared everyone away.

Number 1 dug for traction and turned around, its headlights flitting over the wrecks. His father's car had moved. It sat in the back corner, its roof lopped off, resting like a bent shield on the hood.

He followed the creek upstream, cruising through the high school, then parked and got out. The falls roared. On the bridge the spray was heavy as rain. The creek roiled white beneath him, too fast to fish. His father had told him stories of men trapped in midriver when the dam in Oswego opened its spillway. Their waders filled and held them under; days later they'd wash ashore a few towns downstream, their fingers nibbled to stubs.

The railroad ties were wet, the bushes dripping. He kept to the trail, the falls exploding in the dimness ahead. Water gathered in his hair, ran freezing down his neck. His workboots slipped on the rocks. Straddling a log, he banged his knee. Though he could barely hear himself, Larry called and called. He'd cleared the trees and moved onto the bare ledges by the pool when he saw him.

His father lay fallen on the wet slate, curled on his side like a child. His down vest was gone, his shirt ghostly in the dusk. Larry ran to him flatfooted, careful of the slick stone. He knelt and rolled him over before he could suspect a trap.

He was conscious, his eyes beseeching Larry. His shirt was open. In one hand he held a wooden coat hanger, its crossbar splintered. It was duct-taped in place. His other hand clutched his ribs. Pinned to his scarf was the king of spades.

His father's lips moved but with the water Larry couldn't hear him. He leaned his ear down to his mouth.

"It was him," his father whispered.

"You're okay," Larry said, and pulled his shirt back. In the fading light he couldn't see any marks.

His father gripped his legs as if they were broken. He moved his hand up his inseam and cupped his crotch.

"Where else?" Larry said.

He tried to reach an arm behind himself.

"All right," Larry said, to stop him, and checked his limbs.

"It hurts," his father managed.

"Okay," Larry said. "I'm going to pick you up. You just hang on."

He took his father's arm and wrapped it over his shoulder. He remembered the carry from his first week in San Antonio. He'd never had a chance to use it there. He lifted and his father moaned. He was surprisingly light, as if age had drained him, hollowed him from the inside. As Larry bulled through the brush, away from the falling water, he thought Creeley had made a major mistake. He was ready for the ace now.

Under the bubble light of Number 1, his father's back was crosshatched, the color of a mild sunburn. The skin would fade, he imagined, just as Creeley's had.

On the king, he'd drawn a diagram of an L-shaped ambush. Beneath it he'd written: *Frontenac Point*.

It was a strip of summer camps up the west side of the lake. On the point a rotting lodge looked out over the water, its dock listing, half-submerged. The hospital was almost on the way. Larry needed a weapon and a plan. The first was easy, the second beyond him right now.

He called Mrs. R. from the emergency room and told her his father had fallen but nothing seemed broken. Everything was under control.

"I'll be there in ten minutes," she said.

Larry waited three before leaving. He turned Number 1 down the hill and into town, certain he'd pass her coming the other way. He pulled into his father's drive and turned off his lights but left the truck running. The back door was unlocked. The keys to the gun cabinet were in the den, in the middle drawer. Larry chose a thirty-ought-six and two boxes of ammunition. Leaving, he noticed the red eye of the security system blinking and wondered how much of a jump he had on Clines. Not too much, he hoped; later he might need him.

The moon was out now, a soft halo frosting the clouds. He raced up the lake, passing closed motels and trailers with satellite dishes, vineyards and dairy bars waiting for spring. Coke machines shone in front of dark garages. The gun leaned against the other seat, the barrel distilling the green light of the dash. He noticed his mouth had clamped shut the way it did when the liftships spiraled in. He was afraid of losing his rage, then thought of his father and punched the gas.

Frontenac Point Road was private, barely wide enough for Number 1. It plunged downhill through pines for half a mile, cinders plinking in the wheelwells, then curved just before the shore, a homemade sign reminding drivers it was private. Larry slowed and killed his lights; the rain ticked like sand against the windshield. He rolled over a speedbump, the trays in back clattering. When he tapped the brakes, the trees behind him flared red in the mirror. It was dumb to worry, he thought; Creeley knew he was coming.

The summer camps were battened down, shutters locked, tarps over power boats. Ahead, the road narrowed to a causeway and reached into the lake, black on either side. Far out on the point, the lodge was a dark blot, reflectionless. He pulled Number 1 behind a Winnebago foundered in some-one's drive, its flat tires shrouded in canvas. He stopped the motor and jerked the emergency brake, the cable protesting, and the rifle knocked against the dash. He caught it on the rebound, a film of gun oil greasing his palm. He chambered a round before he opened the door.

His pockets jingled, and he tossed the change into the wet grass. The road turned away from shore, the lots smaller, houses dwindling. He crept through the shadows, keeping the vacant cabins and A-frames between himself and the moon. The patios held skeletal furniture, wire clotheslines swinging in the wind. He crouched beside woodpiles and fat propane tanks, his eyes fixed on the flat stretch of the causeway ahead. At the last house he checked his ammunition, made sure he could get to it. He thought he could see smoke coming from the lodge, the glint of a bumper in the lot. He could block Creeley here, wait him out until Clines arrived, but he saw his father lying by the pool, the smashed hanger and the duct tape. Donna was gone, and Scott.

"Fuck it," Larry said, and moved out.

The causeway was raised and wooden; a guardrail slanted out of the ground and followed it across. A sign listed the maximum tonnage. He crawled along the near rail, his ankles banging the planks. Water lapped at the pilings; he could smell the muddy shallows, the rotting weeds. Moonlight defined the haunches of the car now, the wind ripping smoke from the chimney. If Creeley had infrared, Larry was meat. He clambered forward on his elbows, the barrel pointed toward the lodge, then, paranoid, checked his back. He could barely see the last cabin.

At the end of the causeway he scissored over the rail and slipped into the high reeds. He moved hidden along the shore, the mud sucking at his boots, stinking of fish. He'd circle the lodge, come at Creeley from the water.

His cover gave way just short of the dock. He crouched, sizing up the back of the lodge. Plywood sealed most of the windows, but farther on, one square glowed with the reflection of a fire. He could smell the smoke. The window commanded everything to the water. To reach it, he'd have to cross a few feet of beach, a swath of lawn and finally a brick patio.

The beach was stony; at each step, pebbles clashed like marbles beneath his feet. He crawled up the lawn, knees digging into the cold ground. Inside, the fire threw leaping shadows over the beam ceiling. Next to the window a door was propped open a crack, the light leaking out onto the mossy bricks. Larry waited, training the sight at chest level, then scrambled for it.

He stopped below the window to collect his breath, a hand on the wet shingles. The rain made it hard to hear; he could see his breath. The rifle was useless at this range, and he wished he had his pistol. He didn't think he would get this close. Clines would just be leaving town. He should have waited. He wasn't a hunter like his father, he lacked the confidence, the certainty necessary to kill. He'd never been a soldier, only lucky, blessed with friends, men who had died so he could be here.

Larry raised his head level with the edge of the window. Inside, the log walls shimmered. There was no furniture, the light fixtures bulbless. On the warped floor, Creeley had spread out a bedroll. At the head, the letters etched deeply by the fire, Creeley's father's gravestone tilted like a pillow.

The rifle left Larry's hands before he could turn. He caught a glimpse of Creeley's forehead—the long, livid scar—and suddenly he was blind, a bag thrown over his head, drawn tight. Creeley kneed him. As Larry doubled over, he twisted the canvas about his neck, cutting off his breath, spinning him around. Larry grabbed for his hands. Creeley kneed him again, and his bowels filled with heaviness; he thought he would vomit. His wrist clipped what must have been the door, for instantly they were out of the rain and warm, his heels scrabbling for traction on smooth wood. He planted a foot and dove blindly, but Creeley had hold of the drawstring and yanked him back like a dog.

Creeley hit him in the face, the blow coming from nowhere, blood springing to Larry's nose. Larry swung at nothing, and Creeley twisted the bag tighter.

"Stop," Creeley ordered.

The string cut into Larry's skin, dizzying him, and he thrashed.

"Stop," Creeley said again. "Listen to me now." His voice was slow, the words choked out. He gasped like an asthmatic.

Larry struggled. With a grunt, Creeley twisted and pushed him to his knees, gripped his neck and bent his head to the floor. The blood ran into Larry's eyes; he tried to swallow, but coughed, his breath hot inside the bag. Creeley let go. Larry heard him rack the slide of the .45 back.

Larry rolled to his right, but Creeley dropped a knee into his kidneys and kept it there. Larry could feel the cushion of the bedroll beneath him; the wool slipped on the floor like an unmoored rug. Larry tried to wriggle free but it was useless.

"Stop."

"Fuck you," Larry said.

"You got the queen."

Larry didn't answer him.

Creeley gathered breath. "You got the king."

He pressed the gun into his ear and repeated it.

"Yes," Larry said.

"So you know."

Again, Larry made him work for it. Creeley leaned a knee on his neck. "What was the date?"

"August fifth," Larry admitted.

"Where?"

"The Rao Lao Valley."

Creeley lifted his weight off him. His hand fumbled against Larry's neck, pinched, and with a jerk and a crackle of static, the bag came off.

The stone was inches from Larry's nose. Beneath the name rested his pistol, the blued steel gleaming.

"Take it," Creeley said. "It's yours."

Creeley rolled away and lay on the floor, limbs splayed as if he'd been shot, the fire playing over his face, the scar zipperlike, monstrous in the flickering light. He wore jeans and a cheap parka, tennis shoes. He seemed smaller now, less deadly, a sleeping guard dog.

Larry reached over and clamped a hand around his throat, pinning him. Larry picked up the .45 and weighed it in his palm; it felt like a full clip. He could see better now. A batch of Tylenol bottles and prescription vials stood clumped at the head of the bedroll, a tin canteen cup and some half-eaten C-rations.

"Why me?" Larry said.

"You're the Skull. That night, it was just you and me."

"I don't know you," Larry said.

"It's dark in the jungle," Creeley managed. The words were an effort; it seemed to hurt him to speak, as if his ribs were broken. "Those nights, they're all the same. You've been there for hours, the mosquitoes stinging you. Someone's coming down the trail. You wait till they're in the zone." He paused and swallowed. "You get 'em all, but one guy's still breathing."

"It wasn't me."

"There's always that one guy. What do you do with one guy? He's already all fucked up. What do you do, Skull? What's the right thing to do?"

Creeley smiled as if Larry knew the answer. He lay there, panting, his cheek against the floor. "You know this story?"

Larry could not recall it, but that meant nothing. The nights ran into the days there, the weeks into months. He'd seen the flash in his dreams, the head bursting, spattering the leaves. He'd done what was right, though now he was unsure. He'd tried to be careful, to keep his eyes open and see what he was doing. He didn't know what to do if this was his work, and he thought of his father, the responsibility he felt to the town. How much of obligation was love?

"It's a good story, huh? A real tearjerker."

"I don't remember it," Larry said.

"It's my story," Creeley said. "You're just in it."

He lifted a hand to Larry's wrist and guided the pistol down against his temple.

"You know what to do. It doesn't count if you fuck it up. It's like anything else—you can't just hope, you've got to execute."

Larry made to pull the barrel away but Creeley stopped his arm. He reached into his parka and produced a card. He held it face out toward Larry. Across the ace of spades, he'd written, *Payback is a motherfucker*.

Larry let go of his throat to accept it.

"Do it right this time," Creeley said. "Do it like you're supposed to. Like your father was supposed to. Do your job."

The pistol was slick in Larry's hand. Above, rain thudded in the rafters.

"Turn your head," he instructed, and Creeley released the barrel.

Larry pressed it into the dark hollow behind his ear. In the firelight, Creeley's jugular pulsed. Larry pictured Carl Metcalf at the bottom of the crater, faceless, and his father on the rocks. He thought of Donna and Vicki and Scott, how it would be without them.

He tensed and fired, the bullet chewing into the floor beside Creeley's head.

Creeley jerked and purged himself.

"It's a motherfucker, all right," Larry said, and spat a bloody string at him. He rose and turned to go.

Creeley punched him behind the knee and caught his good foot, bringing him down. He moved inhumanly fast. He rolled over and knelt on Larry's wrist, snatching the pistol.

He held it to Larry's temple, the barrel trembling.

"No slack," Creeley asked, "huh, Skull?" He smelled from fouling himself.

He removed the gun from Larry's head and put it to his own.

"You want to live," he said, as if disgusted. "Not me. I died over there a long time ago. I don't like it here. Everybody's dead, there's no one left. But you'll remember me, won't you? Promise me that."

He fired before Larry could answer. The spray flew and the gun clunked to the floor, his body toppling over. The flames crackled, made a flapping sound going up the chimney.

Larry froze as if it were a trick and Creeley might rise again, but Larry's face was wet, and his forehead, and the floor. Creeley had done a good job. The air smelled metallic, a steely ozone. Wind licked through the door, and the flames guttered. A finger of blood inched across the wood, searching for him. He got up and wandered through the room a minute before checking Creeley to make sure, then retrieved the .45 and the rifle and sat down by the fire to wait for Clines.

IT WASN'T just the names. They wanted him to take pictures. They wanted him to leave things. Trayner gave him a boonie hat soft as a chamois, Mel White a pair of mirrored shades missing a stem. Meredith sent a pocket chess set, Sponge a plastic grass skirt. Larry wanted to take the ace and the pistol, but Clines needed them for evidence. He'd kept Larry's name out of the paper. Creeley was a suicide, the wound self-inflicted, which was the truth. Larry emptied the trunk upstairs. He had Magoo's pictures and Leonard Dawson's cards in a bag in the back of Number 1, along with all of the ward's stuff. His class A's swung from a hanger in the empty racks.

He wasn't carrying anything else. He'd checked the truck out before Marv got in, and now he was well south of Ithaca, tooling through the hills. In the passenger seat, Scott followed the arc of the wipers, cocking his head like a dog. Vicki had forbidden him to go, and Larry had to kidnap him out of class. He kept to the right lane, watched for cops in the grassy medians, the islands of trees.

He'd thought of taking his father but he needed a few days to recuperate. Though the beating had left no visible scars, his body was thick with fluid, his knees and elbows swollen. Mrs. Railsbeck took a tray up to his bedroom. His father remembered Creeley saying something about his mother but exactly what he could honestly not recall. He thought that Larry should have killed him but understood; maybe Larry was right. It was an argument for another time. Scott was a better choice, Larry thought; his father already knew the price of war, the hardest lessons.

It was Wednesday, there was no one on the road, only muddy logging trucks, campers quilted with bumper stickers. They slowed for the little cities —Horseheads, Corning—moved through them anonymously, camouflaged, then turned south into the emptiness of central Pennsylvania. Peeling billboards stood in cornfields; churches advertised their sermons. Miles outside of Mansfield an adult bookstore beckoned to truckers, its front windowless, a heavy grille over the door. Blossburg came, and Covington—towns without stores, houses falling in on themselves. SPEED CHECKED BY AIRCRAFT, a sign claimed.

"I spy with my little eye," Larry said, "something green."

"Tree," Scott guessed, and then it was his turn.

They used up the yellow line, the bridges, the other cars' license plates. In the mountains the radio stations broke up. "Chances are," Larry whistled. The truck labored up the long grades, the needle dipped toward empty. They coasted through the high hunting country, curving above the great reservoirs, the signs promising Williamsport. It cost him thirty dollars to fill up.

They stopped at a Friendly's above Harrisburg for lunch. Larry checked his wallet, then helped Scott down and held his hand across the parking lot. The waitress gave Scott crayons in a cup and an E.T. placemat; she called him darlin'.

"Nothing for Dad?" she asked, and Larry smiled as if he had to resist her. A free sundae came with the meal; Larry helped him with it.

They got back in the truck and drove, the Susquehanna on their left, the low stone bridges and railroad tracks. Larry hoped for a train to show Scott, but when they caught up with one, he'd fallen asleep, his head bent forward, one eye vigilant, the other closed. Larry wedged his jacket under his chin, but a minute later it fell out. He hadn't invited Vicki; now he wished she had come. She was better at planning things.

The rain grew worse as the day faded. South of York, traffic on the interstate stopped, a field of taillights. For half an hour they inched along, merging left. Ahead, a galaxy of police cars blocked the road, their lightbars strobing over the pines. Trucks headed the other way slowed to see what was going on. Larry expected to be stopped and questioned, Scott pulled from the truck. Finally the file slid past an accident, a yellow Corvette broken over the guardrail, its fiberglass nose cracked. The EMTs were working over someone, their elbows jerking. He thought of the grip they'd taught him at Fort Sam, and for an instant, Salazar, then held himself back. If he started now, he wouldn't stop. He wanted to leave everything there, dump it all in one spot like an Arc Light.

Scott slept through dinner. At the Maryland line, a trooper had a Mercedes on the berm, its owner walking a tightrope in the lights. High above a cloverleaf, a Sunoco sign hung in the black sky like a planet. Farther on, high magnesium stanchions bathed a major exchange the color of weak tea; the interstates poured into each other, widening, gaining strength. Semis whined past a few feet beside him, nose to tail like the cars of a train. It was eight, the professionals were out now, the nationwide lines—Roadway, and Carolina, Consolidated Freightways, Red Ball Express. Signs for Virginia appeared, the traffic clotted, and the big rigs veered off, bypassing the Capitol.

On the outskirts, the motel rates tempted him, the truckstops and gas plazas. He didn't know where he was going and he needed to fill up. His eyes burned and his back hurt and he was hungry, but he stayed in the middle lane, avoiding the on-ramps, pointing Number 1 for the city. The signs took him along the river, toward the Lincoln Memorial. He got off and stopped at a gas station, waking Scott.

"Home?" Scott guessed.

It was warmer here, the air rich with mud, as after a thaw. Larry got the pump started and walked to the lit office. The attendant wore a union suit, under it a sweatshirt with a hood. He was younger, his hair in cornrows; he kept a toothpick in one corner of his mouth but didn't chew it. He unfurled a map on the counter but said nothing, and Larry had to ask.

"You mean the ditch," the attendant said, and removed the toothpick. His finger lit on it immediately. "There you go. You won't see nothing though."

Larry bought the map and the attendant drew the route on it with a marker.

Larry had only seen Washington on TV, the protestors and limousines, the marble facades. He remembered the gaslamps from JFK's cortège, the boots turned backwards in the stirrups. It was a disappointment to see it was a city. The corners bristled with convenience stores and panhandlers. Traffic

396

rushed madly from light to light, buses cutting in front of him. He had the map folded into a square, pinning it to the wheel with one thumb.

On the way, they passed a McDonald's. Scott was hungry.

"After," Larry said, and he whined. Larry was trying to placate him when he saw the Washington Monument, the two warning lights on top blinking like eyes. He signaled and pulled to the curb.

The map told him to go around, but the park entrance was closed. They sat idling by the chain with their lights off. The Wall was supposed to be through these trees, but he didn't see anything and double-checked to make sure.

"Okay," he said, and unbuckled Scott.

He helped him down, then went into the back for the bag. He draped his class A's over his shoulder and took Scott's hand. It was still raining, but not hard; under the trees they couldn't feel it. The ground was spongy beneath his feet; he stepped lightly, wary of the roots. In the blackness, Scott squeezed his hand, and Larry wondered how safe the park was. He was too used to Ithaca.

They came to a clearing and stumbled onto a cobblestone path. The bag bumped against his leg. The Wall was supposed to be there, in front of them, but all he saw was an opening and another grove of trees. They crossed the path and a tripwire snagged his shin.

It was a string to keep people off the new grass. Beyond it leaned a snow fence, a slope leading down.

Ahead, below them, a lighter flared, and he could see a figure silhouetted against the Wall. The flame touched a candle, illuminating a face, then just a pair of jungle boots mirrored in the polished stone.

His eyes grew used to the wet reflection. On either side of the candle the Wall stretched indefinitely. It was sunken, the earth contoured to reveal it, ten feet thick in the center, the edges tapering away. It loomed like a whale over the candle, the granite soaking up most of the light. He was too far away to see the names, and wondered how large they were, how small, how many. All, they'd said.

"I'm hungry," Scott whined.

"I know," Larry answered.

They followed the path down to the Wall. It seemed to rise out of the ground in front of them. As they descended, the rush of traffic in the distance softened, then disappeared, leaving only the rain, their shoes scuffing the path. The man at the candle stepped into darkness and vanished as if they'd scared him away.

They moved to the flame and stood before it, holding hands. Larry didn't know the names he was seeing. They looked gray in the flickering light, separated by diamonds. They were small, and most had a middle initial. Someone had loved all of them—mothers, fathers, girlfriends. They had come from towns like Ithaca, from high school, leaving everything they knew. The waste seemed plain. In the tiny patch of light there had to be a hundred. Behind them, looking out, stood the reflection of himself and Scott.

The candle rested on a ledge jutting from the base of the Wall. Between the path and the ledge stretched a few feet of sod heaped with wreaths and flags and heart-shaped pillows, teddy bears and keychains, framed pictures. There were boots and OD T-shirts, helmets with scrawled-on liners, medals in their cases, unopened beer cans and packs of cigarettes. Scott sloughed off his hand and leaned down to pick up a stuffed rabbit, and Larry gently said, "No, champ."

"Here," he said, and gave him his class A's. He had to convince Scott to add them to the pile.

He opened the bag and let Scott take some of his things out—Magoo's pictures and Leonard Dawson's cards, Salazar's list. They walked down toward the meeting of the V, dropping off Rinehart's fatigue jacket and Cartwright's cigar box. In the cracks between the panels, people had wedged snapshots and letters; a few had fallen to the wet grass. They walked slowly, doling out the contents of the bag—the .50 caliber rounds and paper fans, the jingling dogtags. When they reached the end, there was nothing left but the lists and Larry's camera.

He shuffled the lists, though they were impossible to see. In the darkness, he couldn't make out the names on the Wall, and he wasn't going to take the man's candle. He leaned across the offerings and touched the granite, his fingertips tracing the letters. All of them, he thought. They were arranged by date. Somewhere in the middle were his—Salazar and Smart Andy, Leonard Dawson and Bates. The Martian, the LT. He didn't have to look at any list. He knew their names.

Larry took out the camera and handed Scott the bag. They'd given him money to buy film. He stood back, framing the blackness. He pressed the button, and the flash exploded off the stone, dazzling him. He moved a few steps to his right and took another. The letters stayed with him, burned purple in the dark. He made his way down the Wall, flipping the flashbar, jamming it in like a clip. He worried that the pictures wouldn't come out, and at the far end he turned and came back, taking a second set. He wanted to make sure he got Carl Metcalf and Dumb Andy, Nate and Pony and Bogut. He'd get Fred the Head and Magoo. He'd even get Creeley. This time Larry wouldn't miss anyone. This time he would bring them all home.

FOR THE BEST IN PAPERBACKS, LOOK FOR THE

In every corner of the world, on every subject under the sun, Penguin represents quality and variety—the very best in publishing today.

For complete information about books available from Penguin—including Puffins, Penguin Classics, and Arkana—and how to order them, write to us at the appropriate address below. Please note that for copyright reasons the selection of books varies from country to country.

In the United Kingdom: Please write to *Dept. JC, Penguin Books Ltd, FREEPOST, West Drayton, Middlesex UB7 0BR.*

If you have any difficulty in obtaining a title, please send your order with the correct money, plus ten percent for postage and packaging, to *P.O. Box No. 11, West Drayton, Middlesex UB7 0BR*

In the United States: Please write to *Consumer Sales, Penguin USA, P.O. Box 999, Dept. 17109, Bergenfield, New Jersey 07621-0120.* VISA and MasterCard holders call 1-800-253-6476 to order all Penguin titles

In Canada: Please write to *Penguin Books Canada Ltd, 10 Alcorn Avenue, Suite 300, Toronto, Ontario M4V 3B2*

In Australia: Please write to *Penguin Books Australia Ltd, P.O. Box 257, Ringwood, Victoria 3134*

In New Zealand: Please write to *Penguin Books (NZ) Ltd, Private Bag 102902, North Shore Mail Centre, Auckland 10*

In India: Please write to *Penguin Books India Pvt Ltd, 706 Eros Apartments, 56 Nehru Place, New Delhi 110 019*

In the Netherlands: Please write to *Penguin Books Netherlands bv, Postbus 3507, NL-1001 AH Amsterdam*

In Germany: Please write to *Penguin Books Deutschland GmbH, Metzlerstrasse 26, 60594 Frankfurt am Main*

In Spain: Please write to *Penguin Books S.A., Bravo Murillo 19, 1° B, 28015 Madrid*

In Italy: Please write to *Penguin Italia s.r.l., Via Felice Casati 20, I-20124 Milano*

In France: Please write to *Penguin France S.A., 17 rue Lejeune, F-31000 Toulouse*

In Japan: Please write to *Penguin Books Japan, Ishikiribashi Building, 2-5-4, Suido, Bunkyo-ku, Tokyo 112*

In Greece: Please write to *Penguin Hellas Ltd, Dimocritou 3, GR-106 71 Athens*

In South Africa: Please write to *Longman Penguin Southern Africa (Pty) Ltd, Private Bag X08, Bertsham 2013*